I0576267

ONE DROP OF Magic

AMANDA FRESQUEZ

ONE DROP OF Magic

AMANDA FRESQUEZ

Copyright © 2025 by Amanda Fresquez

All rights reserved.

No portion of this book may be reproduced in any form without written permission from the publisher or author, except as permitted by U.S. copyright law.

This is a work of fiction. Any resemblance to actual persons, living or dead, or actual events is purely coincidental.

Edited by Cindy's Fix-It Shop

Cover art and design by Enjoli Hughes/@EnjoliArt

Interior design by A. Fresquez

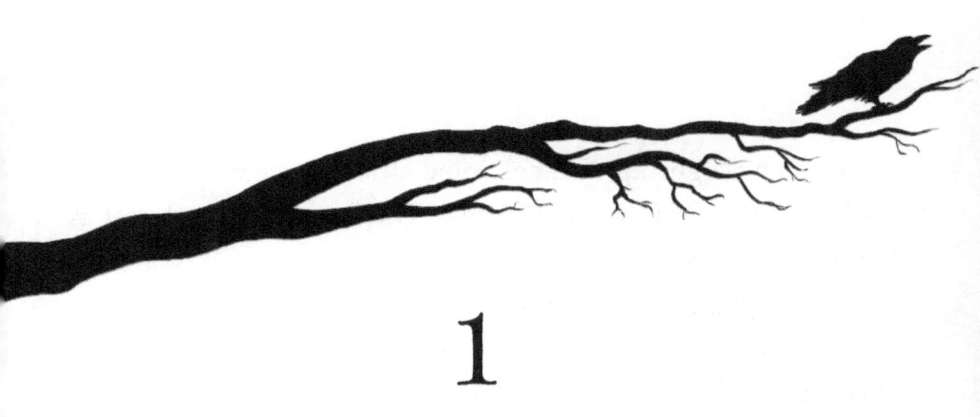

1

CAPE FLATTERY, WA
JUNE 15TH, 2007

EVEN ON VACATION, I'M reminded of those stupid, blood-sucking vampires. The obnoxiously large sensor tower on the distant island stands tall above the neighboring lighthouse, ruining the view. I've always hated them and their alien appearance, surrounding the green zones like high-tech prison bars, even if I am happy they're there. Their low humming sound is comforting, a reminder that they *are* working. If any of those creatures come within a few miles of here, the sirens will sound, giving me time to run. Still, I can't help but see it as a painful reminder of how everything has changed. I choose to leave it out of my drawing as I continue sketching the rocky face of the island.

I sit atop my rain jacket, which I've spread over the wet wooden bench, an open sketchbook across my lap. Looking up at the overcast afternoon sky, I'm surprised it isn't raining.

Crows line the rickety wooden railing overlooking the cliff's edge while seagulls crowd around my feet, awaiting another snack. I toss my last handful of almonds in the crows' direction, hoping to give them a fighting chance. Some almonds go over the cliff, falling to the crashing waves below. The frenzy is over almost as soon as it begins. Seagulls win again.

My phone vibrates in my backpack.

I listen carefully to see if I'm getting a phone call or just a few texts back-to-back. It stops, and I let out a sigh of relief, not in the mood for talking. My family promised me one afternoon of uninterrupted peace and quiet on our two-week-long vacation. Only contact me if it's an emergency, I told them, not thinking it a difficult request. But apparently, I was wrong. The gears in my head begin to spin, already plotting some sort of payback.

I reach into the front pocket, pulling out my old brick of a phone, a hand-me-down from the late 90s, and check my bars, watching as they drop to zero. Phone service has been spotty since we crossed the bridge onto the Olympic Peninsula, but here at the edge of the world—it borders on non-existent.

Three new messages from my mom.

How long are you going to be gone

Are you coming with us to dinner

Brielle is my suitcase in your rental car???

I cackle. Bingo. The perfect revenge has fallen right into my hands.

I guess I have her precious shoes held hostage in my trunk. Should I hide each shoe in a different place in her cabin? Or lead her on a scavenger hunt for them around town? Though, they could get ruined, or lost, that way, and they're way too expensive for me to replace. There's always ransom. Oh, the endless possibilities.

Looks like they're mine now. Sucks for you. XD

My finger lands on the send button, but the screen turns black before I reply. My stomach drops. I try the power button, but nothing happens. The battery's completely dead. I could have sworn I charged this stupid thing, though a quick search of my memory reveals otherwise. Hurrying to the airport this morning, grabbing a quick bite to eat, checking out my rental car...it simply got lost in the rush. The next time I see Mom, there will be hell to pay. I drop the useless, oversized relic back into its place, resigning myself to my fate.

I return to my drawing, realizing as soon as I put down a couple of lines on the paper that my inspiration has faded. After considering starting over on something new, I turn the page, revealing nothing but the cardboard back cover. Out again. I flip the worn sketchbook shut and thread my mechanical pencil through the binder's spiral rings, then slam it down on my lap. I slump against the bench, allowing my head to fall back, not even caring that the damp wood soaks through my T-shirt. A cool breeze passes over my skin as I shut my eyes.

It just doesn't seem real to me. Turning eighteen. Graduating from high school. Weren't these milestones supposed to mean something? When my mom was my exact same age, she was already married *and* pregnant with triplets, yet I still somehow need permission to go out on my own. What was the point of preparing for adulthood if it's just going to be a crappy sequel to childhood, but with bills?

And what does it say that being hours from civilization, alone, with a dead phone and no way to reach the outside world feels like a massive *relief*? More and more, I feel trapped in their perfect little bubble, and I'm running out of air. It's almost like they expect me to live at home forever, to keep acting out the part of the rebellious teenage daughter, as if nothing has changed. As if that could *ever* be enough for me.

Then, something new. A sensation that I can't put a proper name to, as if a weight is being lifted off my chest, and I can breathe a little easier. I listen to the sounds of the waves, feel the silence of the ancient forest, the stillness of the rock beneath my feet. What is this?

Peace.

With no one to tell me what I should be thinking, or what I'm allowed to believe, no one calling me up, criticizing, teaming up against me and picking apart my every little choice...peace of mind. *This.* This is what I want, what I *need*, yet know I cannot have. Not until I find a way to take control of my own life. But where do I even begin? How do you take something back you never gave away in the first place?

Something moves at my feet, and I shoot up straight. Looking down, I find a seagull pushing his luck, nipping at my open backpack. I shake my head, clicking my tongue in disapproval at the naughty little thing, before shoving my sketchbook back in my bag and zipping it.

Just then, all the gathered birds collectively take flight. The commotion startles me, and, for a moment, I'm left puzzled. Did I scare them off? No way. These airborne rats are too ballsy. I watch them fly away until finally, they disappear into the low, foggy clouds.

I stand and head to the railing to look over the edge of the cliff, my eyes dropping to the crashing waves below, a nearly sixty-foot fall.

As the birds' distant squawks fade, I can't shake this sense that something isn't right, then it hits me: The world has gone silent. My eyes move upward to the sensor tower. There's no humming sound, no lights. *The tower is off.* My heart skips a beat before picking up speed.

A thunderous roar explodes somewhere off to my left, and the world shakes beneath my feet, throwing me off balance. A terrifying gust of wind rips through the trees, howling ferociously as it tears them from the soil and topples them over the cliff's edge into the waves below. Sand pelts me as I cling to the weathered wood railing for dear life, feeling it shifting under the strain. When the world begins to settle, I look around, seeing nothing but fallen branches covering the ground. My head spins with fear when I hear faint laughter dancing on the tail of the wind, voices tangling together a short distance away. What in the world is happening?

I hear another, more distant explosion erupting behind me. I turn to look, seeing nothing but tree tops swaying as something rapidly approaches. The tree line bursts open.

"What the—" I utter, before the wind hits me with such immense force that it knocks me off my feet. My hips crash into the wooden top rail as I'm propelled over the edge, tumbling into a freefall. A long, terrified shriek escapes me as I fall head over foot. My hair whips across my face. The dark, jagged waves rush toward me. I shut my eyes, take one last deep breath, and then...impact. Plunging into the frigid waters, my body locks up.

Cold. Too cold. My skin is on fire.

I force my eyes open, but the water is too murky to see anything. Unable to tell which way is up or down, I swim with all my might, unseen forces tossing me, pulling me deeper as my desperation rises. The surface isn't getting any closer. Dizziness washes over me as my lungs burn for air.

Strong arms wrap tightly around my waist, and it feels like someone is pulling me against their chest. Then I'm moving through the water. In seconds, my head breaks the surface. I take a deep, gasping breath, coughing on the droplets of water I inhale.

"I'm going to get you out of here, but I need you to hold on as tight as you can, okay?" a man's voice calls behind me.

He lifts my left arm over him and wraps it around his neck. I reach for him with my other arm, and he grabs my wrist before hoisting me onto his back. I hold on to him tightly, too tightly, practically putting him in a chokehold, pressing the side of my face tightly against the back of his head as I lock my legs around his waist.

Even with my added weight, he moves swiftly through the water with unnatural grace. We narrowly miss sharp boulders, and I'm astonished at how he manages to resist the current slamming against them. We rise high with each approaching wave, and the power of his legs kicking under me, lifts us just enough to stay above the rushing tide as he guides us out of the rocky bay.

It seems like the worst has passed, but I don't see any way to get back up, as steep rock walls line the coast. I hope he knows something I don't because he's headed straight for them. As we get closer, I catch a glimpse of where he's taking us—a small, gravelly strip of exposed shoreline.

I jolt when his feet hit the ground as we arrive on the pebble-strewn shore and I finally release my death grip on him. With one hand under my arm, he steadies me, leading us up the steep incline and letting me go as soon as we clear the water. But my frozen legs give out beneath me, and I slowly sink to my knees, my back to the sea.

"Are you hurt? Did you hit anything when you fell?" he asks, his voice low and steady to my left.

"N-no," I say, racking my brain, not remembering hitting anything but that damn railing. I rub my eyes, trying to wipe away the stinging salt water, unintentionally getting sand in them.

"You're lucky to have missed the rocks," he says with an easy confidence that seems out of place, given the dire circumstances.

"I don't *feel* lucky," I say with a snort. "What about you, you good?"

"I'm...fine," he says through a slight chuckle, seemingly amused by my expression of concern.

My head eases its spinning a bit. Hunched over and blinking repeatedly as I try to clear my eyes of foreign contaminants, I begin to think more rationally about the situation.

"Where did you come from? I didn't see anyone else up there." I laugh nervously, confident I had been alone on that clifftop.

"I was close by," he says, his voice coming from several feet in front of me, no longer by my side. I must be out of it, because I didn't even notice the sound of his footsteps. "I heard you screaming as you fell."

"Huh," I say, finally lifting my head to look at him, my vision still slightly blurred. Am I seeing what I'm seeing? All black, from head to toe: combat boots with cargo pants that would suggest military if not for his black, mid-length leather jacket. His towering, statuesque form faces away from me, revealing the breadth of his muscled back and shoulders. One arm raised, he examines a dripping wet cellphone, so small in his gloved hand that it almost looks like

7

a toy. The wide hood draped over his head completely obscures his face from view.

What. The. Hell.

Am I dead? Is this the grim reaper, come to collect my soul? While he may admittedly look badass, he is *very* off-putting, the most unnerving thing about him being that he's entirely too calm, seemingly unfazed by this life-and-death situation. We need to get out of here before the tide comes in. As I fight the urge to panic, a tempest of anxiety and fear whirls within me. My mind rushes back to the cliff, that freak windstorm, the sensor tower gone dark, the birds scattering...as if fleeing a predator. Is it all somehow related to this man?

"So, how are we getting out of here?" I ask, trembling from the cold, and my nerves, as I pull my long brunette hair to one side and wring it out, water pouring onto the smooth stones I kneel upon.

"Someone's already on the way. He'll be able to help," he says, sounding almost disappointed.

"Does this *someone* have a...boat?"

"We won't need one."

"Why are you being so damn vague?" I bite at him, regret seeping into my bones as soon as the words leave my throat. Welp, that's it. I might have just pissed off Death.

Instead of taking offense, he emits a low, painful sound that resembles laughter.

Nope. I'm out.

I struggle to my feet, turn, and take a few steps back toward the water, scanning the horizon for a boat and looking along the cliffs for a trail that leads up or some rocks that I might be able to climb. At this point, I'd take my chances with the door from *Titanic* over this freak.

"Where do you think you're going?" he calls in a bemused tone.

"I was thinking, how 'bout *you* wait for your friend, and *I'll* try to find us a way out of here," I answer softly, shading over the concern in my voice with feigned warmth as I half-turn back toward him.

And then I see him, from the corner of my eye, a second hooded figure looking down on us from the ledge above. Has he been there this whole time? Before I have time to formulate another thought, he steps forward and plummets roughly thirty feet, landing casually with a soft thud, barely disturbing the gravel beneath his feet—almost as if he were weightless.

The blood drains from my face as the fear paralyzes me. *No, no, no. This can't be happening.*

"Did you really have to do that?" my rescuer says, annoyed.

"Relax. It was just the easiest way down," says the newcomer dismissively. "Care to enlighten me on how we found ourselves in this situation?"

"What do you *think* happened?"

"Don't look at *me*," he says, "unlike some people, I know how to exercise restraint."

Taking a step back, the crunching gravel under my shoe interrupts their conversation, accidentally reminding them that I am standing only feet away. Both hooded figures turn to me at the same time, revealing two pairs of shimmering, blood-red eyes.

"Oh, shit..." the words slip out as everything falls into place.

Vampires.

The newcomer lets out an unrestrained belly laugh as if he finds this entertaining.

"Don't frighten her, just fix it," says my rescuer, eyeing him.

"Always so serious. Does she look scared to you? Besides, she won't remember any of this, anyway."

"What's that supposed to mean?" I snap, trapped between the ocean and vampires, two breaths away from emptying the contents of my stomach onto the tide-washed stones.

"Sleep," the newcomer's voice softly commands, sending out shockwaves that penetrate my skull and instantly still my racing thoughts. *Sleep.* I find myself unable to resist as magic sinks its claws into my mind. My vision narrows and shakes, the two figures growing distant as my consciousness is pulled into the darkness, and within seconds—everything ceases to exist.

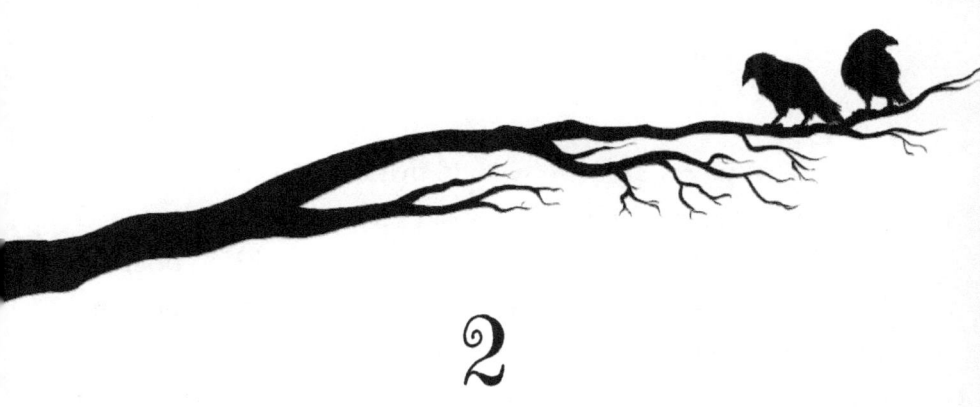

2

Whatever this is, it isn't sleep. There are no dreams in this place, only darkness and the sense that something is weighing me down, almost like an anchor, dragging me further into my mind. The more I fight, the deeper it sinks its claws into me. There's no way to tell how much time has passed when whatever has me bound releases its hold, and I come hurtling back to the surface.

I sit up straight, taking in my surroundings, and have a brief panic attack before I figure out where I am: the backseat of a car—*my* rental car. Warm air fills the small space with the smell of heated plastic and air freshener, as light rain patters against the car's roof. My backpack rests on the center console.

Every inch of me feels like crap. I groan, my throat dry and achy, before grabbing a water bottle from my bag and chugging it down. It feels good getting some hydration in me, though it does nothing to alleviate my headache. Ugh, and what a wicked case of brain fog.

What possessed me to swim in that cold stream, anyway? In my *brand-new shoes*, no less? It doesn't even seem like something I would do. Maybe that was the whole point, though? To be spontaneous? I guess it was fun just jumping in, *frolicking* in the water a while before heading back, dripping the whole way. Of course, without any sun, I had to improvise by using the car's heater to dry off, and, not meaning to, I fell asleep in the back seat.

I rub my face before running my fingers through my hair, hesitating at the touch of something wet and slimy hidden beneath. *Oh God, oh God*...I picture a leech, tiny mouth suckled against my flesh, its ring of pointed teeth latched onto my scalp as it gorges on my blood. Shivering and fighting the urge to gag, it's all I can do not to scream as I pluck it out, tossing the little stowaway in the direction of the passenger seat. *Bastard.*

Reaching through the front seats, I slap on the dome light with my upturned palm, still convulsing with disgust as I emit a squeak at the sight of a liquid-filled bulb of seaweed now riding shotgun. *Not a leech.* Still disgusting as all hell, but a definite improvement. *Kelp*, I console myself, just a harmless piece of ocean vegetation.

The longer I stare at it, the more a strange feeling cuts through my core.

No...No, this is *wrong.* Dread slithers into my mind, leaving the door cracked open to another room where a little voice has been screaming, too muffled for me to make out the words. I try to retrace my thoughts, wondering what about the slimy little thing triggered this rising anxiety. I pinch the bridge of my nose, the headache worsening as I search my thoughts for what could be causing me such distress.

There. A memory, as if partially submerged, drifting at the very edge of my perception. Something tells me to leave it be, ignore it, let it sink back down. Instead, I reach out and take hold, pulling it closer, bringing it into the light. First, I'm overtaken by the feeling of weightlessness, falling from some immense height, and I lean forward, bracing myself against the front seat. My head floods with images of dark waters closing in around me, and I gasp as I feel their icy embrace, my grip on reality fading along with the retreating light.

Chopped-up memories tumble around my head, overlapping, refusing to align. And then, I find it—the one image I didn't know I was searching for.

Clinging to those solid shoulders, feeling the power of each stroke, the smell of leather mingled with salt, and the caress of his hood against my cheek. *Him.* The mysterious man who pulled me out of the water...who I remember nothing else about. My dark savior.

The storm within me calms, my heart steadying as my breathing returns to normal, and I'm back in the car again. I gaze out the window, knowing very little for certain other than this: even though I can't remember how, when, or why, I was drowning...and he saved me. The sound of rain grows heavier as the dying light pulls my eyes toward the clock, which reads 8:14 p.m. My head drops in defeat, having promised to be back before dark. Mom and Dad are probably losing their ever-loving minds.

I climb over the center console into the driver's seat before speeding off on the path back to civilization, tires skidding a little on the loose gravel, as I shove this little freakout to the back of my thoughts. There's no way to avoid dealing with what happened, but it'll have to wait, because right now my time is best spent mentally preparing for the coming showdown with my *royally* pissed-off parents.

Not until I blow past the first speed limit sign do I even bother to check how fast I'm going: twenty over. Easing off the gas a bit, I take a deep breath, settling in for the long drive, glad for every mile I put between me and that place.

The picturesque cabins are a welcome sight. They resemble old-fashioned log buildings, wrapped in dark-stained, exposed timber skirted by a half wall of stacked stone. The lanterns dangling from rustic-looking chains on their porches emit a soft orange glow.

It reminds me of a little village, buildings clustered tightly together, leaving just enough space between them for parking. Pulling into my spot, I notice my parents' car isn't next door. In every imagined scenario, I had them waiting for me. They would run out and start yelling at me, and I would act completely unbothered, like I had no idea what they were so upset about, and head inside. Now, it feels more like they are planning an ambush.

I pop the trunk and hop out, taking my backpack with me. I smile when I see Mom's precious cargo, remembering that I possess all the high heels she brought on the trip. Next to it sits my big, black bag containing my hand-me-down Polaroid camera. My brain formulates a plan just stupid enough to work, but I need to be quick. Mom and Dad could roll up at any moment.

I crack open her rose-pink suitcase and yank out a few pairs of her favorite heels, shutting the lid before staging them in a lineup on top. I snap a shot of my loot, grab the photo that pops out, and slip it into my coat pocket.

Thinking I hear a car coming on the main road, I repack everything and close the trunk. I run next door to my parents' cabin, produce a fine-point Sharpie from my backpack, whip the Polaroid out to write a message on it, and slip it under the door, chuckling to myself. I rush to grab my luggage and head for our cabin next door. Mission accomplished.

Through the closed curtains, I see that the guys must have left every light inside on, as usual. I press my key card to the reader and wait for the click, before turning the handle and slowly opening the door. Immediately, the unmistakable sounds of *MTV's Ridiculousness* playing much too loudly on the television greets me, and the aroma of pickles and garlic assaults my nostrils. To my horror, I realize that I am not alone.

My eyes land first on his messy blond waves, then travel down to those wide, icy blue eyes as they narrow into slits and rake me over with suspicion. Jonathan is tall, toned and—by all means—the hottest guy in our graduating class. However, all I see when I look at him is the most annoying boy I have ever encountered. I find his every action repulsive. Unfortunately for me, he happens to be my brothers' best friend and, somehow, an honorary member of our family. Where once I saw him as the bane of my existence, with time, I've learned to tolerate him somewhat.

"Where have you been?" Jonathan asks through a mouth full of food. He's sunken into the couch like he's been there a while, surrounded by empty containers of local take-out and all the junk food he could get his hands on. His bare feet are propped on the coffee table, dangerously close to an open two-liter bottle of orange soda that wobbles as he speaks.

"I've been out. Clearly. Where is everybody?" I ask, rolling my suitcase inside and shutting the door behind me.

"They all went to some fancy restaurant in Silverdale, but they should be back any minute. You look like crap, by the way," he says, smirking.

I have no comeback for that. I know I must look as bad as I feel. "Why didn't you go with them?" I ask, annoyed.

"I enjoy keeping the food inside my stomach."

"Oh yeah," I chuckle. His motion sickness is usually manageable, but the winding roads you need to travel to get anywhere around here have affected him worse than we anticipated. Thankfully, he rode up here with my parents, so *my* car doesn't reek of vomit.

"Why didn't you text me back?"

"My phone died, and I didn't have a charger. Wouldn't have mattered, anyway. There's like no service out there."

He puts down a slice of pizza and looks at me with unusual sincerity, turning down the volume on the TV. "Seriously, what happened to you?"

"I went for a swim," I say, expressionless. *Frolicking.* Again, the word leaps into my mind, and I have to restrain myself from visibly cringing at it.

He laughs all too loudly. "Come on, Bri. Went swimming, where?"

"A stream. It was...spontaneous. Not the best decision, I admit, but I had fun. Sort of. It was much colder than it looked."

His smile fades as he realizes I'm not laughing with him. "Oh, you're serious?"

I hear a car approaching outside, which can only mean one thing: they're back.

"I'm gonna shower," I say, already headed for the bathroom when I stop myself, listening to the loud thud of a car door outside, voices arguing, and footsteps on the deck. No more running away. I turn to face the onslaught head-on, folding my arms over my chest.

"This ought to be good," Jonathan says, tearing open another bag of chips.

The door swings open, and Mom comes barreling in like a fighter entering the ring, Dad on her heels. Maybe I should have locked myself in the bathroom, after all.

"Brielle Raine Draper! Where have you been?" she hisses, keeping her voice low so as not to get the neighbors' attention. "You were supposed to be back before dark. Why didn't you call me?"

"My phone died—"

"Honey, that's why there are pay phones!" she says, cutting me off.

"I tried, but—"

"You gave your word," my dad says. "That's supposed to mean something. I put that car in my name and agreed to let you use it. I *trusted* you. I can't express how disappointed I am that you thought this was a good time to play one of your bone-headed little stunts."

"First of all, *I'm* paying for the rental, and second, this area doesn't have a curfew. This was no *stunt*," I say in a mocking tone, "It was just an honest mistake. I didn't *do* anything!"

My nosy brothers hover in the doorway, their eyebrows raised, doing their best to act like they aren't listening.

"Well, you should know that we were worried sick about you. We were about to come pick up Jonathan and go out looking for you," she snarls, before looking me up and down. "And why do you *look* like that?"

"I—" I stammer, searching for the words, not even sure what happened, myself.

Mom shakes her head, exchanging her vengeful glare for one of bewilderment as she turns to study Jonathan's fortress of snacks.

"You know what? Everybody, go to sleep. It's been a long day. As for you, young lady, we'll deal with this tomorrow," she says with an eye flutter, sounding more tired than anything.

No. We're not 'dealing with this tomorrow', because there's nothing to deal with. She doesn't just get to decide that I'm in the wrong. They're not listening to me. But what's the point in talking if they're only going to hear what they want?

My dad opens his mouth, no doubt to issue one final lash, but I interrupt him. "Ah ah, you heard the *boss*," I say, leaning down to snatch one of Jonathan's candy bars from the edge of the coffee table. By the looks on their faces, they don't much appreciate the comment. "Later," I say over my shoulder, moving to the bathroom, luggage in tow.

Heavy footsteps pound down the hallway behind me, but they're too late. I've already locked the door. The metal handle jiggles as someone tries it from the hallway.

"Hey. Hurry up, I gotta go," says one of my twin brothers.

I turn the shower handle on, letting the water blast against the wall.

"Go next door, I'm in here," I call to him through a mouth full of chocolate.

"You're such a child!"

18

The tromping footsteps that answer tell me he's going to our parents' cabin, which pulls a devilish little smirk out of me. I'm petrified when I finally catch sight of myself in the mirror. Damn, Jonathan was right, I do look like crap. Staring back are dry, red eyes. The sea green of my irises somehow appears a shade lighter in contrast.

My favorite *Breaking Benjamin* T-shirt crackles softly in my ears as I drag it over my shoulders, the fabric stiff and slightly scratchy like I'd been swimming in seawater. My eyes are drawn to discoloration around my right hip. Twisting my back to the mirror reveals a patchwork of mottled pink-purple bruising running from my shoulder blades down to the small of my back. How did this happen? Why can't I remember it?

When I pull off my shoes, sand spills out onto the tile floor. I bring everything into the shower with me to rinse out the salt. The hot water feels amazing running down my sore back as I close my eyes and relax, letting my mind open. I find myself taken back to the incomplete memory of the water, but it's like a scratched disc that cuts out every time I reach a certain point. The embrace of strong arms, my head rising above the water, holding on to those powerful shoulders. As I nudge against the darkness, the tension plaguing me melts away under the soothing warmth.

"I need you to hold on as tight as you can, okay?" I hear a solemn and dark voice speak, almost as if he were beside me—the man from the water. I replay his words in my head, basking in the sense of security I felt when I first heard them, holding on to them like a lifeline in chaos...

There comes a sudden pounding on the door. I jump, bringing me back to reality.

"Would you stop hogging the bathroom?" Warren shouts.

"Give me two minutes," I call back as I shut off the water, having completely lost track of time. I dry off as fast as I can and throw on my pajamas. The lingering steam wafts into the hallway as I open the door to a pair of amber eyes glaring at me. *Elden, not Warren. Dang.* I must really be off my game, because I haven't gotten them mixed up in a while. In my defense, Elden's usually more chill than this.

I should be able to tell them apart after eighteen years of being their sister. The trouble is that while most identical twins were, at best, highly similar, my brothers are *literally* identical. The way they look, their voices, and even their smiles are the same. It's like they were scientifically cloned in a lab, and they can prank just about anyone except me. All I need is one look, and I instantly know which it is... kind of a sixth sense.

Elden stands with his back against the wall, arms crossed, autumn brown hair disheveled—the practiced pose of a varsity wrestler who spent years trying to look too cool for school. His square jaw and broad shoulders may have fooled some, but all I see is the same kid who used to full-on ugly cry when I beat him in *Diddy Kong Racing*. I hear him draw a breath to unleash whatever lecture he's prepared in the last ten minutes.

"Shut up, Elden," I say before he can get a word out. A slightly dumbfounded look flashes in his eyes before his face twists into the same scowl of disapproval I would expect from my dad.

I shoulder-check him on the way to the living room, feeling his annoyance and condescending attitude. It's strange having this connection with my brothers, always being able to read them, to know what they're thinking and feeling. Even though they don't seem to share the same bond with me. Sometimes, I think everyone just forgets that we're triplets because it's easier that way.

Elden and Warren have always been referred to as the twins, but somehow, I became nothing more than the little sister, even though we were all born within the span of thirty minutes. Of course, it doesn't help that I take almost entirely after Mom. If there's even a trace of my father's DNA in me, I couldn't tell you where it's hiding.

Jonathan's already passed out on the couch amidst his fort of empty food containers. Judging by his light snoring, he just dozed off. It will become worryingly loud as he slips deeper into sleep. I sigh, annoyed with myself for forgetting to bring my white noise machine to drown out his uneven, rattling breaths. I rummage through my backpack till I find my iPod and headphones.

My bare feet move along the cold hardwood floor as I go around the cabin, flipping off all the lights. Now that I've had a minute to soak it in, the little cabin is surprisingly modern and beautiful inside, in stark contrast to the rustic exterior. I hadn't come inside when we checked in this morning. Clean, white-painted walls lined with maritime-themed décor, the TV near a fake fireplace directly across from the couch, a cute little living room with a detached kitchenette, and just enough space for a two-seater dinette table. I wouldn't mind having a little place like this all to myself.

On the way to bed, I pass Elden coming out of the bathroom, wiping off the bottom of his feet.

"What did you *do* today? There's sand everywhere. I thought you were just taking some pictures."

I snort and walk by him. "I'll sweep it up tomorrow."

After entering the dark bedroom, I find it's larger than I expected. My brothers share a king-size bed in the center, while the small daybed against the wall is for me. Warren is already knocked out. I climb under the covers, rubbing my aching bruise as the sound of late-night TV commercials serenades me to sleep from down the hall. I put my headphones in, turn on an *Enya* playlist, and close my eyes.

3

Sleep. The voice reverberates all around me, over me, *through* me. There is magic in his words. In this place, I'm weightless, floating. I've never had a dream like this—one where I'm aware that I'm dreaming yet still trapped between the waking world and whatever lies beneath.

"This is some serious bullshit!" I say, the words echoing in my head.

The darkness trembles in response. Something tugs on my right leg, pulling me deeper into the silence. I reach down, searching in the dark for the culprit. The touch of my fingers identifies the cold, steel rings of a chain coiled tightly around my ankle like a snake, slowly winding its way up.

It's no use trying to pry the creeping, serpentine thing off. It merely re-tightens itself as if it were a living creature. I give up, resigning myself to floating in zero gravity. I can't help but notice my restraints loosening their grip, ever so slightly.

"*Quicksand,*" a voice whispers. It's my voice. At least, the way I sound inside my own head. That's it. The more I fight, the deeper I'll sink. But then, this is all happening *inside* my head. So maybe going deeper is exactly what I need, because where I am now is no place. This stupid chain, as annoying as it is, must be anchored to something.

I grab hold, pulling myself along, gliding effortlessly into the black, soundless depths. It soon gets colder, more difficult to progress as gravity kicks in, and no longer is my iron tether something I can hold in my hand, but it has become enormous, like something you'd see on a ship's anchor. Either my eyes have finally adjusted to the darkness, or there's a faint light coming from above, because now, I can just barely see my hands in front of my face as I keep climbing, using the giant links like the rungs of a ladder.

Then, the top of my head hits the water. Taking a deep breath, I begin my ascent, and then I'm not climbing anymore, but instead—swimming. I soon break the surface, wading in the waves just off a pebble-strewn shore, the mere sight of which triggers a dizzying rush of déjà vu. I swim to it.

I explore the empty beach, the gravelly stones crunching beneath my feet as I move toward a narrow passage in the rocks ahead. Once through, I find myself standing in the parking lot from earlier today.

It's dark again. A starless night sky looms low and heavy. Maybe thirty feet away, my running car, its headlights the sole source of illumination. This darkness is different. It makes me feel vulnerable, exposed, as if countless hidden eyes watch my every move. I sprint to my car, but as I near it, a tall, hooded figure steps into the light, clothed entirely in black, causing me to freeze in my tracks.

"Just be careful this time," his deep, commanding voice says, sounding almost concerned.

It's *him*, the man who saved me.

"When have I ever *not* been careful?" a second voice asks in a cool, persuasive voice that is also hauntingly familiar, as this second figure joins the first, stepping into the light.

"You hit her too hard with the first command. Be gentler."

There's this growing unease in the air, like a rising tension. I fight against the disorienting feeling that strikes me, telling me to turn away, because I *need* to see what happens next.

"You didn't fall from the cliff. You never went into the sea. In fact, you spent the whole afternoon alone. As you were returning from the cliff, you came across a stream not too far from the trail. You went to explore it, and the water looked so enticing that you decided to be spontaneous and go for a swim." I grit my teeth as reverberating waves move through the air, sinking into my skull. "You had a fun time frolicking in the stream, then returned to your vehicle to dry off, and accidentally fell asleep on the back seat."

My savior shakes his head in disapproval.

"Is there a problem?"

"Not your best work."

"If there were witnesses, perhaps the story would need some polishing. We're talking about a lone teenage girl. This should suffice. Besides, you said to take it easy, and I did."

"Fine. Is there something more you'd like to add?"

"Oh yes, you don't remember that business with the wind or anything involving the two of us. All you know is that everything is fine. You're safe. Nothing remarkable happened today."

I pick my jaw up from the floor. "Is this what you did to me, you asshole!? You hypnotized me?" I scream, but they can't hear me. I step forward into the light, and as soon as I cross the threshold, I see what I always knew was there, cradled in the arms of my savior, a young brunette with wavy, waist-length hair. She is unconscious and pale in her Breaking Benjamin T-shirt and barely two-day-old Chuck Taylors, and he doesn't take his eyes off her. I gasp.

The two cloaked figures exchange puzzled glances before turning their gazes toward me, again with those familiar blood-red eyes. Only this time, I'm not afraid of them. Enraged, I open my mouth to give them a piece of my mind, but then the ground dissolves under my feet, crumbling to sand. I sink back into the darkness, those piercing eyes tracking me the whole way down.

4

Port Townsend, WA

A moment of weightlessness startles me awake as I fall, crashing onto the bedroom floor. I release a low groan, brushing the hair from my eyes and unwrapping the headphone cord from around my neck. No movement or sound from my sleeping brothers, despite the chainsaw-like snores emanating from the living room that cut through the silence.

As I lie on the cold, hard ground, still in pain from my rude awakening, previously forgotten details from yesterday piece themselves together in my mind. How he looked at me with those shimmering red eyes, the way I'm still able to feel his penetrating gaze. *Oh no.* I cover my face with both hands. Somehow, I had managed to get through high school without developing a crush on a single boy, only to catch feelings for a friendly monster who lives in a forest.

Hopeless. That's what I am, absolutely freaking *hopeless*.

Then, again, there is the small issue of them brainwashing me, which does nothing but piss me off. "*FROLICKING!?*" I growl lowly to myself, furious. "Freaking vampires, with their stupid, old-fashioned, ugh."

I travel to the least likely place in the world to encounter one of those bloodsuckers, still manage to run into two of them, *and* have them do some weird crap to me. Now, aside from having to adjust my worldview to include vampires having *magic mind powers*, there's the glaring question staring me in the face: Why did they let me live?

Not only had I survived an encounter with vampires, but they went out of their way to rescue me and get me safely back to my car. They aren't supposed to be capable of rational thought, let alone empathy. Every single news story that comes out involving one of those creatures is a horrific, senseless massacre. I'll never forget the first time I saw real attack footage, that soulless, contorted face, the way his fangs extended before he plunged them into the first victim's neck, blood spraying through the air, the ground covered in convulsing bodies injected with venom, left abandoned in a frenzied search for more prey.

Vampires don't help people. They eat them.

No part of me feels up to the task of getting off the floor, but it's freezing, and I need to pee. Slowly, I roll to my side, grab the edge of the bed, and hoist myself onto my knees. I feel around in the dark until I find the alarm clock on the nightstand and smash the button on top. It lights up, revealing the time: 5:14 a.m. Five hours of sleep, wonderful.

My body yearns for rest, but with my mind racing like it is, and Jonathan's incessant droning sounds, there's no chance of that now. I spend one last minute huddling over the edge of the warm, cozy bed before accepting my fate and rising to my feet.

"Well, you always said you wanted adventure," I say to the girl in the bathroom mirror, before throwing on a pair of old jeans, a plain T-shirt, and a basic gray jacket. My tattered hiking boots, the only other footwear I brought along, are frayed and worn, with splits in the seams, and they're a tighter fit than I remember.

The blue hour of the morning has begun, its light spreading evenly across the sky as I head for my car and hop in, no real plan other than to find a halfway decent spot to watch the sunrise and maybe take a few photos. I pause, key in the ignition, wondering whether going out like this is wise, given what happened the last time I went sightseeing. Then, I shrug and start the car. That was over a hundred miles west of here, in a place with no cell service and a human population of effectively zero. Besides, they turned out to be *nice* vampires.

Driving only a few minutes down Water Street takes me past all the stores and out of town. I no longer feel the same excitement I had yesterday while driving this same stretch of road. Instead, there's something more intense, like this elated fear. Anything can happen out here. Many times, I consider turning back, knowing that a solo journey like this isn't without risk, but it's that very absence of safety that spurs me onward, drawing me in like a moth to flame. A part of me hopes to recreate the same feeling of peace I had at the cliffs, and I've already survived one encounter with their kind, so when I see a turn off near some trees, I stop.

I'm surprised at how much darker it gets as I move down the trail, the precious little daylight obscured by dense overhead foliage as I quietly make my way into the woods, wondering what critters I might be able to spot. The forest's wildlife already seems to be active.

Occasionally, I hear snaps and movements as animals scurry away, though I can never quite manage to get a good look at anything.

Eventually, I come to a small clearing that opens on one side to a wide glen, granting a view of the sunrise cresting over the top of nearby mountains. I take my camera out of the case, snapping a photo, the sound of the rollers shattering the morning stillness as they spit out the Polaroid. As I place it in my back pocket to develop, I detect movement from the corner of my eye. Turning my head, slowly, I see that not too far from where I am, amidst the moss-covered tree trunks, there's a tall, grassy clearing where a doe and her fawn are grazing.

Barely able to contain my excitement at seeing something like this for the first time, I swap the Polaroid for a more compact—and silent—digital camera. I adjust the settings for low light and start shooting. Step by step, I edge closer without spooking them, expecting them to dart off at any moment. To my surprise, they just keep eating, probably used to being harassed by the park's visitors, even as I come within just a few feet of them.

Dropping to one knee for a better angle, I raise the camera to take a photo. The fawn steps toward me. I cautiously stretch my free hand toward it, and it sniffs the tips of my fingers. Still holding the camera with my other hand, I snap more photos. The mother deer perks up, her ears twitching. I watch her for a few more seconds before she dashes off, her baby dropping into the tall grass.

"Damn. She ditched you," I say with a chuckle, the first sound I utter in this place, marveling at how well the little things' markings help it to blend into the underbrush. I center it in the frame and prepare to take one last photo of this innocent little creature before leaving it alone, so its mama can return, and *hopefully* learn to be a better parent.

At that instant, I hear the unmistakable sound of a branch snapping behind me, and am suddenly aware of the presence of something else. I spin, then scramble backward on the ground, trying to put distance between me and the large, dark *thing* practically breathing down my neck.

My senses reboot as he steps forward into the pale, blue light that filters into the clearing. Not an animal. Not a thing at all, but *him*. I hold in a gasp.

He's much taller than I remembered, with wide shoulders and a broad chest that tapers down to the tight waist of a body built for speed. Through the opening in his jacket, what I see of his attire appears tailor-made for his muscled physique—well-worn, distressed black leather, fastened with ornate metallic rivets, bearing more resemblance to *armor* than clothing.

My gaze travels up to his face. A neck gaiter constructed from a heavy, woven fabric is drawn up, its top resting on the bridge of his nose. His wide hood, again pulled over his head, casts a shadow over his sharp, angular features. The only parts of him exposed to me are his penetrating, deep-set eyes, sharply arched brows, and a few strands of curly, brown hair that peek out. If he hadn't rescued me from drowning, imagining him as anything other than a villain would be difficult. But I know better, or perhaps, I *hope* better.

The forest sounds have gone silent, like near the cliff yesterday. His unnatural stillness holds a steady tension, like the air just before a thunderstorm, an intense pressure that causes every hair on my body to stand on end. My mind immediately goes to a tightly drawn bow

31

or a coiled serpent, ready and waiting to strike—not a stat-ue—but a living weapon.

He meets my gaze with those fiery red eyes. Unblinking, inhuman...and yet at the same time, strangely alive. Vibrant. Even youthful—like they once belonged to someone my age.

I have to remind myself that he's a monster, and that I should feel disgusted with myself, embarrassed that I looked him up and down the way I had, assessing him. What's the matter with me? Why am I checking this guy—this *thing*—out? Anger and dark resentment well up inside of me.

"What the hell are you doing here?" The words leap from my throat, and I immediately regret them...probably not the most gracious way to greet the vampire who had given me the gift of continued existence.

To my shock, he lets out an amused huff and replies, "Well, good morning to you, too." His voice is soft and powerful at once, having an almost whimsical quality to it. I replay his words a few times, failing to find even the slightest trace of malice in them. It's like he's being...kind?

He extends a gloved hand, and I stare at it too long, deliber-ating whether to take it, before placing mine in his and allowing him to help me off the ground. His grip is firm, but surprisingly gentle, and for a moment, I'm taken back to my memories of the water. He releases my hand as soon as I get my feet under me, and I try to brush the dirt and moss off my pants.

"Aren't you a little far from home? You mean to tell me you literally traveled three hours to Port Townsend...for what reason? Or are you just following me, now?" I accuse, trying my best to keep a steady voice, working to control my breathing and elevated heart rate.

"Yes," he says, matter-of-factly.

"*Yes?*"

"Forgive me if I wasn't clear, but yes...I am following you."

"Why?"

He shakes his head, "Well, certainly not to *bite* you if that's what you're thinking."

"Thaaanks, yeah, that's good to know." I wasn't thinking it, but now I am. "Look. Let's try it again. *Why* are you following me?"

"It's standard protocol to follow and observe humans we run into for a brief period of time. It's, uh—to make sure they don't remember things they're not *supposed* to," he says, squinting his eyes at me. "After I heard what could only have been the sound of you falling from your bed at five this morning, you distinctly said the word *vampire*."

I stare at him, confused, not understanding where this is headed. "Hold on, you *heard* me? Heard me...*how*? From where?" I ask with indignation.

"Oh, no. Don't worry," he says apologetically, "I was well outside your cabin, a good distance away. So far away, in fact, I could hardly see inside your windows."

"Wait, so you have like...super hearing?"

"Well, just average for my...kind." He hesitates. "In fairness, you do speak rather loudly."

"So what? I mean, who even said I was referring to you?" I ask defiantly, "Maybe I watched a vampire movie before bed."

His eyes slowly crinkle from that smile I know is hidden underneath his gaiter.

"You were watching MTV all night. Very loudly."

Damn.

"Okay, well, am I wrong? Are you *not* a vampire? Please, enlighten me what the problem is, because there's obviously some part of this I'm missing."

"The *problem* is that you weren't supposed to be able to remember anything. At all."

"Why, because you and your little friend tried to hypnotize me?"

His eyebrows raise slowly, as if he's in shock. "Forgive me, but I find this somewhat fascinating, exactly how much *do* you remember?" he asks, cocking his head to the side.

"Not much. I guess I was too busy *frolicking* in the stream to remember anything else," I say, not wanting to divulge more information unless he gives me some answers.

I hear either a chuckle or a groan of pain from beneath his mask, I can't be sure...but I get the feeling that he's lost his touch when it comes to human communication.

"How did two vampires get so close to a sensor tower without triggering it? Aren't they supposed to detect your heat signatures or something?"

"Hardly an inconvenience. We can have them taken offline whenever the need arises. In this territory, they're more of a secondary warning system, anyway."

"But they also have a failsafe system, right? Won't they go off if they lose power or someone tampers with them? We learned about it in class."

"Also correct, but even the failsafe mechanisms can be deactivated from *within* the network. For us, it usually just takes a phone call."

"You call the government? You seriously expect me to believe *you* have U.S. military clearance?"

"Well, not exactly..."

"Right, because you're not supposed to be here. Washington is vampire-free. Everybody knows that."

"That's not entirely true. It's more accurate to say that there are no *rogue* vampires in Washington. Every vampire here is accounted for, and we're all working toward a common goal: to keep this territory safe for humans while remaining hidden, naturally."

"That's the most obvious, idiotic lie I've ever heard."

"Is it, now? Think a moment. If we keep the order, the government will divert resources to other causes...like trying to reclaim the red zones, instead of sending their goons after us. We police our own kind better than they ever could. In return, they overlook our existence. Whether you believe it or not, we are the ones keeping the darkness at bay."

This can't be real. How could our government let vampires control a green zone without notifying the public? "Next, you're going to tell me this place is absolutely crawling with vamps."

"Not at all. In fact, there are only a few of us vampires here. The rest of our coven consists mainly of shifters and some...others," he says.

I furrow my brows, unable to restrain the confusion on my face. Other than shapeshifters and vampires, what else is there? I've heard of witches, but nothing about them has been confirmed, at least as far as I know.

"I don't get why you're telling me all of this."

"I need to know I can trust you, so it's only right to gain your trust, first. Since my brother's command didn't quite work as intended, I find myself in need of your cooperation. As you can now see, our existence must remain a secret. Not only for our safety, but for your kind as well."

"Got it. Cross my heart and hope to die. I'll take this to my grave." There would be nothing to gain by breathing a word of this to my family. Even if I could get them to listen to me, they would never believe little Brielle's preposterous tale of the vampire savior.

He raises one eyebrow, assessing me, hands resting in his jacket pockets. The morning light is just beginning to trickle through the tree branches, casting soft shadows on the ground.

"Looks like the sun is coming," I say, curious to see his reaction. We know sunlight doesn't *kill* them, yet they still avoid it like the plague, with nearly all attacks happening at night.

He doesn't acknowledge my comment.

"I'm going to hold you to that promise," he says, the smile returning to his eyes. "Didn't you have somewhere to be this morning?"

Somewhere to be? A gasp escapes as I pull out my phone to check the time. Thankfully, I can still make it. How could he have read the message I scrawled on a photo and slipped under the cabin door? Was this guy standing behind me when I'd written it, looking over my shoulder? Or...had he snuck into my parents' cabin? Ugh, I didn't like either answer.

"Yeah, I need to get going," I say awkwardly, "Oh...and I should have said this yesterday, but thank you. I'd be dead without your help."

"Ah, I'd hoped we could *avoid* the topic, but now that we're on it..." he says, and for the first time, his demeanor falters as if bracing for my reaction. "It was actually one of my brothers who knocked you over the edge."

"I thought it was the wind—" I say, confused. "How could he be responsible for wind?" Then, it hits me. "Wait, *one* of your brothers? Are there more than the two of you?"

He looks around, pretending not to have heard my question—again. I interpret this as a sign that he isn't going to elaborate further.

"How old are you?" I ask impulsively. It might be rude, but it's too late now. "I mean, how old *were* you? In human years, not...vampire years."

"I'm around nineteen, possibly twenty," he says, with slight amusement.

"You don't know your own age?"

"It was a different time."

"The 70s were a different time. What generation are you referring to?"

No answer.

"Pre-twentieth century? Before the Industrial Revolution? How old are we talking?"

Even through the mask he wears, I see his mocking smile.

"Well, okay, whatever." I huff out a long breath and say, "It doesn't matter who did it, I'm glad you saved me."

"You're welcome, Brielle," he says, parting in his words, before turning and beginning down the path. A part of me wants him to stay longer. There are so many things I could learn from him, and I might never get a chance like this again.

"Will you at least tell me your name?" He stops, like he's debating it. I stand there staring at his muscled back for what feels like forever, awaiting his response, but his only answer is to vanish without a trace. One moment he's right in front of me, the next, he's gone. What on God's green earth did I just witness? Did he just *teleport*?

I'm mesmerized, unable to take my eyes off the spot he disappeared from, thoughts swirling in my head about this man, this creature, whatever he is—and how in so little time he'd managed to throw everything I knew about *them* out the window. Until now, I believed they were void of humanity, driven solely by bloodlust. However, his very existence proves they can learn to control their inherent, violent nature. They can act selflessly, show mercy, and tell the truth. My chest tightens as the weight of the sudden realization that vampires don't have to be monsters; they *choose* to be.

Perhaps they aren't as different from us as we like to believe. Every wicked, bloodthirsty vampire was once human, after all.

Walking back to my car, a stupid, traitorous smile spreads across my face. I may have befriended a vampire today...and I can never tell another living soul.

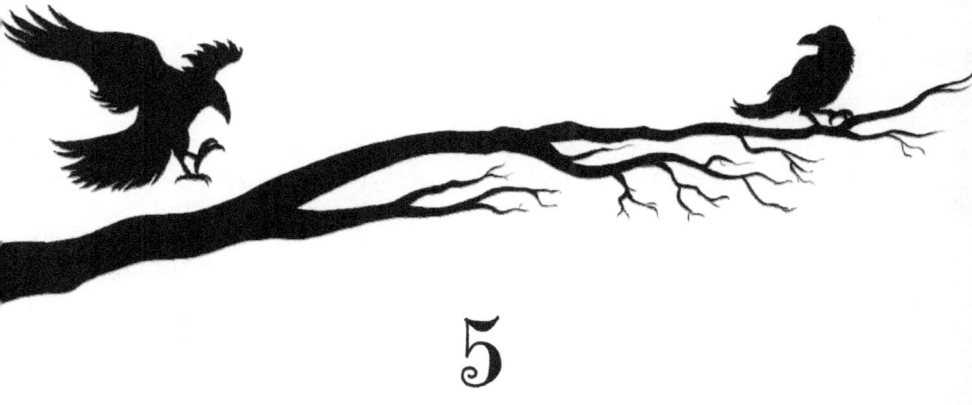

5

I PARK IN FRONT of a tiny hotel on Main Street, a few doors down from the coffee shop where I'm supposed to meet Mom in less than five minutes. Stepping into the warm morning sun feels incredible. I take off my jacket to bask in its glorious rays, allowing the heat to soak into my exposed skin, radiating deep into my bones. To think that my vampire stalker can never again enjoy this sensation saddens me.

Old-fashioned, red-brick buildings line the quiet street, their surfaces still darkened from overnight rain, making their color appear more vivid. As I pass under the tall, untrimmed trees planted along the sidewalks, with their unlikely mixture of red and green leaves, occasional droplets of water drip and land on my head.

Entering the seaside café, the familiar sound of the coffee grinder and the bold, smoky aroma of freshly brewed espresso greet me. There are plain wooden tables, a couple of leather couches in the corner, a pile of board games beside them, and a small gallery on one wall, featuring an eclectic mixture of styles—a way of promoting local artists.

I sit at the table nearest the door, cross my arms over my chest, and lean back in my chair, playing it cool. Given how punctual my mother is, I don't have much time to spare. Before I can get comfortable, the door swings open, and my mom, Evie, enters the scene. Classic white button-down shirt, light-blue skinny jeans, and black stiletto heels with little ankle straps...the same ones from yesterday. She walks toward me like an angry runway model, perfectly styled waves of hair bouncing with each step as I listen, trying to gauge her mood by the sound of those damn heels. Today, she is on a mission.

I smile at the sight of her. Full lips, high cheekbones—beautiful, if not humorously impractical, especially with those hundred-dollar rock star sunglasses, like an incognito celebrity trying to avoid the paparazzi. No matter the situation, she always places fashion above all else, even when coming to negotiate the release of hostage footwear.

With dramatic flair, she abruptly stops beside the table, whips off her glasses, and flicks down the Polaroid I slid under her door last night—like a card in a high-stakes poker game.

I move my eyes to the dark photo, to the words scribbled haphazardly at the bottom, which read:

Coffee shop. 8 am. Come alone.

My smile widens to a grin.

She stabs the center with her index finger, the point of her manicured nail pressed hard enough against the plastic to make an indentation. Depicted in the scene are her shoes in my trunk, situated on top of her suitcase, barely visible in the dim lighting. The chilly night air imbued the film with a greenish tint, altering the colors of her fancy heels to look desperate, malnourished, and in dire need of rescue. Crude but effective. I beam with pride at my handiwork.

"Where are they?" she asks, eyes narrowing, sounding more exasperated than mad.

"Oh, Mom, don't blame me. You walked right into this one," I laugh.

She is not amused.

"I was wondering...have you ever worn the same heels two days in a row?"

"Was this necessary?" she asks as she sits across from me.

"Well, maybe...I saw it as the perfect opportunity to spend a couple of minutes with my mom without the guys around. You know, since it's apparently impossible to have one-on-one time with you without leverage." It sounds so convincing that *I* almost believe what I'm saying.

She shakes her head, a reserved incredulity spreading across her face. Still, she can't seem to muster a quick response. Maybe she is just tired, after all.

"When was the last time it was just us?" I ask, hoping the location is enough of a hint to jog her memory. A long silence follows.

I almost feel where her thoughts are taking her. My high school graduation was three days ago. We had a joint celebration party for me, my brothers, and Jonathan. At no time was it just us. On our eighteenth birthday three months ago? Nope. Another shared celebration, like nearly every event in my life.

"Oh," Mom says, surprised, pulling back on her saucy attitude. Her eyes widen when it finally dawns on her that it has been over six months since she and I did anything together. Just the two of us. Even then, it wasn't exactly intentional. She had taken me out for coffee on Christmas Eve, the morning when all the guys got called in for a big emergency at work.

"Yes. *Oh*," I say, holding my smile while being sure to keep any trace of emotion out of my eyes, preferring not to let it show that it did, in fact, hurt me.

"I'm sorry, hun," she says, her eyes darting from left to right as she searches for something to say, a way to divert the conversation away from the uncomfortable. "So, uh, how was your trip to the cliffs yesterday?"

"It was...great," I begin, wondering what would happen if I just told her everything, before adding, "Are you and Dad still pissed at me?"

She huffs and crosses her arms defensively, lips pursed tightly together. The same look I've seen a thousand times. My parents love to bury things, to let problems fester rather than deal with them head-on. They prefer maintaining the illusion of the perfect, middle-class suburban family over facing the simple truth: there are mountains of serious issues we refuse to talk about. And therein lies the root cause of all our dysfunction. Just awkward silence, a Draper family tradition. A standoff, where the first person to talk loses.

"Well, you look pretty tired, Mom. How late were you guys up?"

She scoffs. "What about you? Did you get *any* sleep? Why are your eyes so red?"

"Not really, I slept like crap, thanks to Jonathan." Even with headphones in and my iPod blaring, I couldn't drown him out.

A smile finally brightens her face at the mention of Jonathan, and I feel jealousy roll through my veins. While not her child by birth, he had become hers, nonetheless. I always wonder what I would need

42

to do to earn a smile like that from her. Maybe they happen, but she's shy about them, only allowing them to occur behind my back or when I'm not around. That is my hope, at least.

"So, has this place changed much in the two decades since you were here?"

"Ugh." She rolls her eyes. "Eighteen years. I was your age. It wasn't that long ago."

"Yeah, well, eighteen years is a long time to me," I say with a laugh.

"Well, hun, it goes by a lot quicker than you think. I remember feeling you guys kicking my bladder in this very café, and now I'm sitting here having a conversation with my *newly* adult daughter, so. Time flies. You won't think it's a long time either when you're my age."

"I don't know, I think it's going to be a lot different. I mean, you were married and pregnant at my age. I'm still kind of waiting for this adult thing to kick in. I'm just not feeling it, yet."

"Your generation is very...*different*," she says, eyeing me. "Having kids and starting a family was just what you did. We didn't have all this technology. And your generation, I don't know, you get your purpose from punking each other." She punctuates her statement with air quotes, then gestures with her eyes to the photo on the table.

Do I tell her that the world, lately, feels too serious, and that we could all benefit from a little fun along the way? I could say something along those lines, but I already know the look she'd give me.

"You want to talk about pranks? Blame your sons and that spawn from hell you invite everywhere. I'm merely an impressionable victim. They were the ones who started the endless prank wars."

"Language, Bri," Mom says halfheartedly, a natural reflex anytime I swear.

"Was humor not a thing in the 80s? Was everything always super serious? Oh, I get it! You must have had no time to do anything fun...You spent it all teasing your hair to ungodly heights." Even *I'm* not sure where I'm going with this, I just love messing with her.

She rolls her eyes again.

I open my mouth to make another remark, but a familiar sight over Mom's shoulder stops me cold. The door opens, and Dad walks in. My exaggerated groan echoes off the walls of the empty seating area.

"You didn't come alone," I accuse, my annoyance shifting to frustration.

"I told him to wait in the car for a couple minutes. I thought we were doing a quick exchange for my shoes. How was I supposed to know you just wanted to hang out?"

"You see? Look at the extreme lengths I had to go through to get..." I make a big production about checking the time on my phone, "...*four minutes* alone with you."

"No, hun. See, I've known you your entire life. Ever since you were itty bitty. You would have done this for no reason at all," she says as she gets up. I nod softly to myself. True enough. Usually, I keep the practical jokes aimed at my brothers, but how can I resist chasing after such easy prey?

I shrug, stand, and clumsily swing my heavy backpack over my shoulder with an audible grunt, then watch as Mom rises from her seat, moving with such confidence, such ethereal grace. I would never have the guts to leave the house in an ensemble like hers. And, if I'm being honest, I could never pull it off. Truly astonishing, given that if my hair were a shade lighter, and she were still my age, we would be every bit the twins Elden and Warren are. How can we look so alike, yet be such completely different people?

My dad gives me a long hug and a kiss on my head.

"Morning, Dad. I was gonna get the guys something to eat. What all is planned for today?"

Dad opens his mouth to say something, but Mom interrupts. "Get dressed for the beach!" she says with a big smile on her face. "Oh, and we're doing the trails, so bring hiking shoes."

"What she said," he quips with a half-smile, never one to get in Mom's way.

I snap my head back to her. "*That's* what you needed your heels for? You're going to break something if you bring those stilettos with you."

"Ha!" she laughs, before giving me a dead serious look, "Never gonna happen."

I smile, knowing that she's right. Her ankles are probably bulletproof at this point.

I carefully place the white paper bag loaded with breakfast sandwiches on top of the donut box, making sure the cardboard will support the weight without caving in, then grab the handle of the drink carrier and balance it all in my arms. I was going to buy everyone breakfast, but Dad stepped in and paid—a ransom for his wife's treasured shoes. There was never a price on them, not truly, but in my book, it still counts as a win.

I open the door to the dark cabin, hitting the lights with my elbow and carrying everything to the dining room table. The place is a complete disaster, with food, clothing, and different bags strewn across the room. It doesn't make sense, but somehow it was cleaner when I'd gone to bed.

"Wake up! Before your nasty hot drinks get cold," I shout into the void, never having been able to wrap my head around the appeal of fresh, hot coffee. Load it up with sugar and put it on ice, though, and now you've got my attention.

Jonathan is still in a deep sleep and rips out another snore, approximately at the volume level of a weed whacker. It's worrisome—that's what it is. Elden exits the bathroom, hair sticking up in every direction like a buff troll doll emerging from his cave.

"Where have you been?" he grumbles. "Why don't you ever wake us up before you go out? We can come with you, too."

"Been there, tried that, but you guys sleep like the dead. Plus, you all take longer to get ready than a bunch of girls."

"And? What was so important that it couldn't wait an hour?"

"I was trying to get some pictures of the sunrise. Kinda time sensitive, just a bit," I say, making a little pinching gesture with my fingers. "Oh, so I found this adorable little baby deer in a clearing, right? And it came right up to me and smelled my finger. I have the photos, do you want to see?" I say with a grin, dangling my digital camera from its lanyard in front of his face, allowing it to sway invitingly.

He looks right past it and straight down at my shoes. "So...is that why you have mud all over the sides of your boots?"

"Yeah, turns out...it *rains* here, and that's what happens when dirt gets wet. Crazy, right? Then again, you'd have to go *outdoors* to know that," I say, furrowing my brows as I inspect my mud-caked hiking boots. I kick them off by the front door, then deflate when I feel my wet socks smacking against the wood floor. Great, another pair of soggy footwear that needs to dry. I could ask to borrow some of Mom's shoes, but I doubt she brought anything practical.

"I wish you wouldn't go out by yourself before sunrise. You know it can be dangerous," he says while his messy hair distracts me from his serious expression.

If he only knew the extent of what's out there.

"Jeez Elden, I was just out enjoying the area, trying to take it all in. Soon enough, we'll all be stuck back in the desert wasteland we call home, burning to a crisp, with strict curfews and nothing cool to do. I mean, what do you expect? I have a car for the *first time*! It's not my fault you just want to waste all your time here sleeping in."

"It's called a vacation," he says flatly.

"If there were any danger, wouldn't the sirens go off? Besides, what difference does it make if I go out alone? Who's gonna fight off a vampire, you?" I ask with a smirk.

I check on the pair of Chuck Taylors I left on the space heater overnight to dry out. Somehow, they're hot but still damp to the touch. What the heck? All the other stuff I hung out is still damp too. I would never have this problem in Southern California. Welp, I guess it's flip-flops for the rest of the trip.

"Look," my brother says, "I know you don't like to admit it, but this stuff is serious. Sure, there haven't been any documented attacks, but a lot of people still go missing in the woods. Even if you forget about, you know, certain *creatures*...There are mountain lions and bears here. Plus, who knows what kind of people you might run into? It's just not a safe place for a girl to be out by herself."

"No, trust me. I get it, Elden. I really do. You think I can't handle myself in the real world."

"That's not what I'm...believe it or not, I would like to hang out with my crabby sister sometimes. And yes, if there were a *real* threat, at least we might be able to buy you enough time to get away," he says.

"So, what? You'd expect me to leave you to the bears? Hell no. Get out of here with this nonsense, acting like I'm some wispy little damsel."

Warren walks into the room behind Elden, wobbling and exhausted. While looking down at his phone he says, "So I guess yesterday afternoon, there were some reports of an explosion up near where you were. Did you hear anything?"

I choke mid-sip on my iced coffee, coughing on the one drop I accidentally inhaled. "Oh. Huh, that's weird. No, I didn't hear anything," I say, clearing my throat.

I eagerly want to change the subject, so I toss them their breakfast sandwiches, then go to the couch and smack Jonathan's exposed shin hard enough to echo in the room. With that, he lets out a grunt and abruptly sits up.

"What's the plan for today?" Warren asks while yawning.

"I'm gonna drop-kick your sister into the next stream we cross by. But other than that, your parents were vague about today's itinerary," Jonathan says, rubbing his face.

"Shut it, Jonathan. If you even try, we'll leave you to walk home. This is supposed to be a drama-free vacation. We have a cease-fire agreement: No pranks, no retaliation," Warren says, eyeing him for a long moment, then his gaze slides to me in warning, as if to say, 'the same goes for you.'

"Fine, whatever," Jonathan says, sipping his coffee.

I give him a smug smile as I turn back to my brothers. "To answer your question, Mom has the beach in mind and the national park that's down that way. So, dress for sunny weather."

"Great, a hike with Mom. Hope you guys are ready to get your cardio in," says Elden with a smirk.

"What's up, man?" Warren asks abruptly, a sober look on his face. I follow his line of sight to Jonathan, who is staring intently at his phone.

"My sister texted me, there was a breach back home, just happened this morning," he says, his voice monotone as he reaches for the TV remote. He flips through the channels until he comes to a 24-hour news station. Everyone stays silent as he turns it up.

I feel numb, holding my breath, bracing for impact while I read the headline at the bottom of the screen. A male news anchor is speaking.

"This is a Red Alert. Devastating scenes out of LA County as a series of vampire attacks wreak havoc on several local communities, unfolding over the early morning hours. The death toll is currently unknown, with many of the attackers still at large. The Department of Supernatural Defense has deployed special forces teams to each of the affected areas and posted an advisory bulletin for the citizenry to shelter in place and report any unusual activity to the proper authorities. Reminder that this is a breaking story, and it remains too early for our experts to estimate containment."

It then switches to grainy video footage, slowed down and set on a loop, voiced over by a female newscaster. "At approximately 2 a.m. Pacific Time—5 a.m. Eastern—disaster strikes. Watch as this refrigerated food delivery truck stops in the middle of the street in downtown Pasadena, blocking traffic moving in both directions. The driver then exits the cab, walks around, and opens the back doors, unleashing a dozen or more attackers. At this exact moment, nearby sensor towers activated, notifying authorities and triggering a citywide lockdown."

"Similar incidents were also reported in Glendale and Long Beach. Though these attacks are suspected to be related, we still don't know who is behind them or what motivated them. Back to you, Jim..."

"I thought they were still looking inside refrigerated trucks at checkpoints," Warren says.

"But...why?" I ask, exasperated.

"Why, what? Why check the trucks? It's one way they work around the sensors..."

"No, I mean, why specifically there, why now? LA is one of the most fortified green zones. They know they're going to get caught and captured or killed within days, so what's the point?"

Elden and Warren exchange glances, not used to me chiming in on matters of supernatural security.

"They're monsters. What do you expect? They don't exactly have a published manifesto."

"Sure, just monsters. Monsters who can think, plan...use tricks to get around our security. I just don't get why they do things like this. It's a pointless suicide mission."

Quiet fills the room as Jonathan turns off the TV. There's nothing more to be gained by thinking or talking about any of this. I'm usually not part of these conversations, and I know Mom doesn't like to hear about this kind of stuff. Dad is even worse, refusing to say a word. Nobody likes the reality of how things are now, but life just goes on.

"I'm gonna go get ready. Bri, you should probably change your pants before we head out. Seriously, did you fall in the mud?" Elden asks.

Heat spreads across my face as embarrassment washes over me, remembering how I scrambled backwards across the ground, getting yet another article of clothing dirty. At this rate, I won't have enough clean clothes to last me through our vacation.

Why did he have to creep up so close behind me? He must have known that would scare the bejesus out of me. But then again, he extended a hand to help me up. Ugh. The heat in my face flares, and I know my cheeks are turning red.

"I...slipped," I say over my shoulder, walking nonchalantly out of the room before anyone notices. I change into my favorite Roxy two-piece bathing suit, but thanks to the bruising on my back, I forego the cute cover-up in favor of yet another ill-fitting T-shirt and a pair of faded denim shorts. I also grab a blue knit sweater, as the late spring weather here is much chillier than I'm accustomed to.

My attempts at a cute messy bun fail multiple times, so I begin a side braid while leaning against the edge of the sink. I try to relax my face, but the furrow between my brows doesn't ease. My thoughts oscillate between my guardian vampire and the monsters running through the streets of Los Angeles, spreading terror so near my home. I should hate every one of those overgrown, blood-sucking leeches...but I don't. Something has realigned in me, but maybe having your life saved by a monster will do that to a girl.

I'm thankful my family has no idea what happened. I'm glad I don't have to explain the feelings I'm still trying to understand. I'm scared to think of how they would react if they knew that not only had I encountered a vampire and led him straight to them, but that there is a growing part of me that very much wants to see him again.

6

I'M ALREADY OVER THIS nonsense.

My family stands gathered at the edge of the ferry, leaning against the railing as they watch the sunset, its last rays reflecting off the choppy waves. For now, I feel more comfortable keeping my distance from the water, electing to remain seated during the return trip from Friday Harbor, the last stop on Mom's itinerary, after a full day of exploration on foot and by city bus.

Now on day three of our vacation, my body is wracked with bone-deep exhaustion from checking off items from her never-ending lists. If yesterday's outing wasn't bad enough, traversing miles of same-looking trails that lead nowhere and trudging across cold and windy beaches with no sun or sand, today we somehow walked even further. Mysteriously, my parents seem unaffected by all of this, lacking neither energy nor enthusiasm.

Jonathan pulls away from the crowd and plops beside me. "I wonder if there's any way to get a hold of some black licorice."

"What?" I say, eyeing him suspiciously. How does he always know my weaknesses?

"Won't that stuff make you puke? Anyways, my plan is...you eat a bunch, hurl your guts all over the place, we'll play into it, and then tomorrow, your parents will leave us all at the cabin...at least until they're sure it's not contagious. We can spend at least a whole day doing absolutely nothing."

I shoot him a look of pure revulsion, but he's just staring off into nothing, wearing the withered visage of a man nearing his end.

"I did not consent to all this walking. I think I'm going to die."

"You look like *you're* about to hurl as it is. Why not just use that as your excuse? I still can't believe you got on a boat on purpose," I say, annoyed, still wondering how long he's known about the black licorice thing, and which of my brothers told him.

"Nah. See, because the thing is, I'd rather you be the subject of Evie's wrath. I can't be seen as the one who ruined her perfectly planned vacation."

"You're hilarious. You willingly agreed to come along, knowing exactly what you were signing up for on this *family* trip, and now you can't handle it. Poor baby."

"Bite me. I thought there'd be downtime. Relaxation. Sightseeing. Not running a whole block to catch the bus, or power walking from one shop to the next. I spent the whole day carrying bags full of things I didn't buy. I'm one hundred percent going to fake an illness in the morning, with or without you guys." He slumps in his chair, letting his head fall back to stare at the sky.

"You don't have to do any of that. Just ask Mom. She likes you more than me, anyway. Tell her to give all four of us a day off. She and Dad can go off on their own."

"No, see, you've always had it all wrong," he says as he closes his eyes, looking dead to the world. Dramatic and annoying from the day he was born. How he had all the girls in school trailing after him is beyond me. "You're the only daughter. You can get away with *anything*."

I stare at him, considering his words, the precious little golden boy who can do no wrong. He should be the one doing this. But since he's too much of a spineless worm...I guess it falls to me. I slowly and awkwardly push my tired body out of my seat, legs barely up to the task as I walk toward my parents. When I reach Dad, I hug him from behind and turn my head, resting my cheek against his back. I feel his hand grab my arm, his only way of hugging me back from that angle.

"Dad, you and Mom need a day to yourselves. I'm exhausted, and Jonathan is about to hurl. We need a rest day, a lazy day."

"No! Tomorrow, we're exploring Seattle! It's the biggest part of the whole trip!" Mom exclaims, bursting with energy from some unknown source.

"Then make it into a date for you and Dad, just the two of you. I'm already getting burnt out with the bigger city stuff. We already live near a big city. I want to stay at our cabin and enjoy the quiet little town."

She looks wounded. Betrayed even, mouth agape. On the other side of Mom, Warren locks eyes with me and mouths, 'Thank you.' I smile at him.

I lean over to look at the water, still holding onto my dad. I don't want to let go. Standing at the edge of the ferry kindles within me a flicker of apprehension, reminding me of free-falling into the cold, dark water. Foregoing the view, I instead close my eyes and enjoy the cool ocean breeze and the warmth of his embrace.

"That would be fine, Bri," Dad says.

Whoa, was Jonathan right?

"See, Mom, now you guys can turn it into a date. Find a club, go disco dancing. Feel young again." I grin, knowing how to poke her where it counts.

"I don't need to feel young again. I'm not old!" she automatically retorts, half vexed, half amused. I see the glimmer of a smile she tries to repress.

"If you say so." Of course, it was always a lie. She is still young. Even when the lines of age eventually show up, she'll always be beautiful.

I feel Dad sigh as Mom laughs and the last rays of sun fade from view, surrendering the skies to the initial phase of twilight.

Back in town, we decide to go out for dinner before returning to the cabins. The guys choose a sports bar that is open late, while our parents go to a swanky seafood restaurant near the water. As everybody settles in, I order a soda and excuse myself to use the restroom. However, as soon as I round the corner, it occurs to me that I could slip out the front unnoticed. Without breaking stride, I push the door open and step out onto the sidewalk, glad I'm still wearing my backpack.

I remember there's a bookstore down the street I wanted to check out, but it wasn't on Mom's schedule. I could go tomorrow, but it's more fun this way, and the guys are probably busy watching football or something lame. If I hurry, I'll make it before it closes.

Quickening my pace, I urge my legs to carry me faster along the sidewalk. Seeing people still out after dark, walking under the streetlights, brings back memories of life *before*. Even though where I'm from is also a green zone, it's nothing like this. Nobody looks nervous or apprehensive, and there are no military vehicles or checkpoints in sight. Experiencing life here makes me feel like I've been lied to for years. Where are the signs of the apocalypse? I'll admit, the idea of vampires watching over this territory to keep it safe is the very definition of foxes guarding the hen house, but I can't argue with the results.

The bookshop's storefront is a series of large floor-to-ceiling windows set into ornate architectural moldings. These showcase shelves full of obscure titles, oddly dressed mannequins, and random memorabilia, all framed with a string of Christmas lights—in *June*. As I enter, I step around two older women bringing in a display featuring books by local authors.

Exchanging greetings with the young cashier, I immediately search for the fantasy section. The musty bouquet of aged wood, ink, and stale glue is intoxicating as I scan the shelves for anything that catches my eye, excited for my upcoming day of rest and relaxation. I reach my destination and turn the corner, only to find a young woman standing in the middle of the aisle, blocking my passage through the narrow corridor. Before I can speak, she looks up from the book she's reading. She is tall and tanned, wearing a yellow summer dress, with wavy black hair that falls softly to her waist, her features stunning and willowy, like someone straight out of a faerie novel.

"You're finally here!" the girl says, grinning as if genuinely happy to see me.

I glance over my shoulder, thinking she must be talking to somebody else, but there's no one there. Her deep blue eyes capture my attention with their almost feline quality and pupils that seem too small for the dim lighting, leaving me to wonder if those aren't colored contacts.

Her smile fades as she returns the book to its place on the shelf. She looks around in mock suspicion before saying in a low voice, "You don't have to worry about him hearing us. I set up a diversion."

I feel like I just walked into the middle of a conversation. "Sorry, are you talking to me?"

Her grin slowly returns. "Of course, silly. It's cool, I already know all about your new friend," she says, winking an eye.

At that, my throat tightens. I feel a hot wave of anxiety flush over my skin. Who is this person?

"Not ringing any bells? Tall, dark, and brooding?" She takes a step toward me. "You recently had a little chit-chat in the forest?"

"How do you—?" I slam my mouth shut, realizing I have already said too much. I gave him my word.

"How do I...know about that? About *him*? We are..." She tilts her head to the side as she thinks it through. "Acquaintances. I'd love to say that we're friends, but he probably sees me more like a manager. Don't tell him I said that."

"You have the wrong person. I'm just here to buy a book."

"I know, I know...cross your heart and hope to die," she says, making an X over her chest with her fingers. "I respect your sense of honor, but you're not breaking your promise to him by *listening*, are you?"

"I—I have to go…" I say, then turn for the exit, nearly reaching the end of the aisle before she speaks again.

"He likes you, you know."

Her words stop me cold. How could he possibly like me? I've been rude to him every time we've met. Besides, what reason do I have to believe anything this weirdo says?

"But he won't…" she says, and sighs.

"Won't what?" I say, looking over my shoulder with suspicion, aware that I'm taking her obvious bait.

"Involve himself…*compromise*. He would never want to get in the way of you living out your normal life, or to influence your choices in any way. He's too much of a gentleman for that."

I glare at her with increased suspicion, not understanding her motivations or how she seems to know what I'm feeling for him.

"It's okay. I wouldn't expect you to trust me just like that," she says with a shrug. "By the way, did he mention he's still following you?"

"Have you considered that maybe I don't want anything to do with him?" I lie, just to see how she reacts.

"That would be sucky," she says, looking devastated at the thought, her expression then shifting to one of determination. "But if that's how you *really* feel, if you don't want to see him again, then do nothing. Walk out that door and return to the restaurant, go about your normal life. Then next week, you get on that plane, and you never look back. Simple as that."

That would be the smart decision, the *safe* decision. The choice that I'm supposed to make.

"But if you did, for whatever reason, want to see him again…you'll have to give him an invitation."

"I'm sorry, a what-now?"

"I don't know what else to tell you. He's old-fashioned. In his day, men didn't just go up and hit on chicks. Women had to open the door first. He's too respectful to bug someone who shows no interest."

"So you're saying I have to make the first move?"

We both laugh awkwardly.

"Honestly, if you give him any indication you don't completely hate his guts, he'll run with it."

"To be clear, I won't be needing to get a fountain pen, and hand-write a letter to him on some parchment—"

"No," she says, snickering.

"—or seal it with wax, deliver it by carrier pigeon?"

She smiles from ear to ear, her eyes sparkling with amusement.

I see the options materializing before me: do I invite the vampire in, or turn away and let this—let *him*—fade into a distant memory? Play it safe or court danger? Oh, who am I kidding? "What would you suggest?"

"Well, you could go out early again, preferably before sunrise, somewhere away from the crowd. Find a place where you won't be seen with him. If you ask him to come to you, he will."

"Why are you telling me this?"

"I know him, maybe better than he knows himself. He's the type who will suffer in silence, forever. A good soldier. But I also know that he's been waiting a very long time for this, and though he doesn't understand it yet, I'm afraid this is his one and only chance."

I think about what she's saying for a while, as well as what she's not saying, what I understand and what I don't, only now beginning to contemplate all the implications.

"Are you, you know—*like him*?"

She shoots me a puzzled look. I watch the gears in her head turn for a couple of seconds before her eyes widen, and her mouth drops open with a gasp, "You think I look like a *vampire*?"

"Shh," I hiss, looking around frantically, "There are people in the store. I'm sorry, I just assumed you weren't human because you're obviously concealing your eye color."

"Oh, no one's listening," she says dismissively, waving a hand in my direction. "Dammit, they're brand new," she laments, rubbing her eyes. "Are they too blue or not blue enough? It's hard to find ones that are natural-looking."

"So, then you're what...a shapeshifter?" I ask, raising an eyebrow. They can easily pass for us in their human form, and unlike vampires, there's no way to detect them.

"Eww."

Wrong again. I feel foolish asking, knowing so little about their world. I must seem like an annoying girl in her eyes, pestering her with questions.

"Witch," she offers with a knowing smile.

Once vampires had revealed their existence to the world, it wasn't long before their rivalry with shapeshifters was exposed, but there are still other things out there. Things we know a lot less about, like the woman standing before me: a seemingly ordinary human, with some sort of abilities. I can't help but wonder what she can do. Is she clairvoyant? Can she read minds? Talk to animals? Fly on a broomstick?

"Wait, how did you know I was going to be here?"

"I didn't *know*, know...let's just say...the chances were very high."

She takes out two books from under her arm and steps toward me.

"Ladies," says an older woman's stern voice from behind me. Startled, I turn to face her.

"Stores closed. We're trying to lock up."

"Sorry!" I say apologetically. She shuffles off, grumbling.

I feel my backpack zipper tugging, notice a weight shift, and then hear it close.

"I picked them out for you, myself. I know you'll love them. Oh, and don't worry, they're paid for. Now you have time to head back before your brothers freak out and come looking for you."

"So, are any more of your friends going to pay me a visit?" I ask in a hushed voice as we move toward the exit.

"Nope, just me."

We step outside into the cool evening.

"It was nice meeting you, Brielle. Sadly, after this, we don't get to see each other for a while."

Huh. Cryptic, but all right. "Well, it was nice meeting you, too..."

"Cora."

"Thank you for the books, Cora," I say, trying not to look as awkward as I feel.

She nods, and I give her a quick smile. There's something about Cora that leaves me with a sense that I wouldn't mind really getting to know her. An air of mystery—

"You really should get going," she says abruptly.

"Oh, crap." I turn and break into a power walk toward the restaurant, throwing a goodbye wave over my shoulder. I sneak through the closing door and slow to a casual pace, slightly winded.

The dining area is mostly empty, and no one notices me as I come in. As I round the corner, I collide with Warren.

"Oof!" He exhales. "What the hell, Bri?"

"Oh yeah, take no blame. You came around a blind corner, too, jeez."

His eyes are wide, alert. It's a side of him I've never seen before. Then, he puts his hands on my shoulders and pulls me in for a hug. I grunt, unprepared for how tightly he squeezes me.

"What took you so long?" he murmurs, voice slightly trembling with worry.

Good grief, I've been gone less than ten minutes. "I went on a side quest," I say with a smile, prying myself from his embrace. "I just wanted to hit the bookstore before it closed." What has gotten into him that he's acting this protective?

"You *left*?" he groans, running his hands through his hair. "We already went to a bookstore today. If you buy any more stuff, you won't have enough room in your luggage."

"Then I'll sneak it in yours since you haven't bought anything," I tease.

Warren gives an awkward, forced smile. I walk past him to the table, only to discover that Elden and Jonathan share the same tense expression. All three appear on edge.

"What's up with you guys? Did something happen?"

"No," they reply in unison. My eyebrows shoot up in surprise.

"We were waiting for you to get back before we ordered," Jonathan says, tossing a menu in my direction. "Wanna do a bunch of appetizers to share? Or order separate meals?"

"I don't care, whatever you guys want to do, but would anyone care to explain why you look like you're about to collectively crap your pants? What happened?"

"Nothing happened," Elden says, seated across from me, adjusting his expression to portray a calm façade.

"First of all, you're a terrible actor, Elden. Look, this better not have anything to do with your stupid job. You were forbidden to bring up work on this vacation," I reply, trying to suppress my growing anger.

Whatever they did when they scampered off with Dad after school or disappeared on the weekends, they weren't allowed to breathe a word of it to anyone, but I'm pretty sure Mom knows more than she lets on. The only person regularly left in the dark—and bored at home—is *me*, and it cuts like a knife.

"Could you try not to ruin everything, for once?" Jonathan says.

"Cut it out, Jonathan," Warren snaps.

"What is there to ruin? Look at you guys, acting like somebody died, yet refusing to talk about it. I'll just head back to the room, see if the Chinese place delivers," I say, digging through my bag for my keys. "You guys can do your thing."

"Bri," says Elden.

"I have my rental, it's fine. You guys can catch a ride with Dad."

"Okay, look, we got a call from Dad. Yes, it has something to do with work, and it's serious. We were brainstorming ways to deal with the issue when we noticed you were gone a while, and Warren said he'd check on you. That's all. None of us expected something like this to come up while we were on vacation. I'm sorry we're always vague, but it's just how work is. If there were any way I could tell you more, I would."

I glare at him, feeling the lingering sting of betrayal and mistrust. He's not lying about everything he said, but he's leaving so many details out that he's told me nothing, all the same.

"We didn't bring up work. You kept pushing the issue," Warren says, avoiding my gaze.

I hold back an eye roll. Fine. Fair enough. I brought it up first. Making it through one vacation without them leaving me out of something was too much to expect, anyway.

"Can we just eat and relax? Today has been exhausting." Elden shifts to a lighter tone. "Let's figure out what we're gonna do tomorrow. Anyone have any ideas?"

"Is there a river nearby to take some inner tubes down or go fishing?" Jonathan suggests, with an annoying gleam in his eyes. I'll bet his idea of fun involves flipping my inner tube, not out of revenge but just for the thrill of it.

"It's not supposed to warm up for a couple of days," Elden says.

"Or we stay in, get some food, and watch movies," Warren says, rubbing his face.

All three turn their heads to look at me, awaiting my input.

"I don't care. I'm going to get coffee early and find a quiet spot to read my book."

We place our order, and after a prolonged silence, the guys begin discussing hunting and fishing in the area, along with local legends about Bigfoot, which surprises me. Like most people, they rarely talk about anything supernatural. Even saying the word vampire in polite company has become taboo, kind of like you're bringing trouble into your life, an old-world superstition revived and repackaged for modern times. Since there's no official evidence that Bigfoot exists, they don't have a problem discussing it.

After dinner, the guys want to walk the storefronts. We pass the now-dark bookstore and a giant water fountain, finally settling on some benches. The sounds of insects, bubbling water, and distant traffic fill the air. For a sleepy little port town, it's quite pretty at night, with string lighting strewn between the buildings, creating an ethereal canopy of amber light. I'd nearly forgotten the safety and stillness of the evening...just one more thing they'd taken from us.

Sitting beside Elden, I link my arm with his and lay my head against his shoulder. But instead of enjoying this rare outing with my brothers, I can't stop my mind from wondering who the man following me is. Scanning the tops of buildings with my eyes, I search for his silhouette against the darkened sky. Would he be up there, perched on a ledge like Batman, watching me even now? The thought brings a silly grin to my face. And more questions. What does he want? Had he returned from Cora's diversion yet? I wonder what he thinks of my strange little life.

Though I'm perfectly aware of the danger he represents, I find myself restless with anticipation to see those strangely beautiful eyes again.

7

I MAKE THE TREK to the living room in silence, the cold hardwood floor siphoning the lingering warmth of dreaming out through the soles of my bare feet. The clock on the microwave reads 4:36 a.m. Jonathan lies sprawled out on the couch, mouth agape, the motor in his throat revving with each strained, gasping breath. Nothing short of a good whack with a stick could wake the poor bastard now.

I open the front door and step out onto the porch, shutting it gently behind me, standing there with my arms folded, unsure where to go from here. What do I know about this guy? After all, I've only met him twice.

Is this what I want? I fumble with the odd shape of the question, as if I've just been pitched a wicked curveball. It's easy to say what I *don't* want: to be pushed around, hiding within an invisible electric fence while powerful beings run free, out there in the wild, beyond the edge of the game board where pieces like me are allowed to move. It sounds like there are still rules he must abide by, but they seem far fewer than those imposed upon me.

The danger of this is obvious. And my choices won't only affect me. There's a teeny tiny chance my snooping family will find out, in which case my stalker's brother will need to erase their memories. I could live with that. Though I'm not sure how well I'd handle it if I want something more, and he, well...doesn't. It could be easier to walk away now.

Nothing frightens me as much as what happens if things *go well*. If we want the same things. If it works out...there's no way for him to become human again. Which would leave only one possibility, and I'm not sure I can fathom it. Yet, as awful as it sounds, the choice between his type of "living" and the life that awaits me is an easy one. Because the only path available to me is to become my mom.

I place my hand on my neck, my fingers trembling, as I think about the painful price of admission. Then I smile, realizing that this is my only reservation. A moment of suffering for an eternity of freedom? Maybe it means I am crazy, after all, but I'd take that deal. All I need to do is convince this sucker to bite me.

"I know you're there," I say softly, aware that if I were to whisper, he'd still hear me. I want him to see me, though. To know that I'm talking specifically to him. "I'm going to walk to the coffee shop in a bit. *Alone.* In the dark. So..." I feel foolish speaking to the air, and scan the surrounding area for witnesses, mortified at the thought of anyone else having heard that.

Silence. Not sure what I was expecting.

I slink back inside and run on quiet feet to the bathroom, stealthily closing the door before flipping on the light, only to be assaulted by the sight of the girl in the mirror. Usually, I don't fuss much over my appearance, aiming for mostly presentable. But today,

I want to try to look...nice, applying my mascara as carefully as possible—the only makeup I brought.

Digging through the mishmash of clothes, I quickly get frustrated: nothing but raggedy outdoor wear, comfy shorts and pants I've had for years, and some baggy band tees. I struggle to find anything half decent, finally yanking out a baby-blue spaghetti-strap tank top and a pair of black skinny jeans from near the bottom of my bag. My Converse are finally dry enough to wear. Lastly, I throw on a cream-colored knit cardigan—almost assuredly stolen from Mom's closet.

The street lanterns glow warmly amidst the silvery fog that blankets much of the town, and the tree branches have become lurking shadows in the mist. I smile at the unexpected beauty of it, as it feels like walking through an alternate reality. The coffee shop's familiar front door is the portal that takes me back.

I order my drink and stand by the pickup window, watching the clock slowly tick by. There's plenty of time before sunrise, but I doubt he's going to waltz into a coffee shop on a Monday morning. Perhaps this was a dumb plan. Or maybe he didn't hear me. Maybe I should drive into the woods again? The lady behind the counter hands me my drink, and I take it with a smile, when I feel my phone vibrate in my pocket.

Crap. Has one of my brothers woken and realized I'm not there?

I pull out my phone, and the small screen displays 1 New Message from an unknown number.

We can meet, but not there.

My heart races with excitement. Cora was right. I rush outside, eyes glued to my phone, mindlessly ambling back to the cabins. How did he get my number? I shrug off the question, sipping my drink, letting the cold, sugary liquid hit the back of my throat and deliver its caffeinated rush to my brain.

> K, where?

Then I wait, slurping my drink loudly, giddy with anticipation.

"What about here?" His deep, even voice comes from right behind me.

My coffee and phone fly out of my hands, bound for the concrete below, as I whip around toward him, nearly leaping out of my skin.

"Dude! What the hell?"

His gaze lowers to his outstretched hands, in which he holds my intact cup and cell phone.

"You dropped these...though, I'm not entirely sure how."

I retrieve them, embarrassed to have made a fool of myself in front of him yet again. Wait, that's impossible. If he was standing behind me, how did he catch my things without me noticing? I think back to the park, the way he just vanished into thin air. Could it be that he moves so quickly...my human senses can't detect him? I shake off the thought, because nothing that powerful could or *should* be real.

He steps into the alley, merging with the shadows until all that remains visible are his eyes, which I can't look away from. I've never seen them so close-up in such low light, and I realize why I keep seeing them in my head, thinking about them. They're...beautiful, seeming to emit their own faint, fiery light, which dances and flickers like the surface of hot embers. Even now, I'm aware of how fearful any sane person would be standing so close to something like him, and yet...

Just then, a loud diesel engine roars and growls from down the street like some mechanical beast, still some distance away. I turn to see the garbage truck in the distance, lurching this way. He heard it coming long before I did. Glancing back down the alley, I can barely make him out in the dark, leaning up against a brick wall, hands tucked into his pockets, maybe fifteen or twenty feet from where I stand. I think he wants me to come to him.

If my brothers only knew I was about to follow a vampire into a dark alley, they would undoubtedly slap the stupid out of me. Luckily, they're back at the warm and cozy cabin, drifting through dreamland as I venture into the shadows.

"Dude?" he asks, amused. "I have been called *many* things, but never that."

"This is the third time you have just—*appeared*—behind me out of freaking nowhere. Do you get a kick out of startling people, or is this something you enjoy doing to me, specifically?"

His eyes narrow ever so slightly. "You know, I hadn't given it much thought," he says, raising a hand to his chin, "Hmm. If I had to guess, though, I'd say it's out of instinct. You see," he says, pushing off the wall, "I like to close in on my prey *without* being detected, this way...I can bite them before they've had a chance to realize they're being pursued. I like to think it saves the victim a little unnecessary...suffering. It seems more humane, wouldn't you agree?"

Hands still in his pockets, his stride casual, he moves slowly and yet covers a lot of ground, having already circled me as he delivers his macabre speech. I refuse to budge an inch or show the slightest sign that his attempt at being intimidating has any effect on me, instead rolling my eyes at his bluff.

"I bet you talk like this to all the girls." Playing it off seems easy enough, even as my tremulous voice betrays my nerves, and though I trust him, I would like to see the facial expressions that accompany these words, to read what is written on his face, hidden behind the mask.

He lets out a low chuckle of smug self-satisfaction, apparently delighting in his ability to instill fear in humans. "You needn't worry, though. Those were the old days. Causing harm to humans is strictly forbidden in this territory. You're safe," he says with amusement, "at least, from *me*."

Although it's not easy to tell in the dim light, I could swear he winks at me.

"Oh, so...if it were the *old days*, you wouldn't have hesitated to sink your fangs in me? To kill me?" I ask with put-on confidence.

"I didn't say kill...I said *bite*."

"Oh, yeah, I forgot...big difference."

"Mm. I can't imagine what kind of savage animal I must appear to be in your eyes. Is this what you humans have been taught?" He lets out a resigned sigh.

"Am I missing some part of the conversation here?"

"Our bite renders the victim temporarily sedated. The wounds heal quickly, without complication or infection. Most human doctors are unable to identify the bite marks. A spider's bite poses more risk than ours. Did they teach you that? Or did they only teach you to *hate*?"

He sounds genuinely concerned with what I think of him, avoiding my gaze. I'm speechless. I never heard anything like this. I don't want to believe he would lie to me, but nothing he's saying can be true, otherwise...everything I've been told about vampires would be—

"Those we feed upon recover soon after with little, sometimes no memory of the encounter, especially if we haven't been seen. Those of us who possess even a modicum of self-control don't need to kill to survive." He brushes off his jacket, straightening the edges and smoothing the wrinkles in his sleeves, then pauses. His shoulders heave as if he's taking a deep breath, then he turns his head back to me.

"My family has always held to our own strict set of rules. You are not the type of human we would feed upon, so no, that would have never happened," he says in a calm and reassuring tone. "Not even in the old days."

"That...goes against everything I know about vampires. I've seen the footage myself."

"No, no. Please don't compare us to those...abominations. In due time, their ilk will be eradicated, even if I must personally see it through."

I gape at him. If he means what I think he means, he's talking about wiping out those mindless creatures, like the ones currently on the loose back home. I wonder how out of my depth I am here.

"From the way you speak...it would seem that you like humans more than your own kind."

"I wouldn't necessarily go that far."

"Then why try to convince me that you're not bad?"

"Because. I like...*you*."

I'm caught entirely off guard. An irrepressible smile spreads across my face. I blush as I lock deeper into those glistening red eyes, not the vacant eyes of a thoughtless killing machine, but open windows to a whole other world where everything looks completely different. How does the loss of humanity change your perspective?

His gaze drops to my lips, still curved in a smile, and then travels back to my eyes.

"I'm glad you wanted to meet again, even if I don't follow your line of reasoning...though I am curious...how did you know I was nearby?"

He asks the question nonchalantly. I'm guessing he's not used to being caught by anyone, like ever. It's probably driving him crazy. Well, damn, now I wonder. Was that encounter at the bookstore supposed to have been a secret, as well? Cora didn't say anything to that effect.

"I was approached by an acquaintance of yours," I say, watching as he sharply raises one eyebrow.

"Oh?"

"Yeah, bumped into her last night. She told me you were still following me, and not much else. Somehow, she managed to be even more vague than you."

"Hmm. That might explain why I spent two hours last night searching for something that was never missing to begin with," he says, "...and that curious smell."

"The *smell*?"

He just rolls his eyes. Didn't know vampires were capable of being sassy.

"I don't mean you. You smell quite lovely."

"Okay..."

"Did she, by any chance, *give* you anything?"

"Yeah, actually, she put some books in my backpack. Is that not good? What would make you ask that?"

"It's nothing. I thought I caught a faint trace of witch around you, particularly near your bag. Would you mind holding still for me, please?"

I swallow hard. Although I can't imagine the reason for his request, I take his asking politely as a sign of respect. As fast as he can move, there's nothing he couldn't do to me, with or without my permission.

"Sure."

He starts off by taking slow, measured steps to my left. I follow him with my eyes until he disappears behind me, hardly visible in my periphery. I can't prevent the image of razor-sharp white fangs from popping into my head. What could he possibly be doing back there? Then, my backpack lifts from my shoulders, and I hear him sniff.

My eyes widen, and laughter bubbles out of me as its weight gently returns. "Did you just...smell my backpack?"

"Ever the interloper," he says, then sighs, now standing where I can see him. "Figures it would be her. That meddling witch loves to put herself in everyone else's business." He huffs and shakes his head, but there's amusement in those red eyes. "What is she playing at with this? Why would she interfere?"

"Wait, you can seriously identify a person just by the way they smell?"

"Yes, we can, at times. Usually, the trails tend to fade rather quickly. Cora, however, has a very *distinct* scent," he says. He stops and resumes his casual stance, as if he forgot that he's supposed to act like a human, putting his hands back into his jacket pockets.

"So," I say dragging out the word, "I can't help but wonder why you're still following me. Did you not believe me when I said I wouldn't tell anyone? I haven't said anything."

"I know, and I appreciate you keeping your word. I trusted you then, and I trust you now."

"Then...why?"

"There is...another issue...something I need to keep an eye on."

"Is this something I'm allowed to know about?"

He looks deeply into my eyes. If I had to guess the expression behind the mask, I would say that it resembles pity. "You truly don't know, do you?"

"Well, yeah, that's why I'm asking." Thought that was obvious. Why is he being weird?

"Since you seem entirely unaware, I think it's best we leave it that way. At least, for now," he says slowly, carefully weighing his words.

"But this issue has to do with me in some way?"

"Yes."

I close my eyes for a long moment before they can roll back into my head. Adding more secrets to ruminate over. Just great.

"Would you at least tell me if I were in danger?"

"You mean, other than your frequent run-ins with vampires?"

Sigh. "Alright, well, how much longer do you plan on hanging around?" I ask.

"Depends. How much longer do you intend to remain in my territory?"

"We're leaving in ten days."

"Then, I'll be watching from the shadows for the next ten days."

I can't help but smile, yet again, at the thought of him hanging around. Watching over me, keeping an eye out. A forgotten feeling comes back to me, another relic from the time before vampires, that of being protected, secure. Unlike my brothers, father, or Jonathan, so long as he's around, I don't have to fear vampires, or the night, or bears...or *anything* for that matter.

"That's going to get super boring for you."

"No, it won't. I find you and your little misadventures...interesting."

I blink at him skeptically.

"Perhaps that's not the right word..." His head tilts.

If he thinks I'm interesting, then he must be one hell of a recluse. "Then, I look forward to you stalking me some more."

As soon as the words leave my lips, I realize they are the kind you think but never speak out loud. My face is on fire, and I consider crawling into a nearby trash can to hide my embarrassment. Always surrounded by my brothers and Jonathan, I'd gotten so used to saying whatever's on my mind, but now, I'm left wishing I had a little bit of a filter.

"Intriguing," he says, "that was the word I was looking for. There's something more to you that I haven't quite figured out, yet."

I stammer, with nothing coherent coming out. Is he just messing with me? We've met three times. The first, I looked like a drowned rat, and the second, I was more pissed off at him than anything. So, I'm not sure what he's seeing...but I'll take it, and hope that he's right, that there is anything more to me.

He sighs, pulling back a sleeve to glance at his watch. "As much as I would like to continue this conversation, you should probably get going. I've noticed you don't like to be seen coming or going by your family, for whatever reason. If you still want to make it back unnoticed, you only have ten minutes until your father's alarm goes off."

"No, it's cool. He gets up at six." I pull out my Nokia and push the home button to check the time. "We still have like half an hour."

"That would normally be the case, yes, but I overheard last night that your parents are leaving early for Seattle."

It takes just a bit longer than ten minutes to walk back. Now, I need to decide whether I want to talk with everybody about why I went out early, by myself again, or I'll have to run the whole way. Great. Just great.

I take a few steps backward onto the sidewalk, leaving the alley, not wanting to go just yet.

He watches me with curiosity, like he's trying to read me, to figure me out. "Of course, you could stay a little longer. I'm sure they can be made to understand, right?"

Ugh. How do I explain the dynamics of my crazed, intrusive, boundary-stomping family to a vampire? "If I don't sneak off, they'll just tag along or stop me from going. I don't get a say in the matter. They don't exactly...listen to me."

"So, you'd rather run the whole way back with a full bag and a coffee in your hand, rather than explain yourself?" he asks, amused. "Again, I don't understand, but I can't wait to see it."

"Even though you sometimes scare the hell out of me, I hope this isn't the last time I see you."

As mortifying as it is to say such a thing, I truly want him to know that I also find him...intriguing. I don't want him to go away. Maybe if I encourage him, he'll emerge from the shadows and talk with me. I wonder if he's lonely, what his family's like. If, despite everything on the surface, we're not quite as different as it seems.

"Tick-tock, Brielle," he says with a smile in his voice.

I down the rest of my coffee and toss it in the nearby dumpster before pulling the straps on my backpack tight. "Later, dude," I say with a smirk, then sprint down the sidewalk, full-on Tom Cruise running back to the cabin. I can't be sure, but I think I hear the faint sound of rich, baritone laughter in the distance.

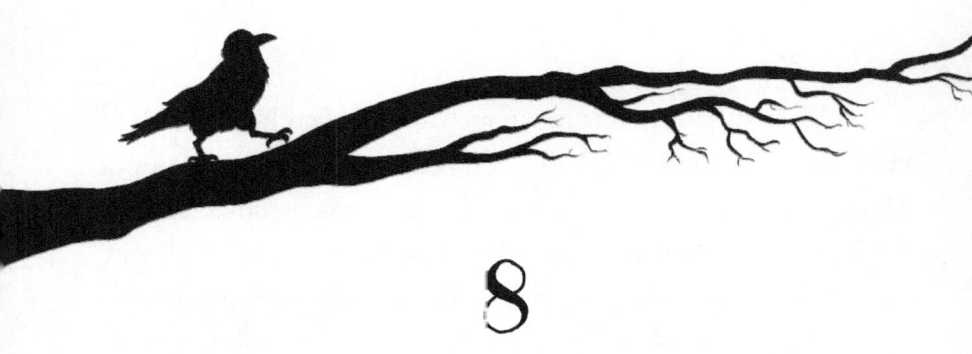

8

I SLIP INSIDE UNNOTICED, cold and out of breath—everything is how I left it.

I set my backpack on a kitchen stool when something catches my eye: Warren's green duffel bag, lying open on the floor at my feet, with a faint, glowing red light emanating from within, shining through the fabric of one of his shirts. As I watch, it slowly fades. My curiosity takes over, and I reach for it.

Right as my fingers touch the cloth to pull it away, there's a loud noise, and I jolt upright, snapping my head toward the entryway. Someone pounds frantically on our front door, repeatedly trying the knob. The silhouette of a tall man appears at the window, visible through the break in the curtains. He peers inside, hands cupped around his eyes, face pressed against the glass. My heart pounds in my chest. When he backs up, the porch light reveals half of his face—my dad's face. I rush and unlock the door, yanking it open. He bursts in, overcome with panic. I've never seen him like this.

"What's wrong, Dad?"

The twins enter the room, looking dazed. Jonathan still doesn't stir.

"You guys all here? Everything okay?" he asks my brothers.

"Yeah, we're good. What happened?" Warren asks, crouched and zipping his duffel bag.

My dad does a double-take at me, the only one not wearing pajamas. "Why are you dressed? Where do you think you're going?"

"Nowhere, yet. I got up early. I was just about to turn a movie on." I try to avoid telling outright lies to my Dad, but I don't see anything wrong with being vague at times. "Besides, what's the big deal? You're not saying anything."

He looks to his sons without acknowledging me, "You two, get dressed and come to my cabin for a few minutes. Bri, I need you to stay here with Jonathan."

"You're seriously not going to tell me why you nearly broke the door down to get in here?"

"We'll talk about it later, hun," he says, trying to placate me. "I just need you to hang tight for a little bit." With that, he turns and takes a step toward the door.

What the heck? "Are you being serious right now? You barged in here asking if 'everyone is okay,' like there was a fricking serial killer on the loose. Now everything's fine?"

"Now is not the time—"

Weird. That's the exact phrase he uses whenever I ask about his top-secret government job. "Does this have something to do with your work?"

Silence.

"You guys are unbelievable," I say as I grab my bag from the stool.

"What are you doing?" asks Elden.

"What does it look like? I'm leaving..."

"You can't—" Warren tries to say.

"Try and stop me," I challenge, knowing none of them will do anything.

Warren scoffs and Elden huffs out a strained breath with Dad only standing there in pained silence, eyes on the floor. He's usually more subtle, even cunning, when excluding me. This has to be related to what happened at the restaurant last night...but how?

"Please, just stay here with Jonathan," Dad says, "You can put your movie on. We'll be back as soon as we can."

"I'm not his damn babysitter!" I snap.

"Come on, Bri, just for a few minutes. Don't make it a big deal, please," Warren pleads.

For a moment, I consider watching the movie...keeping the peace. I've done it before. I could shrink down and play my part to keep everyone else happy. I feel the car keys in my pocket, think about my vampire stalker, my waiting rental car, the fact that I could have died the other day, but for whatever reason didn't.

In an instant, it could have all been over, so what am I even doing? What's the point in worrying about this meaningless crap when *he's* out there, waiting for me?

"No offense, guys, but I think...I'm *done*. I'm *really* done with this. Go ahead and have your little chat," I say. "I'm just gonna head out."

"No," they all respond in unison, only deepening my resolve to spite them.

"Now is not the time to be stubborn," Dad chides, raising his hands but not entirely blocking me from leaving. As I pass him, he softens his tone, saying, "Please. I need you to trust me, this is more serious than you can know."

I stand in the doorway, back to him, arms folded defiantly across my chest, and without looking at him, I say coldly, "Fine, I won't go...*if* you tell me *why* it's serious." I let a few breaths pass, pretending to wait for an answer I know will never come, no matter how many chances I give them.

I turn to him, look him dead in the eyes, and say what I've wanted to say for so long. "It's disgusting. You let *Jonathan* in on all your little secrets, and he's the biggest blabbermouth I've ever known. I'm your *daughter*, and you treat me worse than a stranger. Why would I trust you? What have you ever done to earn my trust? What did I ever do to make you have so little trust in *me*?"

The hurt in his face will stay with me forever, but still, he says nothing. With nothing left to say, I storm out.

Warren's the one to come running after me, but he's too slow. I'm already inside the car. "Go away, War," I say, slamming the door.

He goes to the passenger side, but I lock it before he can jump in.

"Come on!" he groans with exasperation, placing his hands on the roof. "Open up. I know you're not serious about this. We'll make it up to you." He jumps back when I start to pull out.

I crack the window just enough for him to hear me say, "You're barefoot in your pajamas. Get back inside and have your dumb meeting. I'm going to go live my life."

"It's not even six in the morning. Where do you think you're going?" he says as I roll up the window and drive away, no destination in mind. It doesn't matter where I'm going, I just need to go.

My first stop is the gas station at the edge of town, as the fuel light has come on, reminding me that I haven't filled up in days. I run inside, grab a soda and a bag of chips, and hand the cashier a twenty-dollar bill, asking her to put the rest on my pump.

Once I've finished fueling, I climb back into the car, connecting the auxiliary cord to my iPod. Without worrying about the guys' constant scrutiny of my musical tastes, I pull up my favorite Pink album. As the first song starts, I turn it up. It feels like she really understands my mood.

Back on the road, I roll down the window, feeling the rushing wind on my face, hoping it will help calm me. No master plan, no itinerary, and no one to answer to. In a way, this feels like the beginning of me living my life on my terms.

"You are quite unobservant, even by human standards," rumbles a voice from the backseat, and I slam on the brakes, sending my backpack careening onto the floorboard. The cup holder barely holds on to the soda as I come screeching to a stop in the middle of the road. Thankfully, there isn't another car in sight.

"Oh. My. God!" I shriek, my arms extended, white knuckles gripping the steering wheel tightly. Locking eyes with him in the rearview mirror, I demand, "Why do you keep doing this?"

He stares blankly back at me.

I shift my foot from the brake to the accelerator, and the little car's engine groans reluctantly as it struggles to gain speed. I slap on the dome light, giving me a better view of him.

"Well? What do you have to say for yourself?"

"Honestly? This time, the blame rests squarely on you," he says, eyes closed, fingers pressed on the bridge of his nose, clearly frustrated with my reaction. "Most people would notice someone in their back seat. I thought you saw me wave to you through the window when you were refueling the car. The lights even came on when you opened the door. It's not as though I were hiding in the dark."

"Well...jeez, dude. You know, it's not normal for other people to just pop into your backseat unannounced. Give a heads up," I say, my voice shaky.

He lets out a small huff, his wide shoulders sinking as my eyes drift to the passenger seat, pushed all the way forward to accommodate his long legs.

Damn, I am unobservant. How did I *not* notice that? Neither of us says anything for a minute, long enough for me to find some humor in his constant intrusions. Maybe he's been hanging around other vampires for so long that he's forgotten how to act around humans.

"Does it offend you when I call you dude?" I wonder aloud. My pulse is still not ready to return to normal, and I feel my heartbeat in my neck and ears.

"No."

"Then, that will be your new nickname until you decide to tell me what to call you," I say with a sinister grin.

He stares at me, amusement gleaming in his eyes.

I focus on breathing, trying to lower my heart rate as I wait for his retort. The seconds stretch into minutes, but he maintains his silence. I keep glancing at him in the mirror, only to see him staring out the window, seemingly lost in thought. What could he be ruminating over?

"Where are we going?" he asks.

"I think it's called Lake Crescent. I was going to stop there the other day, but...well, you know, I ended up doing some involuntary cliff diving. I'm dying to see it. I hear it's really pretty."

He gives a low hum of acknowledgment.

"I would've figured you'd still be watching over the other situation. Not breaking into girls' cars at the local gas station."

"The other situation doesn't require my constant attention," he says, repressing a laugh.

"So, there's no work-related reason to join in my morning adventure?" I ask with a smug smile, taunting him. He seems relaxed now, at least as much as an immortal vampire can be while crammed into the back seat of a Honda Accord.

"Would you like me to leave?" he asks.

"No, it's not that I want you to leave. It's just confusing. I figured it would be days before I saw you again, if ever. Not less than an hour later," I say, hesitating before asking, "Did you hear our argument?"

"Yes."

"Do you think I overreacted?"

"No," he says in a way that gives me the feeling he doesn't want to elaborate.

Another long silence. This time, he breaks it, saying, "Might I suggest getting into the habit of locking your doors?"

"Because...of your kind?"

"No, because of *your* kind."

Oh. I feel his gaze on me. I wish I could look deep into his eyes, but I'd rather not crash into a tree.

"So, Dude the Vampire," I say, smashing the door lock button, "now that I have you trapped in my car, can I get some questions answered?"

His low chuckle suggests he might humor me. "There are things I can't tell you. Otherwise, I'll be happy to answer any questions you have."

"Such as?" I ask, immediately testing the boundaries, "What, specifically, are you *not* allowed to reveal? So I can avoid those topics." Hearing him exhale in annoyance, I laugh before sipping my soda, contemplating what I should ask.

You know what? To hell with it. "So, why hide your face? Even at night—even in the dark?"

"For the safety of my family and myself."

"What, like, you're afraid someone will uncover your secret identity?"

"It's to hide from humans and your surveillance systems. Your kind has become obsessed with putting cameras everywhere, even out in the woods. We have survived these many years by remaining hidden, operating in secrecy, and relocating when it served our interests. It was easier when we were merely myths. Human memories are short and unreliable. No good can come of having our faces immortalized on a video recording for all the world to gawk at."

"Honestly, it doesn't sound like you guys could have remained hidden much longer."

"No. We couldn't, and we all knew it. We'd seen it coming for decades. The biggest threat to our existence has always been the one thing we require, and now you're evolving too quickly for us."

"Humans. Can't live with 'em, can't live without 'em."

He does not laugh. "Technology, in particular, has been the driving force behind our continued downfall."

"Damn. You almost got me feeling a little bit bad for vampires." Or maybe just *my* captive vampire. "But are you sure it wasn't the mass attacks on our cities that got you busted?"

"No, your government knew of our existence half a century ago."

I glance over my shoulder at him in disbelief before quickly returning my eyes to the road. "Wait, the government *knew*? Fifty years ago? And they didn't do anything? Or at least warn us?"

"Oh, they did plenty. Believe me. If the rumors are true, it was your government's actions that led us down this dark path. We did *not* want our existence known to the world. In fact, the only reason our leaders would have ever revealed our kind was if the alternative was far worse."

"Far worse, *how*?"

"I don't know exactly what ultimatum they were presented with, but they were likely being extorted. Manipulated, forced to surrender money and land, fight in wars, and do favors, all under threat of exposure. Through the years, I've seen it all. For them to have resorted to this, though...whatever they were faced with must have been truly unthinkable."

"Whatever happened to your leaders?"

"They're all dead, now. Destroyed in bombings of our most secret lairs."

Oh. "But wait, didn't you say you were working *with* the government, now?"

"In a way, yes—at least for the time being."

"Shouldn't they be your sworn enemies?"

"It's rarely so black and white. For now, we share the common goal of purging these new would-be contenders for the throne and putting an end to whatever new order they seek to create."

I didn't know vampires had such involved politics.

"So let me see if I understand this: you don't trust humans, the government destroyed your leaders, you don't seem to get along with other vampires, yet you're willing to work with all of them—*and* you're teamed up with a witch. What about shapeshifters? What part do they play in all this?"

"Shifters are a nuisance, at best. Typically, they stick to their people, staying out of vampire affairs. And they have one major advantage that has plagued us for millennia: they can blend in with the human world. Some of them like to worm their way into your politics, using secret alliances with their kin to advance their war on us, teaching humans to hate and fear us."

"Why would shifters have a problem with vampires?"

"That's an excellent question. One for which I have no satisfying answer, I'm afraid. We have always been at odds for some reason or another. Like many feuds among immortals, the reason may have been forgotten with time, but the bad blood persists from century to century."

Who would have known this hidden world would be so complex? I figured it was just a bunch of skeevy dudes in cloaks hanging around in basements. It sounds civilized.

"How'd you end up in a coven with shifters if you guys don't get along?"

"Days before it all started, before our leaders revealed themselves to the world, Cora showed up on our doorstep. We were residing in Quebec at the time, on the outskirts of Montreal—"

"Whoa, whoa, whoa. A *Canadian* vampire? I did not see that coming." I laugh.

"—and she told us that we needed to come to Ashland, a newly formed territory encompassing Oregon and Washington, and that she had convinced the shifters native to this region that they were going to need our talents for what was to come. They granted my family and me conditional residence in exchange for our services. Cora's ability to see danger on the horizon had saved my family in the past. She said she needed us, we trusted her, so we came."

"So, I have Cora to thank for the tall, dark, and moody vampire held captive in my car." If my taunting gets a response, he doesn't let it show. Then again, I *also* have her to thank for getting knocked off a cliff into the frigid waters of the Pacific Ocean, almost drowning, and having my memory wiped. Perhaps she *is* a meddling witch. But...if it weren't for her shifting of fate, I never would have been put on a collision course with the hottest guy I've ever met.

"Indeed, you have become my captor, and though it seems to me a trivial thing to free myself from your naïve restraints, I find myself rather happy to remain the prisoner of such a captivating jailer."

I cackle, probably not the correct response. Who still talks like this?

"Especially one so beautiful."

Oh.

Looking back at me through the rearview mirror, his eyes meet my gaze—deep set, hooded, accented by steeply arched eyebrows. These are my only clues to the face beneath the mask, features that seem, perhaps, more fitting of a villain. It doesn't entirely elude me that I'm being too trusting when it comes to him...or that I'm completely vulnerable in this situation. But damn, if the pull he has on me isn't irrepressible beyond words.

I keep trying to rationalize these growing feelings. Okay, sure, there's a lot I don't know about him. But he did selflessly hold me above the water as the waves crashed around us. There was no reason for him to waste his time saving me, to put his secrets at risk, just as there's no reason for him to accompany me on this drive...and it makes me want to believe that he likes spending time with me.

Plus, he's respectful, even though I'm technically food, and he exhibits kindness and grace in his every action. He even sees the evil in his kind and fights against it, keeping humanity safe in the process, essentially making him a hero...could it be that these are the reasons why my thoughts keep returning to him?

But...no. I know myself better than that. These are all just excuses for a raw desire that is deepening with every passing minute, one I fear I have already indulged too much to turn back from. And for now, I have him all to myself.

His brows furrow at the change in my expression as a giant grin spreads across my face.

9

LAKE CRESCENT

THE UNNATURALLY BLUE LAKE stretches for miles, surrounded by mountains and hills covered in the endless green of towering old-growth forests. We couldn't quite stop at one of the typical touristy spots, but luckily, my prisoner pointed out a back road leading past a dozen private driveways to a secluded trailhead.

I was looking forward to watching a six-foot-something shadowy apparition climb out of the back seat of my Honda and had, at the very least, hoped to get a giggle out of it. But no. He just appears unceremoniously at my side before I hear the *thunk* of the rear passenger door closing. I shoot him a sarcastic look. If he takes note of my impudence, his eyes do not betray it, two smoldering embers blazing through the gray of the foggy morning.

"You might want to watch your step," he says, glancing at my feet. "These paths can be treacherous, even with proper footwear."

I look at my Chucks and let out a resigned sigh. They will never survive this vacation.

We walk side-by-side, but I struggle to maintain a steady pace. With so many exposed roots, fallen branches, and loose stones, I could easily see myself eating it. To my dismay, I find I must watch my step the whole way. Something strange catches my attention: my shoes leave clear indentations in the dirt as I tromp and crunch my way across the forest floor, whereas his steps are silent and light, disturbing nothing in their wake. I roll my eyes.

"We might not have that long to hang. My family has an uncanny knack for finding me when I wish to be left alone. I swear I must share some weird psychic magnetism with my brothers, or something, or there's like a hidden tracking device embedded in me. I honestly have never figured out how they do it."

He chuckles softly under his breath. "Even all the way out here?"

"I wouldn't put it past them."

The cleared portion of the trail ends, and we begin down an overgrown path that appears to have been abandoned. The trunk of a fallen tree blocks the path ahead, and thorny blackberry runners crisscross the muddy ground.

"After you departed, they went looking for you. First, they checked the coffee shop you like to frequent, then they split up from there."

"Figures. They're predictable." And they know my affinity for cold, sugary drinks.

Every movement and step he takes seems deliberate. Confident. His hands are casually tucked into his jacket pockets, and he exudes such masculine grace that I can't help but feel awkward by comparison. In many ways, he's everything I'm not.

"I understand why they feel the need to protect you, but ultimately, you are your own being. You have the right to make decisions for yourself, even if they place you in peril. If you don't mind me asking, have they always been this way?"

Why do I feel so strange when he asks me this? Having someone else take my side, heck, even just acknowledging my perspective, is so refreshing. Why am I having a healthier relationship with a vampire than I ever had with my own family?

"No. Before I was fifteen, everything was somewhat normal. And then, after, well...you guys showed up, it wasn't." I still remember the family meeting where Dad laid out the new rules. No trips out of town. No going places after dark. Any time I left the house, I was to be accompanied by one of the guys. And of course, all my college and travel plans were indefinitely placed on hold. It changed every aspect of my life for the worse.

"I'm sure in time they'll learn to see the error of their ways."

"Doubt it."

"Oh?"

"I don't think things can ever go back to how they were before," I say.

He doesn't respond, but walks beside me quietly, waiting, listening. Does it matter what I say to him? He's a vampire. Who's he going to tell? I could confess a murder to him, and he would likely shrug.

"If...I could get away and start my own life, beyond their reach, I would. It's like they can't see me as anything but this little girl. And it drives me nuts." I sigh. "But right now, and for the foreseeable future, it's like I'm just stuck."

"Stuck?" he asks, seemingly taken aback, and stops abruptly.

My eyes flicker up to him. This is the first time I've seen him break his cool-guy demeanor. I attempt to stop alongside him, but my momentum carries me forward, and my right foot slides out from under me on the mud. I let out a gasp as my arms shoot out in a desperate attempt to regain my balance. It's too late. I'm falling.

But then, his arm is around my waist, instantly halting my fall. I feel his solid body pressing into my side. For a few heartbeats, neither of us moves. He looks down at me with an intense expression, and I can't read this change in his mood. Then I'm upright again. His arm retreats as I regain my balance.

"Why does this stuff only happen to me when you're around!?"

"I've been under the impression that you had a happy life with your family, other than the secrecy surrounding your father's work."

"Well, that's mostly true."

"But now you say that you feel stuck?"

"I'm—" I hesitate, never having told anyone this before, "—stuck living in my boring little desert town. Just like you're stuck here."

"If I weren't happy here, I would simply leave. What is it that prevents you from doing the same?"

He stands there, looking at me expectantly. Uh-oh. How do I get out of this? What does he want me to say? That I'm broke? That I can't get a good job in this stupid vampire apocalypse? That I have no life because of the curfews, I don't own a car, and I have a net worth of five hundred bucks?

"Brielle?"

I try to weigh my words, but he feels so...safe. And then it all just comes pouring out.

"I can't simply leave. I'm not like you. Humans need money. I need a car. Even if I had either, I'd still need to apply to transfer residency to a different territory, and the waiting lists for the safe places are backlogged for years. You can't get a good-paying job without experience, and you can't get experience without a job. Sometimes, I feel like I was just born at the worst possible time. But I'm guessing that vampires don't have to deal with that sort of thing, so you probably didn't know any of this. And I'm sorry if it seems like I'm mad at you. I mean, I am. Mad, that is, but not at you."

"No, it's great. In truth, I find your complete absence of tact refreshing. I've always appreciated a woman who speaks her mind, who doesn't waste time with pleasantries. You're right, as well. I've never considered anything like that before. It sounds terrible."

His gaze drifts off, and for several moments, it looks like he's internally debating something. Then he turns to me, and with a gleam in his eyes, offers his arm. I accept, linking mine through his, and we continue down the trail toward the lake. We come to a large, downed tree trunk blocking the path.

"May I?" he asks.

"Sure," I say, not knowing what the question is. Before I know it, I'm being lifted over the tree and set down on the other side. He hops over effortlessly, takes my arm, and we resume going along the path, my head swimming with the hope that there are more roadblocks ahead.

Before I had his arm to hold on to, my eyes were trained on my feet as I struggled in vain to keep my balance. Now, I study the scenery, practically daydreaming. Is this what it is to have someone to rely on? To *trust*?

I don't know what I expected to find at the end of this little journey, but I couldn't have imagined a more enchanted place. Dense plumes of fog roll down the mountainside, emerging from the tree line and cascading across the water's glass-like surface, shrouding the world around us in fine mist. We've come to the end of a small, creaky wooden dock, and though it's silly to think such thoughts—it almost feels like it's been *waiting* for us.

"It's perfect," I whisper in awe, relinquishing my grip on his muscular arm. I'll forever be grateful for my defiant nature. If I hadn't argued with my father and stormed off, or if I'd stopped to listen to Warren's endless excuses, I'd never have gotten to experience this.

He stands there, motionless, but for the edges of his coat and hood, which sway lazily in the soft wind. I wonder how long he's been, well, alive. Has he seen so many amazing things that he's no longer impressed by the beauty of nature? Or maybe being here has brought back a memory from so many lifetimes ago he can hardly place it.

"It *is* perfect," he says, then looks at me with something in his eyes that makes it feel like the world is shifting around me, "now."

I turn away, hiding my face from his gaze, heat flooding my skin in response.

I hear fabric rustling and look over my shoulder to see him removing his jacket, which he then lays across the edge of the dock at my feet. My eyes travel along his powerful legs, tracing the curves of his thighs upward to his tight midsection, then finally to his sculpted chest. His dark, fitted clothing leaves dangerously little to the imagination. His mask remains defiantly in place, and his dark curly hair falls nearly to his shoulders. Lord have mercy. I've never seen a man crafted like this before.

"Have a seat," he says, his ruby eyes glistening as he reaches his hand.

I place mine in his, and he gently lowers me down before sitting beside me. My feet dangle over the edge.

"Are you sure we're allowed to be here? There's a house right there," I say, pointing to a beautiful little lakeside cabin not far off.

"It's empty," he says. "The owner travels a lot for work. He always intends to spend the summers there but never seems to find the time."

"Huh," I say. How stupidly rich do you have to be to own a house that nobody lives in? I hold my words, examining his pensive demeanor, wondering what he is about to say.

"Say there was a way you could move to a different territory," he begins, his voice dark, heavy, and hesitant. "Ignoring the details, would you *want* to leave your family? Living life on your own in an unfamiliar place where you'd be starting all over...There would be *challenges*."

"What are you saying?"

"I need to know. Would you *really* be happier?"

"Yes. Well, I think. It's not like I want to leave my parents or my brothers, but I can't help feeling that there's a whole other me being drowned out by all their noise. Unless I can go somewhere that they aren't, where I can figure out how to live life on my own, I don't think I'll ever be able to hear my own voice."

"I see. The reason I'm asking you this is that I have certain connections here in Ashland. We move people in and out all the time for every imaginable reason. What I'm trying to say is...if you wanted to relocate here, I could make it happen."

I stammer, but nothing comes out.

"I even have a few houses you could stay at, one in town, others that are a little more...private. Though I'm not sure any of them would be to your liking, I do own a few cars. For obvious reasons, I rarely drive them. I would be happy to see them used."

"You want me to live in your house and drive your car? Are you kidding me?" I say through soft laughter, trying to conceal the shakiness in my voice, as a smile tugs at the corners of my lips.

"What I want...is for you to have another option," he says, "rather than being condemned to suffer a life you would only grow to hate. Besides, I would regret doing nothing for you."

"Seriously?"

He nods.

"Thank you," I say after a long and awkward pause, unable to make it sound as sincere as it should. There are so many questions I should ask, so many details that are missing, but deep down, I already want to accept, though I know I need to be smart.

"There's no rush. I've got all the time in the world," he says with an easy chuckle.

A soft breeze blows through, and the chill of the morning is sharp and bracing. I watch my breath rise like little puffs of smoke with every exhale. For him, though? Nothing. I study him carefully to make sure of what I'm seeing...his chest and shoulders don't move at all.

"Are you...holding your breath?"

"No, not exactly. I forget, sometimes, when there's a lot on my mind."

"You forget *to breathe*?"

"Yes. It stops being involuntary after a while. You see, we don't...*need* oxygen."

"Oh, that's weird." I chuckle to hide my discomfort.

"As a result, breathing ends up taking a surprising amount of focus."

"Then don't, if that feels more natural."

"I wouldn't want to make you...uncomfortable."

"Big deal, you don't breathe. I'll adjust. I wouldn't want you to pretend to be someone you're not. Although, you must breathe a little. Like, when you sniff things or talk, right?"

"When you become...like us...your sense of smell becomes a way of connecting with your surroundings. The ability to track scents can be helpful, but it only tells part of the story."

"So, then, your super-hearing is what you rely on most?"

"Usually, yes, though not always. Say the thing you're hunting isn't moving *or* breathing, and it has no heartbeat. What good is hearing, then? For instance, there could be a vampire in the water under your feet right now, and even *I* wouldn't hear it," he says, peering over the edge into the darkness below.

"Har har," I say, giving him a sarcastic glance and rolling my eyes. Ugh. Why did he have to say that? I slowly pull my feet back onto the deck and fold them under me so that I'm now sitting cross-legged, trying to make it seem natural—like I was going to do it anyway. I already feel uncomfortable being so close to the water.

He throws his head back and laughs, deep and beautiful, startling me more than anything else he's done.

"You're not funny," I say, smirking. How can something like him even exist—a bunch of contradictions rolled up into one gorgeous, perfect mystery? I still don't know what he looks like, and I'm frightened how little that seems to matter.

"I'm just joking. There is no one in the water," he says with a levity I haven't heard from him before, "at least that I know of."

I let out a strained laugh, and when our grins subside, I see he's staring at my mouth with that same look in his eyes that I can't define. As seems to happen often, neither of us says a word.

My backpack buzzes. I wonder how many frantic texts I've gotten from my family. We both look in its direction.

"I never asked, what books did Cora give you?"

"Oh? Oh. I never looked. I was too busy dealing with a stalking vampire."

My bag vibrates again, its sound amplified by the wooden planks. I let out a pained groan as I reluctantly drag my backpack closer and retrieve my phone from its pocket. I'm about to check my messages, but I stuff it into my pocket instead, not ready for my time with him to end.

I lift my bag onto my lap and unzip the main compartment, pulling out a brand-new spiral-bound sketchbook. Exactly what I need since my old one is out of blank sheets to draw on, but how could she have known that? On its cover is an image resembling the scene before me—green, forested mountains blanketed in fog beside a serene lake. Huh. The other book she gave me is an out-of-print fantasy novel I've been trying to find a copy of for years.

"Oh, my gosh..." I say as I inspect it, finding it to be in pristine condition. "But how did she know?"

He slowly nods, his eyes revealing a slight wariness. "Cora is a seer. The most talented one I've ever encountered. Her watchful eye encompasses the entire region, helping us to prepare for danger

101

before it strikes. Whereas many seers are careful not to peer too deeply into the future for fear of altering it, Cora seems to delight in it."

"Has Cora told anyone else you know about, well...me?"

"No, she hasn't, thankfully. And you would know if she did because my brothers are exceptionally nosy creatures."

We enjoy the quiet for a while, watching as the sunrise unfolds and the light gradually spreads behind the cloud cover.

"You know, there's one thing I still don't get. I've seen vampires out in the sun, on the news anyway. I know it doesn't burn you to a crisp, but how come you all hide from the sun and mostly only come out at night?"

He raises one eyebrow.

"Gotcha. I suppose that's one of the few things you can't tell me?" Of course, it only makes me even more curious.

"Where, exactly, do you live?" he asks, changing the subject.

"Castaic, less than an hour outside of Los Angeles."

"What do you do for work?"

I shake my head, knowing that sore spot brings out my bratty side, "Nothing now. I got let go when I put in my request for vacation, so I'll be looking for a new job when I get back. They are hard enough to find, even as it is."

"Has anyone else in your family had the same trouble finding employment?"

"Well, Mom loves her some sales gigs, like Home Interiors, Mary Kay, PartyLite. Ugh. The worst is when she throws Tupperware parties. But other than that stuff, she's a stay-at-home mom...mostly. My dad, the twins, and Jonathan all work some super-secretive government job. They aren't allowed to talk about it, which causes problems. And lots of arguments."

"Why would it cause arguments? Just because they can't talk to you about it?"

"It's more than that. Dad has worked there all my life. He never talked about anything, to the point that I have no idea where he goes during the day or even which branch of the government he works for—just nothing. I figured we would never know. Then, when my brothers and I turned sixteen, my dad had them both apply for summer internships. I begged and begged him to let me put in an application, but he just had all these lame excuses about how there were only two open spots in the budget. I even offered to work for free, but no. He said that he'd keep pushing upper management."

"Unfortunate," my immortal prisoner says, "I'm sorry to hear that."

"Then, a few months later, after I'd all but given up on it, I discovered that while I was waiting for another opening, Jonathan had been hired for the same position as Elden and Warren, right on his birthday. There was another slot after all, and Dad had already decided who he would give it to. He was just stringing me along to keep me off his back about it."

My vampire shakes his head, eyes closed.

"Dad got that little bastard a job, but not his own daughter. I used to think we were so close. I looked up to him. But that betrayal put a huge strain on our relationship, and I have caused a lot of problems in my anger."

"From where I'm sitting, I would say your anger is justified."

"Well, if you ask them, they'll say that I went off the rails, from a well-behaved teen to a complete hellion overnight."

"I find that a little hard to believe."

"I ignored my dad's very existence for months after that. I thought the silent treatment would make him change his mind. But it was met with constant guilt trips from Mom and the guys to stop taking it out on him. Thus began my rebellious phase."

He looks me up and down. "You don't strike me as the rebellious type. Impulsive, perhaps, but not necessarily defiant."

"I started by sneaking out of class a lot. Then, I began climbing out of my bedroom window and just wandering off without saying a word. Sometimes I would even get out of the car at a red light and just...go," I say with a laugh. "I would take off and lead them on a manhunt through stores and whole neighborhoods. Once, I hopped on a bus and just got lost. I didn't even know where I was. But the wildest part was that no matter where I went, they would find me. Still, to this day, I don't know how they do it. Anyway, I did everything I could do to piss them off, to make them as angry as they made me. Immature, yes. Effective? Absolutely. But now, with high school over...I guess I'm just having a difficult time adjusting."

"Your brothers mentioned putting a bell on the window? In case you left in the middle of the night."

"What?"

"That one's true, I'm not teasing you. But from the sound of their private conversations, they truly do want to protect you. I know and can tell you that much for sure."

Well, note to self, they're not private conversations anymore.

"Yeah, well, now you know all about my petty little drama. Why don't you tell me about yourself? What am I allowed to know about you?" I ask, hopefully.

"There isn't much to know. Not anymore. My duty is to keep my family safe, and I don't do much else. A long time ago, perhaps, I was a different person, though I hardly relate to that life now."

"Then start with what you do for fun?"

"When you have all the time in the world, eventually, everything becomes incredibly boring. It was easier before the public knew, back when we could move freely. Even if the story was always the same, at least we could change the backdrop. Now I find myself patrolling the same borders over and over, again," he says, sounding tired.

His version of life is so different than mine. I spent most of my days around people at school, working, and not having time to be bored.

"Just endless days, no sleep, no sunlight. Bound to the night. Sounds tiring," I say.

He gives me a weird look. "Oh, now, that's one of the things humans get wrong. We do sleep, sometimes. Not as much as humans need. Only when we need to regain our strength."

"What?" I ask in disbelief. "Seriously?"

"Don't believe everything you hear."

"So...do you sleep in a coffin?" I ask, smirking.

He groans. "That was a trend. Like wearing bell-bottoms for humans, everybody did it back in the day, but now it seems kind of...lame."

"Wait, you're serious? That's the one true thing?"

"It made sense at one point in history. We could effectively pass for the dead if discovered, and disturbing the dead was taboo. Sleeping in a coffin could save your life, so why not? There were some nice ones too."

"How has all of this been kept a secret? You know what? Never mind, I want to hear more about you."

"Before I saw you, my job consumed my every waking moment. I mean, before you were flung off the cliff. Now, my job is to watch over you, for as long as you're in this territory."

I hope he's keeping something from me because the alternative would mean he doesn't do anything for himself—no days off, nothing to look forward to—which sounds like such a sad, lonely existence.

"Do you ever remember your dreams, Brielle?"

"Usually, mostly the bad ones stick with me. Do you?"

"Always," he says with a smile.

"What do vampires dream about? Are they peaceful, or are they nightmares?"

"Depends. How would you describe a dream where you're searching for the answer to some mystery, a key that will unlock everything, and every time, just as you're about to lay hold of it, you wake up?"

"Sounds like a nightmare to me."

"Is that how your nightmares are?"

"Kind of. Mine are always somehow me back in school. I'm running through the hallways, trying to find a way out, but all the exits are chained shut, and the windows are bricked up. I can't get out. Sometimes, just when I think I'm about to make it out, I wake up."

"Sounds like we're both trying to find something."

"Kinda does."

My phone vibrates again in my pocket, signaling that it's almost time for *this* dream to end. I whip it out and type a message to Elden. With my finger hovering over the button, I look at him in question.

"Go smooth things over with your family. I should be on my way too."

> *What did you guys have planned for breakfast?*

"So...will I see you again, dude?" I ask with a playful grin, eliciting a curious response. I love his reactions to the nickname.

He looks to the sky, letting out a frustrated breath.

"What?"

He rises effortlessly, his movements smooth and agile, never a hint of awkwardness. He offers a hand, and I take it. Then I'm back on my feet.

"I'll see you again," he says, pausing as he looks down at me, humor still in his eyes, "And you can call me by my name: Aldrick."

10

I SWEAR THE SAME chunky seagull has followed me here from Cape Flattery. I see him inching closer in my peripheral vision as I sketch the forest at the edge of the park, seated on the damp grass.

"You already ate the last of it," I say to the greedy little thing.

The ground rumbles with a heavy *thud* beneath me. A pained groan follows the flap of retreating wings and the unmistakable howl of Jonathan's laugh.

Glancing up, I see Warren flat on his back and Elden standing over him with a shit-eating grin. I keep my eyes fixed on him as he lies sprawled on the ground, at least until he starts to roll over to push himself up, to which I breathe a small sigh of relief. Watching them spar has always been nerve-racking. They're always far too rough, acting like they're indestructible. How they haven't broken their necks by now is a miracle.

"Your turn, Bri," Elden says.

"No."

"Come on, you need to keep up on it," says Warren, looking unsteady on his feet.

"No, War, I had my cardio for the day."

There's no way I'm letting them fling me through the air without so much as a mat to ease my landing, though I guess I should count myself lucky for making it this far without them trying to drag me into training.

Elden and Warren square off again. Warren shoots in on Elden, tackling him around the waist and grabbing one of his legs from under him. They both end up rolling on the ground. Thankfully, they're wearing different clothes, or I wouldn't be able to see which is which. Elden kicks Warren off, then they're back on their feet. I hate it when they start kickboxing. Someone always gets hit in the face.

They exchange blows, each looking for the other to make a misstep in their footwork or drop their guard for a split second. When Elden goes for a right cross, Warren avoids it and hits him with a left hook to the jaw. He stumbles but doesn't fall; instead, the two exchange blows until they run out of steam and decide to call it a draw. How they don't both have concussions after that is beyond me.

I look back at my sketch. It's the kind of drawing I do when things are weighing on my mind. It's lifeless, at least to me. I've been thinking about one thing, and one thing only, and have ignored my family since my return from our meeting at the lake. Not out of anger or spite, but rather because my thoughts keep returning to *him*.

Aldrick.

Though appears young, not much older than I am, his name isn't exactly typical of an 80s baby. And the way he uses his words,

I had figured it was maybe a vampire thing or a regional dialect, but now I think he's just not fully caught up to modern English. Considering everything I know about him, he's probably much older than I initially thought. Maybe that should matter to me, but seeing as how, up to this point, I've already thrown all my good sense out the window—I'm not sure there's any turning back.

I might have fallen hard for him. It's such a stupid thing to do. I still have over a week left with him. If I take him up on the offer, how do I explain this to my brothers? Won't they figure out their sister's dating a vampire, and then sabotage my efforts to leave?

"Bri?" Jonathan asks.

I jump, startled. When did he come up beside me? He wears a carefully neutral expression, his tousled hair hanging across his forehead.

"Yeah?"

"So, what are you drawing?"

He wears a fitted white T-shirt, his arms crossed, accentuating his toned biceps, sun-kissed skin glistening with sweat. If he wasn't such a pain in my neck, he might look good. For whatever reason, he keeps shifting from one foot to the other, like he's nervous about something.

"What do you want?" I ask, guarded, taking a sip of my cherry Slurpee.

"I thought we had a truce. Can't you at least pretend like you don't always hate my guts?"

"I don't *always* hate you. You can be cool on rare occasions. But be real, you couldn't care less what I'm drawing. So, can we get to the real reason for your weird intrusion?"

110

"Okay, I'm just going to say it. Since we got here, you've been going out a lot, you're dressing differently...since when do you wear make-up?"

"What's your point?"

"Have you...like, met a guy? Maybe when you were out, getting coffee or whatever?" He looks like he's dying inside.

I'm unsure where he's going with this, but I'm also impressed that he's this observant. I had always taken him for an airhead. I look him straight in his irritating, icy blue eyes when I lie saying, "No. Why do you ask?"

"You just seem...different lately."

"Ugh, why do you have to be so weird?" I drop my eyes to my sketchbook, nearly done but needing to act busy, so he'll hopefully leave me alone. I place my pencil on the page and keep going. Nothing more off-putting than a Jonathan who is acting normal. My skin crawls at the thought.

"I'm not the one acting weird. You're the one who came back dressed all cute and smiling."

"Eww. Don't say those words."

He huffs out a breath.

"You should ask yourselves why you all keep trying to suck the joy out of me? This place is beautiful. I had fun this morning. Just leave it be, okay?" I say, trying to change the subject.

"The Bri I know would be sleeping till noon, any chance she could, hiding out somewhere with a book or watching movies back in the room."

"Jonathan, what's my favorite color?"

"Uhh...I don't—"

"Yeah," I snort, "you know me *so* well."

"I know that you're impulsive."

Dang. That's the second time I've heard that today.

"Your judgment sucks, and I know that you're a horrible liar. What's so wrong with admitting you've been hanging out with a new guy?"

"Even if I were, why would it ever be any of your business?"

He scoffs.

"And it's cerulean, by the way."

He side-eyes me.

"We are going to do a few laps," Elden calls from behind him as he takes off.

"Welp. Fun chat. Later, loser," Jonathan says abruptly as his hand snakes out to smack the sketchbook off my lap, sending it tumbling. Sprinting away before I react, he joins my brothers on their run.

My pleasant mood in shambles, I reach out to grab my sketchbook and freeze as my eyes land on something jotted down in black ink, not in my handwriting. It's just a phone number and a note that reads, "If you need me, call me."

I flip through the pages, but nothing is written anywhere else.

I contemplate what this could mean. A witch, a seer, and a self-proclaimed vampire manager has written her number on a random page of this notebook, so doesn't that mean she knew I wouldn't see it until now? But wouldn't that also mean she should know whether I'll end up needing her? Or maybe this is her way of being friendly?

Either way, I create a new contact for Book Witch in my phone and enter her number, shaking my head and praying I never have a reason to use it.

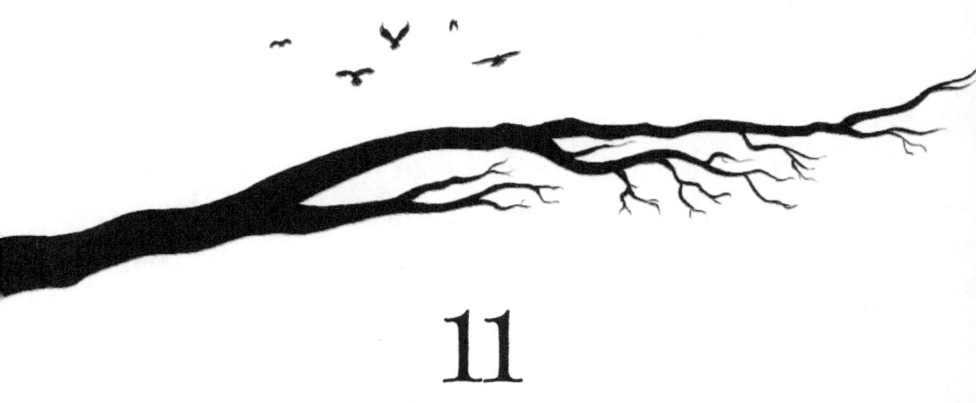

11

I look at my phone through squinted eyes. It's 4 a.m.

Tearing myself away from the bed, I stumble into the bathroom to get ready, straightening my hair and throwing on mascara. Eyeing my suitcase with contempt, I wonder what possessed me to bring every baggy top in my closet? Not a single cute item left to wear. I grumble in frustration, deciding it'll be a *Fall Out Boy* T-shirt and jeans kind of day.

I exit the bathroom, grab my things, and head for the door, skidding to a stop when I see it.

Jonathan isn't at his customary post on the couch. Instead, he's splayed out on the recliner, which has been dragged across the room and jammed against the door, cutting off the only exit from the cabin. The smile leaves my face, my excitement replaced by seething rage that burns through my veins. He's made it so the only way I can leave is to go through him first. Who the hell does this boy think he is?

Do I wake him and scream at him? No, that's what he wants. That way, I'll miss my chance to see Aldrick today, and they can team up and lecture me. My mind goes to the bedroom window, but there's zero chance they haven't boobie-trapped it with some idiotic device. There's only one other way out of this building, but I don't like it.

I glare at Jonathan, a wicked grin spreading across my face. For now, he can sleep. I'll deal with him later.

Back in the bathroom, I lock the door behind me, examining the long, narrow sliding window over the shower. Standing on the tub's edge, I open it as quietly as possible, then pop out the screen and set it down next to the shower. Hoping I fit through this opening, I send my backpack into the void, mortified by the sound of it crashing to the ground outside.

I place a foot on one of the plastic shelves in the shower, which lets out a discouraging creak, pausing to envision the motion of pulling myself up and swinging the other leg out the window. I've done dumber stuff than this. I take a deep breath and go for it, struggling to hold in a squeak as the bottom of the window frame cuts into the inside of my thigh. This is good, though. I exhale and begin squeezing through the opening, tucking my head into my chin and contorting my body until it clears the edge. Okay, we're getting somewhere. More of my body is outside than inside.

There's still the small matter of getting to the ground, which I cannot see. With an arm hooked around the window, I lower my leg, leading me to do the splits as I try to free my other foot, which has unfortunately become stuck. Please, God, don't let the sexy vampire be watching me do this. I lose my grip once my shoe comes off, and I drop, landing in a crouched position.

The loud crunch of the gravel cuts through the silence of pre-dawn. Feeling around in the dark for my lost left shoe, I slip it back on, then find my bag and swing it over my shoulder as I walk in what I think is the direction of the parking lot. I bypass my rental car, having no way of telling what those idiots have done to it.

> *Wanna meet up?*

I text Aldrick, which feels far less dumb than talking to myself and hoping he's within earshot.

Nearing the park, its lights are beacons, brightly illuminating the benches. I plop myself down on one and dig out a plastic baggie full of snacks, tossing out a handful to get the birds' attention. The woods beyond the park lights are shrouded in darkness, but I hear soft chirping in the trees. I remember too late that everything here is always damp, even when it hasn't been raining—my butt is cold and wet as the water soaks through my jeans. I sigh, accepting it, knowing that the damage is already done.

The minutes slip by, and I toss out more treats, watching the seagulls and crows arrive to resume their endless squabbling over the crumbs. My phone vibrates in my pocket. I check it.

Incoming.

I wonder how he'll make his grand entrance, paying close attention to see if I can detect any sign of his presence, noticing as the birds stop pecking at the food, then suddenly depart before I hear the thud of something hitting the ground not far from where I'm sitting, off in the direction of the woods. This is the first time he has given me a gentle warning of his approach.

I see his brilliant red eyes first, glimmering like two jewels in the night. If I didn't know who—or what was approaching me now, I would be abjectly terrified. Heck, maybe I still should be. Illuminated by the soft light of a nearby lamp post, I see his tall, muscular form and the edges of his leather coat. He radiates an aura of danger, his steps slow and deliberate, those of a creature that doesn't need to hurry, one who owns and commands the darkness around him.

"Hello, Aldrick," I say, beaming at him. His attire never seems to change, and I wonder if he owns anything that isn't black.

"Good morning, Brielle." His low, silken voice sounds less bored than usual. "Why the park?"

"It beats a dark alley," I say, patting the empty bench beside me.

He turns and sits on the bench, and the air around me becomes thick with the smells of the forest.

"What do you even do all night long? You smell like you've been up close and personal with some trees."

He huffs, "I'm around. Sitting, listening, and conserving my energy so I don't have to sleep as often. Otherwise, I might miss out on things like, I don't know, the sound of you climbing out of the bathroom window at four in the morning."

Oof. I hope he didn't *see* it.

"Why wouldn't you have used the front door?"

"Because *Jonathan* blocked it off. Intentionally."

I swear that the red of his irises intensifies with a spark of emotion. Could this be anger? Oh. I like it a little bit more than I should. "They just think they're protecting me, I know, I know."

"By trapping you in a room?"

"Look. Don't worry, I'll deal with them."

"I'll admit, the banter between you and your brothers can be amusing at times, but I find Jonathan...irritating."

"Right?"

"Even more so after this."

My eyes widen in surprise. "Really? Because everyone else seems to love him. He only acts like a jerk with me. Girls can't see beyond his chiseled jaw to any of his many personality flaws."

Aldrick snickers at that.

"He liked to go around telling our classmates that I'm a brat, that I'm too mean to my poor, innocent family. Too vindictive. Too bitter." I shake my head and smirk. "To be fair, though, I did say a lot of mean things about him too."

"And your brothers didn't come to your defense?"

"Oh, they would if they heard it in person, but that didn't stop him from blabbing to everyone else in their circle of friends—this massive group of annoying guys. At best, they would do a little damage control. But all that's over now."

"Did you not have friends of your own?"

"I do, although I guess things are changing. I have three close girlfriends, and they all get to leave. Sarah is moving away with her boyfriend. Jen and Abby are going off to different colleges. I don't even have a way of visiting them yet."

"Hmm."

I pour the remaining handful of snacks into my palm, tossing them into the grass, before shoving the empty baggie back into my pocket. They'll be waiting for the birds once the vampire leaves.

"So...yesterday morning, I know you caught the argument between me and my dad. Did you maybe hear anything that would explain why he freaked out like that? What possessed him to rush over and start pounding on our cabin door?"

He lets out a long, resigned sigh. "You must think I'm just like them, keeping things from you. You'll likely be angry with me if you ever find out on your own, but to reveal anything more...for you, it might feel like the ground is giving way beneath your feet. I couldn't be the cause of that."

Everything feels distant as I close my eyes, attempting to process this statement. How big *is* this secret they've been keeping from me? Was I adopted? Are we in the witness protection program? Is my whole life being broadcast on a TV show? What could possibly require this much secrecy?

Opening my eyes, my full attention shifts from my thoughts to Aldrick when his head snaps toward the tree line, every muscle in his body tense and ready. At first, I think he's messing with me, his eyes carefully scanning the horizon as if he's looking for something. I smile, taking a breath in preparation to say something, but he raises a silent finger, and I stop.

A few moments pass before he turns to me and says, "Don't. Move."

I blink. He's...gone, leaving me alone in the eerie silence he carries with him, devoid of the sounds of nature. How can he move that quickly without a sound, not disturbing so much as a single blade of grass in his wake?

Sitting alone on the soggy park bench, without him, not knowing what else might be out there—*watching me*. I've never felt so exposed. With nothing else to distract my mind, I focus on the mounting panic inside and the chill creeping in through the thin fabric of my jeans. As the seconds stretch into minutes, the only thing keeping me from screaming is the thought that no matter what creature might be lurking in the dark, it can't be as terrifying as *my* monster.

"A shifter was here recently," he says from behind me, eliciting a small shriek as I jump to my feet and turn to him. He's...*different* now. This is a side of him I've not seen. Gone is the effortless saunter, the hands buried casually in his pockets, and his carefree demeanor. No, this is *Scary Aldrick*.

"I don't understand how it got through our defenses," he says.

"Are we...in danger?"

His brows snap together. "I don't know. Crow shifters are not native to this region. While we aren't enemies, they still have no business showing up unannounced in *my* territory."

"You mean to tell me that a person in crow form was here? Just chilling, pretending to be a bird? But why?" I ask.

"That's what I'm trying to piece together. We don't lay claim to the skies, so there's a chance he was merely passing over and stopped for a rest."

"Wait, so I could have been *feeding* some random dude while he just stared at me?" My body quivers with revulsion. That's not creepy at all.

"First, there's the situation with your family," he begins.

"The one I'm not allowed to know anything about," I add sarcastically.

He materializes inches before me, no longer in the mood for playing human for my benefit.

"And now a shifter from your territory has slipped in, undetected, even by Cora—and of all places, he finds himself in the same

119

town where your family is staying. A lot of coincidences, don't you think?"

"But what does this all mean? Is this crow shifter something you're going to hunt?"

"No. I'll have to be very careful how I handle this. We wouldn't want to damage relations between our territories." His voice is so deep and commanding that I nod in agreement, though I don't fully grasp what this means.

My eyes widen when I hear his phone ring, my nerves still on edge. He raises a finger to his lips, and I nod.

"I'm tracking an unknown crow shifter at the edge of town. Has Cora contacted any of you?... I followed his trail as far as I could, but he's already in the air...Chetzemoka Park...See you soon."

He snaps the phone shut, shaking his head, his irritation evident in his movements. "You should head back. They're on their way."

"Your family?" I hesitate.

He nods.

"So, this is a big enough deal that you need help?"

"The coven is always notified about any border breaches. Ordinarily, Cora lets us know where and when to intercept visitors beforehand, and we're waiting for them when they arrive. I don't understand how she missed this. She's never failed us before."

"Wait, won't your family smell that I was here?"

"This park is awash with human scent trails from countless visitors; you were here with your brothers just yesterday. Besides, they won't be looking for you."

All I know is that I need to avoid his family, especially after what his brother did to my mind. It might be cool with Aldrick that I know of their existence, but there's no guarantee the rest of his coven would approve.

"You should go about your day as if nothing unusual has happened. I'll be searching for the intruder," he says, softening his tone as he turns to me. Our eyes meet, and I see it: even the vague threat of danger has awakened something in him, bringing some dormant part of him to life. This is what he lives for.

I watch as he assesses me. Without hesitation, he lifts his hand, reaching for a chunk of my hair, his fingers brushing gently against its silky strands, and tucks it behind my ear, exposing the side of my neck. I swallow hard as his eyes move down.

My cheeks are hot, and my heart throbs. His hand moves away from my hair, the back of his finger gliding down the blush of my cheek. His fingertips trace the hollow of my throat before coming to rest on my collarbone.

"You have the most beautiful eyes," I blurt out. My words pour forth, and all I want to do is reach out and gently pull down his mask, revealing his face. But that's not my choice to make. As much as I want to, I'd never ask him to take it off if he has his reasons for keeping his face from the world, his reasons for keeping it from *me*.

The look he gives me can only be described as bewilderment, as if I were the one who caught him off guard.

"And I hope to see them again before my vacation ends," I say, grinning, on a roll with my brazen thoughts.

"You truly are a strange case, Brielle Draper."

12

I STAND DEFIANTLY BEFORE the cabin, solitary and motionless but for a single finger tapping against the cold, plastic wall of the vessel. Steeling my nerves, I resolve myself to the course of action I've chosen and go forth. With each step toward my destiny, the frigid liquid within sloshes around, and I hear the subtle tinkling of the ice. I take a deep breath of the wild, northwestern Pacific air on summer's eve, imbued with subtle notes of cedar, freshly cut grass, and pine, allowing it to fill my lungs—it smells like freedom.

Leaning down to carefully place the drink carrier on the patio table, I catch a fleeting glimpse of a crow taking flight from its perch on the neighbor's porch railing. Side-eyeing the retreating creature, I wonder if the nasty little spy might also be a shapeshifter. Do they know Aldrick's onto them? That *I'm* on to them? It still doesn't compute how a fully-grown man can change into something so small.

I silently open the door to the cabin, pushing it as far as it will go before hitting the back of his chair, maybe an inch, then use the card as a shim to prevent the latch from closing and softly release the handle. There's a chance my efforts will wake him, but with how deeply he sleeps, they may not. Bracing my shoulder against the door, I plant my feet firmly on the wooden deck slats and shove with everything I've got until it won't budge anymore, only moving the recliner another inch or so—time for a different approach.

I lie flat on my back, placing my feet against the door in a squatting position. Digging my fingers between the deck slats for leverage, I push with all my strength. It's working. I scooch closer and go again, inch by inch, slowly getting the door open. I stop when the opening appears big enough to squeeze through. Out of breath, sweating, and undoubtedly red-faced, I right myself, grab the drink carrier, and shuffle sideways into the cabin.

There aren't words to describe the triumphant feeling of standing over an unsuspecting Jonathan, still sprawled on the recliner, fast asleep with his head thrown back. The fool. I quietly shut the door behind me—after all, no need to wake the neighbors.

I place my arsenal on the ground and scoop up one of the four 24-oz cups of ice water I'd grabbed on the way here, having told the barista they were for the guys, every intention of holding to my word. With a flick of my thumb, I pop the lid, grinning as it falls silently to the floor.

Using my finger to open the neck of his T-shirt, I dump the contents through the opening, sending an avalanche of ice-cold water cascading down his firm chest, watching as it spreads, darkening his clothes. It takes longer than I predicted to get a response. When his puny dinosaur brain finally registers the sensation, he cuts off mid-snore with a gasp, quickly followed by the highest-pitched squeal I've ever heard him make. He shoots straight up in his chair, looking around frantically, grappling with what I've done to him.

I reach for the second cup, a devilish grin warping my lips. He *still* hasn't figured out that I'm standing over him. I pop the next lid—this time, pouring it over the top of his head as I jump clear of the splash zone.

He shrieks, flailing out of the chair and slipping on the ice, struggling to keep his balance.

The twins stumble into the room, their eyes wide as they take in the scene. Jonathan is drenched, standing in a puddle of ice water.

"Who the hell do you think you are? You think you have a say in my life? In my choices? Clearly, you must have lost your damn mind!" I scream at him.

"What is happening?" my brothers ask in unison.

"He blocked me from leaving like the psycho he is! Did you two have anything to do with this?" I yell at them, my voice shaking from the adrenaline. I grab the third cup and tear off the lid as my eyes land on my next targets.

"No! He must have moved the chair after we went to sleep."

Jonathan's curses ring through the room as I empty yet another cup on him, scattering liquid and cubes across the room. My brothers watch the ice slide clear to their feet and come to a stop.

"That's enough, Bri!"

"Oh, *now* it's enough? Well, for once, I agree. Because I've also had enough of this crap!"

"I just wanted you to be safe," Jonathan growls at me, hair drenched, face red with anger and frustration, and the white knuckles of his tightly clenched fists clearly showing. Finally, I might have gotten through to him in a way he understands.

"Like you could do anything to keep me safe!" I yell. "Just leave me alone. Let me live my life! I don't need your help!"

"You are such an ungrateful brat! You know that? You should be *thanking* me! You have no idea..." he stops, like his tongue quits working, perhaps realizing how stupid he sounds in a rare moment of clarity.

I glare at him. "I have no idea? No, *you* have no idea. No idea what is out there and how useless your protection is, and I'm tired of living in this shitshow of lies and delusions. What are you going to do, use MMA on a vampire? You guys are a joke. And I hope you remember this next time any of you have some thought of trying to control me. But you, Jonathan, *you* are not my brother, and you are not my family. And even if you were, you still would have no right!"

"Okay! Okay," Warren says, hands up in surrender. "We get it. No more questioning. No more controlling. We'll stop. Right, Jonathan?"

Jonathan's light blond hair, now darker, lays in his face. His soaked T-shirt reveals the well-muscled physique that had driven so many girls in school crazy as he stands mannequin still, dripping onto the spreading puddle at his feet. Those wintry blue eyes move from Warren's face to mine.

"Fine," he says through gritted teeth.

"So, I have everyone's word to leave me alone, correct?"

"As long as you clean your mess," Elden says.

"Then it's a deal."

125

One good thing about my family—we're well adapted to sweeping things under the rug. How we all became so practiced at it is beyond me. Jonathan, on the other hand, takes his sweet time before fully burying the hatchet.

With the day sunny and warm enough not to need a sweater, we decided to plan a trip to Sequim Bay. I dress in my bathing suit, a pair of jean shorts, and a baggy T-shirt to cover the fading bruises on my hips and back. I slip on my flip-flops as the guys finish gathering their things. We drive to the local grocery store to grab food for lunch, cramming everything into a white foam cooler before tossing it into the trunk and heading out.

There's a small convenience store on the water that offers kayak rentals. After paying, we carry them to the docks.

We spend a couple of hours on the water before Jonathan paddles off by himself, becoming a blob in the distance, his light hair the only discernible feature. With him away doing his thing, there's an opportunity to spend time with my brothers. I made sure to bring a few disposable waterproof cameras, knowing that, at some point, they'd drag me along to the lake or ocean. Eager to capture plenty of photos for my album, I hand one to Elden and Warren.

I aim at Jonathan as his kayak gently sways on the waves, paddle resting across his lap. The sun is high, glinting off the choppy water around him. I snap a picture, then wind the camera till I hear a click.

"That's one hell of a swim to shore if he falls in," I say, laughing. Jonathan, in his own words, is 'too cool for a life jacket'.

"Trust me, he'll be fine."

Now that our shared sentence in educational purgatory has come to an end, I wonder what his plans are. "You guys know if he's moving out of his mom's place?" I'm usually one to avoid discussing his home life, which has always been rocky, to say the least. We all know what type of person his mother is; it's the one thing I learned from a young age *never* to tease him about.

"Actually, he's planning on renting a house in our neighborhood," Warren says, his face lighting up with a dopey grin as he waits for my reaction.

"You're kidding, right?"

The twins laugh together.

"Tell me you're screwing with me right now."

"Surprise, we're getting a new neighbor!" Elden says.

"Since you already know, we can tell him to call off whatever creative way he had planned to spill the beans," says Warren.

"It's much better this way. Promise," Elden adds.

My groan, loud and long, can be heard echoing from the distant mountains.

"It won't be so bad. His sis will be moving in with him. You two always seemed to get along great. Maybe you can hang out? Be buddies?"

Ember is nice, but it's like pulling teeth trying to get her to talk to me, so I usually stay out of her way whenever Jonathan brings her around.

"Ugh, why does *he* have this habit of infiltrating every part of my life?"

"Well, what about you? Have you made up *your* mind? Are you moving out or staying?" Elden asks, already knowing the answer.

Leaving is all I ever talk about, but the reality of doing it is another story.

"Oh, shut it. You know this vacation is bleeding my bank account dry. Unlike the two of you, floating around on a lake, using paid vacation days from your cushy job," I say as I slam the ore's flat end onto the water, splashing all three of us. "Like I could even afford my own place."

"Why would you want to leave anyway? We should stick together for another couple of years while we don't have to pay rent," Elden says as he retaliates with his paddle, water raining on my hair.

"I want to get away before I get stuck in some career and end up having no choice but to stay. There are other places I would like to see."

"Come on, Bri. Again, with your dreams of traveling the world and studying abroad? People don't do that stuff anymore. Not with the monster takeover. Besides, why can't you see it's better to stay with us? Don't you want to be with family?"

"I, for one, would love to see you find a dude. Maybe take your mind off all this traveling business," Elden says with a stupid grin.

"Well, there's a lie if I ever heard one! You guys have always tried to scare them away! It's been, like, your *mission* since middle school. Any boy I'd look at, anyone who'd even talk to me! There you'd be. In their face, joking, teasing, all but barking at them."

"No, we weren't," Elden protests.

"Now you're *really* just making things up," says Warren.

"Only last week, at our graduation ceremony, you nearly ripped Jason's arm from his socket for trying to give me a hug."

"Well, *that* was different," Elden says.

"Do you even know Jason? There was no way we would let that guy near our sister," Warren remarks.

"Oh, okay, how about two weeks ago when Matthew from English passed me his number? You ripped it from my hands and set the paper on fire in the hall."

"If you'd heard even half the things that come out of his mouth, you'd have burned the note yourself," says Elden.

"You do know Devin has a huge crush on you. Now *there's* someone you should give a chance to. He's a great guy," Warren insists.

"Yeah, the one who falls for any girl who so much as looks in his direction," I say, rolling my eyes. "Look, you two should just quit trying to play matchmaker. You're terrible at it."

Warren swipes his paddle through the water's surface, cutting through like a blade and spraying all over us. Squinting, my eyes land on Jonathan, who is closing in fast, headed straight for me. Only his unquenchable thirst for revenge could drive him to move with such fervor, his devious intent palpable from afar. Welp, that was a nice ten minutes I got to spend with my brothers, Jonathan-free.

"I'm...hungry," I say, rotating my kayak toward the dock, before adding, "I'm gonna go get something to eat before you guys devour everything in sight." I start paddling, my arms already burning. "Please make sure you get some good pictures!" I call them over my shoulder, booking it for the shore.

"Coward!" Jonathan cries out after me.

My only response to him is to laugh and throw up a middle finger before continuing my escape. Each stroke through the water takes more and more effort, but I press on, knowing that if I ask my brothers for help, Jonathan will rub it in my face for ages. I feel the nose of the kayak crunching on the rocky shore as it comes to a stop, awkwardly scrambling out as it bobs underneath me. With a squeak,

I slip and tumble into the shallow water, hearing the guys' booming laughter echoing in the distance.

I exit the lake, humiliated, and laugh softly under my breath as I wring out my hair, water splattering on the rocks. Yeah, I probably had that coming. It feels like the only chance I'll get to be with my brothers is at an end.

Stretched across my towel, wearing a pair of oversized sunglasses, I spend a while lounging on the beach, drying off in the warm sun while watching the guys play fight with their paddles. Elden's kayak tips over, and he disappears under the water. Warren and Jonathan's squabbling reaches me as they go to rescue him. I shake my head.

My eyes drift to the nearby dock. Not the same one we met at, but it reminds me of Aldrick, nonetheless. I wish he were here beside me, though frankly, I'm uncertain I could explain why. I pop open a bag of chips.

He isn't human, but for whatever reason, this doesn't seem to matter. Even before I could fully remember him, my thoughts kept returning to our time together. Is this normal? Nothing more than what all girls feel when they like a guy? What if this turns out to be a meaningless schoolgirl crush that kicked in a little late? If so, then it's my first.

What do I know about Aldrick? What do we have in common?

Most importantly, does he like me the way I like him?

I shovel a handful of chips in my mouth.

I use this reprieve to take stock and sort out my tangled thoughts. I'd had a near-death experience the other day, and those make people do crazy things...maybe instead of going skydiving or getting a tattoo, my thing is cozying up to a hot, dangerous vampire. Still, I feel no need to overthink this, as time will tell how these feelings for him develop, and whether they will wither to nothing or blossom into something more. But that's not the main thing eating at me.

I watch these three knuckleheads splash each other, giggling like eight-year-olds, and I wonder: what kind of reality-altering information could these goobers have managed to keep from me? It simply doesn't make any sense. Jonathan, the same little boy who once stormed off and rode his bike home when he didn't get to be the red Power Ranger, certainly couldn't have anything to do with this. I mean, could he? The dude leaks secrets like a sieve.

The day passes, and the guys finally return once the last of them has tipped over, dragging their kayaks behind them. Still famished after devouring the rest of the snacks, we decide it's time to head in and get some real food to eat.

The sun dips behind the mountains, its last rays fading as day yields to the chill of the evening ahead. As we're packing up to leave, Jonathan snatches the keys from my hand.

"You know I only get carsick if I'm not driving, you don't want vomit all over your rental car. They'll charge you extra to clean it."

I roll my eyes. He's annoying, but he's not wrong.

The drive back passes quickly, partly due to Jonathan's complete disregard for posted speed limits but also because I'm lost in thought as I watch the trees fly by, considering lies, secrets, and the hidden affairs of vampires. The nature of my feelings for him, *Aldrick*. Finally, a name to attach to the phantom-like object of my affections, something concrete. Not a daydream, but real. Contemplating the potential fallout of our two worlds colliding, my thoughts drift lazily between reality and fantasy as we blast music the whole ride, windows down—likely scaring off any deer within a five-mile radius.

13

WE GRAB PIZZA BEFORE heading in and watch a few *Malcolm in the Middle* episodes. Afterwards, I shower and change into my pajamas, exiting the bathroom to the sweet sound of silence. A quick peek into the bedroom reveals the twins asleep on their bedding. Poor little tykes were too tuckered out after such a big day to get under the covers. I snicker. In the living room, Jonathan lies face down, motionless. It's a perfect opportunity to get a peaceful night's rest.

I grab the key to my parents' cabin, my bag, and an armful of blankets and pillows, and head next door. Inside, it's almost identical to ours, except that the décor betrays someone's pathological obsession with lighthouses.

From the look of things, my mother had rage cleaned before she left. I open the windows to air out the room, still stuffy after such a balmy day, allowing the sea breeze to flow through. I can't get over how fresh the air smells up here.

I switch off the lights, turn the TV on to something boring, lie on the couch, and immediately drift off. Not two minutes after I shut my eyes, I get a text, which I ignore. It can wait until morning. I toss and turn on the lumpy sofa, my mind abuzz. What if it's from him? Giving in to curiosity, I dig my phone from my bag and check the message.

> *Still awake?*

My exhaustion lifts upon seeing his text. I hadn't planned on going anywhere tonight, or I wouldn't have gotten changed into the rattiest pajamas I own and left all my clothes back at our cabin. But then again, wasn't his family supposed to be around investigating the crow shifter? What could he want?

> *Yeah. Why, what's up?*

While I wait for his reply, I visualize meeting him outside in my PJs, wrapped up in a cute blanket. I could make it work.

> *I thought your parents were out of town?*

For a second, I forgot that I was texting a super-stalker vampire—one who is probably watching my parents' cabin as we speak, and he can tell that someone's inside.

> *Oh, yeah, that's me. I broke into my parents' place to get some peace and quiet.*

I lay back, a stupid grin on my face, knowing I must crack him up, even if he's too dead inside to let it show. I'll bet his life has been cryptic, dark, and boring for years. Decades? Centuries? Poor guy. I bet the only excitement he gets is when he's hunting. What's it like to live so long that everyone you knew is gone? To see that it all just goes on without you.

What would I be like as a vampire? The thought bursts in through the back door of my mind, uninvited, like a crazy neighbor. What would I do instead of sleep? What would I wear? Then there's the whole...blood...thing.

"You look comfortable," he says from behind me.

My heart kickflips in my chest as I jerk my head toward the sound's source, propping up awkwardly on an elbow. Aldrick's imposing form darkens the bedroom doorway, leaning casually against its wooden frame.

He strolls across the living room, taking in his surroundings, his heavy leather boots falling feather-soft on the wooden planks. I gain a new appreciation for his body as he crosses in front of the TV. Tall, well-muscled, decked out in black leather, straps, and buckles that seem to serve no discernible purpose other than to look cool. And on him, they do—they *really* do.

Even if he were human, minus the vampy powers, with his size and strength, there would be nothing I could do to fend him off. My mind tries, and fails, to process him in the mundane context of our vacation rental cabin, watching helplessly as our two worlds come dangerously close to one another.

I sit up, smoothing out the fabric of my baggy T-shirt, worn thin and threadbare from a thousand wash cycles, my chest heaving as I try to regain control over my breathing. It's okay, no big deal, not the first time I've been alone with a vampire, or the first I've looked like absolute dog crap in front of him. But why did he have to show up when I'm wearing my old gym shorts as pajama bottoms? I work on regaining my composure while he studies a large ceramic lighthouse on the fireplace mantle.

"Good evening to you too," I say, sarcastically.

He turns to shoot me a curious look, one eyebrow raised. The soft light of the TV screen illuminates only half his face. It hits me only then that he's not wearing his usual mid-length jacket. Which makes sense, upon closer consideration—it's not meant for the weather but rather to shield himself from sunlight.

I pull my pillow onto my lap, still wrapped in my blanket, making room for him on the couch beside me. Once I have his attention, I give him a pointed look, then move my eyes conspicuously to the seat next to me, and then back at him, making a funny face. I see him roll his eyes as he moves in my direction.

"I can only stay a short time. My brothers aren't far from here," he says, accepting my offer and sitting beside me, which he does with implausible grace and fluidity. The cushion hardly compresses under his weight. Oh no. Please don't tell me that I outweigh this beast of a man.

"Is everything...alright?" I ask, sensing his frustration.

"We've made no progress tracking down the shifter. Everybody is becoming weary of the search."

"Cora still hasn't seen anything?"

"No. She believes they are veiled by magic."

"I'm sorry, veiled?"

"Hidden from her vision, covered over."

"How would that even work if she can see the future?"

"It can be done, but it requires extensive and uncommon measures, which only reaffirms my initial suspicion that something is, indeed, very wrong. While you were at the lake, we searched this area. I caught a scent trail outside your cabin, that of another crow shifter...different from the one at the park."

"Wait, there's two of these suckers?"

"Unfortunately, no. They don't travel in small numbers. There are likely more remaining high and hidden among the native crow population. We're only detecting those that have come down from the treetops to get a closer look."

"Have you ever dealt with these crow shifters before?"

He shakes his head. "Like I said, there exists no enmity between our territories. Our relations with the crows are strong. I'm afraid your family must have brought them to our doorstep."

I swallow hard.

"My family? Why?"

He grunts and shakes his head. Of course, he isn't going to tell me anything.

"If someone's following me, why didn't they pounce when I was sitting alone at the park? Or at the cliffs? Unless. Do you think they knew you were close by?"

"I think our accidental meeting has been the only thing protecting you and your family from meeting an unpleasant fate, which brings me to why I'm here. I broke away to come and ask you something."

"Okay," I say with a half-smile. "Ask away."

He leans back against the couch and crosses his arms, and I trace the outline of his biceps with my eyes, my gaze lingering there before traveling back to his face. He's so still that it's unnerving.

"What brought you to Washington? Why Port Townsend?"

I know the answer, but I start overthinking it like it were a trick question. "My...parents came here when Mom was pregnant with me. Well, me *and* my brothers. She was my age. They always talked about the peninsula, how beautiful it was, and promised they'd take us to see it one day, but they just kept putting it off. Then, when we were planning our post-graduation trip, I listened to all the guys' dumb suggestions and put my foot down. If it were to be our last trip as a family, before everybody goes their separate ways, we were going *here*. I just knew it was now or never."

"So, it was *your* idea to come here? Not your father's? Or someone else's invitation?"

"Well, yeah. They didn't want to travel too far from home. I never expected them to get why I wanted to see this place, but I thought it might give me some clue as to the girl my mom used to be—and who I'm supposed to be. A part of me just always knew I would come here. But anyways, yeah, I talked them into it. I was relentless. My one and only other request was that there would be no talk of work, but we couldn't even get halfway through the vacation without interruptions from their dumb job."

He offers only silent contemplation in reply.

"My turn to ask you a question," I say, "Since you only have a little time. I want to make it count."

He lets out a small chuckle, the sound rumbling through me.

I beam at him, desperately wanting to see his smile. I want to see how it forms, the shape of it, and whether it's as striking as his eyes.

"I know I already asked you once why you wear that mask, but what I want to know, what I *meant* to ask, is—why are you still hiding your face from me?"

After a long pause, he says, "I'd rather you not see all the *reminders* of what I truly am."

"What do you mean by that?"

"Many times, in the past, when humans have seen my face, I've been met with panic and screaming. There's something about my face that people seem to find deeply unsettling."

Damn, now I'm truly desperate to see what he looks like. "Well hold up, though. Maybe, it's not so much how you look but your habit of sneaking up behind people in forests and dark alleys. Like it's just a personality thing."

"Perhaps? Although I have tried different methods, styles of dress, and even wearing special contact lenses, regardless of my efforts to soften my appearance, I always managed to make humans uneasy. I guess you could say I don't blend well."

"Hmm. Have you ever thought of wearing, like, really big, dark sunglasses?"

He suppresses a soft laugh.

"I hope you know, no matter what you look like, you won't make me uneasy. Not after I've gotten to know you, the *real* you."

"So you say."

"Try me, then."

He side-eyes me. "Maybe on the final day of your time here, as you're leaving. After we get through this."

Looking closely, I see the skin around his eyes has a more translucent appearance, with thin, faint black lines that resemble veins. He seems tired. "You mentioned needing to sleep before. How long can you go without it? What happens if you don't?"

"When I conserve my strength, I've gone as long as a month without resting. At other times, it might be as little as a few days before I'm completely exhausted."

"What could you do that makes such a big difference?"

"Some of us have certain...gifts. Using them repeatedly can be quite *draining*."

"If you recover strength from sleeping, then why do you need blood?"

"The simplest way to think of it is that life is a kind of magic, passed down from one generation to the next, and in all living things, this magic is carried in the blood. We," he says, motioning to himself, "do not possess the gift of life, so we have to *borrow* it, from time to time."

I laugh nervously at his careful choice of words. "Borrowing implies that it would be returned." Literally sucking the life out of their human victims. Damn. That's even more hardcore than I figured. "But if all living creatures have life, why not drink animal blood or something? Like go drain a gazelle."

"If only it were so simple. Without the need for human blood, vampirism wouldn't be much of a curse, now would it?"

"What do you mean by curse?"

There's pain and resignation behind his eyes as he says, "There are legends, even among vampires. Stories of old magic. Have you never wondered where the first vampire came from?"

"Well, I guess your kind doesn't exactly seem to be the product of natural selection."

I see a smile return to his eyes at this, and I wonder what I said that has amused him so. It's a lot to process. Most humans still want to think of them as a genetic anomaly—a different branch of the evolutionary tree that specialized to feed on human blood with a weakness to ultraviolet light, rather than what they are: supernatural beings we can scarcely understand.

He checks his watch, and I'm brought back to the moment. I have him here and don't know when I'll see him again. I want to open my mouth, but my throat tightens. The butterflies in my stomach are back with a vengeance. Any moment could be my last with him.

"I'll have to tell you that legend another time."

You know what? Screw it. What am I waiting for? "What is this?" I ask suddenly, "I mean, you and...*me*."

"It's my sworn duty to see to the protection of this territory—"

"You could have just called me to ask why we came here."

"I needed to hear it from you, first-hand."

"Bullshit," I say, folding my arms, holding back my smirk to look more serious.

"I don't know what you're expecting me to say."

"How about we start with the truth?"

His eyes dart around, looking for an escape from being put on the spot. Clearly, he wasn't expecting me to be this assertive. Heck, I wasn't expecting it, either. Where's this coming from? It's so unusual to see him this way. It's sort of adorable and sad. How could someone so powerful be so uncomfortable discussing his feelings?

"You could have tried erasing my mind, again. But you didn't. You could have let me drown. You don't have to reply to my texts, nor did you have to come here tonight. You obviously want something from me, and I just want to hear you say it so I can stop feeling like I'm crazy."

He lets out a long, frustrated sigh. "Fine. But know this...I've been trying to avoid leading you into something. Brielle, you're eighteen. You just graduated from high school. You're mortal. You don't know what you want from life yet. As much as I want to, I can't just…A girl who's lived a life like yours is liable to jump at the first opportunity she has to escape her current situation."

"Whoa, whoa…"

"Just let me finish, please. I know what I feel, but I don't want to pull you into making a choice you'd only regret. It would be so easy, you see, to lure you into our world. I can see it in your eyes. You're the type who is drawn like a moth to a flame. I've watched it happen countless times, and they always grow to resent the one who stole them away from their loved ones, took away their life. I could never bring myself to do such a thing."

"You ass! You think I'm just some impressionable waif who can't make my own choices?"

"I'm—just saying that many young women in your position—"

"First of all, get *all the way* over yourself."

He bursts out laughing. "It's too much. I can never predict what wild thing will come out of your mouth next. You possess the unrivaled audacity of a queen upon her throne, yet with what power?"

Now, it's my turn to laugh, but I keep it to a bare minimum, denying him the satisfaction of breaking through my façade.

He hangs his head in quiet contemplation before uttering, "Have you given any consideration to my offer?"

"I have…I mean, I'm thinking about it, if it's even still on the table. It's just. Look, I don't want to be in any more situations where there are strings attached. I'm already stuck with my parents, and it feels like I would only be trading that for being stuck somewhere else, surrounded by people I don't know. As tempting as your offer is—I think I'd rather work to try and find my own way in life where I'm not dependent on others."

He nods. "No strings. In fact, I'd probably just have the titles signed over to you. Consider it thanks for keeping things to yourself and a repayment for what we did to you at the cliffs."

Whoa.

"But this is the trouble. Sure, I can buy you a house. *Houses,* even, with closets filled with new clothes. I've had a long time to accumulate resources, so I can bring you the means to live the life you desire. *But* will you not then feel, at least ever so slightly, obligated to me? Will I not, in effect, be bribing your affections? Will you not come to see me as a means of provision? I ask myself, over and over, what do I have to offer you? And each time, the answer is...nothing.

"Whatever I try to do, we can never be on equal footing. I will always be holding the cards. And even if I appeal to your *sensibilities,* rather than your innate sense of survival, is that not also a manipulation? If I told you, for instance, that I wanted you more than I've ever wanted any other—that I dreamed about you before I ever saw you, that I've been looking for you my entire existence—"

The room spins around me. I feel big and small, hot and cold at the same time. What is he saying to me? Is this just hyperbole? From the tone of his voice and the intonation of his words, I would almost say he's speaking from his heart—holding nothing back.

"So how could it *ever* work between us?" he says, almost pleading. "How could we build a house upon such a shaky foundation? Even though having you would mean that my heart would be glad every day, I could not possibly deceive myself to such a degree as this: to think that I could ever be truly wanted, ever be *useful* as anything other than—"

He stops short of what he's about to say.

"I'm gonna need some clarification on a few points—"

His head bolts to the window. He's heard something.

"I must go. They're nearby, and I've already stayed too long."

I sit there, looking at him, mouth agape.

"We'll finish this another time," he mutters.

The front door softly closes, issuing a final click.

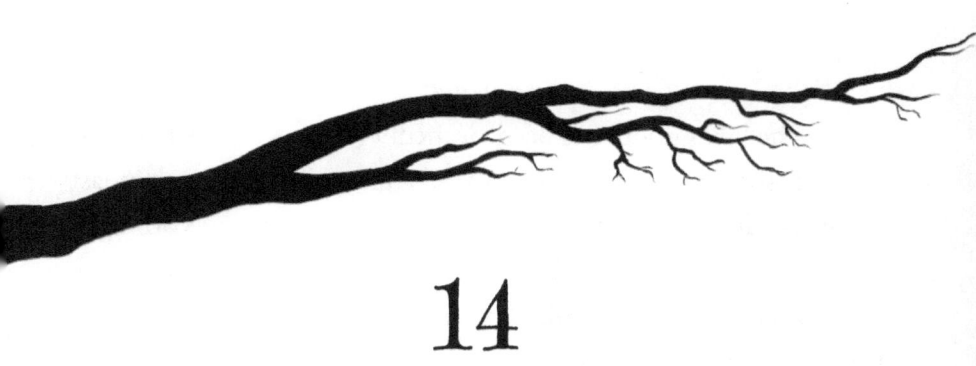

14

THE SILVER-BLUE LIGHT FILTERING through the front window must have woken me. I moan, stiff and achy from lying in the same position all night on the uncomfortable sofa, my left arm tucked beneath the pillow, numb under the weight of my head. I bury my face, not yet ready for the waking world, still grasping for the last remnants of my dreams as they slip through my fingers like fine mist.

It's the first time I've slept in on this vacation, feeling groggy and muddled, unable to remember the day of the week. If not for the siren song of caffeine, I wouldn't bother to get up today, with the words he spoke last night still weighing heavily upon my mind.

I rise slowly, reluctantly gathering my things before departing for my cabin, arms wrapped around the unstable mass of blankets and pillows. When my bare feet hit the cold, damp asphalt of the parking lot, I quicken my pace. It's hard to get used to the fact that no matter how warm the day before, the morning is always cold here. To my surprise, the cabin door's already wide open upon my arrival.

The living room has been cleaned. No shoes on the floor, no trash, or soda cans. The bottle of vodka Jonathan had snuck in last night has disappeared from its station on the counter. Nothing is out of place in the immaculately clean room, which only means one thing. As I hear the rhythmic *click-clop* sound of heels coming down the hallway, I release a prolonged groan of defeat.

"What was that for?" Mom snaps, irritated by my greeting.

"Because you cleaned, and you only clean when you're pissed. And I, for one, would prefer not to be caught in the crossfire over whatever this is about."

She glowers at me, her arms crossed over her chest.

"If you're mad about the alcohol, don't look at me. Run it for fingerprints if you like. That right there is *all* your sons and Jonathan."

She rolls her eyes and shakes her head, letting out a small, exasperated huff. "I'm not mad. I'm fine. Just get ready. We can go get breakfast, just us girls," she says with a smile that doesn't reach her eyes, which are still crinkled in annoyance. She may sound convincing to herself, but I can tell she's seething *just* below the surface.

I don't know how I missed it before, but there are no other sounds in the cabin. "Where is everybody?"

"They *would* have brought you along, too, but you were sleeping," she says, avoiding my gaze. "They went to the police station. Someone broke into our car."

It sounds plausible, but what my mom doesn't know is that, over the years, I became a professional at spotting her lies. Mom can never look me in the eyes while lying, and she has another tell—she becomes restless, like she is right now. She's fidgety as she moves around the kitchen, rearranging things she has already put into place. You'd think that after all these years of bullshitting me to my face, she'd at least have gotten a little better at it.

"Wow, that sucks. I'll let you go back to your cabin, then. Give me a little bit to get ready?" I say, issuing my phoniest smile. I spot her open suitcase on the couch, and thinking quickly, I add, "Oh, and I'm borrowing one of your shirts."

She nods and leaves without a glance over her shoulder, and I squint at her retreating figure with suspicion. I grab the first thing I find in her luggage and head to the bathroom to change. It's a fitted, black, long-sleeved blouse with a scoop neck. I pair it with skinny jeans and complete the look with my mud-encrusted Chucks before pulling my hair into something resembling a ponytail. Ugh, I wish I'd brought my makeup bag.

Mom is full of it right now, but why lie about something so dumb? There's no way their car got broken into this morning. And the way she cleaned this place up, she's upset about something. I finish applying mascara and step out of the bathroom before I have any more time to critique my appearance.

After all that crap about sticking together as a family and just wanting to make sure that I'm safe, they'll pull weird crap like this—leaving me behind without so much as a text. If it was a work emergency, why hide it? Curiosity drives me to pull out my phone.

Where you guys at?

I message each of them.

After a couple of seconds, I hear a muffled sound coming from the bedroom. The guys' bed is made, their neatly folded clothes piled on top of their respective suitcases. I walk to where the buzzing is coming from and overturn his pillow, dramatically revealing Warren's cell phone. I sit on the edge of the bed and grab it. As the screen lights up, I see two unread messages. For a split second, I hesitate, having caught them snooping on my phone before and remembering being livid. *Oh well*, I shrug, my turn now.

The first is a message from an unknown number with our local area code.

> *Call us when it's over.*

"Us?" I say aloud, baffled. Yeah, that's not cryptic. "When *what's* over?"

The other message is from me, just moments ago.

I'd snoop through his other texts, but there aren't any. No call history either. The only contacts listed are our immediate family and Jonathan. Puzzled, I return his phone to where I found it. I search all the obvious hiding spots in the room and find nothing else, realizing he left it behind by mistake. They must have rushed out in a hurry, but why?

I stare out the bedroom window for a while, debating my next move. Either I ignore this and wait to hear the inevitable lies they'll tell when they return, or I can use my rental to go to the police station myself, to confirm what I already suspect.

I grab my backpack and car keys off the counter. If I know Mom, she's sitting on the couch in the living room next door, waiting for me to get ready, and she'll see me if I leave. Good. She can be a witness.

I walk right outside. Even before she says anything, I sense her presence. I could probably ditch her before she gets to the car, but I have a better plan. Mom comes out, and we both get into the car. As expected, there's silence between us as I pull out of the parking lot. She looks a little confused when we don't stop at any of the breakfast places downtown and keep going.

"You know you just passed all the restaurants, right?" she asks.

"Oh, did I? *Dang.*" I feel her eyes upon me.

"You can do a U-turn right—" she says, as I drive past the turnoff.

"You know what I think? I bet the guys are just about done by now. It doesn't take that long to file a police report," I say, rounding a corner.

"Ah, well, no. They were going to go do their thing. I thought you wanted to do something together? You know, a little mother-daughter time," she says weakly, trailing off as she realizes we've just pulled up to the front door of the police station, the only car in the otherwise empty parking lot at seven in the morning.

"Well, that's weird," I say, looking at the posted hours sign. "They don't open until 10 a.m. Don't you think that's *weird*, Mom?"

She just sits there with her arms crossed, looking unimpressed.

"Come on, you have to give me credit. I busted you."

She won't even look at me.

"Hello. Earth to Mom, they aren't here. So where are they *really*?"

Still nothing. Looking at her stubborn expression as she stares out the window at absolutely nothing brings back a flood of memories of times just like this. Things that make no sense, that will never be brought up again by anyone but me. I might as well go ahead and add this morning to the list of things that I made up or never happened.

I shake my head at her and drive off, knowing that nothing I can say will make any difference.

I waltz into my cabin with a giant iced coffee in one hand and a box of a dozen assorted donuts in the other, ready to eat half the container myself. The door swings open behind me, and my mother—who refused to even get out of the car at the coffee place—storms in, silently fuming.

I drop onto the couch and let my body sink in, propping my shoes up on the coffee table. I casually turn on the TV and balance the open box across my lap. "Why are you still here?" I say, as I flip through the channels.

"What?"

Either through mounting courage or growing contempt, I find the nerve to look my mother dead in the eyes and say, "Would you just go away, already? You obviously have no interest in hanging out with me. You probably just got stuck watching me. Well, don't worry, I'll be right here. I don't feel like going anywhere now."

"That's not—"

"Will you please just *spare me*? Quit acting like we have a relationship! I actually hoped this place would somehow allow us to finally connect, but it won't. Nothing ever will. So just stop *pretending* like I was ever a part of this family. All you care about are the guys, so go be with them. I'll be fine without you...because I always have been."

Mom's scowl turns into a shocked expression, and I see a brief flicker of pain flash across her face as she slowly turns away from me.

With that, she walks out the door mumbling, "I think I'll walk down and grab a coffee." The door clicks shut behind her.

My chest aches, and that familiar heaviness returns to my gut. I realize now, and only now, the source of my resentment toward my mother. I needed her on my side all those years growing up in that household with Dad's rules, desperate for her validation. All it would have taken was the occasional eye roll behind his back to let me know I wasn't the only one who thought it made no sense, but she couldn't even do that. Just like this morning, all I needed was for her to acknowledge the bald-faced lie I caught her in, to take my side, to tell me something—anything—but all she offered was silence, the same thing she's always done.

She reserves all her love and support for her husband and has always—will always—take his side no matter what because Dad is *everything* to her. And as bad as it hurt me to say it to her, it needed to be said, though I'm beginning to feel like the bitter person they all claim I'm turning into. No, what they've *turned me* into.

My stomach is in knots, my appetite lost. I shove the box of donuts off me, and it crashes onto the coffee table. I take a series of deep breaths and fight off the tears as they begin to well in my eyes. I don't care what their big secret is anymore or why they lie to me. All I want is to be free of it. I *need* to be free of it. And now, I have a way out, even if it is an invitation from a vampire.

I no longer want this drink, but it's too expensive to throw out. Emotionally drained, I pry myself off the couch and cross the room to put my coffee in the fridge for later, sniffling and wiping the tears from my eyes, resolved to accept Aldrick's offer. I'm done being shy—no more games. The next time I see him, I'm going to wrap my arms around his neck and tell him yes. I snort at the image in my head.

That's when a strange, high-pitched screeching sound comes from outside. First, I think it's the squeal of a loose belt on an old car, but it keeps getting louder and higher-pitched. I set the drink on the counter and place my hands over my ears. And then—

BOOM!

An explosion rocks the building, its force striking me violently from behind, launching me forward. I land hard in the kitchen, face down on the floor, bits of shattered glass and splinters of wood falling around me. I scramble to my hands and knees, shaking from the adrenaline, and twist, fully expecting to see a crashed airplane.

Instead, a single black crow glides in through the opening where the window once was. It reaches the center of the room, and there's a blinding flash of iridescent green light, accompanied by a powerful sucking sound, and down drops a man, his bare feet slapping loudly against the wood floor. His hair is long, black, and greasy. Running down his face from his brow to his chin is a long scar. He's tall, tan, and scary-looking as a toothy grin expands across his face, revealing rows of uneven teeth. There is a beat of silence as I take everything in.

"Why are you *naked*?" I scream at him, too deep in shock to understand what transpired. A strange man has popped into existence in front of me, in the nude, and the entire front end of the cabin is caved in.

"We have a door! You didn't have to do that!" I yell through tears, unsure why I'm even talking to him. I should be running. I will run. As I push off the ground to stand, my hand lands on something cold. I pause, feeling the object and realizing what it is. Good.

"Well, well, figured if we watched long enough they'd leave you alone for at least a minute," he growls, smirking. "Would never have guessed it would take a whole damn week!" he shouts, and throws the couch out of his way with one hand, tromping straight in my direction.

I don't know what I think is about to happen, but when he gets to me, he reaches out and grabs me by the hair and tries to drag me off.

I grit my teeth in pain, grabbing the wooden handle of the object under my hand and shoving the steak knife into him, burying it in his gut. He lets out a pained grunt, releasing his grip just enough for me to break free of his grasp. I run around him, and without looking back I make a break for it, my shoes crunching on the glass as I move past the overturned couch, snatch up my backpack by the strap from what was once a coffee table, and jump over the remains of the front door, sprinting for the car.

I fumble for the keys in my bag, my hands shaking as I shove the right one into the lock, before yanking the door open and jumping inside.

As I struggle to get the key into the ignition, I hear a bellowing cry, followed by that same high-pitched screeching from before emanating from inside the cabin, and then another loud explosion. The walls of the cabin *flex outward* from the force. Nope. *Hell* no. I'm out. I start the car and throw it into reverse, backing it out at full speed the whole way through the parking lot. After jumping the curb, I yank the wheel hard, and the car spins around. I put it in drive and floor it, pretty sure that the laws of the road don't apply when you're fleeing from a scary ass, magical, exploding crow man.

Driving with one hand, my phone in the other, I go to my recent calls, find Aldrick, and speed dial him. "Come on, come on, come on! Please, Aldrick!" The immortal vampire's cell goes straight to voicemail. "No!" I scream into the device.

Cora. The image of the girl's face flashes in my mind. I find the contact I made for her, eyes on my phone. I look up, almost going off the road while rounding a bend, passing the last store in town. I call her number as I cross the center line, passing an old, slow truck, praying for her to pick up.

She does.

"Brielle? Where...are you? I can't see you at all." Her voice is so uncertain.

"A naked shifter just blew up the cabin! He grabbed me, but I got away!"

"Wait, slow down. Who grabbed you?"

"A freaking crow! Look, I'm driving out of town..." I trail off mid-sentence, noticing a crow in the rearview mirror, fast approaching, easily beating the speed of the car. *Holy moly*. I can't go any faster.

"Damn it, no, he's a bird again!" I shriek into the phone.

"I can't see you! I'm so sorry. I don't know how to help you, but everyone is already on their way back. Just hold on! Where are you now?"

"Just outside of town, I don't know! I'm not sure! Why does everything have to look the same?"

The crow veers away from the vehicle, arcing upward out of sight.

"Now he's above the car! What do I do?"

"First, slow down...you *can't* outrun them. You're only making things more dangerous for yourself by driving faster."

"Well, I'm not going to *let* him catch up to me. I'm pretty sure I've seriously pissed him off!"

Something slams into the back of my car with a loud crunch, sending the rear end skidding into oncoming traffic. The driver of the Subaru goes onto the shoulder to avoid a head-on collision, honking his horn the whole time. Screaming, I throw the wheel hard to the left, trying to prevent a spin-out, then I throw it the opposite way, back and forth, until I regain control. I cannot. Believe. That just happened. I reach to buckle my seat belt.

Maybe I can't outrun them, but it's my only chance of keeping out of that asshole's clutches until Aldrick gets here and rips his freaking head off.

"What was that? What just happened?" she yells, her voice a distorted screech through the phone.

"A *bird* did a pit maneuver on me! He tried knocking me into oncoming traffic! How is it so strong!? I'm freaking losing it!" I yell, as I search for him everywhere, leaning forward and peering up through the windshield at the gray skies above me.

"Brielle, it's too late. You need to stop the car before you get hurt or worse."

"Oh God. There's more of them!" I say frantically as I spot the dozen or so crows soaring high above my car in a tight formation. Finally, the realization sinks in...she's right, it's over. I'm done. If one can cause all this mayhem, then this many is unstoppable.

"Pull over! Now!" Cora yells at me.

I obey the voice and slam on the brakes, feeling the car lock up beneath me, but it's already too late. Something strikes the left side of the car even harder than before, sending me spinning completely off the road, too far gone to correct. Closing my eyes, I brace for impact and feel the car spin once, then twice, before slamming into something. Everything comes to a sudden halt with a loud crunch and the pop of glass as my poor car comes to rest on its side. The driver's side window is now level with the ground, my cheek resting on the still-intact glass, unsure of what I hit in the impact. My mind is scrambled, and I struggle to maintain my grasp on reality.

"Brielle? Are you okay? What happened?" Her voice sounds more distant with every passing second, as everything fades into silence, blackness, emptiness—

15

LOUD, IMPLODING POPS ISSUE all around the car, followed by the hollow thunk of many pairs of feet hitting the grassy earth, faint voices speaking in whispers, laughing, and cursing. I lie still, dazed, confused—praying they'll think I died and leave me alone. The weight of the car shifts and starts to creak, crying out with a metallic groan of pain. I hold back a whimper as the Honda slowly turns, coming to a rest inverted, roof to the ground. There's nowhere to hide as I dangle from my seatbelt in the overturned sedan, like a turtle on its back. With one hand outstretched for support, I release my belt buckle and fall onto the ceiling. I huddle in the dark, cramped space, not wanting to look outside, wondering what happens now.

"Please answer me. Are you alright?" I hear a distant, small voice calling to me. *Cora!* I scramble through the debris and find my phone.

"Please help me," I whisper-shout into it, "they're all around me."

"Everyone's already on their way. Don't do anything impulsive. Listen to me: wait for Aldrick."

A horrible, crunching sounds, then the whole car lurches as the driver's side door is ripped off its hinges. A guy tosses it aside like it's nothing to him and squats before the opening, a wry smile on his twisted face—this isn't the guy I stabbed. He's shirtless, with a gaudy pendant necklace dangling from his wide neck. Thankfully, he's wearing a pair of sweatpants. I retreat into the car, trying to duck under the seats to put distance between us, but his powerful hand clamps around my ankle, and with a tug, I'm no longer in the car.

He pulls me to my feet and turns to face the group. My eyes scan their faces as I regain my balance. My vision tilts, and confusion fills me—the man who broke into my cabin isn't among their rank. Counting them, there are eleven in total, including the one holding me. Twelve, if I add the guy who attacked me earlier. That's *way* too many shifters.

One stands outfitted in nothing but a pair of boxer briefs, holding open a gym bag full of clothes; the others grab things out of it indiscriminately, putting on pairs of sweatpants and shorts to cover their immodesty, each one wearing the same ugly necklace.

"How bad you think she's hurt?" one asks.

"I don't know, but that crash was *sick*," another says, laughing as he fist-bumps a buddy.

"Did you *really* have to destroy the car, Derek? We could have used it instead of waiting here."

"Yeah, and it'd be the first thing they look for, numb nuts," says Derek, the guy holding me.

Other than the occasional tattoo, I can hardly tell them apart. They all share the same cocky dude-bro energy, ungroomed hair, and look and smell like they haven't showered in days. The rancid smell coming off the burly man holding me is gag-worthy.

My confusion fades, and I try to pull away from his clutches, but it's no use, so I go for a knee to his groin, but he steps back, avoiding it, ducks low, and throws my body over his shoulder.

"Oof," I huff out, my upper half upside-down, indignation rising within me as I yell, "What the hell is your problem? Put me down!"

I hear laughter from a couple of them.

"Grey should be here soon with another car. Hide this pile of crap in the trees and get everyone out of sight. We don't need to draw any more attention to ourselves," Derek says, ordering the rest of the group his voice rumbling through his body. They hastily comply. I lie helplessly across his bulky shoulder, staring at the wreckage of my poor Honda Accord.

Watching these men fumble the car and clumsily drag it into the woods while pieces of wreckage fall to the ground, laughing and pointing at me while making crude jokes, I find it hard to believe they've made it this far without being tracked by Aldrick and his family.

"What could you possibly want from me?" I yell as I beat my fists on his iron back, trying to elbow his kidneys. If he feels anything at all, he doesn't show it. Damn, I would kill for anyone's help right now, even—and I can't believe I'm admitting this—my stupid brothers or, ugh, Jonathan.

Derek carries me away from the wreckage. Breathing heavily, all I can do is stare at the ground, watching the backs of his bare feet grow progressively darker as the light and noise of the group fade.

We cross briefly through some woods before emerging onto a back road just off the main highway that appears to lead nowhere.

"He's going to kill you, you know. He's a hunter," I say, but he only grunts with amusement. "I mean it. You have no idea how fast he is. His power, what he's capable of. When he finds out you did this to me, he'll kill every last one of you. And he'll enjoy it."

"Who, your little vampire boyfriend?" he says, laughing deeply, sounding disgustingly sure of himself. "Nothing but an old dog on a very short leash. Soon to be neutered."

"You're wrong. He's coming, and he's gonna be pissed. Any second now."

Almost as I finish speaking, Derek quiets his laugh and suddenly halts, turning to face the main road. Then I hear the roaring engine of a car that sounds like it's moving *fast*—and getting closer.

"About time," he says. "Looks like your carriage is here, princess." He lets out another self-satisfied chuckle before adding, "What are your feelings about riding in the trunk?"

Wait, what?

I crane my neck, trying to get a better look at the red sports car screaming toward us, its tires tearing through the loose gravel. Just when I think it's going to run us down, the driver slams on the brakes, and the car skids to a stop less than twenty feet away.

"What the—" Derek says as the cloud of dirt following in the car's wake overtakes us.

When the driver's side door opens, *Jonathan* emerges with an expression on his face that I have never seen before. His icy blue eyes have darkened to storm clouds as he exudes an aura of absolute confidence—his jaw and cheekbones sharp as ever. From the looks of it, he's furious.

160

"Jonathan, run, get out of here! They're shapeshifters! He'll kill you!" I yell, panicking. I can't watch him get hurt—one poor human boy against an army of shifters.

Unphased by my words, he slams the car door behind him, his jacket and hair whipping in the wind as his long legs consume the distance between us. The air feels like it's wobbling around me, like everything's happening in slow motion.

"No! Don't! You need to go!" I scream frantically before turning away and closing my eyes, unable to stomach the gut-wrenching thought of Derek tearing him apart, seeing his motionless body, of losing him—

Derek drops his shoulder, sending me free-falling to the ground. I hit the gravel on my hands and knees with a pained yelp, rocks biting into my palms. What? I spin to face the two men, landing on my butt and crawling backward.

I watch as it happens, and the world as I knew it shatters into millions of tiny pieces that can never be put back together again. The ground has opened beneath me, swallowed me whole, and I'm slowly sinking into it...

Jonathan throws his hands out wide in front of himself as a strange, glowing red light emanates from his rings and necklace, forming waves of energy that flow through the air, spreading and distorting the world around him. At this point, I can't tell if what I'm seeing is real or a wild hallucination from a head injury—but it looks like this energy is responding to the movement of his hands, like he's shaping it—*wielding* it? The field of neon red energy expands around him, becoming more vibrant.

Derek screams, "Shit!" as he leaps into the air and, with an audible pop, shifts back into a crow, abandoning his pants. As he takes flight, they drift lazily to the ground like a falling leaf. The small black bird flies up high and impossibly fast, creating a blast of air that causes the nearby trees to sway, then flips around, beginning a dive-bomb at Jonathan. I cover my ears as that same high-pitched screech begins—knowing what comes next...

The shockwave rips through the air as Jonathan slams his hands together, arms straight out, pointed directly at the crow. The screeching stops. All of the red stuff now focused in one intense, straight beam, which I follow with my eyes to the crow hanging motionless in the air, lifelessly impaled on a thin, red shard of light that extends from Jonathan's hands.

I gasp as the shards of energy retract back to Jonathan like a switchblade, and the crow falls from high above, shedding feathers as his body slowly morphs back into Derek. These red waves surrounding his arms flow back into his rings and necklace and, with a final release, dissipate completely. Jonathan's frosty eyes look at me, and he smirks, just as I hear the dense impact of Derek's body hitting the ground.

Jonathan runs over and pulls me to my feet, putting his arm around me and turning us away from the carnage—I give in to the impulsive thought, though, and chance a look at what's left of the shifter. His body lies twitching, blood oozing and spreading along the dirt and gravel. In the place where his heart and lungs should be...nothing but a gaping hole—a piece of him is just *gone*.

Jonathan just saved my life from the shifter, and he'd made it look almost *easy*.

I stare at the carnage, not comprehending, as he tries to rush me to the car. The damn wobbling air returns, disorienting me and then, the red energy flickers back to life, only this time—I'm inside with him, the waves swirling around us. I watch in disbelief as a wall forms around where we stand, encompassing us in a dome. I look just in time to see the group of shifters arrive, see their fallen comrade, then turn their eyes to us.

The shifters converge on us. I bury my head in Jonathan's chest, expecting an onslaught, but soon lift my gaze to see a bunch of men beating on this barrier he's erected, cursing him and spitting at us, but their attacks have no effect on it. They can't touch us.

I look up at Jonathan, standing there against me, breathing heavily through his nose, still fuming with rage.

"Jonathan, what is this? How are you doing this?" I ask, my voice shaky and hollow.

"Magic," he says, voice strained.

The commotion outside the wall stops, and all the men fall silent, eyes changing from anger to confusion as they turn, their backs to us. Through the gaps between them, I can just make out what has grabbed their attention.

There before them—like a god among men—stands Aldrick.

"Please, listen to me this time," Jonathan starts. "Stay behind me, and for the love of God—don't say anything."

Aldrick looks down at the shifters, towering a full head over them, stepping slowly through their midst like an angel of death, assessing them. He stops for a second to examine the lifeless corpse on the ground before continuing toward us. There's tension in the air, but nobody speaks. Why isn't Aldrick fighting them? Why aren't they running for their lives? Don't they know who he is?

"Stand aside," the command comes, his voice deep and angry. I'm astonished as they do what he says. The shifters move off to one side of the road, gathering near the body of their fallen comrade, a good fifteen feet from Jonathan and me. They all remain alert, their eyes locked on the vampire.

Aldrick walks closer to us, placing himself between us and the shifters.

"You can drop the shield now, Jonathan," he says, looking right at us, his red eyes hard and aggravated.

With a wave of his hands, the shield is gone, red energy retreating into Jonathan's rings and necklace. As it dissipates, a cool breeze glides over my skin. Aldrick watches me, the look in his eyes one of confusion and sadness.

"Are you hurt?" he asks softly.

I go to answer him, but Jonathan sucks in a deep shocked gasp, dropping his arm from me, staggering back a few steps. "No. Brielle, no!" His wide eyes dart from me to Aldrick several times, finally coming to rest on my face.

Another first: Jonathan looks scared.

"What have you done? Out of all people, one of *them*?" he yells at me, horrified, a look of betrayal spreading across his face.

"What have *I* done? Are you kidding me?" I scream, practically hysterical.

He continues to stare at me, eyes wide, shaking his head.

"You used magic freaking powers to make a shield! What the hell was *that*? You blew a hole through that guy!" I point to the corpse of the shifter, my hand trembling. My breathing is becoming jagged, and I know that if I don't stop talking, I'll start crying.

Jonathan's eyes leave mine to peer over my shoulder at something in the distance, and I hear another voice that stops my thoughts in their tracks.

16

"WHAT DO WE HAVE here? If it isn't the little group of *trouble-makers* that crossed into our territory without even bothering to say hello," he says slowly, with a hint of arrogance. "Not exactly neighborly behavior."

The voice brings me chills because I know who it belongs to—Aldrick's brother with the freaky mind powers.

I see three tall, hooded figures emerging from the tree line. They position themselves about twenty feet up the road from us. All three have their faces covered with masks like Aldrick's, wide hoods pulled over their heads, red eyes, and wavy brown hair, though none share the same sharp features. These must be his infamous brothers. The small road is starting to look like a standoff.

"A little far from home, don't you think, guys? Hey," says one of the new arrivals with a put-on enthusiasm, pointing his gloved finger at a shifter wearing a pair of cutoff jean shorts, who looks back at him in confusion. "Love the jorts look. Underappreciated. I keep saying, they're going to make a comeback."

This voice, I do not recognize at all. The third—and tallest—doesn't speak. Instead, he looks off to the side, shaking his head, like he'd rather be someplace else.

"Enough," says Aldrick impatiently. I follow his line of sight and nearly have a heart attack when I spot two more cloaked figures hidden in the trees behind the shifters, staring directly at us. A lovely woman, and an older man whose haunting gaze terrifies me more than anything I've ever seen. With my heart racing out of control and my mind still reeling from the wreck, I feel faint.

Then, the chugging of a diesel engine draws everyone's attention to a giant black Hummer turning off the main road, and coming our way. It stops inches behind Jonathan's car. My dad jumps out first, with Elden and Warren following closely behind. All three wear the same heated expression.

Dad only has eyes for me, pulling me into a tight embrace as soon as he reaches me. I'm still fighting back my panic—and losing the battle—it feels like I'm hyperventilating, and I'm praying that maybe I can pass out if only to give my mind a few minutes to deal with all this overload.

"Why should we have to come to *you* first?" says one of the crows, scoffing. "What business do vampires have getting involved in the affairs of shifters and mages?"

My dad finally releases his grip on me to go and deal with the situation, trying—and failing—to give me a reassuring look. I can tell he's rattled, too.

"*Any* uninvited guests in our territory get Aldrick sent on their heels," says the brother with the hypnotic voice. The others by his side remain silent.

"It's a little hard to tell which of you is speaking since you're too *scared* to show your faces," the shifter sneers.

"I am Gerard Holsten," he responds, placing a hand over his heart. "I assume you're all familiar with my eldest brother, Aldrick. These are my younger siblings, Isen and Dane, and behind you—our parents, Sylvain and Aurelia," he says, gesturing to them, triggering the group of shifters to turn and look over their shoulders.

"And you are...?" Gerard asks in an inviting tone.

But no answer comes.

"*That* is Thorn Ackerman," my father says, stepping into the center near Aldrick. Eyeing the dead body, he adds, "And from the looks of it, he's just been promoted to the leader of their group."

"Do you tolerate bloodshed in your territory? One of our men was just murdered by this boy," he says, pointing at Jonathan, before moving his finger to me, "and another was maimed by that girl!" Thorn hisses.

"Let me stop you there, big guy...Because it kinda feels like you might be leaving out some important details," says Dane.

"The mage girl," he says, pointing at me, "*she* drew first blood."

Six sets of red eyes turn to meet mine as commotion erupts, and I swallow hard.

"Let her speak," says Aldrick, silencing their voices.

"I uh. He uh," I look back at him, stammering as everyone's attention is on me. "One of them blew up the cabin. It knocked me down. He came after me! He grabbed me! So, I took the kitchen knife, and yeah—I stabbed him, in self-defense!" I barely get it out, my face hot, words hitching. I breathe heavily, feeling like a fool.

Frustrated, Gerard presses two fingers against his forehead, "You know that doesn't count. You still attacked first. Which means Jonathan had every right to protect her."

Now Aldrick's brother is on a first-name basis with Jonathan?

"It doesn't matter! It's her word against our brother's, and he's the one fighting for his life right now. We'll see who our people believe."

The look on Dad's face, I've seen it before—as though he's heard something peculiar, but he keeps it to himself. I doubt anybody else would pick up on such a subtle cue.

"Are you sure you're in a position to be making threats?" Dane asks.

My eyes remain on my father, wondering what he could be thinking.

"There might be some sort of misunderstanding—" Dad begins to say.

Thorn's head whips to Dad, and he says loudly, interrupting him, "Interfere with our departure in any way, and you will have a whole host of our brothers descending upon you within the day. This is not a war you want to begin."

Dad looks straight at Aldrick and says, "They're bluffing. They aren't—"

"Oh, Lucas?" Thorn interrupts again as one of his men hands him a phone, and he looks down at it with a devious grin of pure self-satisfaction. "Before you finish that thought—is there something you're forgetting? Or maybe I should say...*someone*? I see your sons, even your daughter, but where is your little wife?"

My father's face goes blank with confusion. He looks at me, silently asking the question.

"I just saw her. She left to get coffee a couple of minutes before they attacked me. The guy said he was waiting for *me* to be alone. I didn't think—" I answer him, confused.

Aldrick turns to the shifters, his tone terrifying and absolute, and demands, "Thorn, tell me you haven't taken a hostage in *my* territory."

There's a beat of silence before the horror hits me. They have Mom.

A small, anguished sound slips from my lips, my peripheral vision flooding with red. The air wobbles, causing a rippling sensation that flows through my core, like being thrown into the deep waters of a crashing ocean, yanking on me back and forth, yet unable to move me. Knowing that Jonathan can do something like this is one thing, but seeing my brothers—my *father*—summon that same strange red energy—it's too much. I need to get away from them. From this feeling.

"Everyone, stand down!" Gerard yells. I know that voice and what will come next. I tense up, bracing for impact. But I don't sense any reverberations in my skull. There is no magic in his words.

"It's no use," Jonathan proclaims. "They possess a stolen mage artifact. It seals all magic, except our own, from being used. None of your abilities will work in its presence."

I stumble backward, running into a tree before changing course, starting toward the main road, in the direction of the cars. I'm roughly ten feet from them, but it's not enough distance to escape the strange pull of their powers. There comes a gentle tug at the end of my sleeve, and I don't have to look to know who it is. I turn to face Aldrick, the only one here I trust. He shakes his head at me, his solemn eyes holding me in their gaze.

169

"Don't leave," he says, "this can be worked out."

"What do you want his wife for?" Gerard asks the shifters, indignant. "Why did you pick the Drapers out of all the mage families?"

"You think we're only going after *one* family? That a single hostage would be enough?" Thorn hisses.

"But invading our territory, armed with a stolen mage weapon? Concealing yourselves from our seers, following a teenage girl for days on end. You're starting a war on multiple fronts—but to what end?" asks Gerard.

"So, uh," I whisper to Aldrick, low enough that hopefully only he will hear me, "This is what they kept from me? That they have magic?"

"You can see why I was hesitant to tell you," he says as I look at my family, red energy swirling around them. Mages? That's what they are? All these years of deception, being excluded—all because I don't have these powers, because I'm not one of them.

The last bit of control I have breaks away. My tears overflow, and I swipe them away angrily. I don't want to cry. I want to scream and rage at both sides, the shifters and my family. *This* is how I find out? Even the vampires knew what they were. I realize that I'm nothing more than the one stupid, oblivious human girl who's been made a complete *fool* of.

"How could you keep this from me?" I shout at them. "Really Elden? War? Do you have nothing to say? Mom knows, right? She has to know."

My father looks back at me and closes his eyes, his face full of pain.

"She knows," Aldrick says softly.

I look back at him, my heart tearing apart.

"They'll be here soon," Jonathan says, peering over into the trees at nothing. What is he talking about? He turns to Dad. "They're bringing her, Lucas."

Bringing her? *Mom?*

"Good news, everyone. Looks like our guest of honor is about to arrive," announces Thorn. "I don't think I need to tell you what happens to her if you do anything...hasty, do I, gentlemen?"

Time is running out, ticking away with every beat of my heart. What will be the outcome once this is over? They walk out of here with Mom? Is no one going to say anything?

Thorn steps forward, addressing everyone gathered, his men smiling smugly behind him, "So here's how this is going to go. We'll bring her out, let you see her with your own eyes. I want you to understand the stakes here. No need to take my word for it. Once we've made it clear who holds the cards, me and the boys are going to hop in our car and ride off into the sunset."

They don't just get to *have* my Mom. We *need* her. I need her.

"No stopping us at the checkpoints, no interruptions, no funny business. Just smooth sailing back to our territory. If you wish to negotiate for her release, *after* this is all finished, you may take it up with our council."

He's *lying.*

"Oh, and Lucas, what was it that you were trying to share with the class before?" Thorn taunts, staring my father down.

Dad lowers his eyes, silent. My brothers look to him and follow suit.

That's it? With their powers, they can't come up with anything? They're just going to give Mom up? Oh, *hell no.*

171

Maybe it's delirium from the car wreck, or my mind has finally snapped under the pressure of all these lies—but before I know what's happening, my legs are carrying me forward. With each step I take toward Thorn, I feel a burden lifting. A finality. Release.

"Brielle!"

Voices cry out from behind me, but nobody else moves.

Wild amusement fills Thorn's eyes as I approach him. He opens his mouth, no doubt to make some snide remark, but I speak first.

"It's me you wanted, right? I'm the one you came for. Well? Here I am."

He narrows his eyes and searches my face as if trying to discern my intent.

"Just let Mom go. Take me instead."

Thorn smirks, peering into my eyes and realizes that I'm serious. "Deal," he says, nonchalantly.

"No!" Aldrick screams, and I turn to see him struggling against three sets of strong hands—all three of his brothers fighting intensely to hold him back from coming to me, their heels digging into the ground as he slowly drags them. "We'll figure this out! I'll fix it! You don't have to do this!"

But it's already done. I've made my choice.

The crunch of gravel under the tires calls our attention as a third vehicle arrives, a pearl-white Escalade. We hear the slamming doors and footsteps approaching. Mom appears shell-shocked between the two half-dressed men, somehow still graceful as she clutches her purse tightly. One man I don't recognize at all; the other is covered in dried blood from his abdomen down to his feet—the scar-faced shifter who attacked me at the cabin—his belly wound appears almost healed. Mom doesn't fully understand what's happening as she enters the scene. She doesn't look my way. Instead, the moment she sees Dad, she runs to him.

The shapeshifters let her go.

At that instant, a strong hand grips my shoulder and something cold and sharp, a knife I assume, presses against my throat. My heart pounds, throbbing in my temple, drowning out the sounds around me, and I feel lightheaded. I hear yelling, pleading, but I'm not listening.

The shifters waste no time moving to their getaway car. Two grab their fallen ex-leader and carry him to the vehicle. I remain at the back of the group, hard steel pressed tight against my neck—a human shield.

"Wait! Please," cries Aldrick, "I will forget this—forget that you exist. You have my word. Just let her go. But if you take her from me, if any harm comes to her...I will follow you to the ends of the Earth, hunt you day and night. When I find you, and *I will* find you...I will tear the still-beating heart from your chest."

"You don't get to bargain," Thorn replies. "You have nothing we want."

"Thorn, are you blind?" Jonathan says, taking a few steps in our direction.

The tip of the knife digs deeper into my neck, and I suck in a shocked breath.

"Don't move, Pembroke," Thorn says, his voice wavering slightly.

Jonathan raises his hands in surrender, trying to appease him.

Thorn moves toward the car again, jerking me along, my feet stumbling as I try to keep up, and not get my throat slit in the process.

"How can you not see it? She's his soulmate!" Jonathan blurts, "*You,* more than anyone here, should know what this means. Please, just let her go."

Dead silence fills the forest as Thorn's body stiffens. Every eye is now on me. Horror etches my family's faces.

Soulmate? Why would Jonathan say something like that? Why is everybody reacting this way, taking his words for fact? Does this have something to do with magic? Looking back at Aldrick, at the conviction in his eyes—I can tell he, too, believes it.

"Don't give her up, Thorn," says one of his buddies.

"Without the girl, we're not getting out of here alive." echoes another.

"I'm aware, you idiots," he growls, continuing to back away.

Aldrick never takes his eyes off me. He manages to break a single hand free from his brother's grasp, and even this small gesture causes Thorn to flinch a little. Then he does something I don't think anybody anticipated. He reaches up and hooks a finger around the mask at the bridge of his nose.

"Aldrick, no!" his brothers say in unison as he pulls it down, allowing it to rest on his neck.

Time stands still.

Something breaks in my chest, and it's painful—the shock radiates through every inch of my being. I always believed he would be a sight to behold, but how could I have known that his face would be so devastating? His eyes alone were always overwhelming, capable of hypnotizing me with just a look...but this—his straight, prominent nose, high cheekbones, strong, angular jaw. He wears a short, neatly trimmed beard, which grants him a slightly rugged appearance. Lastly, my eyes land on his mouth—simply *glorious.*

His lips are shapely, full, delicate...yet undeniably savage. They're perfect.

I see nothing but perfection.

Even if he were human, even if he had a heartbeat, had human flaws and weaknesses, it wouldn't matter. He would still be lightyears out of my league. His face remains hard, stoic, strong—though the look in his eye is something I don't recognize. A shift has occurred, subtle and minuscule, yet present.

There's a tug on my arm, but I refuse to break eye contact. If this is the last time I'll see him, then I will hold on to every second I can get.

Aldrick's head tilts back defiantly, his eyes harden, and he speaks. "Do not be afraid, Brielle. I will come for you."

For just a moment, all my anxieties and fears evaporate like smoke. I forget about the betrayals and the lies as I catch a glimpse of *him*—not my savior *or* my stalker—but the terrifying vampire he truly is, and I think I've finally lost it. Something must be seriously, *deeply* wrong with me. A grin stretches across my face, and a deranged, euphonic laugh escapes my lips.

Everything becomes a jumble of red, swirling lights, men changing into birds, the soft sound of fabric hitting the ground as their pants drop—nowhere to go but down. I watch as they throw Derek's lifeless—and *chest-less*—body into the trunk of the Escalade, laughing again, remembering what his last words to me were.

The red light is still spreading, coming my way. Jonathan's light is the biggest and most brilliant, spreading far and taking shape as it snakes around the vampires, creeping at us like gnarled fingers that flow around the car like licks of flames as the shifters shove me into the back seat and take off like bats out of hell.

By the time I come to my senses, I don't know where we are or how long they've been driving. All I know is that it's an unusually quiet ride. I stare out the window, my mind blank, feeling empty inside, until Thorn finally breaks the silence.

"We have the mage girl *and* the artifact—so why is everyone acting like we just lost?"

"Did you *not* see the look on his face?"

"We're dead."

"Don't talk like that! We have leverage!" Thorn chides.

"You think he gives a damn about leverage? Do you not know who we're dealing with?"

"No, I know *exactly* who I'm dealing with."

"That's literally what Derek said, and now he's worm food."

Silence.

"We stick to the plan," Thorn says.

"No," says the gruff voice of the shifter I stabbed, "We cut and run."

"Grey, what the hell are you saying?" Thorn replies.

"Look, I don't like it any more than you do, but he's claimed the girl. We're burned, and we need to go deep underground."

"So, what if he claims her? We *have* the girl! All the more reason they must come to the negotiating table. We hold all the cards, now."

"Don't you get it?" Grey says, "The archmage was right. We were blind, and now, the Demon of Bremen will not rest until the last of us is dead. Laws and treaties hold no meaning for him. He'd burn the whole world down just to get to her."

So, now demons are real? Hmm.

"What would you have me do? Return her?" Thorn asks.

"No, there's no assuaging his anger. We're past that," Grey says, the smile evident in his voice. "We use him to our own ends. We sell her off—to his *own kind*. Let vampire kill vampire."

"Use his wrath to sow discord among their ranks," says Thorn. "I like it."

"Then we take the money, and while they're fighting amongst themselves, make use of the time it affords us to get out of dodge, regroup. Come up with a new plan of attack."

"Isn't it risky for her to hear us talking like this?"

"Nah, look at her, she's so deep into this, but she still doesn't know a damn thing. I almost feel sorry for her."

"The best part of my plan," Grey says, "she doesn't survive."

Well, that's not ominous at all. Looking back, maybe I shouldn't have stabbed Grey. Maybe if I'd gone peacefully with him in the first place, things would have turned out differently, but what's done is done. My only hope now is that Aldrick—

"Ow!" I jump at the sharp prick in my arm, followed by a burning, stinging sensation. I look to see the syringe in Thorn's hand, empty, all but for a single drop of liquid hanging from the needle's tip.

"What did you—"

17

THE FIRST THING TO register is the sound of a woman wailing hysterically. I realize soon that she isn't alone.

All around me, sobs and moans, whispers and low voices—my dulled senses desperately try to sort out the flood of stimuli invading my consciousness. My limbs and eyes don't heed my commands—instead, refusing to move, apparently not mine to control. Metallic banging rings out, echoing around me, and I hear shuffling on the tile floor—the click of women's heels, rubber-soled shoes, and bare feet, all having a timbre distinctly their own. Awareness returns to me in waves, and I feel my body lying on the cold, hard floor.

Time passes, and my jumbled brain starts to clear. The first thing I remember is a box of donuts, a spilled coffee, an explosion, and my hands protecting my face as I'm thrown onto the kitchen floor. The knife in my hand. Hanging upside-down in a car. Crashing, swirling clouds of neon red magic.

Aldrick.

His devastating, beautiful, perfect face. I hold this image in my mind until I'm finally able to open my eyes.

My vision is blurry, and my eyes shift focus involuntarily, but I make out the low concrete ceiling above me. Dim fluorescent lighting fills the tight, suffocating space, the way I'd imagine the inside of a prison might be. My limbs feel heavy, but at least I can wiggle my fingers now. Where is this place? How did I get here? And why does it reek of piss and vomit?

The last thing I recall was being in the car with all those shifters, listening to them talk about demons, mages, and who even knows what else. As the dullness recedes, I become acutely aware of several aches and pains in my body—the worst on the left side of my skull, the place I suspect my head hit the window in the wreck.

"You're finally moving. Getting some color back to your face too," says a girl's voice nearby, though I can't tell which direction it comes from. She lets out an irritated huff before scooting closer to me, moving into view at my left side. She looks around my age, perhaps in her late teens, extremely thin, with long, dark blonde hair. Something about her reminds me of a person who's led a hard life, but the smile she gives me is genuine.

"Wha...t?" I try to get my mouth to form the words, but my brain and body aren't in sync yet.

"You were drugged. Like the rest of us," she says, though it's hard for me to hear her with all the other noises in the room. "You're the last one to wake up. I thought you were dead till I felt your pulse." She says it calmly, downplaying the situation.

"Wh...ere?" I try again.

"We're in a giant locker room of sorts." The girl laughs humorlessly. "Minus the lockers."

I study her eyes and see the subdued panic behind them; making light of things must be her way of coping.

"There are some bathroom stalls and a couple of showers, but no windows. And only one way in and out—those big metal doors are locked from the outside. At least they were nice enough to leave us some food and water."

I turn my hand over, feeling the smooth surface of the tiles and running the tips of my fingers along the rough grout lines between them.

"Some of these women have been here for days. They kept bringing in more until about a day ago, when they just...stopped. You were the first to be brought in alone. You've been here maybe half a day."

"Who brought us?"

She shrugs. "Men. Who else? They come in here with these cattle prods. Use them on anyone who tries to leave. They have, like, these military helmets that cover their whole faces, so it's hard to tell, but it kind of seems like they're with the government."

Turning my head to the side, I see dozens of women around the room. Too many women. How is this possible? Although they are all adults, their ages range wildly. I see gray-haired women, blondes, brunettes, some dyed with bright colors—nurse's scrubs, prison jump suits, a nightgown, office wear—you couldn't put together a more random group of women.

The majority sit along the walls in silence, some talk to each other, others pace back and forth, and a few cry at the doors—begging to be freed. So, is this the shifter's territory, or have I been, what did Grey say? Sold off to vampires? My heart rate quickens as I think about what vampires could want with all these different women.

"No one," I say sluggishly, "knows why they're here?"

"No, not a clue. I know a bunch came from different women's prisons. Some were on vacation, out shopping, hiking, camping, or on road trips. Even in their beds, sleeping. They all just woke up here," she says, lying beside me, joining me in staring blankly at the ceiling.

We both lie there a while, contemplating in silence, as I do my best to block out the sounds of anguish. I wish I had the power to help, but all I can do is remain here, hoping the tranquilizer will wear off faster.

"Do you know what time it is?" I ask weakly.

The girl lifts her arm, shaking her wrist to move the clock side down. "It's 2:12 p.m."

"Thanks," I whisper. I was unconscious for an ungodly amount of time. One good thing, I guess, is that I didn't get to drink that giant iced coffee yesterday. It wouldn't have been very much fun waking up covered in my own urine. I struggle onto my hands and knees, deciding that I've had enough of the ground.

"You might as well rest some more. There's nowhere to go," she says.

"I haven't eaten since the day before yesterday," I say. It might be easier to crawl than walk right now.

"You're really going to eat their food? What if it's poisoned?" she asks. I peer around at the women, who all appear physically unharmed. I can't be the first to try the food if they've all been here for days.

"Then...I'll be the guinea pig for you," I say, giving her a grin, accustomed to acting like I have more confidence than I do, something I got used to growing up with a bunch of douche wad guys who can practically smell weakness. My stomach drops. I feel the hurt at the thought of my family, the lies—but I choose not to pick at it, at least for now. There will be plenty of time to open old wounds after I get the hell out of here.

I stand, legs wobbly but not giving out, and take a step. If not for the girl, who puts her arm around me, I would have fallen. She guides me to where they keep the food.

"Dig in," she says.

On the ground, piles of hollowed-out boxes once filled with store-bought cookies and pastries, open bags of chips, and mostly empty two-liter bottles of off-brand soda. Cups, silverware, or plates are notably absent—they're feeding the women like animals.

"Is there any water?"

"This way," she says, helping me to a solitary drinking fountain mounted on one wall. The water tastes like pennies.

Hours go by, and I no longer feel the effects of the sedatives in my system. There's no sign of our captors. No new arrivals are brought in. I join the ranks of the silent women who sit along the walls as the girl who has been with me thus far goes to chat with a group of seven women standing in a circle, whispering to one another. The metallic-tasting water I quenched my thirst with now weighs heavily on my bladder, and I scan the open space for the bathrooms—only to be mortified when I finally find them: two green toilet stalls in the corner.

Oh, come on...

On closer inspection, they're what you'd find in a typical public restroom, metal partitions bolted to the ground, only with gaps in the doors that are wider than I'm used to—not only in plain view of the whole room, but with no way to stop people from hearing *everything*. I hold in my groan. There is no other option that isn't even more embarrassing. As I prepare to enter, I tell myself things could be much worse. That is, of course, until I see the state the toilet is in. Ugh.

After that harrowing ordeal is over, I go to exit the stall, bracing myself for everyone's judgmental eyes on me, wishing I had my backpack and the small bottle of hand sanitizer in the side pouch. As I slide the lock open, I hear an even louder sound—that of the main doors opening—and thank my lucky stars for the distraction. I peek through the opening, watching the scene unfold.

In walks a man, covered from head to toe in black, tactical military gear. He removes his helmet, pulling it off slowly, before shaking out his long, thick hair. Then, he looks up and smiles, baring his fangs.

There's a beat of silence before the screaming begins.

I'd never seen a set of their long, pointed teeth in person. Though I'd become somewhat used to their red eyes, there's something deeply unsettling about those fangs—the first thought that enters my mind is the image of a rattlesnake. The second? *Run you damn fool.*

We are all *so* screwed. The women flood against the back wall, slamming the stall door shut with me still inside. I stand, frozen in terror, with nowhere to go. I have no idea what's happening out there. There are flashes of blue light, I hear the crackling and pulsing of electricity echoing off the concrete walls and ceiling, different voices shouting orders.

"Line up! Let's go! You, over there!"

Heavy footsteps coming in my direction. Then, the door swings open. He points to the spot where he wants me, and I oblige, not needing to be hit with ten thousand volts to understand what's going on. They're herding us like the cattle they think we are.

I hadn't noticed the little white squares taped on the tile floor before now, five rows of them, ten in each row. The only one not standing in one of them is me. Thinking back to when the girl said I was the last one brought in, it makes me wonder if I wasn't a last-minute addition to whatever they intend to do with us. What *do* they intend to do with us?

Aldrick, I think, closing my eyes, seeing him in my mind, focusing on his face, and the words he said to me, not to be afraid, that he would come for me. It's the only way I steady my breathing, the only thing that slows my racing heart. Barring some crazy miracle, his finding me and getting me out of this situation seems to be my only hope.

Then, I hear the chains. I open my eyes and watch as four geared-up vamps walk down the lanes, dragging long chains on the ground behind them. There appear to be several sets of high-tech-looking handcuffs connected to the chains, unlike anything I've ever seen before. A woman panics and rushes for the door. A vampire catches her by the hair with superhuman speed and yanks her backward, her feet going out from under her. She hits the ground hard, and he drags her back to her spot, tazing her until she stops kicking and screaming.

Nobody else resists after that. The four chain bearers stand silently at the back of each row.

The vamp who removed his helmet has remained standing in the same place this whole time, and he still wears the same smile. "Wasn't that so much fun!" he shouts, his enjoyment sincere. "And we haven't even gotten started yet. Now, we expect you all to stay calm and collected as you step outside, or we won't hesitate to use these," he says, raising his prod in the air.

"Hands," a deep voice says from my left. I look at the restraints he holds, open and waiting for me to hold out my arms. I comply, consoling myself by thinking that this is nothing compared to Gerard's power—and that I'm already completely powerless before these monsters, with or without the use of my arms. Now, I'm not only at these vampires' mercy, but my fate is now tied to the women ahead of me in line.

Come on, Aldrick. Where are you?

After the last woman is bound, the speaker and the other four vampires stand at the front, each with their own row, holding our chains. I don't know how strong vampires really are, but these ones don't seem the least concerned about their odds of winning a potential tug-of-war with ten panicked women.

"We will now lead you out. Please follow the person in front of you, maintaining this same distance. Stop when you are instructed to. Do not move again until you hear the starting gun. What you do after that is entirely up to you—but you are strongly encouraged to run."

He recites the speech like he's said this many times before, then places his helmet back on his head and turns to face the door.

The first line's leader moves out through the open doors, and the women in his row follow. I cock my head to the side to see where he's taking them, but those in front of me obstruct my view. When a second set of double doors opens, I can tell they lead outside by the light that filters in—and from the look of it, it's about sunset on a dark and gloomy day.

Once they disappear, the second line moves, and so forth. I can't bring myself to watch them being led out. My heart aches. Having been through so much stress lately, it pounds in my chest. Whatever is about to happen to us is a whole lot different than what I anticipated when I got in the car the day before. If this is the end for me, at least I can die knowing that Mom didn't have to suffer a similar fate.

I know that vampires view humans as utterly insignificant, nothing more than food. Some, like Aldrick and his family, at least tried to hold on to their humanity, while others—like these scumbags—let everything good inside of them burn away during their transformation, leaving behind every trace of good they once had.

When the time comes for my row, the last of all, to move, I'm frozen in place, my whole body shaking. Forcing my feet to carry me forward, I stare at the back of the woman before me as we slowly shuffle through the first set of doors, through a short hallway, and then through the last doors, out into the open air.

I squint and avert my gaze downward because even this late in the day, with the cloud cover, it is much brighter outside than the dim room they were keeping us in. Responding to the screeching of metal, I glance over my shoulder one final time. Two vampires in black military gear slide the doors to the concrete fortress shut.

"Halt!" I hear from up ahead, stopping in time to avoid running into the person in front of me.

My eyes have adjusted, and I take in our surroundings—the cobblestone under our feet, a giant raised concrete platform to my right, too high for a person to climb, and above it—coliseum seating, five tiers by my count—not empty. There are dozens in the audience, seated and standing, some talking and others quietly assessing us. All in black robes.

The clicking and sliding sounds of the heavy metal doors come again, but not from behind me. Across the arena sits another concrete building identical to the one we were in. When the first line of men emerges, chained in the same fashion we are, I understand what our captors have done—separated the men and women into two even groups: fifty men and fifty women, or fifty-one in my case. Dread pools in my stomach at the thought of one hundred human souls, taken from their lives, sedated, and brought here for the sake of someone's entertainment.

Something pulls my attention back to the audience. My eyes are drawn to a few particularly tall vampires off to one side, their red eyes glowing in the darkness, when I realize what I'm experiencing and why—the feeling of being watched. In the distance, one set of eyes has been locked on me unflinching, unyielding, burning into me. My heart can't take it. What was it they'd said to us? When we hear the starting gun, we should run. Now, it's all starting to fall into place.

We are prey.

"Welcome, everyone!"

The loud voice echoes from the concrete and stone as two spotlights come on, stark against the evening sky. They reveal a tall, raised platform off to my left and atop it, the only vampire in attendance to wear a white robe. He holds a glittering, golden microphone in his right hand, and his pallid face bears an obnoxious smile that doesn't reach his dead, soulless eyes.

Some of the crowd erupts with applause and shouting, while others barely manage a half-hearted clap. Many don't respond at all.

"Please, please...contain your enthusiasm," the announcer says with a sarcastic bite to his words.

I detect a faint hint of an accent in his speech.

He throws his free arm wide, nearly shouting, "Are you ready?"

A few scattered hoots come from the hunters.

"Look what fine bounty we've gathered here for you tonight! There's even a bonus one in there, I'm told. No extra charge."

I look back to the spot where the one watching me stood, but he's gone—mixed in with all the others.

"From the looks of it..." he says, gesturing with his finger like he's counting, "we are still waiting for a few stragglers. We'll give them another minute before starting the evening's festivities." His excitement is sickening, like this is all just a big game.

There's no sign of Aldrick or his family, no reason to believe that anyone is coming for me, and even if he tracks me down in time, what would I expect him to do in this situation? Save me and leave the rest of these people to die? Could I live with that? Given the circumstances...perhaps even that bleak outcome is wishful thinking.

All I know is that whatever they have planned—we are all center stage.

18

SOMEWHERE IN CANADA

"WELL, I'LL BE DAMNED..." the speaker says plainly, dropping the act for a moment and bringing a hush to the confused crowd, his astonished gaze fixated on someone in the stands, "do my eyes deceive me? Or do we have first-timers in our midst? So nice of you to finally join us after all these years."

I swear his vacant eyes move to me.

"I suppose we've finally stumbled upon something to pique your interest in the games." The speaker says the cryptic words soberly, letting them hang in the air uncomfortably long, before returning to his over-the-top demeanor. "But don't forget that there are rules we all must abide by!"

"First rule: No one enters the field until the timer runs out!" A huge screen before his podium lights up, revealing a stopwatch display with thirty minutes on the clock. "Can everybody see that? Good, good. Second rule! No violence is allowed between vampires and our shifter friends," he says, eyeing the attendees.

"If you break either of these simple rules, *you* become the hunted," he says, putting his hand over his chest, making a sympathetic face. The crowd lets out a mixture of sounds, ranging from booing to laughter. "Yes, yes, heartbreaking, I know. You hate to see it. You hate to see it."

Observing this man on the podium as he tries to entertain the crowd, watching his movements, is like witnessing a reanimated corpse trying to imitate a living creature. Nausea rolls through me, and I pray for the poor soul who sees that *thing* coming for them moments before they die.

The announcer vampire looks at his watch and says, "Well, boys, it's the moment we've all been waiting for! Welcome to the five-hundred and fifty-first annual Summer Solstice Hunt!"

At this, the crowd goes insane.

Suddenly, the air around me becomes heavy and thick. The sounds of the celebration soften, and there comes a ringing in my ears...It feels like I'm about to have a stroke, and then I hear the words.

"Don't freak out, Brielle, it's Dane...Aldrick's much cooler brother," a familiar voice whispers in my ears.

I freeze because it sounds like it's coming from all around me. They came for me. I feel a tremendous weight being lifted. I'm not alone.

"Pretend like you can't hear me. We're here, and we're going to get you out as soon as we can, but here's the thing, you're going to need to survive the next thirty minutes more or less on your own."

What?

"Survive what?" I whisper-hiss, not sure if he can also hear me.

"We've been eavesdropping...and there are...whisperings. Our best guess is that someone plans on having you taken out before the hunt begins, before we can get to you..."

"What do I do?"

"You're going to have to run, Brielle. Run like you've never run before."

Just. Great. I can barely stand without my knees quivering, and now I have to complete a marathon in the fading light, who knows where at. And it's damn cold. So much for summer.

"Seriously, run?"

"You have no choice. Anyone out there with you could be trying to kill you. Don't help anyone. Don't trust anyone. Just run and don't stop running."

Bang!

This weird connection with Dane dampens the sound. I look to the podium to see the vampire holding a smoking gun in the air, a horrific look of glee on his face. A cacophony of metallic clicking sounds comes as the bindings on our hands open and fall to the ground simultaneously. The timer on the screen starts running down.

"What are you doing just standing there? Go! Now!"

Oh, right. I turn and bolt for the concrete building, curving outward as I run along the wall, hoping to avoid the stampede. Behind me there is screaming, commotion, and pounding feet. Once I clear the corner of the bunker, I must choose—go in the same direction as everybody else, to the open grassy field ahead, or head for the trees off to my left?

"Behind you—"

I spin, and a body slams into me, knocking me to the ground. Hands wrap around my throat.

"Freeze," utters the haunting voice.

The reverberations glide right over me and hit their intended target. My attacker freezes in place, a look of terror and confusion locked in his eyes, having lost all control over his body. I drag his hands from my neck, crawl backward from under him, scramble to my feet, and take off toward the tree line.

"Yes, the forest. Go!" Dane whispers. "Keep going in a straight line!"

Heeding his words without hesitation, I break for the trees, running as fast as my weakened legs will carry me. To my right, I see dozens of men and women all moving in the same direction. My arms and legs burn; it feels like they have been asleep. Pins and needles rush through my limbs with this renewed blood flow.

"Why can't you just come get me now?" I shout at him through the invisible conduit.

"That's a no-go. Even *this* is bending the rules. Once the hunt begins, Aldrick *will* reach you before anyone else has a chance. Now save your breath and focus...You got two more hot on your tail."

I glance over my shoulder, spotting them closing in behind me. Damn, he's right. Their footfalls get louder as they near. Despite giving it everything I have, there's no way I can outrun them.

"Okay, you're a lot slower than I thought—"

"You try...getting knocked out...and—"

"We get it. Brace yourself."

Brace myself, whatever that means. I feel a strong impact on my back like a sudden gust of wind, and it rushes loudly in my ears and blows my hair forward. Suddenly, I'm lighter, and I start to pick up speed. Holy crap, I'm really moving. I easily pull ahead of the men pursuing me.

Looking back, one of them, tall and gangly, uses his long legs and huge strides to pass up the other. He's so tall and square-framed that it's like being chased by Frankenstein. We're nearing the trees now. I hope I can outmaneuver him, maybe even lose him.

"Okay, free ride's almost over. I'll have a harder time keeping up the connection in the woods. As soon as you enter, start looking for something to use as a weapon. Sharp, pointy rocks are ideal."

The trees are just mere feet away.

Sure, just find a weapon. No big deal. Just a little fight to the death in the woods. I swear, these vampires.

A beat of despair hits me as I enter the trees. I'm now truly alone and need to survive the next twenty-eight minutes. The weight of my body returns to my legs—it's like running in slow motion by comparison.

These trees are unlike those I remember before; no under-brush blocks the path. I weave through the dark woods, my eyes slowly adjusting to the last remnants of the dying light of day. I've never experienced such an unnaturally long dusk before. My pur-suer must be exhausted from all that sprinting—because he's much slower now, but still coming, as evidenced by the snapping branches and leaves crunching under his approaching feet in the stillness and silence of the woods.

"Quit running...you little skank!" he shouts.

Out of breath and time, I go for the next heavy-looking branch that catches my eye. All I think of is gym class, playing baseball. I tuck a leg and slide across the ground, grabbing it and rolling behind a tree. I crouch, holding it like a bat, waiting until his loud feet come clomping by. I rear back and then swing, gaining as much momentum as I can, smashing it into his knee as he comes by, connecting with a cringe-inducing crunching sound.

He screams as he twists, doubles over, lands on his back, and grabs his knee with his hands. I'm surprised how quickly my terror switches to rage now that I've gained the upper hand. I raise the branch high before bringing it down on the hands covering his knee. I feel the vibrations of breaking bones travel along the wood as his screams pierces my ears, ringing out around me.

"What the hell is wrong with you?" I scream as I swing at him again, but he rolls away before it gets him a third time. I refuse to quit, striking again, hitting him squarely in the back of his head as he tries to stand, watching as his limp body slumps onto the ground.

The relief is over when I hear the slower of the two bad guys headed my way. I need to go, but before I do...I find the perfect rock. Easy to hold in one hand, heavy but not too heavy, with one large, jagged end. I trade my bat for it and take off away from the sounds of the others.

As I press on, the forest becomes less dense. Once I clear the trees, I'll be more exposed, but if I get back out in the open, I'm hoping that Dane can use his wind power to reach me again. Not an ideal trade-off, but at this rate, I'm not sure how much longer I can keep this pace. I'm still exhausted from the sedative and lack of food, my legs are unsteady, and my lungs are burning, unable to get enough oxygen.

"Bri...Are you..." I hear the vampire's voice as if it is calling from a distance. "Alright?"

"Never...been better..."

"You're doing good...keep going."

Minutes pass slowly as I press onwards, barely jogging through the forest. The trees are tall, thin, and too spread out—there's no way to hide behind them. It's too open. I'm too visible. Climbing is impossible with no branches in reach. My thunderous wheezing feels like it is being broadcast to everyone nearby, like a giant flashing arrow pointing right at me. The rock becomes too unbearably heavy to hold in my hands, so I clutch it to my chest as I run. How is it still going? It must have been at least thirty minutes by now. No—it must have been longer. Much longer.

Then, I hit my limit. I hunch over, one hand on my knee, desperately trying to catch my breath. No matter what I do, I can't get enough oxygen to my starved limbs. My head pounds—whether from the run or the caffeine withdrawal, low blood sugar, or all three? Confusion takes over.

"Can you...hear me?" I whisper into the wind, "How much time...is left?"

I wait for the reply to come as the seconds tick by. I might be too far out of his range. Maybe even Aldrick's sonar hearing can't reach me at this point.

"Six minutes..." his voice comes in softly on the breeze. I start to catch my breath a bit, the world around me quiet. Maybe, just maybe...I'll make it out unscathed after all. I take a deep, centering breath—in through my nose and out through my mouth.

You got this. I almost feel—

"Run!"

The voice comes on the tail end of the gust, echoing as it moves through the air. The distant sound of a breaking twig reaches my ears first, then pounding feet rapidly advancing. I take off again, needing to give everything I have, but having nothing left to give. *No, no, no!*

I just need to make it six more minutes, and then I will see him again. I will be free of this hellhole of a hunt.

I have to make it. Only this singular thought, plays over and over. I let it consume me.

I start counting the steps in my head, hear how fast he's approaching, and realize I won't be able to outrun him for even another minute. He's gaining on me too quickly. A quick glance behind me—the man is roughly twenty feet away. Cursing under my breath, I refuse to let him catch me from behind.

With only seconds left, I have to devise a plan quickly. Once he is within ten feet, my time is up.

Heart pounding, I stop abruptly, throw my arms out to get momentum, and spin to face him. My eyes lock onto his as I turn, swinging my improvised weapon through the air, directing it at my target.

My aim is true. I hurl the hefty rock at his unprotected face, smashing into his nose with an audible thwack. He screams in pain and rage as he jerks to a stop. Red fluid streams down his face. I use the opportunity to run at him, dropping to my knees, power-sliding across the dewy grass, and delivering the heaviest punch of my life—directly into his crotch. His screams are cut off with a loud gasp, followed by a groan as he falls over. Picking up the now bloody rock, I take off again.

Looking back in disbelief, I see that even my mightiest dick punch doesn't keep him down for long. He's back on his feet, albeit not nearly as fast. The pounding of my heart in my chest, in my head, in my ears, breathing loud and labored as I run—all these internal distractions are making it impossible to hear if he is catching up.

He cries out. I glance over my shoulder to see him tripping on an exposed root, falling on his face. Holding in my laugh, triumph fills me...I might be able to outrun him.

I hear an unfamiliar thunk as something hard and cold sinks into my thigh. My leg instantly gives out as my body falls, sliding to a halt on my stomach. An agonized scream escapes my lips before I register what has happened as I reach down to feel something metal protruding from my leg.

"Get up, get up." I plead with myself. Panic fills me as I struggle to convince my body to move before he gets to me, but every movement makes the excruciating pain worse. I force myself onto the other knee, gasping in blinding white agony and exhaustion. I look back to see the man, still on the ground where he fell, slowly getting onto his knees—and the manic grin is clear on his bloody, battered face.

I crane my neck to see the source of my suffering—on the outer back thigh juts the handle of a fixed blade knife, sunk to the hilt in the soft flesh. The world is spinning around me.

He's still coming with that hideous face—bloody, broken, and smiling.

I need the weapon. I need it now. I'm out of options.

Grabbing the hilt, I yank as hard as I can, sending a flash of searing pain through my entire nervous system, like fire in my blood, and I am not strong enough to hold in the scream. In my peripheral, I see that he gets off the ground slowly, the rock to the face making him wobbly. So much blood covers his nose and his face, dripping onto his white shirt. I grasp the stone from where it dropped. Jagged gasps come out as I push myself off the ground, rising to my feet, squaring off with him. One hand clutches the dagger tightly, and in the other, the sharp rock.

"Why are you fighting back?" he barks as he tries to wipe the blood from his mouth. "You're only going to die in a couple minutes anyway. I was going to make it quick for you!"

"That's how...you wanted...to spend your last minutes? Seriously?" I yell back at him, rage, pain, and confusion consuming me.

"You don't get it! Whoever kills you...gets to live. And it's going to be ME!" he screams, delirious, eyes wide and crazed. I see the determination flooding him, his face contorting, and I know the clock is ticking—both of our times are almost up.

My whole body shakes; the adrenaline won't carry me much longer. I feel myself crashing out, collapse imminent, and he walks toward me. I'm not sure I can swing the rock again.

I whisper, hoping for a miracle, "Dane, if you can, please..."

Spinning, I push through the pain and force myself to limp away from him again. My focus stuck on the burn of the cold air, the jeans hitting the open wound, and the feel of blood soaking into them. Every jolt, every move of the muscle in my leg sends a shooting pain down through every nerve, sending shocks of pain like electric pulses to the webbing of my toes, up through the hip bones.

There is an explosion in the direction of the arena. The trees in the distance sway wildly, like something is coming, and I have a flashback—the cliff. The wind roars through the woods to the side of us, snapping a tree clean in half, sending it crashing to the ground.

My assassin stares in awe, having no idea what he just witnessed, but I get the message loud and clear—Dane fired a warning shot.

I move as fast as I can for cover. By the time I hear the second deafening boom, I'm throwing myself on the ground behind a tree, groaning as my thigh smacks into the trunk. I cover my head with my arms, listening to the wailing sound as a gust of the same magnitude as the one that threw me over the railing comes through the trees.

The roar of the wind is deafening. Branches crack off the towering trees as dirt and leaves are whip past me. The man shrieks from close behind me as his body soars through the air. My hair flies forward, and I catch glimpses of leaves swirling around me in the aftermath, as if a snow globe has been flipped over.

"Ha! Thank you!" I cry, my euphoric joy bypassing the pain for a moment.

The falling branches and sticks smash against the trees, making their way to the ground. After a hit like that, I had hoped it would be over, but my pursuer's distant, enraged roar is even louder as he returns to his feet. From maybe fifty feet away, he starts running at me, screaming like a lunatic.

His unhinged fury is palpable, causing a surge of desperation within me. I push to my feet, wincing through the pain, before bracing my back against the tree, leaning into it for support.

Please, let there be only seconds left.

He's getting too close, and running is not an option. Anger builds inside of me. I swing my arm with the rock to try to smash him in the face again, but he throws his arm up, blocking it. He smiles and puts his other hand on my neck and squeezes hard, pressing me against the tree, then pries the rock from my hand. It drops to the ground with a dull thud.

My limited training has made me comfortable with practice weapons. We learned which areas not to leave open and which areas to defend. This, though…this is different. It is horrible. And yet, I have no choice.

"I'm…sorry…" I try to squeeze the words out as I aim the tip of the knife upward and insert it as far as it will go into his left armpit.

We both freeze, our eyes locked. In the middle of the dark woods, so far away from any source of help, regardless of whether or not he deserved it…I just dealt him a killing blow.

His face fills with shock and indignation. The pain has not registered in his eyes yet as I feel warmth flooding across my hand.

He releases my neck as he staggers back, and I gasp for air, not realizing that the pressure of his hand was the only thing keeping me on my feet. My injured leg no longer bears my weight, and I slide down the tree, scraping my back against the bark.

The sound of a gunshot rings out in the distance.

This man's hollow, dilated pupils track down to the rock on the ground. I wonder what they drugged him with before they sent him after me. I try to inch away, but I can't move my legs anymore. He grunts as he drops to one knee, wrapping his fingers around the rock. He raises it over his head, his expression blank, his face pale from blood loss and shock. There is nothing behind his eyes as he starts to bring it down on my skull.

But no blow comes. Instead, I open my eyes to see *him*. Holding the assassin up in the air by his throat with one hand, looking down at me with those fiery red eyes, is Aldrick. He flicks my attacker aside with utter disregard, as if he were disposing of a piece of pocket lint, not so much as a glance in his direction.

"Wait, no!" I gasp, moaning in pain, "No! There's blood! I'm bleeding!"

He puts his hand against my cheek, and I close my eyes at his touch. My heart bursts at the feeling, eclipsing the pain for a moment, and my only feeling is relief that I didn't die before seeing him.

"I'm so sorry, Brielle," he whispers, and tears the black robe he wears into strips, using them as bandages to put pressure on my injury.

"Why...didn't you tell me?" I spit out, unable to control my emotions. If I die today, I want to know why yet another person I cared about kept something from me. "Why was I the last to know?"

"You've lost a lot of blood. You're weak. Save your strength—"

"What does it mean? That we're soulmates?" I say through my gritted teeth, the pain growing with each passing moment as the last remnants of adrenaline in my bloodstream fade.

He sits me up and places his robe over me.

"Some souls come into this world whole, needing nothing, while others enter in twisted, crooked, broken, unable to be made right. But then, some souls were brought into existence neither whole nor broken, but rather...in two parts. Sometimes, they come together—as if drawn by some mysterious force—while others drift through life, never finding one another, born at the wrong time, hundreds or thousands of years between them."

"What are you saying?"

"Every time I dreamed, it was always the same. I would be running through some endless forest, searching for something. Then, I would finally arrive at the coastline. I would step out of the darkness and into the light—and there she'd be. I call to her, and just as she turns, she smiles at me. And I wake."

"I don't—"

"I knew the moment I saw you...that day at the cliff, that you were the one I've been searching for all these years...The girl with the sea-green eyes. And when you fell—"

"Aldrick—"

"I feared that if I showed you my face, you'd see it, that you would know...I didn't want what *I* wanted to take away your life, to turn into what I am...I wanted you to decide what your future would look like."

Without a thought, I reach and pull down his mask, then use it to yank him closer, momentarily losing all clear thought. Breathing in his scent, I kiss him. His lips are soft, almost silken, as mine mold to his. My heart thuds, picking up its already dangerous pace, and I run my other hand through his luscious hair, gliding it down to the back of his neck, feeling the strength in his shoulders under my hands. Much too soon, he pulls back slowly, leaning his forehead against mine and breathing deeply. I run my hand along his jaw.

His head whips around. "Stay back, there is blood!"

They don't listen. His brothers come up behind him. I feel surrounded as all three stop on each side of me. One of the brothers covers his nose and mouth with his hand, closing his eyes.

"Either learn to control yourself, Isen, or get the hell out of here," Aldrick snaps as he pulls his mask back into place.

"He's fine." Dane eyes him like he's willing him to be okay.

A high-pitched buzzing cuts through the night.

"What is that?" I ask.

"Nothing good," says Gerard.

"Want me to swat that mosquito?" Dane says.

"Knock yourself out," Aldrick says in a growl.

Dane points his index finger at the noisy little device and drops his thumb like the hammer of a pistol, releasing some kind of shockwave that causes it to explode and fall to the ground, before looking right at me and blowing the barrel of his finger gun. He winks. It's hard to imagine that these men are all related.

"His mind is not right, but I have seen the face of the one who offered him freedom," says Sylvain, Aldrick's terrifying-looking father, with a voice that is equally chilling.

"Gerard!" Aldrick says the name like a command. "He'll help you sleep so you don't have to feel the pain."

"You sure it will work?" I ask.

"Just don't fight it."

"Fight it?" Gerard asks.

"You still didn't tell him?" I ask.

"We've been a little busy."

Gerard looks at the two of us with a raised eyebrow. "Why do I get the impression that I'm missing something?"

"Your command would have been more believable if you hadn't used the word *frolicking* while attempting to rewrite my memories. No one says that anymore," I chuckle, then groan.

Gerard stares at me like his whole world is falling apart.

Dane laughs. "Now that is interesting. A human resisting your command? You must be losing your touch, old man."

"We need to go—now," says Isen as he scans the horizon, the first words he's ever uttered in my presence. His voice is surprisingly sensitive, unlike his siblings.

Gerard crouches on one knee in front of me, softly pressing his hands to the sides of my head, and I feel it start. His words are whispered low, so quiet that I can't hear them, but only feel the reverberation as his words take hold. The pain recedes into nothing; the release is what my body craves. Red eyes are the last thing I see before closing my eyes, letting the words take me away.

19

PORT CRESCENT, WA

"Why isn't she waking up?" says Elden to my father.

"I *am* awake, dumb dumb," I say, sitting at the edge of the bed, rubbing my face. But the little punk doesn't look at me.

"The doctor will be back soon to try something else," Dad responds.

Mom paces, chewing on the tip of one of her perfectly manicured nails. For once, she looks...haggard.

I have no clue how or when I got here. Whether it's blood loss, a head injury or the damn drugs in my system—it's hard to think straight. My vision is hazy, the world coming through only in shades of gray, and the words spoken around me sound slightly muted, like I'm underwater.

I shake the confusion away and refocus on where I'm at: not a hospital, but a room as big as my high school's cafeteria. To my right, an exterior wall, consisting entirely of floor-to-ceiling windows and two sets of glass double doors, leads to a stone balcony, propped open to let in the fresh air. The two adjacent walls feature large windows, inviting light from all three sides. A ginormous flat screen TV is on, turned to a major 24-hour national news network running a breaking story. When I see it, my heart stops.

It's me. Backed against a tree, knife in hand. The man's bloody, mangled face appears in my head. I watch the TV in horror as I sink the blade into him, the gushing blood pouring onto my hand. I still feel its warmth trickling down my arm.

On my feet and walking toward the TV without thought, the words become clearer and louder as I near. The footage shows aerial videos of people running from figures in black robes, being ripped apart, and bodies scattered across the ground.

"For anyone just joining us, this is a breaking story. Something straight out of a horror film. Exclusively obtained footage shows incontrovertible evidence of human captives being ritualistically hunted by robed figures at an unknown location, lending credence to theories about the existence of an underground world of vampiric terror."

A man, a senator, appears on the screen, speaking at a press conference.

"I think we've all known, instinctively, that these, uh...sorts of horrific activities go on, but they've always been shrouded in extreme secrecy. The emergence of these videos heralds a major turning point in policy. This is the final nail in the coffin for peace talks between humans and vampires. We are in a war for survival, plain and simple."

The TV screen cuts to a stunning, blonde female news anchor.

"The story then takes a shocking twist, as at least one human is believed to have taken part in these ritual killings. Drone footage shows her luring this man, identified as thirty-six-year-old Oklahoma resident Douglas Maxey, out to the woods before she participates in his brutal murder. Maxey, who worked as a janitor for the Tulsa school system, was reported as a missing person last week."

I stare in disbelief: they've edited the footage to leave out the part with him chasing and attacking me.

"Believed to be caught up in the seductive world of vampires, this entangled, runaway teen from Castaic, California is named Brielle Raine Draper—and she's only eighteen years old."

"No, no, NO!" I scream at the TV. There is no way. This can't be real. This has to be a dream. My graduation photo appears on the screen.

"Watch as she appears to kiss one of the vampires, wearing one of their robes—what experts are calling an induction ceremony."

"Oh, God! What is happening?" I yell, looking at my family, who has zero reaction. They don't even look in my direction. "Would someone please just answer me, for once? Say something! What the hell is this?"

I look back at the TV, watching an interview with an expert who claims that I'm a psychologically unstable, dangerous victim of Stockholm syndrome.

The TV suddenly goes black.

"I don't want her waking up to this drivel," Dad says.

I turn and see he's holding the remote.

Aldrick ambles into the room, looking terrible. His three brothers trail behind him, their usual masks replaced by sullen expressions. His skin is pale, almost gray, with black veins that spread from under his eyes, visible beneath his skin. His gate is slow—it looks like he's in pain, carrying something. He softly lays my backpack on the foot of the bed.

"Aldrick!" I shout, running to him, but he turns away—probably not wanting me to see him this way.

"Dad," I say, "you know they're lying on TV. That isn't what happened. Please, believe me. Aldrick, tell him! My *face*! My face is all over the news! Everyone will see this! Everyone I know, all my friends! They make it seem like I wanted to be there, that I lured some guy into the damn woods! That is insane!"

Dad stands there, shaking his head slowly, deep in thought.

"Please just talk to me! What do I do? How do we fix this? You work for the government, don't you? Isn't there someone you can call? Please!" I beg. I thought my world was crumbling when I learned of their magic, then again, as I ran through those dark woods...that nothing could ever be worse than that. I'm so stupid. So naïve. This is literally the end of my life.

"Okay, my son, you've seen her once more. The doctor has only just left, and he said she's going to be fine. We'll watch over her while you rest. Delay no longer. You must regain your strength," Aurelia says gently, wrapping her arm under his and leading him out. His brothers follow.

I watch after them, confusion setting in deep. Why are they talking about me like I'm not here?

"Dane, wait!" I call as I rush to catch up. He'll talk to me.

I pass Jonathan on my right, leaning against the hallway wall between two giant Renaissance paintings, his eyes fixed on his phone. I've never been so happy to see him in my life. "Get off your damn phone and *help me*." His head pops up at the sound of my voice. His brows are furrowed, and I watch as his face morphs into shock...and horror. He takes off running back into the room with my family. A totally normal response.

The vampires have vanished, so I follow after Jonathan. He stands over the bed and looks back at me. His face has gone white.

"Hey," Jonathan says to my family, "you guys have been here for hours. Why don't you go down to the kitchen and get something to eat? Cora stocked the fridge. I'll take a shift."

Dad drops the TV remote onto the couch. "Let's go, Evie. You need to eat something."

"I don't want to leave her," Mom whispers, taking a break from her incessant pacing.

"Even if she does wake soon, it'll be a while before she's fully lucid. We'll be back before then."

"Oooh, I get it," I say, "this is some kind of payback, right? For all the pranks?"

Dad takes Mom by the hand, and Elden and Warren get up wordlessly.

"Could you possibly have picked a worse time? My life is *falling apart*! My face is plastered all over the news. Come on, I just got stabbed—" The words die in my throat as the revelation sets in.

I've been running around without pain for the last several minutes. Not even an ache. Nobody can see or hear me...I watch the hazy gray world around me wobble a bit. Oh, no...

My brothers follow our parents out, closing the door behind them with a diffused thud that sounds long and low, like the rolling of distant thunder. The more I look around, the more unnaturally *distorted* things look. How had I not noticed this before?

"Jonathan, if I were dead, you'd tell me, right?" I say, turning to him.

"You're not dead...yet, anyway. You're just—not where you should be..." he says, squinting his eyes, a consternated expression on his face like he's thinking hard about something.

"But you *can* see me?"

"In a way."

"Now isn't the time for your secrets! Tell me what's happening—"

"I can see souls," he says, like it's not the most batshit crazy thing I've ever heard in my life.

"What?"

"Just...look," he takes a step back, pointing at the bed.

"Yeah, a bed. Cool?"

He scrubs a hand down his face, shaking his head as he storms at me, grabbing my wrist and pulling me along back to the side of the bed. He grabs my chin. I attempt to slap his hand away, but it passes *right through* his arm.

"Look!" he commands.

"I'm looking! I—" And then I see it, finally. Jonathan is forcing me to look at a very much asleep, pale version of me under the covers.

He releases his grip on me.

"I'm a ghost?"

"I mean, kind of? Well, look, it doesn't matter. All we need to do is get you back in your body."

"How did I even get out of it?" I ask, panicking.

"How should I know? Just let me help you," he says, reaching out a grubby hand for me.

I jump back from him, "No! You don't touch me with your mage powers! Not until you tell me how I got like this, so I can keep it from ever happening *again*."

He sighs deeply, throwing his head back. "Let me think..." he says, "well, weird stuff like this is common with mages when the power in our blood awakens—usually around the time we turn sixteen."

"So...you're saying I'm powerful now? I can learn to use magic?"

He laughs. "Oh, Bri—no. Not in this lifetime. But...you probably got a hefty dose of it from the blood transfusion they gave you. You're a match with Lucas, by the way. Anyhow, your father's magic might have triggered *something* in you. Think of this like...shocking yourself on a doorknob after rubbing your socks on carpet. Just a discharge of built-up power."

Darn it. Just when I get my hopes up.

"Okay, so now you have your answer. Let's get you back in your body before things get, shall we say, *weird*."

"Fine. Do what you gotta do. This sucks anyway." I fold my arms impatiently. I don't have to sound like such a brat. After all, he is trying to help me. But on the other hand, it's *Jonathan*.

"Ready?" he asks.

"Yeah, whatever, just get it over with," I say, rolling my eyes.

"Brace yourself."

"You know, I'm really starting to hate that phrase."

He raises his hand, placing his open palm over my forehead, and closes his eyes. He recites strange words, barely above a whisper, and everything around us darkens. Red waves of energy move along every surface. When he opens his eyes again, they're solid white. Then he smirks.

He lightly touches my head with two fingers, and then the world blurs and twists on its side as I'm flung through the air, slamming into my body.

I jolt awake, a strangled sound escaping my throat. Every inch of me feels like it's been run over by a train, then drop-kicked by a horse. No wonder my soul was trying to escape.

"Oh, crap, I'm so sorry...I've never put a soul back *in* before."

"Does that mean you normally take them *out*?" I say, then groan. My throat feels bruised.

"When I need to."

I roll my eyes, wanting to limit my words; it hurts too much to talk.

"Let me go get your parents."

"No. Wait," I say, taking a deep, painful breath, "I saw myself on TV. How screwed am I?"

He huffs slowly, sitting on the edge of the bed. "It means...you can't show your face...like, anywhere. At least not for a long time. You'll have to put this whole fierce independent girl thing aside for a while. No getting a job, no trips to the coffee shop—no nothing."

"What if I just dye my hair blonde and wear colored contacts?"

"I mean, sure. Couldn't hurt. But the thing is...it's not humans that you need to be worried about. Anyone who has ever had beef with Aldrick's family—and that's a long list—that to get to him, all they need to do is get to *you*. You are his greatest weakness now."

"I'm his weakness?" I repeat, my heart sinking. What have I done to him? Is this going to ruin his life? Get him killed? This isn't

212

what was ever supposed to happen. Can't two people just be together without the whole world trying to come between them?

"I could ask the witches if they have any ideas about concealing you," he says. "Speaking of which…"

He stands and walks to the nightstand, retrieving a shot glass of clear liquid.

"This is from Cora. She brewed you up some witchy stuff, should take the pain away," he says, handing it to me. I reach for it, but he draws it back.

"Now, just because you'll feel better, doesn't mean you'll *be* better. Your body still has a lot to recover from. The medicine they'll give you will speed up the healing process, but it'll still take weeks before you're back to normal."

He hands the stuff over. I down the shot, expecting some horrid taste, but there's none. It just tastes like sweet water. I feel it move through me quickly, every ache and pain fading as it spreads.

"I need to text your brothers. They'd want to know that you're awake."

"Can we wait? I really don't feel like being bombarded with questions. Not yet."

"I'll go talk to them, get them to hold off until tomorrow. I think they'll just be happy to know your eyes are open."

"I'd also appreciate it if you kept my…soul…walking to yourself. If that's even possible for you. You blabber every damn secret."

"For you, I'll keep it a secret," he says and slugs my arm.

20

To my shock, Jonathan keeps his word. Not only does he pretend that I hadn't just used some donated blood magic, but he also shuts down my family's attempts at dredging up topics I'm desperately trying not to think about.

However, when the next day comes, I know they're ready and waiting to pounce. It's difficult to express my surprise when the first person to come through the door isn't my emotionally distraught mom, anxious dad, or one of my brothers, but Dane. And he's rolling in a TV stand with a flat screen mounted to it. I watch wordlessly as he pushes it across the wide room, wheels squeaking the whole way, and sets it up near the foot of my bed. Below the television is a thin metal shelf, upon which sits a Nintendo 64 and four controllers.

"What—are you doing?" I ask meekly.

"Lightening the mood. Everyone's being so serious, it makes me want to hurl," he says, inserting the game into the slot and turning it on. I instantly recognize the music.

"Goldeneye? I mean, I guess...if your goal is to make everyone start arguing and cussing a lot."

He chuckles. "It can't be worse than when Gerard and I play."

The mental image of two centuries-old vampires playing video games together strikes me as odd, but then I look closer at his unmasked face, younger than Aldrick's, no more than seventeen years old. I wonder if they're forever stuck at the same maturity level. Teenagers for all time?

I think about Aldrick, Aurelia leading him off to rest, how he tried to wait for me to wake, again putting his concern for me above his own needs, and I wonder how long until I'll see him again.

"So, uh, how long do you all usually sleep for?"

"Already missing old Aldy, eh? Oh, to be young and in love..." he says with a smirk, "usually a day, give or take. Really, it just depends on how far we push it. Given the state he was in, I'd say at least another twenty-four hours, maybe more."

"That sucks," I say, clearing my throat nervously. "I've been meaning to apologize for bringing all this to your doorstep. You should never have had to get involved. I'm so sorry."

A smile plays on his lips. "I do wish big bro had looped us in a tad sooner. I understand why he wanted privacy, but we could have started snooping around, maybe figured out the crows shifters super-secret plan before, well—you know. Hopefully, after all this, it'll finally penetrate his thick skull that he does need our help. And that we'll always be here, no matter what."

"So you're not angry?"

"Shit happens," he says, shrugging, "we've been through worse. Besides, you really shouldn't be worried about us, not when you have *mages* to deal with this morning."

He hands me a controller.

"Are they here?" I ask, taking it.

"They just pulled up," he says, then heads for the door.

"I didn't get to thank you—for the wind. That was pretty badass," I say.

He laughs. "Anytime."

"I'm serious. Shoot me in the back *one* more time, and I'm going to drop-kick your ass into another realm," Warren snaps. He's lying on his stomach, controller in hand.

"Payback's a bitch," Elden replies with a stupid grin on his face, seated cross-legged next to me, leaning back on a mountain of pillows.

"Who the hell is top right? Why aren't you moving?" Jonathan says, sitting at the edge of the bed in front of me. His untamed blond waves block half the screen from my view.

"Fricking Bri," says Elden, "she's probably on too many pain meds to keep up."

"No, I'm not," I lie, nearly dozing off.

The TV goes black. Mom stands nearby, arms crossed, with a remote in hand.

"Dude," Warren says flatly, glaring at Mom.

"We leave in an hour," she says. "You guys have had enough fun for now."

"Wait, you're leaving?" I ask, having thought that their pacing and visible stress were due to my refusal to talk.

"We need to return home, but not before we have a discussion with you," Dad says as he comes to sit on the edge of the bed, trading places with Jonathan.

"But I don't wanna," I say, feeling petulant.

"I don't get it, hun," says Dad, "you've been asking me for years what I'm hiding from you, and now that I'm ready to give you the answers, you just don't want to talk about it?"

"What else is there to learn?" I erupt, "You have magic. I don't. I'm not in the cool club. I get it."

"It's not—you don't know how long I've wished I could tell you. How long we..."

The guys remain silent, and they don't move from their spots. Seems like they've been waiting for this moment too.

"At least listen. Just let me say what I need to say to you, then I think you'll understand."

"Fine, whatever," I say as I cross my arms reluctantly. Not like I can exactly get up and storm out of the room.

"You must understand, we are under a pact, preventing us from giving away our secrets by powerful magic. Even though I've wanted to tell you about our family, these powers, this world every day of your life, I *couldn't*. There are very few exceptions to our laws, instances where we're permitted to reveal our powers to the uninitiated—and one of those ways is to save an innocent life in mortal peril. *That's* how Jonathan was finally allowed to use his powers in front of you."

"A magical pact which, by the way, you're going to need to go sign up for pretty soon," says Jonathan, taking a bite of an apple.

"You were born to mages," Dad goes on, "a people imbued with magic in our blood, passed down from generation to generation. For reasons lost to the ages, we can only have sons. This is how it has been for *thousands* of years. In fact, in all our recorded history, there has only ever been one female child fathered by a mage. That girl, Brielle, was you."

Great. The one girl born to a powerful, ancient line of mages...and there's still not a damn shred of magic in me. Figures.

"We were elated when we found out we were having twin boys. Yet, it wasn't until the birth that we discovered we were having a third child...and that you were a girl. It was a miracle. Nobody knew what to make of it. Some imagined you might grow to exhibit tremendous power, while others feared this could be an ill omen for our people. What nobody predicted was that you'd grow up to be a normal, healthy girl."

"The council has had you DNA tested like, five separate times. If you're wondering, you are *one-hundred percent* his daughter," Jonathan interrupts with a laugh.

"*Jonathan!*" Mom hisses. "That's not funny. It wasn't about paternity; it was about checking for magic."

"What is it that you guys are even able to do?" I ask. "Shouldn't mages be, like, shooting fireballs, or enchanting brooms to sweep your garages for you?"

A beat of extremely awkward silence as the guys exchange glances, deciding who is going to go first.

"Let me try, Dad," Warren says, then looks at me, "The best way to explain it to you, at least for now, would be that it's like we can distort space. Bend it into different shapes and densities. What you saw was Jonathan using it as both a weapon and a shield."

"Huh. That's not what it looked like," I say before taking a sip of my drink.

Warren and Elden look to Dad in question.

"What do you mean?" Jonathan asks as he stares at me, suspicion in his eyes.

"It just looked like he was controlling that red stuff that came out of his rings."

"You can *see* it?" Dad asks with a grin.

"Uh. Yeah, should I not?"

"No," say all the guys in unison.

"No, you shouldn't be able to see or feel it. Not at all. Our fighting techniques are feared precisely because our attacks are undetectable, and thus unavoidable."

"So, what does this mean for her?" Mom asks, and I swear I see the faintest trace of a smile tugging at the corner of her lips.

I scan their confused, excited faces. For the first time in my life, I've done *something* they approve of: demonstrated some sign that, perhaps after all, I'm not as big of a disappointment as they thought I was. Apparently, using magic is the only thing that I could ever do to gain their approval—something I have no control over.

And then, a gut-wrenching wave of guilt hits me, as I realize that I'm sitting here in this bed, drinking a caramel iced coffee, surrounded by my mage family in what looks to be a *vampire mansion*, hearing people guess what, if any, powers I might have been born with.

Because despite everything, the injuries I've endured, the lies I've been told, and now being faced with the prospect of going into hiding—maybe forever—I'm going to be okay. I *made it*, unlike all those other people who died during the hunt. People who will never see their families again.

I think of the blonde girl who watched over me, carried me. She was brave, kind. I never even bothered to ask her name. And now, she's dead. All for the sin of being a powerless human.

"Hold on a minute," Elden says, as if deep in thought, "Even if she can't wield the energies, *only* mages can perceive realm phasing. That proves she has *something*—"

"It doesn't prove *anything*," Jonathan says.

"No, wait. Let him talk, Jonathan. What are you saying, Elden?" asks Mom.

"Okay, look. All our tests for magic have come back negative, right? And yet, she is clearly exhibiting some ability. This proves that our tests aren't conclusive. What if her magic is hidden, locked up somewhere so deep inside, even we can't find it? What if—"

"Or," says Jonathan loudly as he walks around the bed, "there's magic in her, after all, but it isn't *hidden*. It's faint, barely there. So weak and inconsequential that it essentially amounts to nothing." He places his hands on the footboard and locks eyes with me—intense, cold, and winnowing.

"And that's why our tests can't detect it," says Warren, crestfallen.

"What are you saying, man?" Elden asks, his earlier enthusiasm deflated.

"Maybe...just maybe," Jonathan starts, locking eyes with me, raising a hand, pinching the air with two fingers like he's holding something impossibly tiny, "there might be one drop of magic blood in her whole body."

"She probably stole it from us in the womb," Warren chuckles, and Elden joins in.

"Well, that one stupid little drop hasn't done me any good. You can have it back." I roll my eyes.

"I have a question," Mom says. "How did you manage to encounter a vampire in the first place?"

"What are you talking about? This place is crawling with them! How could you guys not have known?"

"Our intel placed the Holsten residence in southeast Oregon, on the Nevada border. I would never have condoned this trip if I thought there were any chance of encountering them," says Dad.

"That still doesn't answer my question," says Mom.

"I...uh...fell off a cliff the first day we were here."

"What?" Mom yells.

"He jumped in and pulled me out of the water. I would have drowned without his help. And then, we started meeting up in the mornings."

Jonathan laughs. "No wonder you looked like shit that day."

"You...*fell*...off a cliff?" Warren asks doubtfully.

"Yeah, it was an accident."

"Between Aldrick and the shifters, it finally explains why our detectors kept going off," Jonathan says as he pulls out the necklace tucked under his hoodie. Dangling on the end is a dimly glowing red gemstone.

Elden produces a similar necklace, and says, "If one of these babies glows, it means there's a supernatural within a hundred yards."

"Closer they are, brighter it gets," Warren adds.

"So, I'm still confused. What is this business about you being soulmates with a vampire?" Elden asks, looking at Jonathan and then me.

"Does that mean you're going to...try to *be* with him?" asks Warren, sounding unsure of how to word it.

Jonathan snickers. "Jeez, guys, exactly what part of this are you having trouble grasping?"

Warren and Elden shoot him a betrayed look.

"Whose side are you on, anyway?" Elden snaps.

"Oh, I don't know...fate?" he says with an obnoxious grin.

"We haven't had the time to have that sort of conversation yet. I haven't talked with him since Tuesday night." It's only been three days, and it feels like an eternity has passed.

"Wait...Tuesday *night*, as in when you went over to Mom and Dad's cabin by yourself?" Warren accuses.

Whoops.

My mom gasps, "You were with a guy, alone, in—"

"No, it's not like *that*! He just came to update me on the crow situation. *Speaking of which*, it would have been really nice to know you had beef with shifters, instead of leaving me in the dark to wonder why I was being followed." I feel my cheeks heating.

"Oh. Yes..." Dad says. "That was, in part, our fault. We work closely with the crows in our territory. Unfortunately, there was a group that stole something from their own people, committing murder in the process. In the end, they were exiled. It was to be kept under wraps. They didn't wish for others to know there was trouble within their ranks. Showing weakness opens us all up to attack. The Holsten's couldn't have known about the exiled group. Never in a hundred years would I have guessed they'd try to take members of my family hostage."

"Well, maybe you guys should think about being more open with neighboring green zones, establish relationships. Communicate. Aldrick could have just annihilated them if he had known. None of this ever should have happened."

"And we plan on it. Once the girls are rescued and we find the perpetrators, we intend to open communications with this territory."

"What do you mean...rescue what girls?"

There is a long silence.

"Do you remember when Thorn said one hostage wouldn't be enough?" he says, and swallows hard, "The same time they went after you, other men in their group executed attacks on different locations inside our territory. Two others were taken. They tried to take a third—one of our witches, named Vanya—but she killed them, sacrificing herself in the process."

Elden interjects saying, "It was an all-out attack on our territories' leaders. As the only female mage ever born, you were a target. That's why they were willing to come this far."

"You mean a lot to us," Warren says.

"And to our people. You signify the possibility of something new," Jonathan says.

"Is that why you treated me like a pariah all throughout high school?"

He laughs. "You dished it out every bit as much as I did. If anything—I showed restraint."

"Oh, that's some bull—"

"Let's not lose focus," Dad says sternly. "We got the call this morning. We've received a tip on where the girls are possibly being held. Once Aldrick awakens, he'll be joining the search party."

"I can't believe you're leaving me. Again. In this condition. I don't even know where I am."

"You'll be taken care of here until it's safe enough for you to travel. You need to rest."

"Fine, whatever. But could you at least do me a favor?" I ask.

"Sure, hun," he says, "anything."

"I'm gonna need Jonathan to stay here with me."

21

Watching my brothers climb into the back of the car and drive away is an unsettling sight, neither knowing what danger they'll be in or when I'll next see them. I've never been away from them for more than a day.

How many other missions have they done without me even being aware?

"Why are you making me miss out on hunting these crows down?" he says, resigned, grabbing my hand and lowering me back into the wheelchair. I insisted on standing to hug everyone goodbye, but in hindsight, it was a bad idea.

"If I get *stuck* again, no one will be there to help me," I say, attempting to be vague, not entirely sure I want the vampires in on our secret just yet.

"Oh. And uh, what makes you so confident that it could happen again?" he asks with genuine concern in his face.

I shrug.

"Well, if I'm going to be holed up in a vampire's castle for a while, I'm going need to make a quick trip to the store," he says, as he turns us around and heads up the stone path that leads to the entrance.

Their enormous house appears to have been designed to resemble a modern castle in an enchanted forest. It is constructed with dark stone and features turrets and numerous balconies. Giant windows adorn all three floors, while vines with white flowers climb along the walls.

Movement grabs my attention. Gerard stands in the doorway, just inches from the sun, wearing a pair of slacks and a polo shirt. I might have taken him for your average rich kid if not for the red eyes.

"I can't help but notice the Drapers left you here without transportation. If you need a set of wheels, you're welcome to the garage. I'm sure you'll find something down there to suit your tastes. The keys are on the wall. I'll take Brielle from here," Gerard says with a million-dollar smile, all perfectly straight, eerily white teeth—though his canines do appear slightly sharper than they should.

"Oh, hell yeah," Jonathan says, eager to hand me off.

"You're just going to ditch me? Then what was the point of agreeing to stay behind?"

"Relax, I'll be back in no time," he says to me, before looking to Gerard, "Which way to the garage?"

"Ugh!"

"In the foyer, you'll find an elevator. It's the first level basement."

"Be right back!" he shouts as he takes off, jogging.

"Who'd have guessed? Shiny cars are all you need to serve as a distraction for an archmage," remarks Gerard.

"And *why* would you want to distract him?" I ask, crossing my arms, suspicious.

"Well, to give us a chance to learn about one another, of course! Our dear older brother went to such great lengths to hide you from us. Naturally, we're all a bit...curious."

He walks behind me and begins pushing my wheelchair.

"Out of the way, Gerard. It's my turn to give the tour. Plus, let's face it—she likes me better." A thud sounds behind me, presumably as Dane knocks him aside.

I snort with laughter, unable to see what's happening back there.

Entering through the grand double doors, marble floors that stretch across a spacious, open first floor greet us. A double staircase leads to a second story, and there are doors everywhere, so many that I can't guess where they all lead.

The brothers' tour begins inside as they circle the bottom floor. The kitchen looks untouched, with so much stainless steel that it reminds me of a hospital. The refrigerator is ironically large considering it's likely empty most of the time.

Next is a dining hall, with a mahogany table that stretches across the room, easily seating over two dozen. Paintings line the walls, alongside shields and swords, flags and crests that all look distinctly European, authentic, and old. A large fireplace is against one wall, spotless inside, as if it's just for décor.

Exiting through the far end, we enter a living room where couches are positioned directly across each other, with coffee tables between them.

"Do you use this area often? I didn't think vampires were all that social."

All three brothers laugh.

Wait, three?

I turn to find that we've been joined by Isen, the only one still dressed in black. He stands tall and gaunt, clearly the youngest of the brothers, and he keeps his distance like a shadow in the corner of the room.

"Ashland doesn't have many vampires. Our numbers are made up mostly of *other* supernatural beings. They could hardly tolerate us in the beginning. But my brothers and I have been carving our way into their hearts," Gerard says with a chuckle.

"They learned pretty quickly how much they needed us—and our abilities," Dane says. "Well, except yours, Isen. They hate yours."

"Everyone does," Isen says with a twisted smirk.

Yikes.

"This is the game room," says Dane, pushing me into a dark space.

My eyes adjust to the dim lighting, and see the room split into two sections. The first looks like the inside of a bar, complete with a pool table and a dart board on the far wall. The second is like a home arcade loaded with pinball machines and a bunch of noisy game cabinets so old I don't recognize them.

"Does anyone use all this stuff?" I ask.

"Have a look," says Gerard, gesturing to a nearby screen. The high score initials all belong to Isen.

"So, is your ability being really good at video games?" I say to Isen.

"No, I just have the best eye-hand coordination."

"Yeah, yeah," Dane says.

"And the fastest reflexes."

"I'll bet you're not faster than Aldrick," I say, grinning, which seems to wipe the smile off his face. Oops. "So, um, I know Dane controls the wind, and Gerard has some kind of magic hypnosis..."

The guys chuckle.

"But what is your power? And why does everyone seem to hate it?"

"Maybe it's easier just to show her," Gerard suggests.

"Show me what?"

"Let's get some fresh air," says Dane as we start moving again. All three grab long cloaks and cover themselves moments before entering the sunlight.

We leave the house, which immediately opens to a beautiful paradise. On either side is a garden with every type of flower I can imagine, planted in tiers, featuring fountains, hedges, statues, and ponds. Everything looks so vibrant that it seems like a painting brought to life. Everything is in bloom. The smell hits me. I recognize the lavender, wisteria, and roses, but the rest is just an overwhelming symphony of everything sweet and pleasant.

"How can this be real?" I say, feeling intoxicated by the beauty.

"This is mother's garden," says Dane, as we stop in front of a long, rectangular pond flanked by several fountains, the air filled with their delicate babble.

"I was banned from Mother's Gardens for a month after I accidentally killed three of her plants," Isen says, looking over at me, as he steps over to a large weed protruding out of a crevice in some nearby rocks.

"Not exactly a green thumb, either, huh?" I remember trying to grow little house plants on many occasions. Never did I ever figure out what I was doing wrong.

"No," Isen says, a sudden dark edge to his voice, "—quite the opposite." He reaches down to the base of the weed and plucks it with two fingers, then lifts it to show me.

From his hand extend dozens of black, misty tendrils that wrap around the plant. I watch in disbelief as it wilts, turning brown, then black and withered, right before my eyes. Finally, it collapses into dust.

"What did you just...*do*?"

"Did Aldrick really tell you nothing of us?" Gerard asks.

"No. Not a word. All I had was the implication that there was more than one of you."

"Our little baby brother here has a remarkable talent. He can suck the life force out of any living thing just by touching it," says Dane.

"Anything?"

"That's right. Animals, plants, vampires...*humans*."

"Quit trying to frighten the girl, Dane," says Gerard, impatiently, before turning to me, "you have nothing to fear from our brother, Isengrim. He's—"

"Don't—" says Isen, too late.

"Isen...grim?" I repeat, not sure I heard it right.

He sighs, pinching the bridge of his nose. "I thought we'd agreed to stop using my *full* name in mixed company."

Dane chuckles. "Yeah, well—I don't know how far you've thought this through, Grims, but Brielle here just might end up being your new sister-in-law."

"Whoa," I say, "you guys are getting way ahead of me."

"That's highly uncalled for, Dane," Gerard lectures.

"What did I say? Everyone sees what's going on here. Aldy's been hanging on to his serial bachelor status, always searching for the one. Now, finally, after all these years, Mr. Desperado has met his match. Sparks are flying. What's not to love?"

Oh, no. My face is getting hot...

"What about the lady's feelings? Have you considered that?" Gerard says, low, through gritted teeth.

"Are you kidding me with this? Have you heard the mouth on this chick? She cusses like a sailor. She knows she's got a rocking bod—"

"Dane!" Isen shouts.

There's a tense moment between them, which I break by letting out a strained, nervous laugh. I feel their eyes upon me, but nobody says anything. Just the sound of the fountains.

"How are you guys even related to Aldrick? You seem so different compared to him. So much more...*carefree*."

"For many years," says Isen, "Aldrick carried the burden of providing for our family, protecting us. It was expected of him as the eldest. I guess you could say that he's always shielded us from the worst."

"Well spoken, Isen." says Gerard, "Our brother has always been there, putting himself last, shouldering the load, even when it was too much for our parents."

"It gave us a chance to live a little, find things to do to pass the time, read a book, watch a movie...you know, *experience* the world. Live a little. I don't think...I don't think he ever learned to do that," says Dane.

"He was always fighting. Sometimes, I think that's all he knows how to do," Isen says.

This moment is too heavy for me, too much for right now. I just blurt out the next thing that I can think of to change the subject. "So *why* did you kill three of your mom's plants?"

Dane snickers.

"My ability will sometimes trigger...unintentionally. When I'm attacked, that is," Isen says, glaring daggers at his brothers.

"You were attacked in this garden?"

"Well, at the time, Gerard was launching a pumpkin at the back of my head—revenge for something, I don't even recall what—while my hand was brushing up against a rose bush."

"Oh, yes, the way it flew through the air—like a bullet, really," Gerard says with self-satisfaction as he stares into the distance, replaying the memory in his head.

"Huh," I say, keeping my eyes on Isen's hands while trying to hide my rising panic, which he picks up on like a hawk.

"Don't worry, you don't need to be afraid," he says with put-on confidence, "We've done a lot of training since then. I've gotten much better at controlling it. Besides, I learned how to reverse it, too, put the energy back in." He smiles, proud of his accomplishment.

"Yeah, sure. So long as he doesn't *break* the connection, after he's done ripping the life out of you, he can put it back in. Most of it, anyway," says Dane.

"That's very reassuring," I say blandly, remembering that the first time I saw Aldrick, I thought death had come to claim my soul, when the whole time Isen was out here being the actual grim reaper.

"I think I've had enough of the great outdoors," says Gerard, "let's resume the tour, shall we?"

Inside, the guys remove their cloaks and place them on hooks. Then they wheel me up to a pair of bookshelves against a wall in a little study and stop, leaving me to look around, puzzled. Then Dane smiles, and tugs on the corner of an old, yellow book with red lettering on it—upon closer inspection, it says *Dracula*. I roll my eyes as the two bookshelves slowly split apart, opening to a set of elevator doors.

The guys laugh heartily as Gerard pushes me in, while Isen and Dane remain outside.

"Aren't you guys coming?" I ask.

"It's kind of a tight fit, plus with Isen, a little personal space is always advisable."

Oh, yeah.

The doors close, leaving me in a small space with only Gerard. He presses the second-floor button. It's quiet, except for faint music played through a tinny speaker. The elevator itself looks like an antique, jumping and jolting as it noisily climbs.

"The second floor is ours. The third has our parents' room, as well as Aldrick's...well, whatever you call that thing."

With a loud ding, the doors slide open, revealing his two brothers waiting.

I lose track of all the history and stories as they show off paintings and tapestries that line the halls. They claim to have stolen them from different European castles throughout the centuries, works by famous painters that nobody had ever seen. They have ancient artifacts that came into their possession before they crossed the Atlantic, coming to America for the first time.

Gerard loves to talk the most, regaling me with tales of fame and fortune, making deals with nobles and merchants—like a highlight reel of his finest moments. Dane comes second in terms of verbosity, with Isen mostly staying silent. He doesn't come across as shy, he laughs plenty, but he rarely speaks unless someone drags him into the conversation.

It is a bit of a shock when Isen shows me his music room, the first truly messy one I've seen in the house. Musical instruments are scattered everywhere. Guitars hang on the walls and open books and music sheets that spill onto the floor clutter the desks. String instruments rest on a stool before a grand piano, while very old, hand-carved pieces that look like they belong in a museum line the shelves. A large wooden harp leans against one wall. Everything modern and medieval all intermingle in one big room.

Dane's room is essentially a home theater. A giant, windowless space with a projector screen, every video game console known to man, and an endless DVD collection containing everything from Hallmark movies to obscure, subtitles-only Chinese martial arts films. He goes on for a long time about who would win in a fight between Jet Li and Jackie Chan. I see movies in French and German on his shelves, which makes me wonder just how many languages he and his brothers have picked up over the years.

Gerard's room surprises me the most. It's just an ordinary bedroom. A very spacious one filled with expensive-looking furnishings and having an insanely gorgeous view of the water, but nothing you wouldn't see in any average millionaire's home. A tasteful nude painting here, a generic piece of art there...and while I'm sure they all have stories to go along with them, they don't reflect the same level of passion as his brothers'. The way he gazes out the window, though, holds each precious trophy of his storied past as he recounts the lore behind it, I think I begin to understand him—that he yearns for adventure, forever seeking the next, taller mountain to climb.

It's interesting to see what is important to each of them. Not seeing them just as the three brothers, but as individuals. I still have so many questions for them, mainly about Aldrick. How did they fit together as siblings? Why was he so often alone while they were always together? What was their life like before they joined this territory? And before that, when they came to America? I can't even fathom that they were alive before this nation was founded. Not yet. Maybe not ever.

Drifting off in thought, my mind starts to wander as we move silently through the halls of their massive estate, and I begin to wonder what *his* room would be like. What secrets lie there? Are there things he's never shown anyone? Not even his family? Would it be like him...dark, inviting...what would it *smell* like?

At the end of the tour, we head up to the third floor.

"And lastly, Aldrick's room."

We arrive back at the one I've been staying in.

"Wait, no. *This* can't be his room. It's just a big, empty white box with windows," I say, confused, looking at a few stacked moving boxes in the corner. "Where's his stuff? His clothes? It doesn't look like anyone even comes in here."

"Nobody really does," says Dane, "I mean sometimes we use it for storage. The space comes in handy for events."

"He's never home?"

"Nope. He's always out. Patrolling," says Gerard.

"Or showering or sleeping. Sometimes, he'll pop in for a minute just to see how things are going. But that's about it," says Isen.

In the silence that follows, a coldness runs through me as a breeze filters in through the open doors that lead to the balcony. The space is so barren, so clinical, *so* devoid of life...No books, no journals, no art displayed on the walls—not even so much as a T-shirt dropped carelessly on the floor beside the bed.

There's nothing of him in this place.

How could someone live like this? Always out, always working, fighting...is there truly no comfort or warmth in his life? For how long has he been this way?

I feel the loneliness seeping in from the walls, and my heart starts to break.

22

I GRAB THE RIMS on my wheels and push, my forearm muscles already burning as I begin another lap around the first floor. My mind wanders through places and time as I breeze by ancient suits of armor, trinkets, and artifacts more rare than anything you'd find in a museum collection. The aroma of bacon and potatoes wafts from the kitchen, tempting me back to reality as Jonathan gleefully prepares breakfast in the estate's fancy kitchen. The only thing in this world he loves more than being a royal pain in my ass? Cooking. And right now, he's in heaven.

The sound of masterfully plucked guitar plays off the marble and stone columns, a soundtrack to my swerving—still only a fledgling wheelchair pilot. I find a place to rest near the source of the music. My eyes lock on Isen, sitting on the couch, his strong fingers gracefully dancing across the strings, producing a mesmerizing song that is old, foreign, and sad. He seems oblivious to the sun's rays inching closer to his exposed arm with every passing minute. They do so much to avoid the sun, yet they won't speak of why. It's driving me just a little crazy. It's so close to hitting his skin. Just another minute, and I might get to see *something*. I move nearer, eyes widening with anticipation as the light inches across.

He stops abruptly, lifting his head and placing his palm on the strings, silencing their song. It's like he's listening for something, then he smiles pleasantly. He moves his arm, so naturally that it comes across less like he's intentionally avoiding the sun, and more like instinct.

"Do you know how to get down to the garage, Brielle?" he asks in his soft, monotone voice.

"Yeah," I say, unsure of *why* he asks.

"You may want to head that way. I believe lover boy has finally awakened from his slumber."

"Aldrick is awake?"

"I can hear him in the tunnels."

A stupid smile spreads across my lips, hardly able to contain my excitement as I awkwardly maneuver myself around in the direction of the elevators.

"Wait. Did you say *tunnels*?"

"Yeah. You know, for emergencies," Isen responds flatly.

"Emergency tunnels, as in more than one," I repeat in a skeptical tone of voice.

"Whole network of them," he says, and then resumes strumming his guitar, like there's nothing more to be said.

As I fly down the hallway, arms searing, racing to the entrance of the emergency tunnel network to meet my vampire, finally awake after sleeping for two days straight—it occurs to me just how bizarre my life is becoming.

The elevator doors open to the underground level, Jonathan's favorite place to slip off to and spend hours drooling over their fancy cars. Dozens of shiny vehicles line the walls of the dimly lit concrete room, some I recognize, others I don't, but every high-end make and model you could ask for is stored in this garage.

There is only silence, other than the hum of the fluorescent lighting, and then comes a loud, mechanical whirring from a far wall. I see a small piece of the ground drop down, before disappearing completely from view. A figure leaps from the opening, landing gracefully.

Oh, my...

It's like seeing him for the first time. He looks freshly showered, his still-wet hair brushed back, looking almost black as he stands there in a simple, clean white T-shirt and pair of blue jeans. When he looks at me, I can't hold back my grin, which makes him smile in return.

There's a touch of innocence in his smile, but I can't say the same for his eyes, which despite their glimmering, ruby red luster and the absence of any visible signs of aging, harbor a sort of weariness—like he's simply seen too many things—and maybe it's just wishful thinking on my part, or head trauma. Still, I swear life comes into him when our eyes meet.

He strolls toward me, holding my gaze, his bare feet silent on the concrete.

"Finally!" I say emphatically, "Those were the longest two days of my life!" I lock the brakes, pushing myself to stand so I can walk to meet him. I gasp as I'm swept off my feet before I even get them under me. I wrap my arms around his neck. In the air, there's a faint, lingering trace of golden light between where he was and where he stands now—like nothing I've ever seen, before.

"Brielle," he breathes, a mixture of relief and regret, "are you...alright?"

Shivers run through my body. Oh, do I love hearing him say my name. "Yeah. No pain, no infection. So far, so good," I say.

"Damn!" he huffs out.

"Damn?" I ask, wondering what could be displeasing about my recovery. But then I hear it: the elevator is coming. Well, that certainly was a lovely thirty seconds we had all to ourselves. He gently lowers me back into the wheelchair as the door slides open, from which Sylvain and Aurelia emerge without hesitation.

Aldrick's father, Sylvain, looks exactly how an eight-year-old me would have imagined that a scary vampire would look: his eyes are deep set with steeply arched eyebrows, the large bridge of his nose is wide, but tapers down to a point. His lips are thin and his mouth extraordinarily wide, exposing too much of his ever-so-slightly pointed teeth for comfort. The most haunting of all, though, are his tall upper eyelids—which appear to be in a permanent state of retraction, granting enormous real estate to the whites of his eyes.

"Good morning, my son," Aurelia says softly, almost musically. She is gorgeous, with long, flowing dark hair and a round face with sharp, feminine features, like a queen of old.

Glancing back and forth at the two of them, it's clear how Aldrick somehow has movie villain features, yet still manages to be hauntingly beautiful.

"Good morning, mother. Father." He nods at each in a way that seems oddly formal.

"The Drapers departed yesterday. We have a possible location for the hostages. We're meant to join them upon your waking. Come, my son, the plane is already waiting," Sylvain says in an accent I've never heard before, stressing only the wrong parts of each word and phrase.

"Of course, you'll have a few minutes to say farewell," Aurelia adds with a slight bow of her head, her English much more refined.

Sylvain's hand lands on my shoulder as he looks at me and says, "Rest and heal, Miss Draper."

I nod, unable to form coherent words while looking into those terrifying eyes. It genuinely surprises me that he doesn't end each sentence with evil laughter.

With that, they turn and depart. I wait until the elevator doors close to say, "I knew you had to leave, but nobody told me we wouldn't even get five minutes together."

"I know things seem bad, but I promise you, after this is over, I will make this right. You *will* have the life you want. What's most important now is that these families have their loved ones returned."

Of course, I wouldn't dream of interfering with the rescue of someone else's wife or daughter out of a selfish desire to be with him. "I know, you have a job to do. And I am glad you're going to help those people. Maybe it's for the better, anyway I'm not sure I want you seeing me like this," I say half-heartedly. I know lives are at stake, but my whole world is crumbling around me. Maybe there's something horribly wrong with me, after all, but deep down I don't care about the world and its problems. Not right now.

I just want him to stay.

"Please...be careful," I say, standing, and putting all my weight on my uninjured leg. He closes in, wrapping his arms around me. I breathe in his scent deeply. He gently lifts my chin using his thumb and forefinger, tilting my head back to kiss me. My heart races as my mind is wiped clean of everything else, and I am completely stuck on the feel of *him*.

He pulls back and brushes the hair behind my ear before smiling and saying, "I'll be fine. I just need you to be safe. Everything else...we can figure out later."

I lean in, resting my head against his chest, soaking up every last bit of these fleeting moments I have with him.

23

I HAD NEVER KNOWN what true boredom was until now. Their library, expansive as it is, doesn't seem to contain a single title published in the past two decades. Some of the old, dusty tomes on their shelves look like they might disintegrate at my touch. Everything from architecture to music theory, woodworking, herbology, and an entire *section* dedicated to maritime superstitions...all these books, filled with such rich knowledge of the world, yet that's not what I seek. I long to escape from the thoughts in my head, my reality.

Escape...From the heaviness that weighs on me every moment I'm stuck here, alone...from the images that keep invading my thoughts, like the face of the girl who waited beside me as I woke up. Did she die that night, out there in the cold, alone, with no magical vampires to save her? I hadn't bothered to ask her name. Every day, I watch all the leaked footage that airs, but she never appears on any of it. I like to imagine that she got away, too—one of the "lucky" ones, like me.

On my way to the garden to go bug Jonathan, I pass through the living room, only to find three vampires lounging on the sofa, watching a movie. When I see what's on screen, I do a double-take: *Legally Blonde?* A chick flick? Huh. It's funny how they'll act like normal teenage guys—minus the raging hormones, of course—but then I'll catch them doing the oddest shit, like playing backgammon and shuffleboard, or building a ship in a bottle. After observing them in their natural habitat, I'm beginning to wonder what is happening inside those heads of theirs.

"Morning!" I call to them as I continue outside. If they respond, I don't hear it.

Aurelia's gardens are truly a thing of wonder, and not just because she's a horticulture expert—but it turns out that her touch has the ability to push life into things—the opposite of what Isen does. For some reason, though, she only uses it on plants, and I'm too afraid to ask why.

I lock the brakes on the wheelchair when I see magic swirling in the air near the giant fountain, a sign that Jonathan is nearby, doing his daily mage exercises. As I walk to where he's training, there's only a slight limp in my step. It's been getting much better day by day.

There sits Jonathan, cross-legged on the fountain's edge, moving his hands around, causing the waves of red energy to expand and shift. At first, I'm not sure what he's doing, but as I watch closely, I see he's guiding a long, snake-like section through rings floating in the air. As it disappears into one, it emerges from another. As he does this, the muscles in his arms move and flex tightly, a sheen of light sweat on their bronzed surface. On his face, a look of intense concentration. Showy bastard.

I sit, far enough away not to distract him. Only the falling water disturbs the silence as I watch the white lily pads drifting lazily on the surface.

"It looks like a big worm," I say, examining it.

He drops his hands, and the red magic becomes formless clouds, slowly trickling back into his rings...like fine sand drifting in the air. His breathing is heavy. I can't guess what it takes out of him to use his powers.

"Hey, let's sneak out and go for a drive? I need to talk to you," I whisper.

He lifts his hands again, and the energy changes paths, spreading out and forming a dome over us. It gets quieter and quieter, until I can't hear the fountain anymore. I examine the place where the shield of red energy cuts through the water, appearing to be about a foot thick. I reach out and put a hand on it. It feels like...solid nothingness.

"There. Now they can't hear us."

"Hold on, so you can just create a soundproof shield whenever you want?"

"Yeah...?"

"And you couldn't have mentioned that before?"

"Why, what's the big deal?"

"Ugh. Okay, look...I don't think my borrowed magic is gone. I keep seeing *things.*"

"What sorts of things?"

"I saw this streak of golden light near Aldrick, and I think I'm seeing traces of magic from the brothers. I see a silvery haze around you sometimes, at least I think I do. It's only there for a second.

Or I'll look at you, and your eyes will be solid white, but then you blink—and they're back to normal."

"Probably just some lingering effects. I wouldn't waste too much time stressing about it, especially since it won't last much longer."

"What makes you so sure?"

"Put simply, your body doesn't produce magic, and you're burning through what little you got from your father with this rapid healing you've been doing."

"I thought that was from Cora's special witchy brew?"

"That stuff cuts your recovery time in half. Instead of taking two months to recover, you'd have been better in a few weeks. For you to be on your feet after seven days is nothing short of a miracle."

"Oh..."

He glances at me with a cocky look. I know that look. He's going to start talking shit.

"I bet you're probably *dying* to see your little boyfriend, huh?" he says, almost sounding disgusted.

Typical Jonathan. Unfortunately, I can't hide my smile as I tuck my hair behind my ears. *Boyfriend.* I'm not sure what we are. A modern label would be nice, something concrete as the rest of my life spirals out of control.

"Gross, you're blushing."

"Shut up. I miss him, okay? I would love nothing more than to jump in the car and go hunt him down," I say. I elbow him and add, "C'mon, don't be a wuss. You up for it?"

"Once you've healed enough and the hostages are recovered, sure. In the meantime, it's best if we stay put. This is the safest place for you. You'd only be putting everyone in jeopardy if you showed up now."

I sigh, and we both sit there in silence.

"Only *you* would fall for a fricking vampire. It's still so hard to wrap my head around it," he says, letting out a heavy sigh of his own. "I probably should have seen this coming when you started having a crush on Sephiroth."

"No, I didn't," I say. Sure, I might have filled an entire notebook with sketches of him, but then again—I was twelve.

"Do you even know what they call him?" he asks, lowering his voice.

"Who, Aldrick?"

"Yeah."

"Uh-huh, his brothers nicknamed him *Aldy*. I think it's adorable."

"No, Bri. A demon."

I furrow my brows and scowl at him, but then the words return to me. Something I heard in the car with the crow shifters... "Actually, now that you mention it, Grey said something like that. 'The Demon of Brennan'. Is that another supernatural territory name, like Ashland?"

"It's *Bremen,* and it's not a territory. It's a port city in Germany. It used to be this huge crossroads for trade and commerce in the seventeenth century."

"Okay...and? What does this have to do with him?"

He merely side-eyes me, his expression dour, before continuing as if I hadn't spoken, "Many tried to conquer it, but it remained a free city throughout the Thirty Years War, even after the surrounding territory was taken."

"Cool? But I didn't know you were *capable* of paying attention in history class."

"Oh, this isn't in your history books. He is in ours, though."

"You're still not answering my question. How does this relate to Aldrick?"

"Listen, I just read this yesterday. Let me tell the story before I forget it—Swedish soldiers were sent to pressure Bremen into submission, but the ones stationed in the surrounding countryside came to fear the night, because that was when it was said that a red-eyed devil with the strength of one hundred men would appear to terrorize their camps—"

"Seriously, the *seventeenth century*?" No way. I know he has to be old...but *that* old? What would he be doing there? Then I think about Gerard's stories, the treasures scattered through their palatial estate. *Oh, no...*

"You're not thinking straight, Bri. He brutally killed countless men who were just doing their jobs to help the city's rulers win a war, in exchange for treasure and blood to drink. Where do you think they got all this money? Your little Romeo is a killer for hire."

"You're wrong, you don't know anything about—"

"Have you even asked his age?"

"Well, yes *and* no..."

"What the hell were you talking about, then? Or *were* you talking?" he says, waggling his eyebrows suggestively.

"Shut up!" I say, and sock him in the arm. "Oh, yeah? Well, Grey called you an archmage. What's the story behind that, huh?" It's well past time to change the subject. If I'm to hear any more about this, I need it to come directly from Aldrick's lips.

He gives me a long, pensive look. "Fine. You deserve to know the truth. Our ranking is determined by the level of magic in our blood. Mine is about as high as it gets, which makes me an archmage. After that are mages—like your father and brothers, lesser mages, and acolytes."

"What rank of mage will I be?"

"Likely, you'll be an honorary acolyte, like Evie. Essentially, it's a fancy word for secretary," he says with a smug grin.

I've never wanted to slap him this badly.

The smile quickly fades as he says, "One day, probably sooner than I'd like, they'll push me to become one of our leaders, like your Dad or my father before me."

"Wait, your father was one of their leaders?" All I ever knew about him was that he died before Jonathan was born.

"Yeah. Dear old Dad. When I came of age, they told me about him. That he was a *very* powerful mage. Not the greatest guy, though," he says with a pained smile, "I still haven't learned all his crimes. No one likes to talk about it, especially around me, but he killed people—*a lot* of people. He had some crazy master plan to do something unspeakable. Many mages joined him. He and his adherents took on their whole world order. They lost, of course...and he was killed in their final battle."

Never in all my years of knowing this boy has he ever opened up to me about his family.

"Well, that sucks."

"Maybe it all worked out for the best. I got to grow up without having to know what a piece of garbage my father was. Lucas and Evie stepped up to the plate, took me in, introduced me to their sons...and their annoying, crabby little sister...made sure I always had a place to go when things got bad with Naomi. It scares me to think who I might have become, had things been different."

My heart sinks. In my eyes, he'd always been the whiny little punk who stole my brothers away from me, always sulking until he got his way. I never understood why he was always there, wherever we went—eating all the cereal, swiping the last slice of pizza, hogging the couch, stinking up the bathroom, leaving his crap everywhere. Now I see the whole picture: all those years, he had just been a lost boy in need of a family. And instead of being the sister he needed, I treated him like a burden.

Damn. I've been the villain the entire time.

"I'm...sorry, Jonathan, for treating you like dirt. I—" I can't believe what I'm saying. *Me* apologizing to *him* goes against everything I hold true in this world.

He eyes me in disbelief, unconvinced of my sincerity, and who could blame him? It seems like this is as touchy-feely as he's willing to get.

"What did you *really* come out here for? What elaborate prank are you setting me up for, this time?" he accuses, aiming those pale blue orbs at me.

"To talk to you, silly," I say with an artificial smile.

His expression remains blank.

"And to see if I could borrow your phone."

"What's wrong with yours?"

"Supposedly, my phone number got leaked. I started getting so many calls and texts that it froze and shut down. Then, Gerard came and broke it. He tried saying that someone could trace it, like, is that even a thing?"

He hands his cell to me and lowers the shield. The breeze returns, blowing his blond locks into his eyes as he gives me a curious look, "Of course that's a thing. Don't you know how cellphones work?"

"Shut up," I say, jerking it from his hand. Still sounds like bullshit to me. I text Aldrick.

> I'm severely disappointed in the lack of coffins here.

> Then you haven't been looking hard enough.

I grin. He's probably joking...but what if he's not?

"How far does your shield go?" I ask Jonathan, "Could I use it to do some proper snooping around the house?"

"It doesn't work like that. You need to be close to me."

"No offense, but that's kind of lame."

"Not as lame as you. I'm not the one who got stabbed in the ass by a middle school janitor."

To think I actually apologized to him. "It wasn't my *ass* you ass, it was my thigh," I say, almost laughing. "I felt that in my *bone*." I'd like to see how *he* would handle a blade slicing through his muscle. I bet he wouldn't think it was so funny then. What I wouldn't give to wipe that stupid smirk off his face.

> *What happened to your phone?*

> Gerard destroyed it.

A few moments pass, during which I like to imagine that Aldrick is calling Gerard and giving him a piece of his mind. I watch Jonathan doing some stretches.

> *I'll have Dane set you up with a new one.*

> *Thanks. XD*

I delete our conversation and hand Jonathan his phone. He shoves it back in his pocket before raising his hands and bringing the magic back to life, and I marvel at the shapes as they whirl and flow around him, hardly able to guess what he's trying to do, or to deny that it looks pretty cool. I'm not sure whether he's really training or just trying to look impressive.

Eyeing him, absent the anger I usually feel when around him for more than a few minutes, I get a creepy feeling. Whether it had occurred slowly over time, or all at once, I couldn't say for sure, but I try to pin down when I had stopped hating his guts. When did he stop despising me? What happened between us that reversed a lifetime of bitter resentment?

Just a month ago, he was flipping me off in the hallways of our school for spreading a rumor that he was working on a rap album. I don't see the same boy in front of me anymore. Had I changed, or had he? It was wrong of me to say to him that he wasn't my brother—not my family—and one day, perhaps, I'll even have the balls to tell him.

24

ALDRICK HAS OFFICIALLY BEEN on this rescue mission more than half the time I've known him.

However, instead of allowing myself to wallow in the misery of having my whole life torn to shreds right in front of my eyes, of being separated from him time and time again, I force myself to remember how lucky I am, just how much the good outweighs the bad.

I know I shouldn't complain. After all, while the world out there is burning, here I am on the balcony of a castle in the middle of an enchanted forest, overlooking the sea. I spend my days wandering through a magic garden and, if I want anything, I need only to ask for it. It's the closest thing I've ever experienced to being a princess—and it's incredibly boring.

Two weeks. Two excruciatingly *boring* weeks.

I sit in the shade, staring at my empty cup of coffee, watching the ice inside melt. Condensation runs down the sides, pooling on the table's glass top, as I lift my hands—imitating what I've seen

Jonathan doing—focusing as hard as I can, trying to use my leftover magic to make the plastic container move, even just a little...

There's got to be something lingering in me. I still clearly see traces of magic everywhere, strange colors, sounds, smells. So, regardless of Jonathan's repeated insistence that I have zero magic, it must be there...somewhere. All I need to do is find it, figure out some way to bring it out.

First, I try closing my eyes, visualizing the red energy swirling around the cup. Then, I clear my head of everything but the image of the cup, and open my eyes, staring intently at it without blinking. I swear it moves once, but I'm disappointed when it turns out to be the wind.

"You gotta get a hold of yourself," Jonathan says out of nowhere, startling the bejesus out of me. "I know you're going through stuff, but you need to man up...and clean this mess." He comes in hot with an ornate, silver serving tray loaded with plates and sets it on the glass table so roughly I'm surprised it doesn't shatter. He grabs a plate bearing a fat, juicy-looking burger and fries and sets it on the table before me.

I fold my arms and lean back in the chair. "I'm not...going through anything." I lie. "I'm just trying to figure out how to use this magic. Just once would be cool."

"I thought you were trying to keep it a secret."

"Cats out of the bag. Gerard already commented how they should stock up on mage blood in case I get hurt again."

He snorts. "Lucas wouldn't say no to that."

"Can you just tell me *how* you do it? Like, is it all in your head, or—"

"Oh, my God!" he says, rubbing his face with one hand, "*How* many times do I have to tell you before you listen? There isn't enough magic in your veins to do what we do. Even if I wanted to—"

"Dude! I saw your power before the transfusion."

"Okay, sure, you can sense magic and maybe do a few other odd tricks. So what? Even common witches can do that and more, still they would *never* claim to be mages."

"So now you're calling me a witch?"

He snickers. "No. In fact," he says, taking keen interest in my empty drink on the table, "I'd say you're more like that." He gives an indicating nod in its direction.

I squint at the cup, wondering what he could be prattling about now.

"All ice and no coffee," he says with an easy confidence. "I'd help you if I could, but I can't teach you to control what isn't there. So no, there won't be a training session, no fighting leathers or finding your inner something-or-another. This isn't one of your fantasy books. Soon enough, the last remnants of what you absorbed from the blood transfusion will fade, and you'll go back to what you've always been: an empty vessel."

I roll my eyes at his attempt to be authoritative, pick up my burger, and then watch as Jonathan serves two plates to himself. What does he know, anyway? There's never been a girl mage before, so I might as well pretend that none of their so-called rules apply to me. I know what I'm feeling, they don't. There's something in me, and it's getting stronger.

He drops into the chair and wastes no time shoving a burger in his mouth, juices from the meat and barbecue sauce dripping in large globules onto his platter, which holds not one or two but *three* burgers—the other plate solely for holding his mountain of steaming, hot fries. I can't help but scrunch up my face in disgust.

He smirks as he opens his mouth and chews loudly, groaning with pleasure as he crams in more food, downing everything quickly as if we had somewhere to be. Though he's always eaten like this, I've never understood why, treating every bite like it could be his last.

A loud revving of a car engine comes through the air, which is odd because Jonathan is usually the only one who drives anywhere.

"Is there someone else here?"

"Oh, yeah. A bunch of people. They're all downstairs, having a big secret meeting," he says, miffed.

"Who?"

"The coven."

"Ooh, I wanna see!" I say, eagerly jumping out of my chair. Finally, something is happening around this place.

"Whoa! Take it easy."

"If you're worried about my leg, it's healed, if you haven't noticed." I mean, we went rollerblading through the gardens just this morning. It should be obvious. "Come on, let's go. I need you to introduce me."

"I wouldn't go down there if I were you."

"And why's that?"

"If you think Daddy Vamp is scary, you'll find some of the shifters even creepier." He chuckles.

"Are you coming or am I going down there by myself?" I stand, my arms folded, an impatient look on my face.

"They won't let you see them," he says, his mouth full, "because you're not part of their coven."

"Neither are you, but you still got to go in and meet everyone."

"Nope. Why do you think I'm up here with a loser like you? Neither of us are invited to party with the cool kids."

"How do you know how creepy the shifters are, then? Hmm?"

"I saw them during our stay here."

What's he talking about? Nobody has been here in two weeks except for Cora and Aldrick's family.

"I haven't seen anyone," I say, puzzled. "When was this? While I was sleeping?"

"No. Every few days, a different group drops in. They're extra careful to avoid being spotted, hanging around, keeping their voices low, exiting rooms before we enter," Jonathan says smugly.

"So, then, you saw their souls?"

He nods.

So, I *was* noticing strange things, after all.

"Why are you only telling me this now? Do you have any idea how creepy that is? My God. How many of our private conversations have they overheard?" I ask, mortified.

"Dude, relax," he responds blandly, "not all of them have vampire super hearing."

"Wait, does this mean you can see people's souls *through walls*?"

He grins at me.

I don't know how to respond. Random supernaturals have been skulking around the house, watching, listening—and there I was, idiotically thinking I've had this whole place to myself. And now, I've just pieced-together that Jonathan has X-ray vision. I've had all I can take of being the last to know everything.

"Why are you like this? Why can't you just fill me in on things?"

"C'mon, admit it. It's a little bit funny."

"Funny? You know what—"

"I don't like that tone of voice on you," he says. "What are you thinking?"

"Where downstairs are they?"

"They're all just hanging in the living room."

I eye the door, debating.

"I'm telling you, I wouldn't do that," he says.

"Why? What are you going to do, stop me with some stupid magic forcefield if I try to leave?"

"No, I would never—ugh, listen," he says, lowering his voice, "I'm supposed to keep you up here. Please? Please don't embarrass me in front of everyone. They'll hear you coming down the stairs, especially with those big-ass Sasquatch sandals of yours," he says, looking down at the pair of platform flip flops I'm wearing. "It's going to get more awkward than you can possibly imagine if you just trapse in there. This isn't one of Evie's Tupperware parties."

"Fine," I say, looking toward the balcony, "I won't take the stairs."

"Elevator is even noisier," he says, squeezing a massive blob of ketchup onto his plate, the plastic container making a sputtering fart sound as red splatters everywhere.

I grin as I walk to the balcony's edge, now self-consciously aware of the loud smacking sound of my footwear. I've wanted to do this from the moment I saw the wooden trellises traveling up the sides of the house. I kick off my bigfoot sandals and hop up on the thick concrete railing, then look down over the edge at the three-story drop, and shrug. I've survived worse. I test the sturdiness of the wooden slats by pulling on them. Like I thought, these vampires don't do anything cheap. I'm sure it will hold my weight.

"What are you *doing*?" Jonathan says, choking on his burger as he gets out of his seat.

I look down, planning my route. The tricky part will be avoiding Aurelia's intertwining vines without getting my leg caught.

He scoffs as he comes over to me. "Like, what goes through your head? How is this a solution to anything?"

"Relax, dim-bulb, I'm just climbing down. See? It's like a ladder. I'll be fine."

"Here," he says, extending his arms, "I'll help you down—"

I swat at his hands. "Get off me! You don't have any say in my life, remember? If I want to climb down the side of a castle, I'm going to," I say with a smirk. I grab one of the boards with both hands and take a deep breath before stepping onto the trellis. It feels fine. I'm going to be fine. Jonathan's wrong, yet again.

"Okay. This is happening," he says, devoid of all emotion.

Ignoring him, I begin my descent, carefully lowering myself. My arms are a bit shaky, and my legs still wobbly from weeks of disuse, but in all, it's easy. In fact, I want one of these installed on my house, one day. I look up to see Jonathan's eyes wide with terror, and show him my widest, most defiant smile. With only maybe fifteen feet to the ground, I could handle a fall from here.

I'm not sure if my hand slips, or a board breaks, exactly—because it happens too fast, all I know is that in one confusing moment, the sky and the ground switch places. There is a brief, horribly familiar sense of falling, then a crash into a pair of strong arms.

Aldrick? I think for a split second, but no—it feels all wrong, and it smells like Axe body spray and suntan lotion. I open my eyes—and leap out of *Jonathan's* arms, landing painfully on the ground, possibly bruising my butt in the fall. Around him, ripples a swirling red haze that seems to distort reality.

"Are you insane—"

"How did you do that?" I cut in, watching as the color dissipates. "Did you use your magic to get down here?"

"No, I ran down the stairs as soon as I saw you slipping," he says in a low voice, rubbing his face. Not even a convincing lie. "You know, if you ever die of anything, it'll be from your own stupidity."

There is no way he cleared three stories in a few seconds. Does this mean I can add literal teleportation to Jonathan's abilities? Or is it something else? How powerful *is* this little brat?

"Oh, shut it, are you not the same guy who used to bet money that I would fall climbing those ropes in gym class? This should be something you'd laugh at, something you'd make fun of me for. Why are you suddenly acting like you care about my well-being?" I say.

"Okay, yeah...maybe I used to hope you'd get hurt—hope you'd fall, hope something would put you in enough danger that one of us could finally save you. And then you'd realize the truth, and you'd have to admit how wrong you were about me...to stop hating me."

That stops my thoughts in their tracks. I think back to all the times he'd push me to do stupid things, dare me to jump, to climb up on something, the way he'd always be so giddy about it. I thought he was smiling at the thought of seeing me in pain. But as I sift through memories and see his motivations in a new light, I'm not entirely sure I like what it implies...Maybe I don't know the first thing about this guy.

Perhaps I don't know myself at this point. I look at the balcony on the top floor, where I'd just done something that in hindsight seems incredibly dangerous and dumb. And I have to wonder: were all these habits, these impulsive tendencies, only a part of me because I was being egged on to take pointless risks my whole life? I recall my brothers doing the same thing, not just Jonathan. Heck, even my Dad encouraged me to hop on a dirt bike a few times.

What kind of woman would I have grown into if I hadn't been lied to or constantly manipulated?

I push off the ground and walk to him, an apologetic look on my face, before socking him in the arm full power and saying, "You jerk!"

"What the—" he says, grabbing the spot on his arm, like it actually hurt. Always the drama.

Before he has time to protest, I turn away and move softly along the paved stone in the direction of the living room, my steps as quiet as any human can make theirs. I peek around the corner, and—seeing nobody out on the patio—travel along the wall like a ninja until I begin to hear voices. Unfortunately, I have to stop short of the window, hidden behind a potted plant, not wanting to come into view of those inside. I would love to sneak under it, but no...they couldn't have normal windows like other people, rich vampires need floor-to-ceiling glass *walls*. I crouch and listen carefully to their conversation through the open patio doors.

Jonathan comes up behind me, silently. Huh, maybe he's just as curious as I am.

A man's voice, loud and boisterous, stands out above the rest. I haven't heard this one before. "His body is displayed, along with the rest," the deep voice rumbles through the air.

Some voices are crystal clear, while others speak more softly, so it's hard to make out every word.

"It's just a reminder of what is coming for them all."

"Pass that over—"

"Any news on Luna? Or Katherine?" a woman asks.

"This one I made—"

"Kat is fine, not a scratch on her. I haven't heard an update on Luna. Was she hurt, Gerard?"

"No, our mother said neither of the girls were harmed," he responds.

They found them? A grin stretches across my face. It's finally over.

"From the sounds of it, they will be there for a while. They could use your help, too."

"There is one issue we came here to discuss."

"The wine goes better with this—"

"You need to tread more carefully. We have kept this a secret, have kept *you* a secret. What if they decide to make a public display?"

A faint distortion in the air comes whipping around the opening of the double doors, encircling us.

"Heard enough, little mages?" Dane's voice asks.

I jump in surprise, and a small gasp escapes before I can place my hand over my mouth. Over my shoulder, I see that Jonathan's lips are pursed in annoyance.

"What was that?" a woman's voice asks.

We jump to our feet.

"Someone just used magic."

"I apologize. I was creating a better cross breeze, it's getting a little stuffy in here," Dane says.

I whisper, hoping only he and his family can hear me, "Dane, what the hell! You couldn't have told me the girls were found?"

"You have about ten seconds to get your ass out of there before Tobias comes out for a cigarette. Try not to kill yourself on your way back, please."

Jonathan rolls his eyes at me before we run along the house, clearing the corner without being seen.

"They found the girls! We don't have to be here anymore!" I say, excited.

"Cool," he says, not sharing my enthusiasm. "Let's head back upstairs. I wasn't done eating."

"Why are you acting like such a buzzkill? Aren't you ready to ditch this place and go do something?"

"We'll just go in through the kitchen. I'll throw up a shield, they won't be able to hear us."

"Oh, so *now* you can use your shield? I wouldn't have had to risk my life if I would have known we could have taken the damn stairs—"

"It's not a toy, Bri. Besides, if they can't hear us, we also can't hear them...plus it doesn't make us invisible."

"I guess. Why don't you just *teleport* us up to the room?"

He throws his head back and sighs, his magic coming to life and encircling us with a barrier. "Just for once in your life, please, respect a boundary. There are some things you're not ready for."

I don't think I can ever get used to the dead silence inside the bubble.

"Forget your food. Let's borrow one of their cars and get out of here. They won't miss one. Go get your puking meds while I pack our bags."

"That's an objectively terrible idea," he says.

"Why?"

"First of all, it's like a twenty-hour drive through some of the country's most barren stretches of highway, and we've got a dozen airborne crows out for our blood. Oh, and I almost forgot—every person in the country has seen your face by now. Road travel isn't an option for us."

"So, let's catch a flight."

"That's an even worse idea," he says bluntly. "Why can't you just wait until we resolve the situation?"

"Damn it, no!" I shout, "You listen to me, good and hard, mage boy. I have been waiting my whole life for one thing or another, and now I have finally learned the truth about our family, and what have I done for two weeks? Wait." I point my finger at his chest, "And now the girls have been rescued, and I've recovered, and what do you want me to do? Wait.

"Don't you get it? I'm just going to be waiting forever! Nothing is ever going to take care of itself. Nothing is ever going back to normal. So, either we're going, or I'm going by myself. I'm done sitting back and hoping for things to happen. And now that I have you on my team, no one is stopping me."

"Fine," he says.

"Fine?"

He shrugs. "I agree with you. All our old leaders prefer to hide us away, letting the world outside go to ruin," he says, his cold, blue eyes staring off into an impossible distance. "You go gather your things, I'll pull some strings and see if I can't get us a private jet."

"A what now?"

"Mage air—the only way to travel," he says with a smirk.

25

CASTAIC, CA

THIS WAS A TERRIBLE idea. Why don't I ever stop to think things through?

"How am I even going to get inside without the neighbors seeing three vampires and America's Most Wanted traitor coming home?" I say, my words muffled by the hoodie I have pulled up, covering half my face. I should have snatched a damn ninja mask from Aldricks closet when I was taking one of his hoodies.

"You look ridiculous, by the way," Jonathan says. "You couldn't have picked an uglier pair of sunglasses, either."

"Dude, there were cameras everywhere!" I hiss at him. "And they happen to be *your* ugly sunglasses, you dummy. I stole them from your bag during landing."

"Does Aldrick know you're such a raging klepto?" he says as he rips them off my face.

I pull the hood further down and sink into my seat, vanishing deeper into the oversized sweatshirt.

The Holsten brothers insisted on tagging along after they learned of our impromptu visit to California. Their coven agreed that sending them to help restore order to a neighboring green zone is the best course of action, maybe even establishing them as new allies.

"Don't you think the house is being watched?" I ask. Everyone in our city knows me, who my family is, and where we *live*.

"No. If there's one thing I can guarantee—it's that we can trust our neighbors," Jonathan says.

"And how would you know that?"

He gives me a cocky grin.

I sigh. More secrets. "So what's this whole mage council meeting thing going to be like?" I ask nervously.

"Normal stuff. You say a few words, they put an unbreakable spell on you and issue you an assigned parking space."

The thirty-minute drive from the airport goes by quickly, with nobody seeming to have much left to say. The car lurches violently as Isen hits the accelerator, the engine growling as we race against the rapidly approaching dawn. Outside my window, I marvel as the blue hour silently overtakes the desert, gradually revealing the barren, rolling hills of my desert home.

Only, it feels different now.

Having spent so long amidst the endless evergreen forests of the Pacific Northwest, I see it with new eyes. This place has its own sort of beauty, like a quiet simplicity. It's easy to see how someone would want to live here. I would just never be one of them.

As we round the last stretch of a drive I've done hundreds of times, I'm lost in silly daydreams—Aldrick taking me in his arms, all of this being over, no longer having to worry about danger, just living. When I see the Lake Hughes Road exit sign, I snap out of it, realizing we're almost to town. I sit up and strain my eyes, looking for the blue Castaic Inn sign in the distance, finding something else, something bizarre and unfamiliar instead. I gasp.

Gerard and Dane whip their heads to me in alarm, following my line of sight in confusion. I can't take my eyes off what I'm seeing.

"What is it, Brielle?" Gerard asks, confused.

A dome. At first, it's hard to gauge the size in the dim pre-dawn light, but as we grow nearer, its monumental size becomes clear. It moves like clouds, almost like the surface of some distant planet, and though the red color is hard to make out, I don't need any better look to recognize it for what it is: one giant, city-sized mage shield.

"Earth to Brielle, care to clue us in on what you're seeing?"

"Jonathan, how is this possible?" I say, hushed. "How can it be so big?"

"Is there something we should be made aware of?" Gerard asks Jonathan.

"If you're to be allies, then you should know. We maintain a continual field barrier around the city, day and night. Nothing enters or leaves without us sensing it."

"You're saying that there's a shield over the *entire* town of Castaic?" Dane asks as his eyes dart around, searching for it.

"Yes. It takes quite a few of us to keep it in place. We rotate in long shifts to protect our city. We're not in danger, though, it's not a physical barrier—unless it needs to be."

"It's like your own mage-powered sensor tower," says Isen.

"Oh, shoot," says Gerard, reaching for his cell phone, "that reminds me. I need to call before eight and have the towers taken offline for another day. They get pretty uptight if you forget."

"You never saw this thing before?" Dane asks, looking me over.

"Um. No. I never even knew magic existed till vacation," I say, thinking back. "Actually, the first time I dealt with it was after I broke through your brother's command thingy."

"You used magic on her?" Jonathan asks, incredulous, "And no one thought to tell me?"

"Yeah. I thought it best to leave that part out," I laugh, "Just chill. It worked out for the best."

"Wait, you're trying to tell me that you resisted Gerard's persuasion?" Jonathan asks, intensely curious.

"Why? Is that supposed to be hard?" I ask, almost able to keep from betraying a smile.

The three brothers look at each other before suddenly bursting into uncontrollable laughter, which perplexes Jonathan.

"Very few can resist Gerard's ability," says Isen, "even those with powerful magic can still have weak minds."

I swear he glances at Jonathan, who rides shotgun.

The red wall is fast approaching, triggering anxiety in me since we're traveling at almost eighty miles an hour. I hold my breath as we approach. The car passes through the shimmering veil without issue, and I exhale in relief, only for my nerves to start acting up. Now I have to meet the mages, and who knows what kind of dickheads they're going to be. Ugh, my life.

"Now there's a sight for sore eyes," Jonathan says, eyeing the fast-food joint on the corner as we enter town.

Neither of us has to point the way. Isen takes all the right turns leading to my home. Jonathan's grin grows as we get closer. It makes sense now why he has always been content to stay in this city, with no plans to move out or find his purpose. Same with my brothers. The realization is slowly hitting me. They have everything they need here—the mage community. It's always been their future.

That's also why they never wanted me to leave. They know this is the only place in the world they could ensure my safety. Hidden under their protective dome, living out my life, getting married, raising two little mage boys, and finally, dying—all inside a literal bubble.

We pull up to my house, and the vampires jump out of the car, making no attempt to cover their faces, red eyes and pale skin on display for the whole damn neighborhood to see. What are they trying to do? My eyes dart from house to house, nervously checking to see if anyone's watching us.

"Dude!" I say, panicking as I climb out of the backseat, drowning in Aldrick's hoodie.

"It's quite all right, Miss Draper," Gerard says with a knowing grin, echoing Jonathan's reassurance that we can trust our neighbors. What is nobody telling me, this time?

Before I can say anything, the front door of my house swings open, and my mom comes out, sprinting and slamming into me, nearly knocking me off my feet. I grunt as she squeezes me.

"Oh, my goodness... Oh, hun, I've missed you so much! I've been worried sick."

"Don't be. Everything is fine," I wheeze out.

"You've been gone so long," she says, releasing her hold on me.

"It's only been two weeks," I say, before sucking in a deep breath. Who is this woman, and what has she done with my mother? I missed her, too...but a mixture of fear, guilt, and heartache stirs within. Seeing her act like this...I can't deal with it right now. "Mom, we need to hurry and get everyone inside—"

Then, the twins are there, hugging me tighter than seems necessary. Is there something wrong with me? Why don't I feel what they're feeling? Why am I forcing a smile? Sure, I also missed my brothers, but having Jonathan around strangely felt like there was a piece of them with me. When did I start to be okay with seeing him as family? Why doesn't that upset me as much as it used to?

"How are you healing?" Elden asks as he steps back.

"I'm great. My leg is better. No need to worry."

"Of course she is; she's a mage," Warren says, patting me on the shoulder.

"Come inside, we're about to start breakfast," Mom says with a smile, before heading inside with the guys. I tag along a few steps behind them, hearing their laughter, seeing the joy in every step as they return to the place they belong, their perfect little world where everything they've ever needed or wanted is.

I come to a stop on the front lawn as they disappear into the doorway, folding my arms as I stare up at the purple sky, the swirling waves of strange, arcane energy, casting an eerie, twilight hue over the otherwise familiar scene.

I look up at the bedroom window I've climbed out so many times, at the basketball hoop over the driveway that Warren bent when he learned to dunk, the front lawn where we used to run through the sprinklers and feel...*nothing*. Like I've never been here before, or maybe the memories belonged to somebody else.

My breath hitches when I sense his presence, and I turn to meet his gaze. A golden aura surrounds him as he comes straight for me. There are so many things I need to say to him, questions to ask, but before I open my mouth, his body crashes into mine, and he sweeps me off my feet, twirling me around once, twice. I wrap my legs around his waist, holding on for dear life.

My heart beats wildly in my chest as I stare into his savage eyes, breathing in his sharp, metallic scent, like the air before a killer thunderstorm. I become intensely aware of the location of his hands and where they seem to be travelling.

"I'm so...so sorry," I blurt out, to which he raises an eyebrow. "All of this, I dragged you into it. I was willing to accept the consequences of getting involved in your world, but I never would have imagined that I would bring this on you, on your family—"

"Shh," he says, unexpectedly placing a finger over my lips. "Nobody was dragged into anything. This *is* our world. Kingdoms and nations are always fighting over this and that. If anything, I failed to warn you sufficiently about the dangers we face."

"Well, we haven't exactly had much time to talk. Seems there's always something coming between us."

"There's nothing between us now," he says, his powerful arms pulling me tighter against his solid body, as I feel his fingers weaving through my hair, drawing my head toward him. I close my eyes as our lips draw near...

Thunk.

The sudden sound attracts my attention toward the driveway, where a wide-eyed Jonathan is closing the car trunk after grabbing the last of his luggage. I watch in horror as he crosses the yard without a word, pretending not to notice us, and disappears into the house.

I sigh and whisper, "Did you know he was standing there?"

He grins.

Note to self, modesty is not one of his strong suits. He closes the space between us and claims my mouth with his kiss.

26

AFTER BREAKFAST, WE'RE SOMEHOW running late for our meeting with the mage council. I scramble to get ready, thankfully having access to my closet, and throw on my favorite blue skater dress and pair of Docs. I run a brush through my hair, slap on some red lipstick, and call it a day. Everyone's already waiting for me by the time I reach the garage: the twins, Jonathan, Aldrick, and Mom.

"Is it just us? Your family isn't coming...along?" I ask, out of breath from the run downstairs, nearly stalling mid-sentence as I do a double-take at what Aldrick is wearing: full-on military combat gear, like what the vamps had on before the hunt. Under his arm, he carries a matching helmet with a full-face visor. "What's all that about?" I ask, gesturing with my finger.

"You mean *this*?" he says, tapping a couple of times on his metal chest plate. "It's just what we wear when it comes time to have a little fun in the sun," he says with a devilish grin.

"I thought that's what you had those coats for?"

"Those are more like...casual wear," he says, donning his helmet as the garage door opens, latching it on tightly. When he turns his head to face the harsh light of the desert sun, I see that it bears the DSD insignia—the official symbol of the Department of Supernatural Defense. He's disguised himself as a government agent charged with defending humanity from his kind. Is there anything I've been told all these years that wasn't a lie?

As we're pulling out of the garage, my brothers keep shooting glances at me with those stupid grins of theirs. I'm the only one who puts my seatbelt on. Instead of leaving the neighborhood, Mom takes a turn into a cul-de-sac. We slowly roll past the manicured lawns with bikes lying on the grass, a basketball hoop on the curb, the house that still has action figures in its gutters to this day. I would ride my rollerblades up and down these same streets, following behind the guys on their skateboards.

When we arrive at the end of the block, she pulls into some random person's driveway and keeps driving, continuing down the paved path that wraps around the side of the house to their back-yard.

"Mom! What the hell?"

"Language, Bri." She responds halfheartedly, having to know by now that it was a losing battle. The boys laugh as she pushes a garage door clicker, and the side fence slides open. We drive through, and I look back at the automatic opener as it closes behind us, then ahead as she curves around and begins driving toward the house.

I don't even bother protesting as she inches toward the sliding glass door leading to their kitchen. Why shouldn't a family of mages drive a minivan into a house? When we pass right through the wall and I watch it ripple like a hologram made of water, I'm not even surprised. The building inside looks completely different, with solid concrete walls, like the inside of a warehouse.

"This...is your...mage headquarters?" I ask skeptically.

"No," says Warren.

"This is just the elevator," adds Elden.

The whole car shifts, and a metal railing pops up around us. We slowly lower, which feels incredibly weird. I watch as the floor rises to window level and then above, as we descend a vertical shaft. Mom clicks on the dome light. Elden and Warren keep snickering to themselves, and she shoots them a look in the mirror. After a minute, we arrive at a wide underground structure which looks a lot like an airport parking garage.

When we settle at the bottom, the railing finally drops. Mom starts driving again as if nothing out of the ordinary has occurred, and parks near a set of double doors leading to a corridor in a spot that says "Reserved – Draper" on a bright blue sign.

"Okay, we're here," Mom says with a cheery smile.

"We're here...in our neighborhood? You mean to tell me that you guys leave in the mornings to go like twenty houses down the street?"

"Yep, and we just passed my new house," Jonathan says with a grin. "Just a quick two-minute walk to work. Can't beat that."

"Well, this is not creepy at all," I say sarcastically to cover my rising nerves.

Mom's clicking heels echo as we move through the corridor. The impossibly long hallway consists of an endless run of black and white checkered tile floor, polished oak wainscoting, and a migraine-inducing floral pattern wallpaper, all lit by Victorian-style wall sconces that must have been installed in the 1920s. We pass countless unmarked, identical wooden doors and occasionally, cross another intersecting hall no different from the one we're traveling down. Even the thought of getting lost down here unlocks a whole new form of anxiety in me.

I'm relieved when, up ahead, I see Dad awaiting us, standing before a pair of ornate, hand-carved wooden doors that open as we approach. Mom and the guys go around him, entering the room beyond. The murmuring voices of a crowd of people fill the air.

"Welcome, hun," he says, hugging me.

"What is this?" I ask, peeking around his shoulder.

"This is our meeting hall. C'mon, I can't wait for you to meet everyone," he says, leading me onto a red carpeted area. It takes a moment for my eyes to adjust to the lights, but I soon realize I'm standing on the stage of an auditorium, looking out at rows of seats—and that there must be three hundred or so people staring back at me.

Aldrick and Jonathan stand on either side of me as the men and women take their seats, with some of the kids sitting on the floor, mostly sitting still, as everyone falls silent. Dad walks to the center to address the crowd, but I don't follow what he's saying.

Instead, confusion clouds my thoughts as I scan the faces in the crowd. I see my neighbor, Mr. Ashford, and another neighbor, Mrs. Thomas, searching until I've spotted every person from my block—no, from the entire neighborhood. I even see the pastor of the local church, the police chief, and the mayor.

They'd lived around me my entire life, and I had no clue that all these men were mages. Even the little boys on my block, including the ones I'd grown up with. I'm reminded of a complaint I voiced repeatedly throughout my life: there were never any little girls my age to play with. Of course, it all makes sense now. They couldn't have daughters even if they tried.

I continue to look for familiar faces and find boys from school—some who graduated years before me, some from the lower grades. I count nine from my graduating class, all a part of my brother's weird group of friends. We ate lunch together at the same rusty tables. We went on all the same field trips. We had birthday parties. We had block parties. Never once did I suspect they were different. My eyes are too wide with shock, and I cannot conceal my true feelings. I knew most of their names and all of their faces.

A light squeeze on my hand pulls me back to the present, and as I look down, I see that Aldrick's fingers are intertwined with mine. Still, even his touch isn't enough to calm me. My heart feels like it's beating out of my chest.

I look at Jonathan, and whisper-shout, "This whole time? Everyone I know is here. My *teachers* are here!"

He leans close and says, "The funniest part was every time you snuck out your window or ran away, the whole neighborhood was watching you, reporting on your whereabouts." Jonathan smirks, his eyes gleaming like he's been dying to tell me.

I feel Aldrick's grip tighten, just a little.

Every person in this crowd has known a secret about me for my entire life; they've been secretly watching me, talking about me without me knowing. What I'm feeling goes beyond humiliation, beyond betrayal.

"Only you would sneak out to do the lamest shit possible. To go for walks. Getting Slurpee's, going to the library, Blockbuster, the park just to feed the damn birds," Jonathan says with a smirk.

For once, I don't find his teasing even the least bit funny. There is no jest in his words, no irony to fall back on. No. I am a fool. I am *the* fool. Everybody's fool, the last to know everything, always. I am a joke to these people, an oddity. So far from being respected, even snot-nosed little children are treated with more regard. To them, I'm just an empty vessel—nothing more than a defect.

I'm startled by a sudden roar of applause as everyone gets to their feet.

Up walks the only man in this place I don't recognize. He has a gentle smile, kind brown eyes, long brown hair, and bronze skin. He extends an outstretched hand to Aldrick, and there is a beat of hesitation before he returns the gesture, firmly shaking his hand.

"I want to thank you again, Mr. Holsten, for bringing Luna back to me. So long as the sun rises on this land, this will not be forgotten."

Aldrick nods as the man turns to me.

"It is nice to finally meet you, Brielle. I am Alonso, chancellor of this region, and on behalf of my people, I would like to extend to you an apology. You have always been a friend of crows. I take responsibility for not watching Thorn's group more closely. I am truly sorry that you were involved in such ugliness."

"It's not your fault," I say, still too shaken to give him a thought-out response.

Another cheer rises from around us, echoing off the vaulted ceiling.

Aldrick leans in close to my ear and whispers, "It's time, though, I'm curious if this will work on you."

"What are you talking about?"

"Their binding spell, to keep you from sharing their secrets. Will it work, or will it crumble like Gerard's?" he whispers softly.

I turn, studying the determined grin on his face, trying to consider what he's implying.

"Go to him, let's get this over with," he says, pointing to my father, who is smiling, motioning for me to come over, and so I do.

"Why are they standing?" I ask Dad, confused as to why everybody is still clapping.

"They're proud of you, sweetheart—we are all proud of you! I should have told you that last time I saw you."

"Proud of me for doing what?"

"For what you did for your mother. That was brave of you! Very few people would have had the strength to do that!"

"I—"

"You didn't give up. You fought until the end."

"I *killed* someone, Dad. It's not something to be proud of. H-he looked drugged out of his mind. Have they not seen the news stories?"

"No, hun, they know the truth," he says, "And now it's time for you to be recognized as one of us!" He turns to the audience, "Mrs. Driscoll, would you do the honor?"

A woman seated in the front row stands. Her skin is dark, her hair short, and she walks with a confidence I only wish I had. I don't know what goes through my mind as she approaches, but before I know it, she's standing before me, looking at me with a questioning gaze. The entire room goes silent when she raises her right hand.

"Do you know what this is all about?" she asks me.

"I can only speak with those who already know. Seems easy enough," I say, shrugging nervously.

"The spell I'm about to place you under will ensure that much, but this ceremony is about more than that, Miss Draper. You are now a part of our order, and as such, you are to protect our people, our ways, and our secrets—even if it means giving your life."

I get the impression she isn't joking.

"Surely, you wish to protect your family, don't you?"

"Yes. I mean, of course. I would do anything."

"That's good enough for me," she says, smiling warmly, eliciting a chuckle from the crowd. She lifts her hands as she steps closer to me, a weird purple energy swirling around her fingertips. I back away, causing her cheery expression to dissolve into a look of disappointment.

"It's okay, she's just nervous," says my father. I turn to him, and for whatever reason, all I can think about is the pain I caused him when I stormed off back at the cabin. All the times I was cold to him. The months I refused to speak to him... All because he was forced to undergo what they're trying to do to me, now.

My mouth goes dry as I eye the nearest exit—seriously considering running for it. I feel like a caged animal, desperately looking for a way out. I look to Aldrick. He'll have my back if I don't want to go through with this, but that will only make his life harder. I peer deeply into his eyes, remembering what Jonathan said—that I was his *weakness*. I can't let that be true. If he isn't afraid, then neither am I.

Steeling my nerves, I smile at him, and he nods solemnly in response. I turn back to face this woman, recalling what Isen said about Gerard's persuasion abilities in the car earlier. Few could resist his powers, but I did, and that was before I even knew what magic was. How much different could this be? Borrowing on Aldrick's confidence, I make my mind up right here, right now. This binding, sealing—*whatever* it's called—isn't going to work on me. I won't let it.

I take one last deep breath and step toward her. She looks at my father, then me, and sighs in relief. Resuming her spell, she lifts her hands and presses her fingertips against the sides of my head, whispering indecipherable words. Nothing happens for several seconds, causing me to wonder what they'll do if her magic doesn't affect me. So subtly that I almost don't notice it, a soft wind sweeps through me, taking my thoughts away on the breeze with it.

Hidden in a dark corner of my mind, I study her magic as it erects a barrier, carefully observing its construction, trying to understand its true nature.

"You think the crows will come attack here?" I ask, popping another piece of toffee in my mouth as I sit on the edge of Dad's desk in his fancy office, raiding his candy dish. I toss the wadded-up wrapper at Warren.

He merely rolls his eyes and says, "Feel free to grow up any time."

"Doubtful," says my father. "They know better than to attack one of our fortified cities. No, by now, I suspect they're in the wind. They lost all the leverage they had when we recovered those hostages. Now they're just fugitives. Still, we can't be too careful. As long as Thorn's men have the sealing stone, underestimating them would be a grave mistake. That's why we're keeping everyone underground until this is over."

"Bummer," I say, hopping down and going to a bunch of old black and white photos in a big glass display case against one wall, containing framed pictures of construction workers, uniformed soldiers, and men in crazy looking wizard robes. One of them is Linus Draper, my grandfather.

"This is like some kind of secret society doomsday fallout shelter, isn't it?" I say, examining the dates on the photos. "You could probably ride out the end of the world down here."

"I like to think we've made it a little more comfortable than that," Dad says, "you might even enjoy your time here. We've got a movie theater, a roller rink, and even a shopping mall—if you can believe that."

"*My* time here? What are you talking about?"

He cocks his head to the side and gives me a funny look, like he's trying to read my mind.

"What are you—" he starts to say.

"I tried telling you, Dad. She isn't going to want to stay down here," says Elden.

"Whoa!" I say, "No, that's not happening. You can't honestly think—you are not going to lock me in a hole!"

"This is far from a hole. We're doing this for your safety. For heaven's sake, Bri, you were nearly killed!" Dad exclaims.

My blood boils as I shake my head, silently fuming. "Where's Aldrick?" I demand.

"Oh, c'mon," pleads Warren, "we're not keeping any secrets from you, this time. Why are you being like this?"

"Because I'm not like you! I'm not okay with spending my whole life inside your big, stupid bubble, stuck with the same people day in and day out, never going anywhere, or seeing anything new. If you want to live your life that way, then fine—go ahead, and do it. I wish you the best."

I've never seen my father and brothers so uncomfortable. They exchange skeptical glances, looking more offended than anything else.

The door swings open, and in walks Jonathan, having undoubtedly sensed an opportunity to gang up on me, to join the others in trying to convince me to stay here and rot in this dungeon.

"Stay out of this, Jonathan," I snap at him before he can open his annoying mouth.

He looks at the twins, then asks, "I take it she's not loving the idea of staying here?"

"Have any of you ever considered asking her what she wants?"

Every eye in the room locks on Aldrick, who gives me a sly smile as he strides to my side. I feel their judgment, see the disapproval in their faces—the utter disappointment in seeing me next to him. Yet in his presence, they bite their tongues. For once, they've found a way to keep their opinions to themselves. I could get used to this.

"If you don't want to stay here, what else did you have in mind?" Aldrick asks.

"Why can't *we* all just stay put somewhere. At least until Thorn's men are spotted." I say.

"Because I'm not taking the chance of losing you again. I can't let you go out there while those animals are still at large. We have no idea what they're capable of, what they're planning," Dad says, running his hands through his hair.

"Surely, you must have safehouses with tunnel access?" Aldrick says to Dad.

"Yes, but I wouldn't call them safe anymore. These are our former allies we're talking about—they know all the locations. They'll have the element of surprise on their hand."

"And I don't suppose you plan on letting my family reside within your walls?"

"Well, no, we'd figured you'd make your own arrangements. No offense, but I don't think that would go over too well with my people, asking them to keep their children among vampires."

"What the hell, Dad! You're kicking them out?"

"It's okay, Brielle," Aldrick says, "I would do the same in his position. After all, he has a responsibility for his people, a burden with which I am most familiar. However, I might suggest that Lucas is forgetting that you no longer fall under his purview."

"Excuse me! That's *my* daughter you're talking about. She lives under my roof!"

"No, Dad. He's right," I say calmly. "And so are you...about the dangers out there. But I'm *not* staying locked up anymore. I can't. I won't live like this for the rest of my life."

"There is one safe house that might be a suitable compromise. It's close to town, outside the wards, has tunnel access," Jonathan says. "It has a lot of windows, but on the plus side, you'll be able to see them coming from any direction. If we need to evacuate, we can alert the crows, let them come and deal with their own."

These supernatural beings and their tunnels.

Dad shakes his head. "I am not going to hang you out like bait!"

"We'll go with her," Elden says.

"Six vampires and three mages against what's left of Thorn's crew?" Warren adds, "Dad, that's not bait. That's a bear trap."

"Are we all in agreement?" Jonathan asks, followed by a long silence.

"I still don't like it," Dad says, "but sooner or later, I suppose I will have to face the fact that I can't always be there to keep you away from the evils of the world." He rises from his chair, walks to Aldrick, and extends his hand.

"Take care of my daughter," he says.

Aldrick grabs his hand and shakes it. "On my honor."

What in the world was that?

"Cool. Glad that's settled," Jonathan says in a dry tone. "Now, if you all don't mind, I'm going to go grocery shopping and meet you guys there."

27

"I KNOW YOU'RE PISSED, Bri, but it's not as bad as you're making it seem," Elden coaxes.

"You couldn't have warned me that everyone in the whole town would be there?"

"The spell will only let us reveal so much—"

"Just shut up and get out," I say, sandwiched between the twins in the dreaded middle seat.

"Isn't this what you wanted? No more lies, no more secrets?" asks Warren, trying his darndest to minimize my humiliation as he exits the vehicle.

I refuse to acknowledge his question, scooting out from the back seat of the car into the scorching midday sun. The air is positively stifling, thick and heavy in my lungs as I squint through my newly acquired pair of designer sunglasses—courtesy of Mom's glove compartment—at the absolute monstrosity of a house which stands before me.

Set upon a hill, surrounded by miles of flat and lifeless terrain in every direction, the peculiar structure has a clinical appearance, all hard angles and concrete with random bits of discolored metal and several tall, slender windows. It's...*hideous*, the antithesis of everything a house should be. Dad must have sent us to the ugliest place they had, figuring I'd take one look at it and beg to be taken back to their mage dungeon.

Not happening.

I throw the car door shut right as Jonathan's busted green Miata pulls in beside us, top down, worn brakes screeching in protest. He sports a Van Halen T-shirt and jeans, looking more like the fresh-out-of-high-school boy than the all-powerful arch-mage as he hops over the side of the car like a wannabe movie star.

Nearby movement catches my eye, and I blink and look again at the lone, crispy tumbleweed that rolls past me on the hot breeze before continuing its unhurried pace into the desolate plains.

"Why are you refusing to talk to us?" Elden asks.

"I'm pissed off. At both of you," I say with a measured voice, too drained for a heated exchange, then release a long, slow breath as the oppressive sun beats down on my shoulders.

What could have convinced me to leave behind the beauty of the forest to return to this god forsaken, dust-blown hellhole? A tingle at the back of my neck alerts me to his presence, as if in answer to my thoughts. I turn my head to see Aldrick standing at the front door, scanning the horizon for threats, shrouded in his golden aura, and just like that, every wound, mistake, and sacrifice—everything that has led me to this point—all make perfect sense. I go to him, brushing off my brothers.

The twins are hot on my heels, still not ready to let this whole thing go.

"If we don't find a way to talk about it, we're never going to get past this—"

"Were you intentionally trying to set me up to go out with your mage buddies?" I ask without turning to face them, not slowing my stride. "Is that why you scared off every guy who talked to me? To try and keep your precious bloodline intact?"

Aldrick's head slowly turns to me. Seems *that* got his attention. Even though his helmet completely covers his face, I know the expression behind it, those beautiful eyes wide with amusement.

Warren laughs awkwardly, "Could we maybe talk about *that* another time—"

"Why? What's the big deal? Everyone in the freaking world already knows my business. You want to talk? Fine. Talk. C'mon, I want to hear you admit it."

"Okay, sure, we might have steered you toward our people, but that has nothing to do with any bloodline. It's the only other way you could have found out the truth," Elden confesses.

Aldrick opens the door and holds it for me to enter. A wall of cold air embraces me as I enter the cavernous foyer with vaulted ceilings and uncomfortable-looking couches. Every window has been covered. To the right is a large kitchen, separated from the living area by an island with a few low-back bar stools and a couple of cute pendant lights dangling an impractical distance.

"Move!" Jonathan calls from behind as he comes barreling through, arms loaded with overstuffed grocery bags that he dumps all over the island's countertop. I don't think he's ever taken two trips to the car in his entire life.

"Bri—" Warren says.

"Don't Bri, me! You've been playing stupid games my whole life. Do you think I'm just some pawn to be pushed around by you supernatural losers?"

"Can't we just chill?" Jonathan whines.

The smell of food hits me as he begins pulling foam clamshell containers out of a flimsy plastic bag, along with a little bag of limes, radishes, and small containers of salsa.

"We tried to chill, we had a vacation, and you ruined it with your secrets and *lies*."

"True. But there is one thing we didn't have on that whole vacation," Jonathan says.

"And what was that?" I ask, rolling my eyes.

"Tacos," he says, opening both containers and pushing them in our direction, a dealer peddling his wares. The smells of seasoned chicken and beef, and freshly grated cheeses fill the air. He's right about one thing...the food in the northwest was extremely bland compared to SoCal.

Aldrick vanishes from his spot, leaving nothing but a trail of flittering golden energy in his wake. I follow along to see it disappear into a hole in the middle of the living room floor, next to an open hatch. Probably the entrance to one of their beloved tunnels. Even in this small space, his speed doesn't cause a shift in the air, not the slightest sign of disturbance.

Everyone accepts Jonathan's heartburn-inducing peace offering, piling food onto fancy square plates he pulls from the cabinets. My brothers open chip bags as Jonathan reaches into a cabinet and produces a bottle opener, then pops the tops of several glass bottles of Coke. I bask in taste utopia as the cold air from the AC blasts around me.

"I can't take this; it feels like you blame us for everything," Elden blurts out, seemingly from nowhere, which causes Jonathan to throw his head back and drop his shoulders.

"I get it, I do," I say, sarcastically, "I can't imagine how difficult this must be for you. After all, *you're* the true victims here. Forced to lie to your human sister, to *conspire* against me in secret. How exhausting it must have been for you to keep me in the dark all these years. Having magic powers sounds like such a tough life."

"We didn't choose this, either!" Warren grits. "Our options were limited."

"Uh huh, sure."

"Telling you about magic wouldn't have solved everything, Bri. And you need to quit acting like it would have," says Elden. "You've always had a target on your back—"

"Elden, please don't," mutters Jonathan.

"She has a right to know!" he shouts at Jonathan, which takes me aback. I've not seen him get worked up like this since...I don't remember when.

"The news of your birth spread far and wide, *despite* our attempts at secrecy. You're the only girl ever fathered by a mage. Look at how far Derek and his cronies went to get to you. At some point, you need to grow the heck up and accept that you could never have had that normal life you always wished for. And *the second* you set foot out of the bubble you seem to hate so much, *something* will always be coming for you. That's not on us," Elden says.

"And yet, because we care about you, every time you run off, put yourself in danger—which you seem to love—we always end up getting roped into it," adds Warren. "It gets old."

"Then go home! Nobody asked you to come. You volunteered—"

"You're our sister!"

"Hey! Check this out," Jonathan's laughter breaks through the tension as he fires off the mini blowtorch in his hand, roasting a marshmallow skewered on a long fork. "Who wants s'mores?" His cheery tone and forced smile are admittedly infectious, but not enough to get this trainwreck back on track.

There's a beat of silence as I try to wrap my head around Jonathan playing the role of peacemaker. He used to throw in against me every time, acting like the third Draper boy. Not anymore. It's like he's becoming his own man.

"Yeah, I *am* your sister, and yet I've had a target on my back all my life and my own damn brothers couldn't find some way to warn me?"

"We took an oath—"

"Then you break it!" I yell at Warren, "That's what family is supposed to do! I would have found a way for you!"

"Guys! Just leave her alone," Jonathan says, "it's a lot to take in. Put yourself in her position for one minute, okay? She has good reason to feel the way she does. And maybe we're not blameless in all of this, maybe we could have done something differently? Well, guess what? It doesn't matter. What's done is done. The past doesn't matter as much as you think."

My next outburst dies in my throat as I glare at Jonathan. I desperately want to snap at all of them. Tear into each of these lying turds. But what difference does it make at this point? He's right. Nothing any of us says will change what's already happened. I shake my head and break away from the confrontation, walking towards the couch, but stop when I hear a muffled laughter echoing through the tunnel below.

A suited-up vamp leaps through the hatch, landing silently on the floor. Dane flicks his wrist, slamming the front door with a brush of his wind, and yanks his helmet off, revealing a head full of disheveled hair. One by one, the rest of the vampire family emerges from underground.

"What took you guys so long?" I tease, attempting to break through the tension in the room.

"We nearly became lost. It's a labyrinth down there," says Isen.

Without warning, my feet are scooped out from under me. Aldrick carries me over and drops onto one of the couches, sitting me sideways across his lap. He unlatches his helmet and removes it, and I get my first eyeful of his sharp fangs as he grins.

He goes to say something but is cut off when we both feel the phone vibrating in his pocket. He rolls his eyes, and pulls it out.

"What now?" I ask as he checks the message.

"It's from your father," he says, his brow furled and eyes narrowed. "He says Thorn's group has been spotted at a motel north of Reno. He wants me to head back immediately to go over preparations."

"Well *that* was quick—" Jonathan says, examining his phone.

"Should we pack up now?" Elden asks.

"What for? You know how long it takes us to make arrangements for field missions outside the territory. Once you bring the crows into anything, double that. And that's if the council will approve a resolution to cross into a red zone in the first place," says Warren through a mouth full of food. "I'd be surprised if we get there by next week."

"I'll go speak with Lucas and Alonso. Everyone should finish eating their lunches. Get comfortable. This could be good news," Aldrick says to the room, then looks at me. "I'll be back soon." His lips are on mine too briefly before he slides me onto the cushion beside him and gets up and turns to me. I crane my neck to meet his gaze as he runs a finger through my hair, tucking it behind my ear, his thumb brushing lightly across my cheek.

"I'll text you as soon as I know more," he says with a wink before fastening his helmet. As he goes to the open hatch, Aurelia and Sylvain approach him. They speak, but their voices are too low for me to hear. He nods, and the three descend into the tunnels. Gerard places a foot on the lid and shoves it closed, issuing a loud slam, then he grabs the remote and turns on a movie.

Elden clears his throat, "Bri, you should come and get some food before Jonathan eats it all."

"Save some room, I'm trying this new quick creme brulee recipe," Jonathan says with a smirk, pouring yellow goo into a dozen ceramic ramekins, "and you're going to be the first test subjects."

I pull up a barstool to the island and sit beside Elden. Other than the loud movie, it's quiet. Warren grows restless in his seat as the minutes pass.

"Just say what you need to say," I tell Warren.

He drops his taco back on the plate, takes a deep breath, and says, "I'm sorry. All the crappy stuff you went through growing up, the insanity on this vacation. I'm partly to blame for all of it. We all are. And you're right. I didn't even try to find a way to warn you."

I can't tell if I want to say something to make him feel better or lash out at him again. His voice is on the verge of cracking, so I know he means what he's saying.

"I wish I could go back and not push you, not constantly lie to you, not try to steer you one way or another without you knowing. We never gave you a choice. We just thought we knew better. Now that I think about it you might not have wanted to leave us so badly if we had just backed off. In the end, we were the ones that drove you away. We drove you right into the arms of a freaking vam—"

He cuts himself off, rubbing his face in frustration. He must have forgotten our current company for a moment.

"No. You don't get to take credit for that," I say with a smile, "that was me *and* Aldrick, searching each other out. I can't expect you to understand that now but try to think about it. The first moment of freedom I got in my adult life, I jumped in that car and drove to the edge of the world. *I* found him. I mean, well, maybe he found me first, I'm not sure. But my point is that yes, you did do everything you could have done to drive me away, but my choices were still my own. And if you believe in fate, which I'm beginning to, then it doesn't really matter anyway. This was always going to happen, all of it. And it all has a reason. Even if we can't see it, yet."

It's the way my life isn't in shambles whenever he's around. I need his presence. I crave him. I always felt like there was something missing, and I know now that he holds that missing piece. I only hope that I fulfill something similar in him.

"But I don't get it, you barely know him," Elden says with a confused look on his face. "Other than those few hours you ran off in the mornings, when did you spend time with him? It worries me. It's like you're just rushing into something—"

"You might be right. I could be making a huge mistake. Things could turn out badly. But they could also turn out amazingly. If those crow guys didn't come to ruin our vacation, I would still be there, meeting up with him, getting to know him like I should have been able to. And now that this whole thing is pretty much over, I plan to pick up right where we left off. I'll be wherever he is."

"Wait, you're not planning on going *back* to Washington?"

I just smile.

"Bri, that's insane!"

"No, it's not," I say, as a sense of melancholy washes over me. "Insane is knowing that you have one life to live and not living it because you're afraid. Like a turtle that never comes out of its little shell, or a mage that never comes out of its bubble." I chuckle, gesturing to them.

Jonathan snickers, "I can't wrap my head around this whole thing. Where *did* you meet up with him during those times? You just took a stroll in the park with a vampire?"

"The ocean was the first time. After I fell off the cliff. He rescued me. Then, the second time, he found me in the forest taking pictures of a doe and her fawn. The third time, *I* went out looking for him. I ended up following him down a dark alley," I say with a wistful grin as Elden chokes and sputters on the soda he is drinking. "The next was when he broke into my car—"

Dane's howl echoes off the empty walls, drowning out Gerard's chuckles.

"But that was the same day we met in the alley, after my fight with Dad. The next was just a quick meetup at the park. That was where he first detected the crows. And the last time was at Mom and Dad's cabin. Damn. You're right. We've barely spent any time together."

My stomach twists. Ugh. What's in this carne asada? A strange tingle ripples through me.

Huh.

I scan the room, looking over all six guys, but I detect no weird colors or visual distortions in the air, nothing that would explain this sudden *off* feeling.

"What is it?" Warren asks as he eyes me.

My ears suddenly need to pop, and it feels like there's a shift in the atmosphere around me. The air seems thinner, harder to breathe, like it's being sucked from the room. "Dane, are you doing something to the air in here?" I ask, getting up from my chair, nearly swooning with lightheadedness.

He only looks at me curiously and shakes his head no.

"You guys seriously don't feel that?" I ask, going to the dining room window to peek through the blinds. Nothing but clear blue skies as far as the eye can see. I've never felt this way before.

"Maybe you should lie down," Jonathan says, "I'll crack a window in the bedroom. You can take a nap. Can you guys turn down the movie?"

Gerard turns the TV off, which makes it easier to hear the ringing in my ears. I'm startled by the scrambling sound of the Holstens jumping to their feet, watching as they grab their helmets from the coffee table and slam them on.

"Can someone tell me what is going on?" shouts Elden.

"Will everyone please shut up!" shouts Dane, and dead silence follows.

"What is that?" asks Isen. "Sounds like...a tea kettle?"

"Oh God, it's the crows! They're here!" I scream, covering my ears to block out the high-pitched screeching. But it's useless. The sound comes from inside my head. I dive under the dining room table and scream, "This whole place is gonna blow!"

"What is she talking abou—"

The explosion comes from overhead, blasting wood and plaster into the living room as chunks of the roof crash onto the coffee table and couches. The blinding high noon sun pours in through the opening.

The house rattles again, and this time, little cubes of glass rain down around the table, glittering like thousands of diamonds in the sun.

Explosion after explosion blows out the windows above us, the sunlight streaming in through each new opening. Crows shoot in like bullets, their claws extended, zipping around the room, tearing the window coverings off and letting them fall to the floor. Within seconds, they have stripped the coverings from every window, high and low. My eyes widen with horror at seeing the three vampire brothers retreating to the only corner of the room still shielded from the sun's rays.

The crows swoop down, shifting into human form with green flashes of light, gathering in what used to be the living room.

A red glow attracts my eyes to the kitchen. Elden and Warren have shields, not big red spheres, but medieval-style shields made of energy on their left arms and long, glowing lances in their right hands. I hardly notice the strand of Jonathan's magic snaking across the kitchen floor until the bubble forms around me, trapping me under the table.

Someone kicks in the front door, and three more dark figures enter, all wearing dark tactical gear. At first, I think Aldrick and his parents have returned, but the cocky way they move reveals otherwise.

In all, I count nine bare-naked shifters in human form and three bad guy vampires. And one more odd thing, a strange glowing light emanating from the chest of one of the shifters—Thorn. Is that his *soul* I'm seeing?

"STOP!" Gerard yells.

This draws only laughter from the group, still protected by the stolen mage artifact.

"Well, it was worth a try," Gerard says, shrugging his shoulders.

Some of his crew starts clearing the debris from the middle of the room, uncovering the hatch entrance. The vamps toss a heavy-looking duffle bag to one of the crows, and as they throw open the tunnel's lid, two of them hop inside, taking it with them.

"Keep an eye on those mages," Thorn barks at the three vamps, "especially Goldilocks there. They so much as move a muscle, I want them and that sister of theirs past tense."

Why doesn't Jonathan just blast them right now? I don't understand why they're hesitating.

He then turns to the Holsten trio. "Three little vampires, cowering in the shade," he says, stepping toward them with his cronies. "What's the matter? Not so tough without your superpowers?"

"Are we going to do this, or what?" says Dane.

Gerard adds, "I must agree with my brother. As much as I appreciate a good villain monologue, I've heard it all before."

"No matter how it begins, it always ends the same," says Isen, a chilling, resolute calmness in his voice.

There's a loud explosion sound, distant and rumbling beneath me, getting closer, louder. Two crows come barreling out of the hatch, followed by a giant fireball. A shockwave spreads through the room, not even phasing the supernaturals. The table I presently cower under goes flying against the wall behind me—exposing my hiding spot. As I look up, I realize why my brothers haven't made a move yet.

Crows. Dozens of them. They're on every windowsill, on the chandelier, surrounding the hole in the ceiling, and circling above the house.

"Eyes in the sky," Thorn says, "create a perimeter. Nobody enters, nobody leaves." A few more crows take flight as he turns and gives me a toothy grin. "Sorry, sweetheart, but I don't think your boyfriend is gonna make it back in time."

"Enough showboating," growls Grey, "remember the plan. Let's go!"

Thorn gives him a sneer behind his back.

"Everybody ready?" Thorn shouts, and a chorus of crows squawks, caws, erupts, filling the room. If not for the shield around me, it would be deafening.

I look at my brothers' faces as they try to look strong, but I see the fear in their eyes. On the other hand, Jonathan seems eager for the action to begin—a devilish smile curling at the corner of his lips. I watch as not one, but several slender tendrils of energy extend from him like creeping fingers toward the battlefield, poised and ready to strike—his glowing red eyes unreadable. My God. If I didn't know him so well, I might think he's a dark sorcerer, commanding the very powers of hell.

"Well? What are you waiting for? Let's get this over with!" shouts Thorn.

28

PINNED INSIDE THE BUBBLE, all I can do is watch in horror as the swarm of crows descends like a black cloud, claws out, eager to rip us to shreds.

"No, no, no!" I scream, covering my eyes. I can't watch my brothers or Jonathan die.

Shrill shrieks of pain fill the air—not human, but avian. I open my eyes to a gruesome scene of blood-soaked feathers as Jonathan's red spikes lash out like rapid-fire scorpion stingers, piercing his opponents, tossing them against the walls. How is he controlling them all? There must be seven or eight moving independently. The few birds that breach his wall of death are intercepted by Warren and Elden, who move like warriors of old, swatting them away like *insects*.

A loud noise near my head shifts my focus to those attacking me. By now, they've realized I'm surrounded by an invisible barrier, but remain persistent, taking turns flying high and dive-bombing the bubble—each hit sounding like small rocks tapping a glass window.

I swallow hard as I observe the shield wavering unsteadily from the relentless barrage.

Back in the kitchen, there's a crashing sound and a flash of light as one of the asshole vamps bursts in through the window in Jonathan's blind spot. He doesn't even flinch. Warren pivots on his heel and throws his shield, *decapitating* the vampire, splattering a thick tar-like substance all over the white cabinets. The body falls lifelessly to its knees, then slumps on the tile floor, oozing black goo from the neck hole as Warren leaps over the island and retrieves his shield, posting up guard between Jonathan and the new opening.

The unexpected sound of raucous laughter draws my attention toward the giant hole in the roof. The Holsten brothers crawl on the ceiling like spiders, cracking the electrical cords from the pendant lights like whips, whacking airborne crows out of the sky.

But the fun and games don't last much longer. Crows begin punching through the wall behind the boys like cannonballs, narrowly missing them. They drop to the ground, and Jonathan forms a bubble over them. It doesn't seem like he can attack and shield simultaneously, but the crows don't give him a chance—if he drops the shield, he's dead.

It's at this point that everything goes sideways.

Without Jonathan's constant attacks keeping them on their toes, the crows take control of the battle. They swarm the Holstens, ripping them from the ceiling and tossing them into the middle of the room, in full sun, where they're encircled by a mob of shifters in human form. Even worse, most of the crows Jonathan hit with his attacks are not dead but merely wounded. As I think back to Grey, stabbed in the gut with a steak knife and walking it off the same day,

I count maybe five or six dead crows out of dozens, with even the injured ones still seemingly ready to fight.

So many crows have joined the great kitchen offensive that it's become a fluttering mass of feathers and flapping wings. Even my attackers relent in favor of joining the assault as Jonathan's shield over me weakens with every passing moment. Thank God the shifters don't know that. Yet.

Think, damn it. I can't focus, all I can think of is Jonathan, Warren, Elden being torn apart by those freaking birds...and after that, once Jonathan's shield falls...if I'm going down, I'm taking as many of these suckers out with me as I can. What I need is a weapon.

I search my surroundings for something I can use, a broken chair leg? Too light. A shard of broken glass? Tch. These things fly through windows for fun. I need *metal*. A smile tugs at the corners of my mouth when I see it, dangling from the hearth set: a wrought iron fire poker with a solid grip and a sharp end thingie.

The cool air wafts around me as the sound of fighting increases. My shield is dissolving, which means Jonathan's power is fading. I reach, feeling nothing but thin air. If there's still a chance of saving them...I sprint for the fireplace to snatch the fire poker, then turn back and charge straight at the kitchen.

"GET OFF OF TH—"

A burst of energy pulses through me, pushing me away, then pulling me in, disorienting me in a way nothing ever has. The crows in the kitchen are *gone.* So is Jonathan, the headless vamp corpse, no sign of my brothers, either. If not for a few feathers floating in the air, the blood, and a puddle of black goo, there would be no sign that they were ever here.

Slam. I'm tackled from my right. We crash into a hutch loaded with dinnerware with what feels like bone-crushing force, his arms like steel cables squeezing the breath out of my chest. The fire poker is in my right hand, but only my left arm remains free. I hand it off behind my back, gripping the shaft tightly, and jab the pointed end into his eye.

As soon as he loosens his grip, I break free and spin, bringing the fire poker up against the back of his head, embedding the hook into the base of his skull. Blood streams out of the opening, and down he goes, taking my weapon with him, his body shaking and trembling uncontrollably.

The shifters in the middle of the room erupt. I see why they're cheering as one of them hoists Isen in the air, hand around his throat, without his helmet. He beats on the shifter's arm, kicking and thrashing wildly. He seems helpless. Like all the strength has been drained from his body.

Wait a minute. That's *it*? All the sun does is make them as weak as a normal human?

In the corner of the room, I see that brilliant, shining orb again. Not a soul, but a pendant, hanging from Thorn's neck. He's surrounded. *Protected.* It's so obvious now that I don't know why it didn't occur to me before. That necklace must be the stolen mage artifact, but they all wear similar necklaces, so nobody can tell which is the real one. The stone stopping the Holstens from using their insane powers has been *right-freaking-there* this whole time.

Now, if there were only something I could *do* with this revelation. Because, as it is, I've already been spotted by several of the shifters, who exchange glances and give each other eyebrow raises and smug smiles as they wordlessly debate who gets the next shot at killing me. As a couple of them saunter toward me, my focus shifts to something even more terrifying.

A figure made of shadow takes form above Isen, floating in the air. It circles the crowd around Isen, looking down on the shifters, and I swear it stops when it sees me staring at it, looks right back at me and smiles, right as two others phase into existence on either side of it.

And then, it flips me off.

I try for the fire poker, but can't free it from the shifter's head, having somehow gotten my only weapon lodged in bone on its first use. They're closing in. The kitchen! There's always something sharp in a kitchen, I dart for it, tearing open drawers—silverware, kitchen gadgets, junk mail, nothing—a bright red reflection in the microwave commands my attention...

Now engulfed in a red energy that moves in waves like fire—mage stuff—two shiny silvery threads extend from each of his palms and stretch toward the approaching shifters. As these white strands of ethereal magic pass through the two men's chests, their faces first register shock, then become devoid of life as their bodies collapse to the floor.

It must be Jonathan.

The swirling energy gathers and grows, becoming brighter and more unstable around him. How can they not see it? It fills the room with its unnatural red light, then collapses into a ball about the size of a cantaloupe. It's so brilliant that I can hardly look at it...like he's holding *the sun* in the palm of his hand. And then, he lets it fall.

I don't know when he shielded me, again, but I'm glad for it this time more than any other. There's a blinding flash, followed by a red shockwave—a burst of magic—that sends the bodies of every shifter and vampire gathered in the middle of the room flying like ragdolls. Many of them go through the walls and end up outside.

The only ones in the room left standing are those he bub-bled—the Holstens and myself—as the shadowy figures touch down, materializing into Jonathan and my brothers. I smile wide, thinking that the battle is over, when he drops his shield over me and falters, Warren and Elden helping to support him. He looks *terrible.*

Angry shifters and vamps start piling in through the doors, and my heart sinks at the realization. This freaking fight isn't over by a longshot. All Jonathan did was—quite literally—level the playing field. And now our star player appears to need a break.

My brothers and the Holstens go on the offensive. One of them tosses Isen his helmet, and he joins the fray.

"Come on, come on, come on!" I whisper desperately to my-self, *don't be useless*! What the hell do I do, though? I stare at the block of kitchen knives. No. A flying bodies slams into the island, sending the cabinet flying open and several glass bottles of alcohol rolling across the floor. A vampire lands in a crouch in front of me, crushing one of the bottles, spilling liquor all over the floor.

Not a friendly vamp. A grody, animalistic growl comes from under the helmet, sending a shiver down my spine.

Isen flies over the island and lands atop him, then suplexes the not-nice vampire. The two roll away, fighting. He's still weak from the sun. He needs my help.

My eyes land on the towel hanging from the oven door handle, the pungent odor of spilled vodka filling my nostrils, and I get an idea—a horrible, stupid, and incredibly *painful* idea if anything goes wrong. I snatch the cloth and tear it in half, then use it to soak up some of the spilled spirits on the ground. I grab one of the fallen bottles with the widest mouth, unscrew the top, twist the cloth, and shove it in. Then, make one more.

I turn on the stovetops gas burners; they keep clicking but won't light... "Come on!" I yell. Please, if there's anyone up there...I need fire...

A manic smile tugs at the corners of my mouth as my eyes behold the mini-blowtorch Jonathan was using to roast marshmallows earlier, near the fridge, right where he set it down.

I snatch it from the counter and pull the trigger, unleashing its roaring blue flame with a loud click. With outstretched arms, I reluctantly bring the torch tip to the frayed edge of the fuel-soaked cloth, which instantly flares up, engulfed in bright, hot-orange flames. When the intense heat slaps me in the face, so does the realization that I have made a *terrible* mistake. I've got to get rid of this thing. Now. Without thought, I shove the torch in my pocket, my attention divided between the growls and pain-filled screams that fill the wrecked house and the Molotov cocktail in my right hand.

"Move!" I scream at Isen, who shoves the other vampire and scrambles to get away when he sees me coming with my haphazardly constructed implement of destruction. I hurl the burning bottle at the bad vamp's back. It explodes on contact, the resulting inferno devouring his upper body in flames that shoot up several feet. I don't wait for my shock or horror to take root. I can't afford to hesitate.

I snatch the other bottle from the counter and grip it under my arm as the vampire flails on the ground, ripping off his burning gear, which gives me an idea. I grab the ankle of the burning vampire's pants with one hand and start dragging him. My assumption is right, he's much lighter than a human.

"Go help them! I got this!" I shout as Isen jumps into the air, intercepting an incoming vampire before he can dissect me. I cough and choke at the nauseating smell of burning plastic and hair as I pull him over the threshold out into the sun. He kicks and struggles, growling inhumanly, clawing at his seared helmet, working at the latch. He breaks free of my grip and starts swinging indiscriminately at the air.

I take a few steps back and light it up. At the same time, he manages to get his helmet off. I pause for a second, arm raised, ready to throw—but only because I know this face, distorted as it is from the burns...remember his glee as he ordered all the women into lines, as they tazed us and herded us like cattle—a vampire from the hunt. Why would *he* be *here*?

Red eyes and bared fangs stare back at me, as he *hisses*...not a sound that human vocal cords can produce, but something else...something not of this world. How can Aldrick be the same species as these creeps? When he comes at me on all fours, I let him have it. He rolls and burns, twisting and contorting, making sounds that will haunt my nightmares forever. And then...he stops.

I did it. I, a *human*, have killed a vampire.

Unfortunately, I don't get a chance to celebrate my victory. Through the flames emerges a crow, who shifts into human form mid-flight, right before my eyes, landing with his hands around my neck. My feet fly out from under me as he lifts me clear off the ground, choking as he peers at me with his gray eyes, muscles flexing beneath his skin as he tightens his grip.

I reach into my pocket, then bring the lit torch to his face and shove the burning tip right up his nose. In terms of biology, I have no clue what that does to a person, and—judging from his reaction—I'm probably better off never knowing. He places his hands over his face and screams in agony, releasing his grip on me as I fall to the ground.

Stumbling and coughing, I see an opening, thinking back to the most illegal martial arts move I can come up with—and deliver the most brutal oblique kick I can directly to the side of his knee with the heel of my boot, attempting to break it. It feels like stomping a tree trunk. I narrowly avoid his backhand by ducking, which whiffs by me so quickly that I feel the wind, leaving me with little doubt that a single punch from this guy will leave me unconscious or dead.

Everything I've done up to this point has only made him angrier. Without the element of surprise or something heavy and sharp, or fire...there's no way for me to defeat them.

He stomps toward me, raising his fist, with a look in his eyes that suggests he's going to enjoy killing me. Before I can run away, he stops, the rage in his eyes fading into a cold nothingness, color draining from his cheeks, the expression melting away from his face as he becomes a corpse before my eyes. As he collapses, I see Jonathan standing behind him, his eyes glowing white, a silvery, glowing thread of light extending from his outstretched hand to the fallen shifter.

I hunch over, hands on my knees, feeling like I'm gonna hurl. He moves his eyes to the crispy corpse of the vampire, then back to me.

"You...ripped out his soul?" I ask.

He nods, as he grabs my arm and says, "Come on. I'm getting you out of here. They're going to hold them off as long as possible."

"No!" I say. "I'm going back in. I need you to cover me."

"We're outnumbered. We can't win!"

"Yes, we can! We need to get the artifact. I know where it is!"

"You can see it?"

"Yes, moron, now put your shield on me and get out of my way."

He hesitates, running a hand through his hair, huffing out his anxiety.

"Quit wasting time! Bubble me!" I shout. "I'm going in."

Surrounded by red energy, I storm through the chaos, forcing my way through the crowd, bodies bouncing off Jonathan's shield, searching for that shimmering star of light, which leads me to Thorn.

"Well, boys, what do we have here?" he jeers. "Sorry, sweetheart, but we're done with the whole 'take me instead' thing."

"NOW!" I shout, and he gives me a weird look, since only I see the shield dropping. I grab his shimmering necklace, yanking it clear off him. There's a moment of shock from him as my shield falls back into place, and he lunges at me, hitting a solid barrier. I smile fiendishly when I see that he realizes how screwed he is.

"Get her! Now!" I hear him growl over the cacophony surrounding me.

As I bolt for the door, I see the twins holding steady, fighting side-by-side with the Holstens atop the kitchen island, looking confused as all hell as I rush across the room with the necklace, laughing. I fly out of the front door, passing a waiting Jonathan, and my shield dissolves. I hear chaos behind me, glancing over my shoulder to see him erecting a massive red wall.

"Run!" he screams.

And run I do, straight down the road we came here on, with everything I have in me—and then some. No one ever told me the artifact's exact reach, but I should be out of range by now.

Off in the distance, on the horizon, I see a glint of light, like the sun reflecting on a windshield. Only brighter. Even farther in the distance, over the tops of the mountains, a mass of black dots fills the sky. It looks like birds...hundreds of them. More crows?

Oh, *God*.

The gleaming, golden light moves faster than any car, like a blazing star shooting across the desert. There's only one thing I know of that can move that quickly.

Aldrick.

Come on, please!

A deep rumbling shakes the ground under me, accompanied by a sound like an oncoming train, as the wind suddenly picks up. My hair and dress whip in the direction of the house. I glance over my shoulder at the house and fall to my knees when I see it embroiled in a twisting wall of dust and debris, as the roof flies off into the sky.

Dane has created a tornado.

Furniture, parts of the house, and bodies are thrown through the air, tumbling and reeling out of control, with flashes of green inside, as some of the shifters turn back into crows, struggling in vain to break free of the pull of the monstrous twister.

There's something like green lightning within the clouds, and a handful of crows break through and start heading straight for me, moving in formation. I see another burst of green energy, then another...each time they get closer. No, no...not closer, the crows are getting *bigger*.

"Dammit!" I say, scrambling to my feet, shoving the stone in my dress pocket.

Aldrick is much closer now. His tall and beautiful form is still covered and safe from the sun's rays, engulfed in his heavenly aura, as he runs to me. There's no way to tell him I have the artifact until it's too late, until it strips him of all his power.

Jonathan's words return to me, that I'm his weakness. His *weakness*. That no matter what I do or how hard I try, I'm going to be the death of him. I don't want it to be true. But in this moment, it seems like it will be.

I hear the flapping of their pterodactyl wings, feel them getting closer, ready to swoop down at my exposed back. At this rate, I may never reach Aldrick; so near and yet so damn far. I don't need to see these winged behemoths to know it's a fight I can't win. There's no point turning to face them, just as there's no way to outrun them...I don't see a way to win.

Sharp talons sink into my shoulders, cutting into muscle, hitting bone. The shock steals my breath as my feet lift off the ground. I reach up, trying to pry the claws out of me as the heavy wingbeats pull us higher into the air.

An earthshattering growl erupts from the incoming bullet of a vampire, unleashing a shockwave of energy as he leaps through the air. The next thing I'm aware of is a horrific, unnatural crunching sound coming from the crow, spinning wildly in the air like an out-of-control carnival ride, an agonized death knell as it releases me from its clutches. I tumble weightlessly, blood streaming from my open wounds as I fall to the ground.

I slam hard into a pair of arms as Aldrick catches me, but then those arms are gone, leaving me to fall the last few feet, landing on the ground hard enough to knock the wind out of me. I roll to my side to see him inside one of their beaks—giant mutant crows, so far from anything in nature that they don't even look real, possessing an uncanny quality, like animatronic abominations conjured forth from the abyss. Nearby, an armless shifter hits the ground headfirst, folding over into a scorpion position, followed by two severed, enormous black wings.

Aldrick breaks free of the bird's grasp and falls to the ground, rolling and dodging their pecking, stabbing into the solid ground like steel. They manage to snag one of his arms, then the other, and pull them apart, forcing him to his knees.

"No!" I scream as I get up, my vision blurring in and out, my body already going into shock.

"Oh, yes," says Thorn from behind me. I turn to strike, but he catches my fist in his hand, then punches me square in the gut. All the air leaves me, my lungs seize, and I collapse onto the ground, heaving.

More crows land around us. In the distance, I hear my brothers screaming my name.

"We don't have long, so we're gonna make it count," Thorn says. "Get her up. She's gonna watch this."

Grey's hand wraps around my throat and pulls me to my feet, then spins me and holds me against him. "Remember this?" he asks, holding up a steak knife where I can see it, its wooden grip stained with blood—the same one I stabbed him with at the cabin. He kept it all this time.

"Everyone," Thorn says, "may I present to you..." He unlatches Aldrick's helmet and rips it off. "The Demon of Bremen!" Another behemoth crow circles overhead and lands behind Aldrick, folding its wings and taking its position behind him.

"No, please!" I choke out.

"Sorry, sweetie, but he said it himself. So long as he lives, he'll keep hunting us."

"Don't you touch her," Aldrick growls.

"We know, we know...you'll burn the whole world down. We get it," Thorn says, sounding more tired than anything else. He looks at the crows coming in the distance, then back in the direction of the house. There's fear in his eyes. I can tell things aren't going the way he planned. It gives me hope.

"Finish it. We need to get the hell out of here." he says. "Looks like Alonso sent in the cavalry."

My heart thuds and my blood runs cold as the crow behind Aldrick positions its open beak over his head. No, no, no. This can't happen! I squirm and fight against Grey, not even caring about the knife that he presses harder and harder into the side of my neck.

"I'm so sorry I ever showed up at those cliffs, it's my fault you're here. You should have just let me drown," I say as my throat tightens.

He's going to die, after surviving for centuries. All because of one stupid human girl. Because of *me*.

Thorn approaches me, a look of withering contempt on his face. His eyes move down to the leather cord of his necklace, dangling from the artifact in my pocket.

"No," he says softly, at peace, as if having already accepted his fate. "It took me this many lifetimes to find you, and even though our time together was brief and marked by so much pain... I would gladly do it all again."

"It's not over, you ass!" I say, my eyes becoming blurry with unshed tears. I can't let this happen to him. I won't let it.

A small, indulgent smile forms on his perfect lips. "It's never *over*, because death is not the end—I'll find you in the next life...my love."

"Touching," says Thorn, sneering and shaking his head with disgust as he ties the artifact back around his neck. "Now can we rip his fucking head off, already. We need to leave five minutes ago."

The creature standing over him rears back its gargantuan head, opening its beak wide, exposing the hideous red insides of its fleshy, gaping maw as it prepares to strike.

Something moves within me, just beneath the surface. Rising. Waiting.

The last vestiges of magic in my blood, though not my own, still heed my call. I know what I want from it, what I need for it to do. I reach my outstretched hands toward him, willing the purple energy that appears from my fingertips toward him, praying that it will be enough.

When the crow strikes, I avert my eyes, unable to watch it happen, not willing to spend the rest of my life—short as it may prove to be—with the image of the man I love being killed seared into my mind.

I still feel his presence, like he's next to me. I snap my head forward and see Aldrick, unharmed, his body surrounded by a paper-thin membrane of glittering, violet magic—my magic—as the goliath crow tries to crush him. I did it. I *actually* freaking did it. I made a shield. What else can I do? I think back to what Jonathan did in the house, releasing the burst of raw force that put everyone on their asses. That's what I need, and I need it right, freaking, now.

I put everything I have, everything I've ever had and everything I ever *will* have into that shield. At least Aldrick will be protected from the blast.

I let go of my grip on it. The magic does the rest.

The crow that was biting Aldrick gets the worst of it, since the epicenter of the explosion was inside its mouth, its head splitting open down the middle. The two that hold his arms in place are thrown some fifteen feet back from him. I don't know where Thorn or the others end up, all I know is that I pick up my feet, becoming dead weight right before the blast strikes me, allowing me to slip out of Grey's sweaty, oily grip.

Using that opportunity, I lunge for Aldrick's nearby helmet and chuck it to him. Thorn is the first back on his feet, emerging from a wall of dust, running straight for me. He pulls me up to use my body as a human shield as Aldrick latches his helmet.

My vision tilts, I my skin feels cold even under the summer sun. There is blood dripping off my arms. Something is really wrong with me.

"Make one more move, Holsten, and I'll slit her ear-to-ear!" he says, flashing the knife, sounding crazed and desperate. The two enormous crows attack him again, barely visible in the cloud of fine sand that envelops us. Aldrick leaps straight at one and kicks in the beak hard enough that it cracks, sending splinters of shattered bone flying. The mutant bird's screech of pain makes my skin crawl as he lands, then sprints at the other and slides underneath its beak just as it snaps—issuing a sound like a gunshot as he moves under it, sliding on his back, he throws out his fists into its thin legs, releasing a sound like a falling tree snapping—causing the hideous beast to collapse, warbling, groaning.

Both birds shift back into human form, rolling on the ground, writhing in pain, and cursing him.

"What are you doing? Take him out!" Thorn screams.

But nobody else steps forward to fight Aldrick. Instead, many shift to crow form, deserting Thorn, leaving him with only a handful of fighters, all too paralyzed with fear to step up.

Aldrick starts coming our way, his wide steps quickly covering the distance between us, never breaking his stride—showing no signs of hesitation whatsoever. Thorn, on the other hand, keeps backing up.

"Stay away! I swear to God, I'll do it. I said—"

Aldrick grabs the whimpering Thorn's knife hand and pries it away, allowing me a chance to break free. I fall to my knees, drained and delirious. Behind me, there's a wet crunch, a strained grunt, followed by a squelching noise. I feel the earth pattering like someone's dumping liquid on the ground. I turn on my knees and gasp in horror as I behold the gruesome scene.

My eyes track upward along his outstretched arm to see it, held high in the air—like a trophy—Thorn's heart in his hand. Still beating.

He just ripped out a heart.

Like a proper vampire.

I collapse onto my back, swooning from the blood loss, rubbery limbs no longer able to support my own weight. Thorn's men turn tail, run for their lives, and take to the air, only it's far too late. Alonso's forces eclipse the sky above me, swooping in, seizing them with their talons and tearing them to pieces.

Aldrick kneels beside me and casts the fleshy lump aside, I watch as it rolls along the desert floor, gathering a clumpy layer of brown earth on its slick surface. Dust to dust. He removes his helmet and sets it aside, surveying the damage to my body as dead crows and severed limbs rain down from the sky.

"No, the sun!" I choke out.

"Shh..." he says, removing his gloves, gently slipping a hand beneath my head. There's pain in his eyes, but it's overshadowed by something else. I try to decipher it as the edges of my vision darken and the sweltering day becomes cold.

I only rest my eyes for a moment, but when I reopen them, there's a group of mages surrounding me. When did they get here? When did they put the blanket over me?

"Stay with me," Aldrick commands, his voice like rolling thunder, and his hand caressing my cheek.

"Where else would I go?" I eke out, confused.

"Hey," Jonathan says to me, snapping his fingers softly, demanding my attention, "I'm going hold on to your soul for a little bit, just to make sure you stay put. If you see anything...weird, ignore it. Keep your eyes on me, kay? We're bringing in a healer, it's only going to be a few minutes."

Jonathan's eyes are white, again; silver strands of ghostly energy extend from his palms, entering my chest. Oh, my. That *is* weird. The feeling is indescribable, almost like—

"Mother, can't you at least try? She's bleeding out."

"You know the risks. You might be willing to accept them, but is she?"

"Why don't we just *change* her?" Isen asks.

"No!" the mages *snap* in unison.

Like before, the world around me becomes gray and muted as they bicker around me. And then, I see it. Warm and inviting. It overwhelms me, like the smell of freshly baked apple pie, warm sunny days beside the pool, putting on a fresh pair of socks right out of the dryer. Everything bright and lovely and pure is calling to me.

"No, no, no, no! Damn it, Brielle! Open your eyes!" Jonathan says, shaking my shoulders, "The light is not your friend!"

I'm looking right at him. What is he talking about?

"Mother…"

"They're just over the hill. We only need a few minutes!" Jonathan cries.

"Mother, it's the only way," Aldrick pleads.

"…understand, my son," Aurelia says, sternness in her voice, "I will *not* be held responsible for what comes of this." She sits on the ground beside me, crossing her legs. I can't see her face through the helmet's visor, only my own reflection as she removes one of her gloves, lifts the edge of the blanket and then pauses.

"Forgive me," she says, then lightly touches my wrist with the tip of a finger.

Electricity shoots through my entire body, as if every molecule has been sent into overdrive. I open my eyes, only now realizing that I've been unconscious, lingering in the in-between, Jonathan was able to keep my soul here, but my body is rejecting me. I feel every wound, every cut and gash, every fractured bone, but I'm too weak to scream.

Delirium, or something like it. I wonder…perhaps this is what hell is like? The sound of tires crunching on the dirt. Doors opening, voices. The next moments are a hallucination, a blur of the most intense sensations possible, a full-body migraine.

"Wake up, Ms. Draper," a woman says softly, as the ringing in my ears subsides.

"I've been awake," I say, eyes closed. At least I think I was.

She raises an eyebrow. "How are you feeling?"

319

"Like every bone in my body has been taken out and shoved back in."

"Sounds unpleasant," she says. "Not surprising, though, given the extent of your injuries and the...*questionable* aid you received before I arrived."

A metal roof has now replaced a sky filled with circling crows. Based on how things jostle and bounce, and the equipment surrounding me, I'm in the back of a military ambulance. I follow the tube hooked up to my arm to a blood bag hanging overhead.

"Mage blood?" I ask.

She follows my eyes and smiles, "Only the finest. You should know that we've transfused over half your blood volume. You're more other people than you, now."

Ms. Driscoll sits beside me, strapped into the chair's harness, arms out, both her hands hovering above my body. It's so strange to see her again, only hours later, under such different circumstances. Her eyes are closed in deep concentration. Fine, feathery threads of magic flitter out of her hands, moving across my injuries.

"I've always enjoyed this," she says with a slight grin. "Unfortunately, you don't get the chance to work with wounds this deep very often. Very challenging. I'm afraid there will be some visible scarring, but I'll do my best."

"Glad I could be of service."

"They told me that you used magic for the first time. Very exciting! A word of advice? Never use all of it the way you did. You risk spending the very energy that keeps you alive."

"There was no other option. I was dead either way."

"Yes, well, my advice as a medical professional would be that you avoid situations like that in the future. For your health."

When I think we've arrived at a hospital, the back doors open, revealing our driveway. They brought me home? They help me into the house and sit me on the couch.

"Wait, that's it?"

"Your injuries are completely healed, Ms. Draper," she says, wiggling her fingers with a theatrical flourish. "I would dare say that's quite enough." She turns and departs.

"See, I told you it would work," Jonathan yells, passing Ms. Driscoll in the entryway, socking Warren's arm as they both try to squeeze through the front door simultaneously. "All that freaking out for nothing. Mom is losing her mind."

"She's *here*?"

"No, she's underground with Lucas. The council is in full damage control mode after the underground bombs went off. People in the neighborhoods thought we were having an earthquake. Oh, and then there was the tornado. You know, Six Flags is right over the hill. People riding the rollercoasters probably saw something."

"Where's Elden?"

"They needed to take him to our version of the emergency room. He's still with the healers," Warren says, looking ho-hum.

My heart thuds. "Wait, how bad is he hurt? What happened?"

Jonathan shrugs. "He'll live. Everyone got banged up," he says, lifting his shirt to show several deep bruises across his midsection. "Battle wounds."

I'd forgotten how good it feels to roll my eyes at his nonsense.

Someone pounds several times on the front door and shouts, with a voice like a military drill sergeant, "Pembroke, Draper, we have a debriefing in ten minutes. Let's go."

"Catch you later," Jonathan says.

Warren half smiles. "Feel better."

When the house is empty and quiet, with everyone in town but me attending to important mage business, I shower off the blood and change into my favorite pajamas.

As I'm watching TV, while eating a tub of ice cream, I sense Aldrick's presence. I turn, leaning over the arm of the couch with my chin on my knuckles, watching as he enters silently through the front door, helmet under his arm. The surprised look on his face is priceless. So, he *does* sneak up on me on purpose. We lock eyes from across the room, but neither says anything for a few breaths. There are no words that seem to fit.

"How are your brothers?"

"No worse for wear," he says, coming over, placing his hands on the back of the sofa, and leaning in, looking me over as I twist to meet his gaze. I bite the edge of my lip and squint lightly, trying to order my thoughts.

"How, though? How did any of us make it out of there?"

He gives a crooked smirk and nods. "My brothers...they may seem young, immature, and at times, even silly, but don't let them fool you. They are strong, adept warriors, especially when they're together." He smiles proudly. "From the very beginning, I trained them *not* to rely on their gifts."

The silence looms, heavy with expectation. There are too many questions to ask, too many things that need to be said. Much of what once seemed simple no longer is. But I need to start somewhere.

"There's something that's been driving me crazy. The sun. What does it do to you?"

"Hmph. When the light of day touches our skin," he says, "we are stripped of all our power, losing our strength, speed—even our immortality."

"Does it hurt?"

"No, in fact, that's the worst part of all. It feels...pleasant. But it is our one and only weakness, the part of the curse that has always kept us in the shadows."

I place a hand on my throat... "Thorn's men, are they all dead?"

"Every last one."

"Why was one of the vampires from the hunt here?"

He circles the couch and plops down. I lift my feet and place them in his lap. He runs his hand over my shin.

"They wrote us a strongly worded letter, said that rescuing you the way we did violated the *spirit* of the games. They declared it an insult, a betrayal of our kind, of the old ways."

"So then, we're still in danger? Sorry, I'm confused."

"There's always danger. Over the years, my family and I have accumulated quite an impressive list of enemies. There are many who wish death upon us. Now, that list will only grow. Our union represents an unprecedented alliance between vampires and magekind, and for his daughter's safe return, Alonso has vowed to send aid whenever we call."

"What does all this mean? For us?"

"It means we've become one of the most powerful factions in North America."

"That's great, right?"

"It certainly holds promise, but with power comes conflict and responsibility. We will be forced to make difficult choices. The first of which...how to respond to this attack. What message do we want to send?"

His face is alight as he speaks without any detectable trace of boredom. I think back to what the boys said. There would always be something after me, some enemy of Aldrick's coming to exact revenge, using me to get to him. From the looks of it, he would love nothing more than to spend the rest of eternity in glorious battle.

I wanted to break out of my bubble, to live life my way. To be out there, wild and free beyond the prison bars of my little world. So does that mean I have to spend the rest of my life fighting?

"I just want to know when this will all be over."

He gives me a warm, reassuring smile. "For now, it is."

29

Dinner at the Draper household has never been more awkward.

I sit at the head of the table, near Aldrick, who shares one side with his three brothers, Dad and the twins opposite them. Mom sits at the other end, arms clamped tightly across her chest, glaring at me with subdued rage. I feel the hurt seeping out of her, spreading like a heavy blanket over the dining room. She must have seen my packed suitcase at the foot of the stairs.

The front door slams, followed by Jonathan's big feet loudly stomping through the house. He places a stack of five pizza boxes in the center of the table, his wide grin retreating after one glance at Mom as he takes the only remaining chair to my left.

The guys serve themselves enthusiastically while the Holstens remain unnervingly still. Nobody says a word.

"Well?" Mom challenges, leaning in, eyebrows raised—daring me to respond.

"Well, what?"

She scoffs loudly, rolling her eyes with exasperation. "When were you planning on telling me?"

"I *guess* I didn't make myself clear enough, but...yes, I am going back with Aldrick."

"You barely know him!" she erupts, "You just got home this morning, and now what? You're flying back?"

"After dinner, yeah. Look at them. They need to get somewhere safe and rest. There's no reason for us to stay longer."

"You freaking *died* today!" She slams her fist on the table, rattling the plates.

"Don't overexaggerate—"

"Do you have any idea what it's like to be told that your own daughter's heart stopped beating?"

"Technically, Bri's right. Her soul never left her body," Jonathan mutters, angling his face away from her wrath.

"See, Mom? I was fine," I say, lifting a slice of pizza onto my plate.

"She's been set on leaving since she was a kid," Elden says, not looking away from his plate.

"You don't think you're skipping a step here?"

"Wait...what are you thinking this *is*? Because I'm—"

"So, you're *not* moving in with him, hmm?"

I turn to Aldrick, the look on my face a silent plea for help.

"Not at all," he says, clearing his throat, "In fact, that's precisely what we came here hoping to discuss. Brielle's new title, that is as Ashland's Emissary. If we are to have formal dealings between us, we are in need of someone to act as a liaison between our territory and yours. Your daughter is in a unique position, you see. Mage by birth, friend of crows, and soon to be—"

"A vampire?" snickers Jonathan.

"—a member of our coven," Aldrick says.

"Who? Me?"

"Who else would be a better fit?" Dane asks.

"She can be counted on to represent all sides, fairly," Gerard adds.

"Besides, she can't exactly rejoin the human world," Isen murmurs.

Mom looks unconvinced.

"Seriously?" I ask. It seems too good to be true.

"I promised you that you would have the life you wanted. It comes with good pay, a place of your own, and a car—no strings attached. We can fly here a few times a month," Aldrick says.

"They can stay here with us. We have the spare bedroom," says Dad.

"You're okay with this?" Mom asks, surprised at Dad's response.

"She's an adult, Evelyn. She can make her own choices. And if there's anything we've learned, it's that she's impervious to our control."

Dang. Dad dropped the full first name on Mom. This is getting intense.

"Fine, whatever...but why does she have to leave *tonight*? I don't get what the big hurry is if all they're going to do is sleep."

"Because I want to. Go with him, that is."

Mom looks around the table, seeking a sympathetic face. When she finds none, she leans back, dropping her shoulders, unable to garner any support for her crusade against my independence. For once, she is defeated.

"I still need to introduce her to the members of our coven, show her around, let her get acquainted with how we do things. We're only taking her away for two weeks. You won't even notice her absence."

"I don't know…it makes me nervous," Elden says with a smirk.

"Yeah, things might actually be peaceful around here," adds Warren.

"Har, har."

Jonathan pulls out his phone.

"There's one thing I still don't understand," I say, eyeing the device in his hand, then looking to Dad. "Before the attack…you texted Aldrick, said Thorn's group was north of Reno. How did you guys get it so wrong?"

"That message wasn't from me."

"I saw it with my own eyes."

"*Someone* sent it. I still don't understand all the details, but my tech guys tell me it's not that hard to pull off with the right tools. I still can't believe a band of rogue shifters was that sophisticated."

"Thorn's forces were nothing but a bunch of thugs," Gerard says. "It's whoever helped them plan this assault that has me concerned."

"They hit us in every blind spot we had," Lucas says, ruminating.

"You guys were pretty badass in that fight, though," Jonathan says, raising a plastic tumbler to the Holsten brothers. "I might even say I had a good time, you know, if our opponents were wearing clothes."

All the men chuckle.

"At one point, I got slapped across the face. That pissed me off. Who does that? But when I looked down, it was a disembodied arm that hit me. It's gonna be a while before I get that out of my head," Elden recounts.

"Did you guys get a good look at that giant mutant bird thing?" asks Warren.

"Must have missed it. I was too busy saving your necks," says Jonathan, grinning.

"Lucky you," I say, *fully* expecting them to become recurring characters in my nightmares.

"I did see the carcass of the vamp Bri took down, though," Warren says. "Hey Mom, get this: she made a Molotov cocktail out of random stuff from the kitchen." He laughs. "See? Told you GTA wasn't a bad influence on us. All those years of stressing out for nothing."

The mortified look on mom's face mirrors my sentiments. I recall the scene in flashes, trying to shove the memory down—his screams, the smell. That one will haunt me for years to come.

"Damn. Looks like I'm taking a few slices to go," Jonathan says, looking back at his phone.

I wonder who keeps blowing it up.

"Why?" Warren asks.

"Ember wants me to come pick her up. She says she doesn't want to stay another night with that woman. Can't blame her, neither would I."

He's never referred to his own mother as mom, only Naomi. He reserves that title for our mom.

"You guys are always welcome here," Dad says.

"Thanks, but I think we're going to spend the first night in the new place."

"Do you even have furniture in there?"

"Not yet, but it wouldn't be our first time sleeping on the floor."

"Jonathan? No! You guys, go get the air mattresses." Mom orders Warren and Elden out of their seats. They look at each other and shrug before disappearing through the garage door.

"I appreciate it, I'll stop over and grab them when we get back," Jonathan says as he heads for the door. "Thanks for everything, guys," he calls out over his shoulder on the way out.

Ugh. He *knows* I'll be gone by the time he gets back, and he's not going to say anything? What a little punk. My chair legs squeak as I rapidly leave the table. I need to jog to catch up to him on the front lawn.

"Wait!" I shout.

He turns, looking surprised and confused.

Neither of us seem sure of why I'd just chased him down as we squint at each other beneath furrowed brows. Maybe it's because he's become more than just my brothers' annoying best friend. He became my annoying best friend, too.

"What?" he says, looking at me like I'm crazy.

"You've been with me for, like, the whole last month. A lot of stuff has happened."

"And?"

"And...I just thought I would say...bye."

He scoffs. "You're not going away for that long. You'll be back soon enough. Gah—"

He grunts as I wrap my arms around him and say, "I know. But still, thank you for being there for me...and...I'm sorry. That it took me this long to see how crappy I was to you."

He snorts and wraps his arms around me in a tight embrace.

"It's not a big deal—"

"I should have treated you better, and I hope you can forgive me one day."

I let him go and back up, his face is carefully controlled, his eyes narrowed.

"Enough mushy shit. I'll see you soon."

"Whatever. Oh, I need you to promise me one thing, though," I say, smiling.

"And what would that be?"

"That you go to a doctor and get that damn sleep apnea fixed before it takes you out. I need my soul-sucking mage in tip-top shape. From the sounds of things, I'm probably going to need your help again."

"You are so annoying," he groans as he turns to leave, throwing out two fingers in a peace sign.

I don't understand what I'm feeling. How do I reconcile my perpetual annoyance at the Jonathan I knew with these newfound feelings of admiration? It's too late to get to know the kid who was hiding under all those secrets, the boy long since turned into the man walking away from me now.

I watch him climb into the minivan. And just like that, he's gone.

30

LAKE CRESCENT

THE PENCIL IN MY hand stills against the page of my sketchbook.

There's a subtle stirring, a shift in the world. Warmth, like a dying fire, has been rekindled. Confirmation of something about which I was previously uncertain, but now I know—I can sense his essence. The only question that remains: is it his magic I've become so attuned to or his *soul*?

When we arrived last night, taken the turn off down a dark, familiar road, I was confused why we seemed to be returning to the dock from weeks prior. But instead of going down the slope, we continued straight, leading to a lakeside cabin. Turns out, it had been one of his properties all along. That was how he'd known nobody else would be around.

I sit in a wooden chair on the deck of Aldrick's—*my* lake house, my eyes tracing the tips of the trees on the mountain across the water. The sun dips below the horizon and out of sight, bringing a chill to the air as I fold my sketchbook shut. This scene will still be there tomorrow.

"At the bookstore," I say to Cora, seated beside me, breaking the long silence between us, "you said you wouldn't see me for a while. Did you know what was going to happen?"

"You think I'd have let you nearly *die*? No, I didn't know *exactly* what was to come. I just saw how protective he was being with you, so I tried to look ahead, but both of your futures were clouded, there was so much I couldn't understand. Out of all the possible outcomes, the only way you both survived was, well, together."

"You only knew the way things would end?"

"Thanks to that pesky little artifact, yes. I was only getting glimpses of the rest. I was flying blind when it came to you two. But I knew him, his code and his honor. He was never going to make the first move. Then I saw your family, how they surrounded you with walls. I knew you both needed a nudge, so that's why I intervened," Cora says.

"I'm glad you did. He's the one good thing to come out of all this mess."

"I'm not sure I would agree. From where I'm sitting, it looks to me like you got everything you ever wanted. Your own lakefront cabin. A car...a job. So, why do you still look like you're missing something?"

"It's nothing. You're right. I can make my own choices now. Well, within reason," I say with a subdued smile. I still can't show my face in public, but I can work around it with my new job. "It's just...I thought I'd feel like an adult when I got here. And I don't."

Cora throws her head back, laughing, cackling like the witch she is, willowy and beautiful in her movements.

"What's so funny?"

"I'm twenty-three, and I still don't feel like an adult. You're always going to feel young and immature and make stupid choices. That's just how life is. Give it time. Maybe a few decades."

I breathe out a long sigh. "Then it's normal to have no clue what you're doing?"

"Yes! Try to think back. When was your first day here?"

"June fifteenth," I say, confused.

She looks up to the sky in thought, "That was...twenty-six days ago, not even a whole month. In that time, your life has been turned completely upside down, you've survived utter chaos *and* lived to talk about it. Seems pretty grown up to me."

"I'm just not sure what I'm supposed to do now."

"You'll figure it out. *Later.* Now is the time for you to heal mentally. For you to finally get back on that path you were on with Aldrick," she says with a wide smile.

"Finally," I breathe out.

"See? That's what you do. Pick up where you left off."

"Sorry to break up the soap opera," Dane blurts out, startling me, "but your boyfriend's almost here."

"Which means our shift has finally come to an end," says Gerard.

"Remember, you have all the time in the world. Enjoy it," she says with a grin.

"Not yet, she doesn't." Dane's grin is far too wide as his fangs slowly slide out. "She has one more important step to take before that can happen."

"Eww. Put those things away," Cora says, getting to her feet, "or you're going to have to find another ride back home." She glances back to me and says, "See you at the meeting tomorrow."

"Have fun, little mage," Dane says suggestively, winking at me.

Isen grins, and Gerard laughs as he retreats.

"Uh huh. Run along now. Go get your precious beauty sleep," I say.

"Already on it," Dane calls as they leave, disappearing into the trees. Only Cora's delicate footfalls can be heard over the shifting water behind me. There is a long beat of silence, and I don't have to look to know he's approaching.

"Good evening, Brielle," beckons his molten voice through the heavy night air. He emerges from the house, wearing a white, button-down shirt and fitted gray slacks. "How are you liking it here?"

"It's perfect...now," I say, grinning, drawing a smile from his lips.

My eyes move to his mouth, particularly his teeth—involuntarily raising my hand to the side of my neck.

He sighs. "Don't listen to Dane."

"Well, he does have a point. Sooner or later, we have to talk about it."

"About you being one of us?" he asks, slowly leaning in closer to me, running is hands up my arms, over my shoulders...

I nod, caving in to his touch.

"Is it what you desire?" he asks, meeting my eyes.

"Well, yeah. You don't?"

"Why wouldn't I? To have you by my side, to keep you with me, always..."

"Do you think it's possible? Can mages become vampires?"

"Hmm." His voice rumbles through me. "I don't see it being a problem, but we can have your blood tested. See how it reacts to my venom," he says, trailing a finger down the side of my throat. He must be able to feel my heart beating.

I swallow hard, and say, "I'm worried I won't be able to do this job...to bring these territories together." The words just fall out of my mouth.

"You're going to have them wrapped around your finger," he says, lifting my chin gently.

"When I've done that, when I'm not needed anymore, I'll join you then," I say, reaching up and sliding my hand up his muscled chest to his thick neck.

"I'd never given much thought to the prospects of dating an *older* woman," he teases with a grin, then kisses me softly for just a moment, banishing all thought from my mind, relaxing every muscle in my body. Only now does it occur to me...something he said. That their saliva knocks people unconscious. His kisses are literally a drug.

I lean my head against his heaving chest, listening for a heartbeat that isn't there.

"So, I understand you can *see* magic?" he says, a smile in his voice. "What does it look like?"

"Everyone's is different. Mages have this red energy that moves in waves. The crows flash green when they shift. Dane's power just distorts the air around it. Isen's touch is just like this black smoke."

"What about mine?" he says. "How does it look to you?" I pull back and look deeply into his glowing red eyes, his expression gleeful, expectant. "No one has ever told you what your magic looks like? I highly doubt that."

"I have never met someone who could see magic before you. So, no. Please, I'm dying to know. How does it look?"

"It's this glowing, golden aura that surrounds you. It's beautiful and brilliant...like the light of the sun."

He closes his eyes and smiles softly.

"What are you thinking?" I ask, not understanding this reaction.

"For many centuries, I have been described as some diabolical creature. A demon. The picture of me that you paint with your sweet words is quite different. You almost make me sound like..."

"...like an angel?"

"There's something I want to try," he says, reaching his hands out for mine. I interlace my fingers with his, wondering what I'm getting myself into this time.

"Tell me what you see." he says, as the golden aura spreads over him, then runs down his arms. To my surprise, it keeps going, traveling up my arms and engulfing my body in its light.

"It's on me, too," I say. "How does that even work?"

"Who cares," he says, scooping me up in his arms. "How would you like to watch the sunset?"

"The sun's already gone down," I say.

"Not on that mountain top, it hasn't," he says, looking across the lake.

Before I can speak or even formulate a thought, the scenery around us shifts, the forest becoming nothing but a green blur as he moves, taking large bounding steps that cover huge distances. He leaps into the air, his feet landing on the tops of the evergreens, vaulting us forward at impossible speed. It feels like *flying*, only there's no icy wind on my face, no rushing in my ears. Not so much as a hair fluttering out of place. His golden aura seems to allow us to slip *through* the air as if it wasn't even there.

Within seconds, we've gone from the lakeside cabin to tree-tops and endless sky. He sets me down gently and has a seat, his back to a tree trunk, pulling me in close to him, arms around my waist. It's as he said...on this side of the mountain, the sun is only just about to set.

"Do I still haunt your dreams?" I ask, leaning back against him as he kisses the top of my head.

His laugh resonates in my skull. "You are still there, just as you were the first time I slept after turning. I knew I would have to wait a long time for you. Whoever you would be to me—the woman standing at the end of the world—wearing such strange clothes."

"I'd guess that pants weren't a common thing for girls in the Dark Ages."

He barks a laugh, "I'm not *that* old."

"Hard to tell."

"All those years I'd searched for the meaning of the strange markings you bore on your shirt, drawn it over and over, paid scholars to tell me what it meant, but they couldn't. Until five years ago, when Isen dragged us all to a music store, and I saw an album with the same symbol. But I really knew the time was nearing when Cora brought us to Ashland."

"How so?"

"For centuries, I had searched every inch of coastland I could find, looking for the right spot. It wasn't until recently that I found it. I had to believe you were real, and that I hadn't missed you yet. Every moment I wasn't on patrol, hunting, fighting, I was there, waiting. I had to trust in fate."

His lifeless room comes to mind. He really was never there because the whole time, he was waiting for *me*.

"Then you were there. I had to get closer, to see you, so I called in and had them shut down the sensor tower. But you got up and walked to the railing. My God, it was the moment from my dream, and it hit me, and I felt the pull—the connection of our souls. I knew for certain right then and there that you were *meant* for me."

I try to pay attention, but his free hand grazing my exposed skin is distracting. How could he have waited so long? For an unknown outcome? How could anyone hold on to faith in *anything* that long? I can't understand. It doesn't make sense to me.

"When Danes' first blast happened, I ran back, I had to stop him, but his second one was already out before I could reach him, and it was too late."

"I thought I had died when I saw you. That I had met death, himself."

"I should have focused on keeping you safe; I almost lost you the moment I found you."

I spin and kneel on the ground in front of him, my eyes level with his.

"But you didn't. I'm alive, and you've given me everything I've ever wanted. And I didn't have to wait long for any of it. It seems you got the shitty end of the deal," I say, reaching out and stroking the side of his face.

The most beautiful smile spreads across his lips, and he leans closer.

"I will cherish you forever, my love. While you are human, and when you become one of us."

"Oh, so you're ready for me to annoy you for all time?"

He lifts my chin as his lips meet mine, our souls intertwining.

As the countdown to the end of my human existence begins to tick away, my life with him has only just begun.

Acknowledgements

I thought the blurb was hard to write, but this is somehow even worse.

First and foremost, I would like to thank my husband. Who, through his endless shit talking, helped me fill numerous plot holes, rein in my constant info dumping, and pointed out every single damn echo word in the manuscript. He is the best beta reader I could have ever asked for. I should have let him read it long before the first draft was finished. It would have saved me yet another rewrite. My bad.

To my parents, I love you guys. Thank you for always being there for me and always believing in me. And to my sister Terrah, I wish you lived closer, so I could bug you daily. And to my big brother Markie, who isn't here to read and make fun of the book, I put a couple of things in here that only you'd know about. You would have gotten a kick out of it.

To Enjoli, my best friend whom I've annoyed since before kindergarten. Through the years we spent growing up and figuring out our way in life, including the awkward preteen days, you were there with me through everything. Thank you for creating such an incredible book cover!

To Jenna, thank you for being there for me, for all the long conversations while the kids played, you saved the last bit of sanity I have. You are such an amazing person and friend!

An apology to my eight beta readers. I still want to crawl into a hole, knowing that I sent out the roughest, sloppiest, jumbled mess that was my first draft. Oof.

To my editors, I can't thank you ladies enough!

About the author

Amanda Fresquez resides deep within the heart of the primeval woodlands of the Olympic Peninsula with her steadfast consort and their four spirited young apprentices. When she isn't teaching them to master the arcane arts or leading them on daring adventures, she can be found reading, writing, and playing either her Lore-Master or Hunter in The Lord of the Rings Online.

www.amandafresquez.com

www.ingramcontent.com/pod-prcduct-compliance
Lightning Source LLC
Chambersburg PA
CBHW022033120726
47899CB00001BB/164